Personal Justice

A Marc Kadella Legal Mystery

by

Dennis L. Carstens

Previous Marc Kadella Legal Mysteries

The Key to Justice

Desperate Justice

Media Justice

Certain Justice

Personal Justice

Delayed Justice

Political Justice

Insider Justice

Exquisite Justice

www.denniscarstens.com

A very special thanks to the genius of Charles Dickens who brought us Marley's Ghost with the universally true warning about the chains we forge in life and will eventually wear through eternity; a warning which very few us adequately heed.

ONE

Mackenzie Sutherland followed the wheeled aluminum bier down the center aisle of St. Mark's Catholic Church in St. Paul. It carried her husband's coffin toward the church's front entrance on Dayton Avenue. The bier was guided by six young men, all of whom were sons of old friends of her husband.

She walked slowly down the aisle loosely holding the arm of her personal lawyer, Cooper Thomas. Her face bore an impassive expression; appropriate for a funeral. Anyone looking at her through the black veil attached to her black hat and covering her face would think nothing of the look she wore.

Behind her, having been uncomfortably seated on the same pew with Mackenzie, were her three stepchildren. Robert, the eldest, and his wife, Paige sat with their three unruly children. Then came the youngest, Hailey and her latest *oh so cool, chic and hip bohemian-artist* boyfriend, Chazz. Bringing up the rear of the dysfunctional family was the middle child, another son, thirty-eight-year-old Adam. Of the three of them, Adam was easily the most useless. His problems with drugs and alcohol made gainful employment problematic at best, if he had ever been so inclined toward self-sufficiency in the first place.

Mackenzie's husband, William 'Bill' Sutherland, had been a well-known, respected businessman for almost forty years. Bill and his first wife, Beth, had worked and sacrificed to build a chain of successful grocery stores. *Sutherland's* were high-end stores known for their quality and service. Three months before his death he opened the seventeenth and final store in Duluth. Bill had always treated his employees well, in fact a little too well judging by how it was affecting the company's bottom line. However, because of this there was not an empty seat in the church.

When they exited the church, Cooper Thomas gently led Mackenzie toward the Cadillac limousine first in line behind the black hearse. While the casket was being loaded into the back of the big vehicle for Bill's last trip, Mackenzie took a moment to look up at the sky.

March in Minnesota can be less than pleasant depending on how long winter decides to linger. The driver of Mackenzie's limo stepped aside to allow Cooper to open the door for her. As he did so, a slight, involuntary shiver went through Mackenzie.

"Dreary day," she remarked as she entered the car.

She slid across the seat to allow her escort to get in next to her and close the door. While they sat waiting for the other guests to get in line and form the procession to the cemetery, Mackenzie pushed the button to raise the car's privacy glass behind the driver.

"I'll be glad when this is over," she quietly said.

"You're doing fine," Cooper said patting her right hand with his left. Mackenzie had placed the hand on the seat between them and Cooper held it as if to comfort her.

"Stop," she firmly admonished as she removed his hand and placed hers in her lap. "I don't need consoling, Cooper. I need this business to be done."

Despite his marriage, Cooper Thomas was thoroughly smitten with the very fetching Mackenzie Sutherland. Even dressed in widow black she was still a fine-looking woman. Hiding his disappointment at her admonishment he said, "Soon, Mackenzie, just a few more days. Everything is arranged."

"I know," she sighed. "I'm just tired of his damn kids bugging me about money." Mackenzie turned her head to look out the passenger window as the rain began to lightly fall. She placed her veiled forehead against the window and looked upward toward the gray sky. The limo's tinted windows made the rainy day darker, gloomier and even feel colder. While watching the rain streak the glass, waiting for the procession to start up, a slight smile curved her mouth upward.

While the two of them were silently chauffeured to the cemetery, Mackenzie retraced the route she traveled to reach this destination. Now in her early forties her crusade began almost twenty years ago.

Mackenzie Lange, her original maiden name, graduated from the University of Minnesota in her early twenties with a marketing degree. A very attractive young woman, borderline beautiful, Mackenzie had little trouble finding employment. She quickly learned she could use her looks, charm and intelligence to excel at sales and she found she liked it. There was something about manipulating people to do what she wanted that gave her a rush.

After a few years, Mackenzie suddenly moved to St. Petersburg, Florida. She had saved enough money, so she could live without a job for at least two years, if necessary. Having done her research before leaving to move to Florida, she knew exactly where she would work and in six months the job was hers; new car sales at Bauer Cadillac. It was also the location of the corporate headquarters for Bauer Enterprises, the owner of twelve car dealerships in the Tampa-St. Petersburg metro area.

Mackenzie, using her smooth legs and ample cleavage, shot to the top of the sales board in less than three months. It wasn't long before she caught the attention of the company owner, Joseph Bauer, whose office was in the same building.

Immediately smitten with this beautiful young super saleswoman, within two weeks they were dating. Three months later the angry first

Mrs. Bauer was filing for divorce and three days after it was finalized Mackenzie became the second Mrs. Joseph Bauer.

Along with a very profitable business, Mackenzie became a stepmother for the first time. Joseph had two sons, Samuel a mere two months younger than Mackenzie and David, the spoiled Mama's boy of the family.

Everything went exactly as Mackenzie had envisioned it. Having been married to a Jewish Princess for over thirty years, the sexual wild ride that Mackenzie brought to the conjugal bed turned Joseph into a pliable puppy.

Suddenly, a month after changing his Will, which cut out both sons, Joseph was found slumped over his desk. At the ripe old age of fifty-five, his heart gave out. Because he was a Jew and had a history of heart problems, no autopsy was performed. Three months later the grieving widow sold the business for seventeen million dollars. The amount was probably half what it was worth, but she wanted a quick sale and a quicker exit from St. Pete. The four-million-dollar beach front house was mortgaged to the max. Since her name was not on any of it, Mackenzie did a quick deed in lieu of foreclosure and she was on her way back to the Midwest.

During her marriage to Joseph Bauer, Mackenzie had become acquainted with an old college friend of her late husband. They had socialized several times and Mackenzie had taken every opportunity to flirt and flatter the well-to-do widower. Of course, when Joseph died suddenly this friend, Kenneth Hayes, had flown immediately to Tampa-St. Pete to help the poor widow, console her through her time of grief and help handle the estate proceedings. Although Mackenzie required no help or grief consoling, she was all too happy to let him do it. By the time she cashed out and moved to Milwaukee where he lived, Ken Hayes, soon to be husband number two, had been reeled in and landed.

Hayes, whose first wife had killed herself while driving drunk several years before, was a partner in a mid-size investment firm. In good times and bad, bull and bear markets and even through recessions, the firm made money. The firm's clients might not have always made money, but commissions were always paid.

Mackenzie had done her due diligence and had a fairly accurate estimate of the man's net worth. Knowing she had him hooked, for appearances Mackenzie played the part of the grieving widow for almost a year. Unknown to poor Ken Hayes, she even began scouting out the man who would become husband number three.

Almost exactly a year after the death of Joseph Bauer, Mackenzie was the new Mrs. Kenneth Hayes. Along with the ring came a six-bedroom, seven bath home with both an indoor and outdoor pool on the shores of Lake Michigan.

Being married to Joe Bauer had been easy. Bauer had little interest in socializing which left Mackenzie with time to do what she wanted. Ken Hayes was another matter entirely. Being a partner in the firm required a constant stream of entertaining well-heeled existing and potential clients. If she wasn't planning an event in the lakeshore home, they were going to one at someone else's. And as if that wasn't boring enough, Ken was heavily involved in the state Democratic Party. Being apolitical Mackenzie could not have been less interested in any of it. She was also finding out Milwaukee and her husband were about as interesting as warm oatmeal. To top it all off, the cherry on the sundae, were the three dull, useless progeny. The oldest, a married daughter Carol, was a year older than Mackenzie, a son, Kenneth Jr., was a few years younger and the youngest was a spoiled party girl, Faye.

The marriage lasted until at death they did part, not quite eighteen months after the wedding. The Milwaukee police found Ken slumped over the wheel of his Mercedes on the side of the freeway. A quick autopsy revealed a sudden and unexpected heart attack followed by cremation less than forty-eight hours later.

Of course, a few days after the memorial service, when the Will was read, Mackenzie was shocked—she almost fainted, a nice touch that was—to find Ken had recently changed the Will. He had left fifty thousand dollars to each of his children and the rest to his loving bride, Mackenzie. In addition, there was a three-million-dollar life insurance policy the firm held on each of its partners. The three million was used to buy out the stunned, grieving young widow from any claim in the firm. The final tally was a little over fifteen million, including the house. Shortly after, Mackenzie, who was still only thirty-six, moved to Chicago.

Target number three was an old money Chicagoan by the name of Wendell Cartwright. Wendell Cartwright was the great-grandson of a Chicago Robber Baron, Philemon Cartwright. Fortunately for Wendell, Great Granddad had amassed a fortune the old-fashioned way; by ruthlessly crushing any potential competition. At the turn of the twentieth century, the old crook was the principal owner of the Chicago Stockyards and almost one-third of the real estate in what would become downtown Chicago.

When he turned twenty-one, Wendell's share of the old crook's estate, a family trust fund, became available with almost one-hundred million dollars in it. During the next forty plus years, Wendell had managed to reduce it to approximately forty million by the time he met

McKenzie. Wendell had a definite weakness for the ladies and the good life.

Mackenzie would be wife number five. Wendell's four ex-wives were all living quite well on the alimony payments they received each month. In addition, there were two adult children to support. The first child, a forty-year-old woman from his first marriage named Dorothy, was about to divorce husband number three, a twenty-eight-year-old biker who had introduced her to the joy of methamphetamines.

Wendell also had a son who was thirty-three-years-old when they married named Phillip by wife number two. Despite an excellent education provided by Daddy, Phillip was all but totally useless as a human being. Bothering with employment had never been high on Phillip's to do list. Why should it? The example dear old Dad had set for him had done its job. Phillip was following right in Daddy's footsteps and Dad kept the monthly checks rolling. That and Phillip's drug business kept him living fairly well. He would have lived better still but for his usage of his own products.

All of them, four ex-wives, two adult children and Wendell's hedonistic lifestyle were totally dependent upon the trust money. Getting a job for any of them was out of the question. Because of the way the trust was set up, Wendell could not make lump sum payments to everyone and be done with them. Instead, they all would live off of monthly payments until Wendell's death at which time the trust's remaining principal would be paid out to the named beneficiaries.

Within six months of relocating to the north side of Chicago, Wendell Cartwright was wrapped around Mackenzie's little finger. Wendell was absolutely convinced that the over-sexed Mackenzie was his longed-for soulmate. Little did he know how much she really despised him for his weakness and self-indulgent, indolent lifestyle. Less than a month after Mackenzie's thirty-eighth birthday, husband number three was discovered in bed dead from a massive heart attack. A perfunctory autopsy, a quick cremation and a shocked young widow was forty million dollars richer.

During her brief marriage Mackenzie had come to know the ex-wives, the two children and the amount each of them were being paid every month. When the Will was read, the exes and the kids discovered that the spigot had been shut off. On the surface, Mackenzie appeared shocked and assured them she would do what she could to take care of them. All the while thinking that bankrupting this gang of leeches was the best part of being married to the old fool.

Lawsuits were filed by all of them. Because the divorces were set up with no provision for securing the alimony payments, the lawsuits would be eventually dismissed. Wendell's responsibilities died with him.

And to be clear that leaving all of them out of the estate was not an oversight, he made provision in the Will that each were to receive the sum of one hundred dollars.

The local media had a field day with it. The story had everything the public could want, and they ate it up; an attractive young wife, a rich old man, a huge fight over millions of dollars. Unfortunately for Mackenzie, her picture was in the news at least weekly and it was not long before an enterprising reporter tracked her back to Milwaukee. Just about the time the death of her previous husband came to light, the liquidation of the Cartwright estate was finalized. Once that was completed, Mackenzie disappeared to Europe for six months before coming home to St. Paul.

TWO

The drive to the cemetery, even with the motorcycle police escorts, took almost thirty minutes. Mackenzie made a mental note to give the two motorcyclists an extra two hundred dollars each because of the rain. It was a cold, wet, miserable day to be on a motorcycle. The long procession snaked its way through the Catholic cemetery in Mendota Heights. The hearse finally stopped near an open area alongside Augusta Lake. Bill Sutherland had purchased a quarter acre plot overlooking the lake expecting the entire family to eventually be buried there.

A 20 x 20 awning had been set up over the gravesite. A large marble angel resembling the Virgin Mary faced the street in front of the plot. It was set on a concrete base with the name **SUTHERLAND** prominently displayed.

The chauffeur parked and quickly hurried around the limo to open the door for his passengers.

"You okay?" Cooper asked Mackenzie.

"Yes, Cooper, I'm fine," she quietly answered through the black veil.

The chauffeur had a large, black umbrella open and handed it to Cooper Thomas. He held it over Mackenzie as she exited the car. She took his arm and he guided her to her seat in the front row under the awning.

The fifty chairs under the shelter quickly filled up and at least another two hundred people stood in the light rain. The Sutherland children sat in the front next to Mackenzie. She had always been kind to them and they to her; each masking the reality that they despised each other.

Being a Navy veteran, Bill's coffin was draped with an American flag. The casket was centered over a hole next to Bill's first wife, Elizabeth, the mother of his children. Beth, as she was known, had died four years ago from cancer. Mackenzie had never met her, and it was obvious the children all resented Mackenzie marrying their dad. No doubt believing it would mean less money for them.

When the priest had finished, and the service was completed, one of the pallbearers brought the folded flag and handed it to Mackenzie. Holding the flag out she stepped over to the oldest son, Bob, and held it out to him.

"I think your dad would want you to have this," Mackenzie said.

Startled by this sudden and unexpected display of empathy, Bob could only mutter his thanks, all the while Mackenzie was thinking, *don't thank me yet, that's about all you're going to get.*

Three days later, still clothed in stylish black, Mackenzie took a chair in front of Cooper Thomas's desk. She was a half-hour early for the appointed time to read the Will of this most recent dearly departed husband.

"It's not necessary for you to be here," Cooper reiterated for at least the fourth time. He had taken his chair behind his glass-topped desk and was trying to avoid the sight of Mackenzie's crossed legs.

"I know, Cooper," she answered him. "I told you, I want to see their faces."

"Why?"

"That's not your concern," Mackenzie icily told him. "Is everything ready?"

"Yes, including the security guard," Cooper replied.

"That won't be necessary…"

"I'm taking the precaution anyway. People can get pretty worked up over these things."

Barely twenty minutes later Cooper's secretary buzzed him to let them know the Sutherlands were waiting in the conference room. Cooper thanked her and a minute later he opened the conference room door for Mackenzie and the two of them joined the three people already present.

The younger ones, Hailey and Adam, were already seated. Bob was pouring himself a glass of water from a carafe on a credenza. Before the door finished closing behind them, a serious looking man in a dark business suit came into the room. Without a word he sat in one of the chairs along the back wall as if to observe.

Mackenzie smiled slightly at her stepchildren and pleasantly said hello. Cooper took the chair at the head of the table. Mackenzie sat in the one to his immediate right. All three of Bill Sutherland's children made a point of ignoring their stepmother as Bob took the first chair to Cooper's left.

"We may as well get right at it," Cooper began looking at the three children. "Your father came here and secretly had me change his Will three months ago, unknown to his wife, Mackenzie."

"I don't believe that," Hailey said glaring at Mackenzie.

Mackenzie leaned forward, her forearms on the table top and her hands folded. She stared right back at Hailey and said, "I knew you wouldn't believe it but it's true. I had no knowledge of it."

"It's true," Cooper continued. "He told me this himself and swore me to secrecy."

"We're about to get bent over here, aren't we?" Adam said looking back and forth between Mackenzie and her lawyer.

"Not by me," Mackenzie quietly replied.

"Let's have it," Bob said holding up a hand to cut off his younger brother.

Cooper cleared his throat then said, "First of all, you need to know that there is a 'no contest' provision in the Will. What that means is if you contest the Will and lose, you get nothing.

"Your father left each of you the cash gift of one hundred thousand dollars. The residue of the estate, including the house in Crocus Hill and all of the personal property goes to his wife, Mackenzie."

"That's it? A hundred grand each! This is bullshit…" Adam yelled.

"Shut up, dummy," Hailey snapped at Adam. "We still own ten percent of the business. That's worth at least three or four million."

"What you have," Cooper continued while Mackenzie sat quietly waiting for the hammer to fall, "is twenty thousand shares which was a gift from your father."

"Yes, we know," Bob said. "We each hold ten percent of the common stock."

"Yes, except, the gift provision provided for the company to repurchase those shares, whenever it wanted to do so and at its sole discretion, for par value at any time. Par value was established as one dollar per share," Cooper said looking directly at Bob. "Your father never changed this."

"What the hell does that mean?" Adam yelled. "She can buy the goddamn stock back for a buck a share? That's bullshit!"

While Adam said this, his brother and sister stared at Mackenzie who sat with an impassive expression yet thoroughly enjoying the show.

"My parents worked their ass off for forty years growing a chain of grocery stores into a successful business. Then you come along and steal it. You fucking bitch!" Bob snarled, his voice rising in anger. "First you murder my father then…"

"Stop!" Cooper said. "You had better be careful making allegations like that."

While he said this, he noticed out of the corner of his eye the man along the wall stand up and step behind Bob. The man stood there, his hands folded in front of himself.

"Bob, I know you're upset but your father had a heart attack. There was an autopsy…" Mackenzie started to say.

"You bitch," Hailey snarled. "We all know you did it…"

"And if I find out how, I'll get you for it," Bob said as he stood up. "I should do it now," he snarled.

Cooper held up his left hand to stop the silent security man from interceding. "That sounds like a threat." Cooper said.

"A promise," Bob viciously retorted. Cooper Thomas stood and faced Bob Sutherland. In his hand he held three envelopes, one for each of the Sutherland children. In each one was a copy of the Will, the stock gift document and a check in the amount of one hundred twenty thousand dollars. He handed them out and without another word, the three Sutherland children, obviously steaming, stomped out of the conference room followed by the security guard who escorted them to the elevator.

"That went well," Mackenzie smiled after the room emptied.

"Did you enjoy it?" Cooper asked as he was picking up the papers he had placed on the table.

"Not as much as I thought I would," she replied. "What about the sale of the company?"

"You just destroyed that family..."

"The sale of the company?" Mackenzie repeated.

"Everything is set. The contract will be sent by messenger to their lawyers this afternoon. The money will be transferred into your account at Ameriprise within forty-eight hours. They're getting a bargain..."

"We've been through this," Mackenzie sternly interrupted her lawyer. "Twenty-seven million is plenty. I told you, I didn't want to drag this out for a year for another five to ten million more. Let me know if you need me for anything else," she continued as the two of them stood to leave. "Oh, and by the way, I didn't do anything to that family. Their father did it. He despised them." *And*, she thought, *they didn't get anything they did not deserve.*

THREE

Marc Kadella stared out the open window of his second-floor office. He was a sole practitioner who rented space along with two other lawyers from a fourth lawyer, Connie Mickelson. Connie inherited the Reardon Building on Lake Street and Charles Avenue from her father twenty years ago. Connie moved her practice into this space when the previous tenant was disbarred for stealing client funds. Marc had been with her almost ten years along with the two other lawyers and the office staff. They had created an informal working arrangement, and all became great friends over the years.

Marc was in the office a little early watching the traffic go through the intersection on the street below. The weather geeks were predicting a beautiful Minnesota spring day; sunny and mild with high's in the mid-seventies. Their prediction only increased his sour mood since he was going to be indoors all day.

"Hey, gloomy Gus, you want some coffee?" he heard Carolyn Lucas, one of the office assistants say.

Marc spun around to face her and said, "Sure," as he held up his cup. "Let me ask you something," he continued when Carolyn finished pouring. "You're a woman…"

"What gave it away?" she sarcastically said.

Marc laughed then said, "Don't do this to me. Anyway, I need your opinion about something. I have my twenty-fifth high school reunion coming up in a couple weeks, June second, and I don't want to take Margaret…"

"And she's really pissed about it," Carolyn interjected.

"Yeah, would you be?"

"I don't know," Carolyn shrugged "John and I went to high school together, so we go to the same reunions."

"Oh, high school sweethearts. How nauseating," Marc cynically replied.

Carolyn scratched her nose with her middle finger which made Marc laugh again.

"I don't know why she would want to go to your high school reunion. Even when John and I go we don't hang out together. He has friends he wants to see and so do I," Carolyn said. "If she goes with you then you have to hang out with her and she won't know anyone."

"Exactly," Marc agreed. "I told her she's being unreasonable, we had a big fight and I left."

"Uh, oh," Carolyn said. "It sounds to me like more than just this reunion business."

The two good friends looked at each other for a few moments then Marc quietly said, "Yeah, you're right. It is more than this. She's getting a little clingy and I'm not sure I like it."

The office door to the hallway opened and they heard voices of officemates arriving.

"If you need to talk, I'll be here," Carolyn said.

"I know, thanks. I'll tell you what though, I'm going to this reunion and I'm going alone. I'm not going to hang out with her all night," Marc answered her.

"Good luck," Carolyn said as she turned to go to her desk.

Marc heard Carolyn greet one of the other lawyers in the office just before the man appeared at Marc's door.

"Good morning," Chris Grafton said. Grafton was several years older than Marc and had developed a successful corporate practice for small business clients. He also rented space in the office.

"Hey, Chris," Marc replied.

"Do you want me to come with you this morning?" Grafton asked.

"I don't care," Marc answered with a puzzled look. "You can if you want to but there won't be anything for you to do. Why, is Dan Haney going to be there?"

Dan Haney was a business client of Grafton's and the owner of a chain of successful dry-cleaning stores. Haney's sister was in some fairly serious trouble and Grafton had recommended her to Marc. The good news was the brother, Dan, was paying the fees.

"Yeah, Dan will be there," Grafton said.

"If you want to come along and hold his hand, it's up to you."

"I think I should," Grafton said. "He's been a good client and…"

"Then ride down with me. I'm coming back to the office afterwards. Unless you want to drive…"

"No, you drive."

"Okay," Marc said getting out of his chair, "let's go."

Unable to get into the government center underground parking, Marc found a spot in the ramp across the street on Fourth Avenue. The two men walked through the skyway ramp connecting the two buildings.

"You okay? You seem a little on edge," Marc asked his friend.

"I don't like this criminal stuff. I don't know why, but it makes me nervous," Grafton replied.

"Relax," Marc laughed. "You're not going to jail, she is."

"You don't think you can keep her out of jail?"

"No way, I'll be lucky if we can get her to do time in Hennepin County and not the women's prison in Shakopee."

A few minutes before the scheduled time of 9:00 A.M. the two men went into the courtroom. Marc's client, Michelle Winters, and her brother were already there seated along the back wall. They all greeted each other, then Grafton took the chair next to Dan Haney while Marc went to check in with the court clerk. Marc walked past the table where, to Marc's surprise, the assistant county attorney was already there conversing with a female defense lawyer Marc knew.

The prosecutor, Paul Ramsey, looked at him, politely smiled and said, "You're next." At the same time the defense lawyer, Peggy Sims, said hello to him.

Marc took a seat in the jury box and looked over the almost empty, sterile courtroom. There were only a half dozen defendants, most of whom were represented by the public defender's office whose representative was not present yet.

Less than a minute after taking his seat the two lawyers stood up. They started to go back to chambers when Marc asked, "Who's the judge Paul?"

"Arnold Shelby," Ramsey answered him.

"Arnie's okay," Sims said.

"I know Arnie, Peggy," Marc politely replied.

Five minutes later they came back into the courtroom. Sims walked through the gate and motioned for her client, a well-dressed young man to follow her into the hall.

"You ready for me?" Marc asked.

"Yeah. In fact, I'm looking forward to this," the prosecutor said.

Marc took the seat vacated by Peggy Sims. When he did, he leaned forward and whispered, "You are flying solo now?"

Paul Ramsey was a rookie with the county attorney's office. He had been second chair for a recent trial Marc had done. Marc had gotten to know him a bit and genuinely liked him. Paul seemed to be a bright, capable young man who would likely become a first-rate lawyer someday. He was also a descendant of the namesake for Ramsey County which held the state capitol across the Mississippi.

"I won't be trying it alone if that's what you're wondering. Not against you. What are you looking for today?" Ramsey asked.

"An apology for the inconvenience to my client," Marc said.

"Would you like it in writing?"

"Hey, that's good. A year on the job and you're already as sarcastic and cynical as the rest of us. Congratulations," Marc laughed. "What are you offering?"

Ramsey read the notes in the case file, smiled at Marc and said, "Your client made the top ten list for balls this week. We want a felony plea and a gross misdemeanor DWI. We'll ask for a departure to twenty-four months. She's lucky she didn't kill someone."

A little disheartened Marc said, "She needs treatment."

"She's had treatment, a couple of times," Ramsey interrupted.

"She needs it again," Marc continued.

"The cops are pissed..."

"They're always pissed," Marc said with a dismissive wave of his hand. "Let's go talk to Arnie and see what he thinks."

While the two men waited outside the door to the judge's chambers, Marc said. "You have to admit the whole thing is kind of funny."

"My favorite case so far," Ramsey said with a smile. "Still she is lucky she didn't kill someone."

"Good morning your Honor," Marc said as the two of them approached the judge's desk.

They took chairs and Ramsey told Judge Shelby what case they were there for. Shelby found the correct file from the pile on his desk and put on his reading glasses. The two lawyers waited patiently while he read the police report. When he finished, barely able to suppress a laugh he looked directly at Marc.

"Let me see if I have this straight. Your client, Ms. Winters," he began, "was pulled over by three cops each in their own squad car after a ten-minute attempt to get her to stop. Then, instead of getting out of her car she takes off and hits one of the squad cars, barely missing one of the officers.

"She then leads them on a high-speed chase through the streets of Minneapolis for another thirty minutes. They have to ram her car to get her to stop. And again, she refuses to get out and cooperate. According to the police she sits in her car, giving them the finger, and says through the glass and I quote, 'Give me a minute, I want to finish my beer. It's my last one so just hold on.' She drinks the rest of her beer before finally opening her door and surrendering.

"Then they arrest her, take her to the Fourth Precinct where she blows a point two three. Is that about it?"

Marc nodded his head a couple of times then said, "Sounds about right."

Shelby opened the file again while asking, "Is there a probation report?"

"Yes, your Honor. She needs serious jail time. We want a plea to the felony resisting and the gross misdemeanor DWI. Twenty-four months," Ramsey said.

"Judge, she needs treatment," Marc said.

"Obviously," Shelby said. "Tell you what. How about she pleads to the felony resisting and the gross DWI. I give her a year in county. Does she have a job?"

"Yes, judge, she does," Marc said.

"Okay, she can have work release. She agrees to treatment. I hang an additional twenty-four months over her head for five years. If she completes treatment and stays sober and law abiding at the end of the five-years the whole thing drops to a misdemeanor. Plus, a three thousand dollar fine.

"I'll give her a chance, Marc, but she's running out of them. Mr. Ramsey?" he asked looking at the prosecutor.

"Reluctantly, we can agree," Ramsey said.

"No one will want to put her in prison for two years, Paul," Shelby said. "But," he continued sternly looking at Marc, "if she screws up again and ends up back in front of me, I'll give her the two years."

"I understand, your Honor," Marc said while thinking *yeah, bullshit.*

Marc explained the agreement to his client, her brother and Chris Grafton. A very happy and relieved Michelle Winters actually hugged him. Marc had previously told her the prosecution wanted four years in prison, so this looked like a huge win.

They took the plea in chambers and Michelle and her brother went to court services to pay the fine and arrange the jail time.

On the way back to Marc's car Grafton asked him how much time the prosecution was really requesting. Marc smiled, told him and they both got a chuckle from Marc's little deception.

FOUR

"Bob," Bill Sutherland yelled out from his bedroom to his oldest son. "Make sure the front door is locked before you leave."

Bob Sutherland was closing the door of an upstairs bathroom in his father's house when his dad yelled out to him. Bob thought the request to check the front door was a bit odd since virtually no one ever used the front door.

"Sure thing, Dad. I'll check it. Good night and I'll talk to you tomorrow."

"Good night, son. Drive carefully."

Bob went down the curved stairway and when he reached the bottom took three or four steps toward the front door. When he got there, he reached for the door knob with the locking mechanism in it and found the entire thing was gone. What was left was a large hole in the door where it should have been.

He heard what sounded like scratching noises coming from the outside. Bob leaned down to peek through the hole when suddenly, a woman's hand appeared. It was silently moving about as if trying to grasp something and it missed Bob's nose by inches. Bob straightened up, gasped then put a shoulder against the door to prevent the woman from entering the house and yelled for his dad.

"Wake up!" Paige Sutherland almost yelled frantically shaking her husband. "Bob, wake up!"

"Ahhh!" a startled Bob Sutherland shouted as he jumped and fell off the bed onto the floor.

Paige quickly crawled to her husband's side of the bed and looked down at him. He was propped up on his elbows, a frightened expression on his face as his eyes darted about in the dark of the bedroom.

"Are you all right?" Paige asked.

Bob did not immediately answer her, so she asked him again. He looked at her, blinked several times then finally said, "Yeah, I think so."

"You were having that dream again, weren't you the one with the hand through the door of your dad's house?"

Bob was sitting on the floor now, still a little bewildered. It took a few seconds for him to respond. "Yeah, I was. It's really bizarre and I don't know what it means. I'm really getting tired of it."

"Maybe you should talk to that woman that Rolly knows. It can't hurt," Paige said as she reached out to hold her husband's head to comfort him.

"I think I will," he said. "You're right, it can't hurt."

The next morning, Bob arrived at work and went to his office. The grocery store company had been sold by Mackenzie to a national food wholesaler who wanted to get into the retail business. Because of Bob's experience he had been retained and even promoted.

One of the store managers was a man Bob knew since high school, Jim Rollins who everyone called Rolly. Bob had told Rolly about his weird dream and Rolly claimed to know a woman who interpreted dreams and offered to introduce Bob to her. A phone call to Rolly and ten minutes later Bob had set up a lunch date with the woman, Rhonda Priestly, for later that day.

Bob Sutherland arrived at the restaurant a half-hour early. Having decided to try this, he was anxious to do it and possibly find out what the dream meant. A few minutes before noon he spotted a woman by herself come through the front door. She fit Rolly's description to a T and Bob hurried to the door to greet her.

Rhonda Priestly looked like everyone's idea of a friendly, favorite aunt. A plump woman with graying hair in her mid-fifties who scurried to keep up as Bob led her to his table. When the waitress left Rhonda got right to it.

"Tell me about your dream."

For the next few minutes, Bob explained it to her while she quietly listened. When he finished, she silently thought for a minute then told him to tell it to her again.

This time, she asked several questions to clarify a point here and there. When he finished, she reflected again for another minute.

"Have you had any stressful occurrences in your life lately?" she asked him.

The waitress brought their meals and while they ate, Bob told her about his father's death, the funeral and his stepmother. When he talked about Mackenzie his anger, indeed his hatred of her, became more and more apparent.

When he finished, Rhonda said, "The woman at the door in your dream is your stepmother, Mackenzie. She's trying to get in and you keep stopping her."

"What should I do?" Bob asked.

"Next time, let her in. Let her come in the house. You'll wake up and the dream will stop recurring."

Bob sat back in the booth, looked at her skeptically and said, "Seriously? That's all I need to do?"

"No, but the dream will stop. You obviously have some serious, unresolved issues with her. Those will still be there. In fact, you may even start having a new, different dream," Rhonda told him.

"Great, then what?"

"I suggest you get into professional therapy, Bob. I'm not a psychologist. Your anger at your stepmother and what she did to you and your family needs to be dealt with."

Bob thought it over and said, "You're right. And I'll try to stop the dream. How do I let her come in through the door?"

"In your dream, when you are walking down the stairs, stop before you go to the door, your conscious mind will tell you to do it. When the door opens, and she comes in, you'll wake up."

That night the dream came again, and he did exactly what Rhonda suggested. While he was walking down the stairs toward the front door, he stopped, the door opened and as Mackenzie started to enter, Bob woke up, sat up in bed and felt a calmness come over him.

At breakfast, he talked it over with Paige.

"I think I broke the dream and it's gone," he told her, "I still think that bitch killed my dad and…"

"I've told you a hundred times, you need to go see Simon. Talk to him, tell him what happened and see what he thinks," Paige told him.

"You're right," Bob said. "I should have done it by now. I'll call him today."

At 3:15 that afternoon Bob Sutherland settled into the plush leather chair in the waiting area of the lawyer he was seeing. Simon Kane was the primary corporate lawyer for his father's business. Only a couple years older then Bob, Simon had inherited his old man's client base when his father retired. Simon's dad had been a senior partner in a forty-lawyer firm. Simon was a partner himself but was scrambling and fighting a losing battle to keep the *Sutherland's* grocery store chain as a client. The new owners did not seem inclined to use him.

Simon Kane was not looking forward to this meeting. He assumed it was once again about the Will and the sale of the company. He had been over this with all three of the Sutherland children a half dozen times. Simon had even assigned one of the firm's law clerks to research the issues and legally, there was not anything that could be done.

Bob was paging through a current Time magazine when Simon's assistant, Tamara, came for him. Following the shapely Tamara back to Simon's office would be the best part of Bob's day. She opened the door to Simon's office, smiled and stepped aside for him. The two men greeted each other, shook hands and Bob sat in one of the matching expensive client chairs.

"Always a pleasure to walk behind Tamara," Bob said with raised eyebrows.

"Don't even joke about that. I can probably get sued just for you saying it. Besides, believe it or not, she's incredibly good at her job and I would hate to lose her. So, what did you want to see me about?"

"I want to have my dad's body dug up. What's the word for it?"

"Exhumed."

"Right, exhumed."

"Why?"

"Because that bitch killed him. I know she did it," Bob said, his temperature rising.

"Easy, Bob," Simon said to calm him. "Do you have any evidence of that?"

"Jesus Christ, Simon. That's why I want him dug up. I did a little research and learned there are drugs that can cause a heart attack. Dad's heart was fine. All of a sudden he has a massive heart attack and dies. It's bullshit!"

"There was an autopsy…"

"There are drugs that a normal autopsy wouldn't find," Bob said.

"Yes, I've heard of that. Well, let's find out what it would take to exhume a body. I've never done it, so let's check the statutes," Simon said as he turned to his desktop.

He quickly did a search for Minnesota exhumation statutes, found what he wanted and took a couple of minutes to read it over. When he finished, he turned back to his client and said, "Well, it's as I suspected, you need grounds that the death was not natural or the permission of the next of kin."

"I'm the next of kin."

"Sorry, legally you're not. Mackenzie is," Simon told him. "You think she'll agree?"

"Pretty unlikely since she'll know I'm looking for evidence that she murdered him," Bob admitted. "What would it cost?"

"I don't know," Simon said. "Let's see if we can find out online."

He turned back to the computer and a minute later found it. Again, he read it over then read the pertinent parts again, out loud for Bob.

"Says here, getting to the chase, just to dig him up and then rebury him, ten to fifteen grand. Then there's the cost of the autopsy which will be at least another four or five depending on lab costs. Of course, Mackenzie will fight it, so you can figure another ten grand for that."

"You assholes are too expensive," Bob growled.

"No shit. Why do you think I don't get divorced? I can't afford it," Simon laughed. "Do you have anything other than your suspicions?"

Bob sullenly thought about the question for a moment then reluctantly said, "No, not really."

"Then it would be tough to convince a judge, especially when an autopsy was already done."

Bob sat quietly for a minute or so thinking what he had been told. "I guess I kind of expected that," he finally said. "Let me think it over and I'll let you know if I want to do it."

That night Bob slept straight through until morning. He awoke at 6:00 A.M. slightly puzzled. After a minute he realized why. The dream had not returned.

FIVE

Marc Kadella drove his Buick SUV into the parking lot of the Maplewood Community Center. On the drive from Minneapolis, he replayed the most recent argument he had with Margaret Tennant. It also occurred to him, looking back over the past few weeks, their relationship had become a bit strained. Marc began to realize that she was becoming more and more judgmental. Criticizing little things, he did for no good reason was becoming common and tiresome.

Marc was a few minutes late for the start of the class reunion. The parking lot was almost full, and he had trouble finding a spot. He parked his car, reflected again about Margaret and the way she was acting toward him.

"Maybe it's time to move on," he sadly said to himself.

While standing in line to check in and get a name tag, Marc said hello to a few people. Because Marc had done a few highly publicized trials, he had been on TV and in the papers many times. Several classmates came up to him to shake hands and acted like they were old pals. Without the name tags, he would not have known most of them and even with the name tags he only remembered a couple.

He reached the table and having prepaid, looked over the prepared name tags expecting to find his. As expected, he found it among the 'K's and as he picked it up one of the women at the table recognized him.

"Marc Kadella! Oh my god! It is soooo good to see you!"

Marc smiled at her, took a quick peek at her name tag, remembered the name and said, "Hello, Sofia. How are you?"

"You wait right there," she said as she started to come around the table.

As she came after him, her arms outstretched, Marc thought, *Holy shit. Sofia Kowalski. She must've gained a hundred pounds and now I have to hug her.*

"You come here. I want a big hug and a kiss from our celebrity lawyer," Sofia said.

While he tried to hug her, he continued thinking: *Now I have to kiss her? Dear God, strike me dead.*

After they separated she grabbed his hand, led him a few feet away and whispering said, "I have to tell you something. I still remember the hayride we were on when you and I were making out sitting on the hay. Do you remember?"

"Was I drunk?" Marc asked.

"Well, yeah, a little," she said.

"That explains it," Marc said then quickly added, "why I don't remember it."

"I even told my husband when we saw you on TV once," she added.

"You told your husband?"

"Well, yeah. He was kind of proud, you being a big shot lawyer and all."

Marc paused not quite believing what she said while thinking, *thank God we didn't have sex.*

"Listen, Sofia. It's great to see you but I need to ah, you know, circulate and say hello to other people."

"Of course," she smiled. "Save a dance for me."

"I'll, ah, do my best."

Marc extricated himself from the hungry-eyed Sofia and headed straight for the bar. When he got there he fell in with a small group of men, all of whom he knew and still occasionally socialized with. Marc paid for his Vodka soda and turned to the guys.

"So, you and Sofia," one of them said.

"I remember a hay ride when you and her..." another chimed in smiling.

"She just reminded me, John. Apparently it was the romantic highlight of her life," Marc said.

"You didn't..." John started to say.

"No, I didn't, thank God. At least, I don't think so and I'm pretty sure she would have reminded me."

This last statement brought a hearty laugh from everyone.

For the next hour, Marc made the rounds through the crowd. Of a class of almost six hundred, there appeared to be around three hundred in attendance. One of Marc's friends, a guy he had known since he was seven years old was on the committee that put the reunion together. He told Marc that at each reunion there were fewer and fewer people so half was about what they expected.

Marc was back at the bar talking to a woman he had briefly dated when he felt someone tap him on the shoulder. He turned around and looked directly at a pair of beautiful, brown eyes.

"Hello, Marc. You're looking well," the woman said.

Marc smiled and said nothing for several seconds while he looked her over. Finally, he quietly said, "Mackenzie Lange. You look fabulous. How long has it been?"

"I'd say about twenty-five years," she laughed. "How are you?"

"I'm good, Mac. How are you?"

"You know," she smiled, "you're the only one I liked to call me that."

"Mac? You're kidding. Everyone called you that," Marc said.

"I know but I never really liked it except from you."

Marc looked at her, a bit puzzled then merely said, "Okay."

"I thought of you as a friend. You always treated me like you liked me as a person. Like a friend," she said smiling.

"I did," Marc replied

Marc bought each of them a drink then guided Mackenzie to an empty table. The two of them sat talking for the next hour or so, bringing each other up to date. At least, Marc did. Mackenzie made a vague reference to being a widow then politely told him she did not want to talk about it. Believing it was a sensitive subject, Marc let it go.

The two of them first met in seventh grade at Wilson Junior High. Mackenzie's last name, Lange, starting with an L and Marc's starting with a K, alphabetically put her right behind him in almost all of their classes. Being twelve years old and recently discovering girls, Marc was smitten the moment he laid eyes on Mackenzie, the prettiest girl he had ever seen.

At the ripe old age of twelve, Marc was an awkward, insecure boy who couldn't imagine her feeling the same way toward him. Not realizing that everyone at that age, including the pretty girls, felt exactly the same way, he never acted on it.

They became friends and Mackenzie turned into one of those girls who matures, both physically and emotionally, sooner then her peers. By the time they reached high school and transferred to Central High, Mackenzie was one of a handful of "hot chicks". Like most girls that age, the attention she received from older guys, seniors, made her realize something; she could hunt for bigger game than the boys her age.

It wasn't long before she gained the reputation as something of the class slut. Marc, of course, heard the rumors but not knowing whether or not they were true basically ignored them. A lot of it he knew was likely teenage jealousy by other girls.

While they talked, friends and acquaintances would stop, pull up a chair and join them. Usually, he or she would stay for a couple of minutes then move on.

Once Marc returned from the bar with drinks for the two of them and found another man in his chair. He recognized the man as Jerry Smits, the captain and quarterback of the football team. Jerry had the same high school jock attitude he carried around in school but the good looks he once had were rapidly leaving. Obviously, Jerry was hitting on

Mackenzie despite the white tan line on his finger where his wedding ring had recently been.

Marc stood next to him for almost a minute listening to him remind Mackenzie of his football exploits. He finally paused for a breath and Mackenzie quickly used the opportunity to introduce Jerry to Marc. Smits stood up to shake hands with Marc who had set the drinks down.

"Sure, I remember you, Kadella," the paunchy ex-jock said. "Weren't you on the badminton team," he said laughing at his attempt at humor.

"Wow, that's really funny, Jerry," Marc deadpanned. "Did you think that up all by yourself?"

Ignoring the insult or more likely not getting it, Jerry asked, "So, Kadella, what've you been up to?"

"Marc's a lawyer," Mackenzie told him.

"Really, ambulance chaser, huh?" Smits laughed.

"Another example of that rapier wit I remember from school," Marc said.

"Marc was sitting there, Jerry. We were talking. Nice to see you again," Mackenzie said in dismissal.

Jerry looked back and forth at the two of them as if he was wondering what Mackenzie could see in an ambulance chasing attorney.

"Oh, sure, I get it," he said. "Well, see you later Kadella and I'll see you too, Mackenzie," he added with a sly wink.

Marc took his seat and said, "You didn't date him, did you? Please tell me you didn't, even if you have to lie to me."

"No, I didn't," Mackenzie laughed. "And I don't have to lie about it. I wasn't into the big jock guys."

"He was an idiot then and he's an idiot now," Marc said holding up his glass to her.

She touched hers to his then took Marc's hand and said, "You know, you were my first real crush."

"Seriously? I had no idea," he said.

"Yep, first day of class in seventh grade. Homeroom, Mrs. Anderson…."

"You remember the name of our homeroom teacher from seventh grade? That's actually kind of sad. Why didn't you tell me how you felt about me?"

"Because I was an insecure twelve-year-old girl," she laughed. "And I didn't think you liked me that way."

Marc leaned forward, lightly kissed her and said, "I was crazy about you and too insecure to do anything. Then when we got to high school, we kind of drifted apart and you were dating older guys."

"It's not true, you know," she said.

"What?"

"I wasn't the school slut."

"I never thought you were," he quietly said.

"Are you involved with anyone?" Mackenzie bluntly asked him.

Marc hesitated a little too long before answering.

"That means you are," Mackenzie answered for him.

"I have been, and I suppose still am," he said sounding a bit disappointed. "To be honest, I'm not sure where we are right now."

For the next two to three minutes Marc gave her an honest overview of his relationship with Margaret Tennant.

"A judge, huh? I better stay out of Hennepin County," Mackenzie weakly tried to make a little joke out of it.

"Yeah," Marc said.

An awkward minute of silence passed between them while each took a sip of their drink. Mackenzie looked at her watch then set the half-full glass on the table.

"It's getting late and I should go. Do you have a business card?" she asked.

"Sure," Marc said. He gave her one from the card case he carried. He took it back, asked her for a pen and she found one in her purse. He wrote his cell phone number on the back and gave it and the pen back to her.

"I'm surprised you don't have your cell number on the card," she said.

"I do criminal defense. I don't need these idiots calling me day and night. We have an answering service. If I want to talk to them, I'll call them back." Marc tapped the card she was holding and said, "You can call me anytime."

Mackenzie smiled and said, "Walk me to my car."

When they reached her shiny, new BMW, Marc opened the door for her. They gave each other an affectionate hug and a brief kiss. Then Mackenzie said, "If you figure out where you are with the judge, call me."

"I will," Marc told her.

Marc finished brushing his teeth and while he wiped his mouth with the hand towel, looked at himself in the bathroom mirror.

"Mackenzie Lange," he said out loud. "She looks better than when we were kids," he continued. He paused for a moment then said while still looking at himself, "And you, my friend, are more than a little smitten."

SIX

"Hey, bro," Adam Sutherland said when his brother entered Bob's office.

"Get your feet off my desk," Bob growled at the younger man. "What are you doing here?" he continued as he sat down in his executive chair.

"I need to talk to you," Adam answered. "I talked to Hailey and we're both gonna need money and soon."

"You could try getting a job," Bob said.

"As what, a grocery store clerk?"

"It's an honest living," the older brother replied. "You're a smart, educated man. You could work your way up."

"To what, become a store manager someday? I should have inherited enough so I wouldn't have to work. It's not fair that bitch gets it all!" Adam whined.

"Christ, you should hear yourself," Bob said with disgust.

There was a long pause between them then Bob said, "I've been thinking it over and I have an idea to try. I'll talk to Mackenzie, 'that bitch', tonight. There may be a way to get our share."

"Really? What, how?"

Bob held up a hand, palm out, and said, "The less you know at this point the better. Let me talk to her and I'll call you tomorrow and tell you how it went, okay?"

"Okay, great," Adam replied.

Mackenzie was seated on the sofa in the large living room quietly staring at the logs burning in the fireplace. She was in the Sutherland family homestead in the Crocus Hill area of St. Paul, a five-bedroom, six bath, twelve room Tudor she inherited. Mackenzie never really liked the place and was going to be rid of it as soon as everything settled down. There wasn't a mortgage on it and she figured another seven hundred grand easily. *That should set off Bill's kids,* a thought that caused her to smile.

Earlier that afternoon, she had received a call from the oldest Sutherland, Bob. Of the three of them, Bob was the only one she could barely tolerate. A little on the dull, boring, slow-witted side, he was at least employed and employable. The other two, Mackenzie believed, as did their father, were a waste of breathable air.

She was dressed in a light gray, cotton skirt with pockets and a baby blue sweater. The day was cool and wet from a constant drizzle of rain coming down. Mackenzie checked her watch, saw that Bob was five minutes late, then heard the front doorbell ring.

"Hello, Bob," Mackenzie greeted him when she opened the door. "Please come in."

Bob followed Mackenzie into the house through the twelve-foot-wide foyer and onto the marble-tiled main floor. To their left was the living room with the fireplace against the exterior wall and the informal dining area by the patio doors. Directly ahead was the open stairway leading to the second-floor bedrooms. On their right was the formal dining room with the mahogany table set for ten people.

"Let's go into the living room. I have a fire going. I've been chilly all day. It's June sixth and it just seems wrong to turn on the furnace in June," Mackenzie said.

You can certainly afford it, Bob thought.

"Please, have a seat," Mackenzie said indicating a Queen Anne that matched the sofa Mackenzie sat down upon. The chair was to the right of the fireplace and when Mackenzie sat on the couch, she was directly facing him.

"What did you want to see me about?" Mackenzie asked as if she did not know.

Bob hesitated for a moment, looked around the living room he knew so well then said, "I don't think it's right or fair that you inherited everything my parents worked for and achieved."

Mackenzie sat quietly, her legs crossed at the ankles, her hands folded together in her lap.

"It's not right Mackenzie and you know it," he repeated hoping for a better reaction.

"It's what your father decided. I don't think you know this, but he was not pleased with how the three of you turned out. You know what Adam and Hailey are like and you, quite frankly, he considered an underachiever. And after your mother died, he was sad, depressed and lonely. I brought him happiness the last few years of his life. Other than be born, what did the three of you do?"

Bob, obviously taken aback by her stinging rebuke, sat angrily staring at her for several seconds. "That's not true and you know it," he finally said.

"Do I?" Mackenzie laconically replied.

Annoyed by Mackenzie's seeming indifference and attitude, Bob leaned forward and stared at her. This posture actually impressed Mackenzie because she did not believe he had the backbone for it.

"You murdered my father," he said.

"That's quite an accusation," Mackenzie calmly replied.

Ignoring her non-denial, denial, Bob continued, "There was nothing wrong with his heart and there is no family history of heart problems."

"First of all, that's not true about his heart being healthy which is obvious since he had a heart attack. Plus, there was an autopsy," Mackenzie calmly reminded him.

"I've been doing a little research. There are drugs that can induce a heart attack that would not be found in a routine autopsy," Bob said.

Mackenzie heartily laughed then said, "Chemistry was never my favorite subject. I wouldn't know about such drugs."

"I've talked to a lawyer. He said we can have the body exhumed and another autopsy performed."

"Really?" Mackenzie said with a sly smile.

"Yes, we can. And this time we'll have them look for those drugs. Or..."

"Or what?" she asked.

"Or, you pay us, me, Adam and Hailey our share of the sale of the business. I heard you got twenty-seven million. We each want two point seven million," Bob said.

"And if I don't, you'll dig up your father's remains and try to prove I murdered him. But if I pay you the two point seven million, you'll drop the whole thing. You believe I murdered your dad but you're willing to let it slide for a total of eight point one million for the three of you."

"Yes, that's right," Bob admitted thinking she was coming around.

"Are you wearing a wire?" she asked.

"A what? A wire? You mean like for the police to listen in?"

"Yes, exactly. Are you wearing a wire?"

"No, of course not," he angrily proclaimed.

"That's good because you just admitted to a felony."

At that moment, Mackenzie shivered as if a chill had come over her.

"Be a dear, Bob and stir the fire a bit, will you please?"

"Sure," he said. He stood up and took the iron, brass handled fireplace poker from its stand. He bent over the fireplace, his back to Mackenzie and stirred the logs sending sparks up the chimney and causing the fire to flare up.

When he straightened up, he turned to find Mackenzie standing a few feet away, a pistol in her hand pointed at his chest.

"What..." he started to say.

Mackenzie fired the small handgun twice in rapid succession. The first bullet struck him in the sternum; the second went through his heart.

The impact of the bullets drove him back into the side of the fireplace, crashing through the fireplace utensils and up against the bricks surrounding the fireplace. His heart was mangled and no longer beating but there was still enough oxygen in his brain to allow him to consciously wonder what happened and tell his lungs to breathe. Not yet dead, he stared at Mackenzie, an uncomprehending look on his face as he tried desperately to breathe and try to understand what just happened.

Mackenzie stood watching him, waiting for him to die. Just before his lights went out, she leaned forward and said, "You should have kept a tighter leash on your brother."

When it was obvious he was dead, Mackenzie tossed the .38 Smith & Wesson snub nose revolver eight to ten feet to her right. She left it on the carpeting and walked into the dining room, pulled out a chair from the table, took out her phone and dialed 9-1-1.

"Oh my god! Oh my god!" Mackenzie frantically started when the 9-1-1 operator answered. "Please, help me! I, I, ah shot someone in my house. He was going to kill me. Please, send the police."

"Calm down, ma'am," the operator coolly said.

"I think he's dead but maybe not. Please, send an ambulance," she almost hysterically yelled. "He was so mad. He threatened me with a poker. A fireplace poker. Please hurry."

It took almost a minute for the operator to get a stammering and stuttering Mackenzie to give her the address. She assured Mackenzie help was on the way and the call ended.

Mackenzie looked at her watch, waited a few seconds longer than two minutes then dialed a number off of a business card she held. The phone was answered on the second ring and Mackenzie repeated her performance for Marc Kadella.

Twenty minutes later Marc parked on the street several houses down from the Sutherland's. Being Crocus Hill, an area of St. Paul with more money than most, the cops were there in force. There were at least six squad cars, an ambulance and a vehicle from the medical examiner's office. Marc would have to walk up the sidewalk in the rain to get to the house.

On his way he was stopped three times before finally reaching the front door. Each time he politely explained to the officer who he was and that he was there for his client. Marc also told each of them to keep an eye open for a tall, attractive, brunette woman, a private investigator that worked for him and would be arriving any minute.

Marc entered the house and saw Mackenzie sitting meekly to his right in the dining room. She was by herself and looking very frightened about the chaos taking place in her house. Marc waved to her which caused her to slightly smile as if in relief. He held up an index finger to her to indicate he would be with her in a minute. Marc then found the detective in charge and introduced himself.

"I don't want anything moved or disturbed, detective," Marc told her. "I have an investigator coming and I'll want pictures myself."

"No problem, counselor," Anna Finney politely replied.

"Did you try to question my client?"

"When we first got here, yeah," she said. "She told us she had called a lawyer, he was on the way and he had told her not to talk to anyone or answer any questions. So, we left her alone in the other room."

"Okay," Marc said. "Let me go talk to her then I'll find you."

Another cop tapped him on the shoulder and Marc turned around to face him. He was the officer guarding the front door.

"Your P.I. is here and you weren't exaggerating. Can I get her phone number?" the man asked.

"You'll have to ask her," Marc smiled.

"I'm afraid to try. She'll probably laugh," the cop said.

"Let her in, please," Marc said shaking his head at the 'Madeline effect'.

Madeline Rivers came striding up to him a few seconds later.

"I hate her already," Anna Finney whispered to Marc when she saw Maddy coming.

"Maddy Rivers, Detective Finney," Marc said introducing them. The women shook hands and Maddy produced an excellent Nikon digital camera from a bag.

"Don't disturb anything but take all the pictures you need," Finney told her.

While Maddy began taking photos Marc went into the dining room to talk to Mackenzie. As soon as he reached her, she stood, threw her arms around his neck and began sobbing.

Marc managed to calm her down and over the next twenty minutes, while Marc asked questions to steer her through it, Mackenzie told him her version of what happened. Just as they were finishing, Maddy joined them. Marc introduced the two women.

"Did you get everything?" Marc asked.

"Yeah and I did a video of the room with my phone," Maddy said. Maddy had taken a chair next to Mackenzie and placed her hand on one of Mackenzie's. She then politely asked, "Were the two of you in any other room that I should photograph?"

"No, um, just the living room," Mackenzie replied. "We went there after I let him in."

"Okay," Maddy smiled.

"Wait here," Marc told the two women.

He walked back to the living room and found Finney and her partner together. Finney introduced them then Marc said, "We have a self-defense case here…"

"Good, we'll talk to her now," Finney's partner, Dale Kubik said.

"No, you won't. I'll bring her to the police department tomorrow morning. How's ten o'clock sound?"

"Fine," Finney politely replied.

"That's nice of her," Kubik sarcastically interjected.

"I'd like someone from the county attorney's office present," Marc continued ignoring the snide comment from Kubik.

"Shouldn't be a problem," Finney replied. "We'll see you then. Ask for me when you get there," she said and handed Marc her card.

Marc went back into the living room and told Maddy and Mackenzie about the next day's meeting.

"I don't want to stay here tonight," Mackenzie said.

"Will you take her to a hotel for me?" Marc asked Maddy, thinking it would not be a good idea for him to do it.

"Sure," Maddy said. "There's the St. Paul Hotel or Crowne Plaza downtown. Which one?" she asked Mackenzie.

"Either is fine. Let me pack a bag."

"I'll call you in the morning," Marc said.

SEVEN

"You made the paper again today," Carolyn told Marc as he came strolling into the office.

"And this morning's news shows," Sandy Compton, the other office assistant chimed in.

Carolyn held out the A section of the Minneapolis Star Tribune to Marc. "Front page headlines," she said.

"Can I have your autograph?" Jeff Modell, the office paralegal mockingly asked.

"I just want to bask in your glory," Sandy added fluttering her eyelids.

Marc ignored the sarcasm and took the paper into his office. He hung up his suit coat, sat down and began reading the account of the previous evening's events. Before he finished the intercom buzzed.

"Hey, Gabriella Shriqui is on the phone. You want to talk to her?" Carolyn asked him.

"I guess so, put her through," Marc answered her.

"Plus, you walked off pouting..."

"I am not pouting."

"Whatever. Anyway, you have a dozen messages from other media types. You want them?"

"As I recall you have a perfectly good shredder out there. Feel free to use it."

"Will do, here's Gabriella."

"Good morning, Marc," Gabriella Shriqui said. Gabriella had been the on-scene court reporter for a local TV station. She interviewed Marc several times during trials Marc did and they had become casual friends. Gabriella was now the host of her own local show, *The Court Reporter*. She was also a good friend of Marc's investigator, Maddy Rivers and it didn't hurt that she was stop traffic gorgeous.

"Hey, kid," Marc replied. "What's up?"

"I see your name's involved with the shooting of one of the Sutherland kids by their stepmother, Mackenzie. Are you representing her?"

"No comment," Marc said with a smile Gabriella could not see.

"Don't give me that 'no comment' bullshit," she said. "You owe me..."

"Why is it I always owe you? Why don't you ever owe me?"

"Because of all of the great free publicity I give you. That and I always wiggle my ass for you when I know you're watching," she laughed.

"You are a shameless hussy," Marc jokingly chastised.

"Come on the show this afternoon and I'll wear a short skirt," she laughed again. Turning serious she continued, "This Sutherland shooting is great stuff and I want the inside scoop."

"You're starting to sound like Melinda Pace," Marc said. Melinda Pace was the original host of Gabriella's show. No one would have nominated Melinda for an excellence in journalism award.

"Seriously?" Gabriella asked with legitimate concern.

"Keep it in mind," Marc said. "Look, for now, and this is completely off the record, Mackenzie Sutherland has a solid self-defense claim."

"That wasn't in the paper," Gabriella said.

"That's shocking that they didn't have all of the facts before they rushed to put it in the paper and on local news," Marc sarcastically replied. "Here's what they have, and I'll quote," Marc continued reading from the paper, "Informed sources close to the investigation claim the shooting is part of an ongoing dispute over the estate of William Sutherland, the founder of *Sutherland's* grocery store chain. Who are these informed sources they are using? Somebody whispers this to a reporter, that reporter runs with it, then pretty soon you're all using it. It's bullshit, Gabriella, and sloppy journalism."

Carolyn opened his door, stuck her head in and quietly said, "Maddy's here."

"Maddy's here," Marc told Gabriella. "I have to go. I'll call you later and if it's okay with my client I'll come on your show in the next day or two. Okay?"

"All right," Gabriella agreed. "Say hello to my buddy for me."

"Will do."

Even at the tail end of rush hour, traffic on eastbound I-94 between Minneapolis and St. Paul was heavy although moving fairly well. Marc and Maddy made a little small talk, mostly about the scene at the Sutherland house the night before.

"Do you believe her?" Maddy bluntly asked as they crossed the Mississippi River bridge into St. Paul.

Marc turned his head to look at her for a second then resumed driving while he thought about his response.

"That's a strange question," he said while Maddy continued to look at him to check out his reaction.

"Do you?" she asked again. "You know her, I don't."

Marc glanced at her again then said, "I'm her lawyer. Yes, I believe her Ms. Cynical ex-cop. Don't you?"

Maddy laughed her delightful, genuine laugh then said, "Yes, I do. I just wanted to get your reaction. Plus, I went over all of the pictures I took and unless the cops come up with something different, the forensics support her story. The fireplace poker was on his lap. I suppose she could have planted it but that's a stretch."

"Cynical ex-cop," Marc repeated with a smile.

"Something's bugging me, though," Maddy continued. "There's something about her. She looks familiar to me, but I can't place it."

"Happens all the time, Madeline."

"True enough," she agreed and dropped the subject.

They picked up Mackenzie from the hotel she stayed in and made it to police headquarters at 9:45 A.M. The three of them checked in, received visitor badges and a uniformed sergeant escorted them to the meeting room.

Waiting for them were the two detectives from the night before, Anna Finney and Dale Kubik. Also present was their immediate supervisor, Lt. Randall Evans and two lawyers from the Ramsey County Attorney's office, Heather Anderson and Wade Keenan.

All of the officials from Ramsey county and St. Paul were seated along one side of a conference table. At one end, facing the chair at the opposite end of the table, was a video camera. On the wall behind the camera was a one-way mirror; a window for a room where people could watch.

"Hi, Heather," Marc said greeting the assistant county attorney.

Introductions were made then Mackenzie took the chair at the head of the table facing the camera. Marc took the first chair to her left, Maddy, the one next to him. Heather Anderson, the lead attorney was to Mackenzie's right. Evans turned on the video camera when Anderson indicated she was ready.

Anderson spoke everyone's name into the record; gave the date, time, place and purpose of the meeting then turned to Mackenzie and said, "Now, Mrs. Sutherland..."

"Before you start," Marc interrupted her. "I want to put something on the record."

"Sure, Mr. Kadella, go ahead," Heather smiled.

"Mackenzie Sutherland is here voluntarily. She has no legal obligation to be here and tell her side of the shooting of Robert Sutherland. In fact, it is her constitutional right not to do so. I want to make sure she understands that if she chooses to do so at any time, she can stop this and refuse to answer any more questions. Or, if she wants to take a break to confer with counsel she can do so. Do you understand that?"

"Yes, I do," Mackenzie quietly replied.

"Okay," Marc said.

“Mrs. Sutherland, we want you to tell us in your own words, what happened yesterday that led to the death of your stepson, Robert Sutherland.”

“Okay,” Mackenzie started looking a little nervous, “Bob called me…”

“By Bob you mean the victim, Robert Sutherland?” Anderson asked.

“Object to the use of the word victim,” Marc said.

“Marc, we’re not in court,” Anderson said.

“I don’t care,” Marc said. “Words matter. At this point he is not a victim of anything.”

“Okay, point taken,” Heather said. “Please continue, Mrs. Sutherland.”

“Yes, Bob is Robert Sutherland. Anyway, he called me around 4:00, 4:15 somewhere in there. He said he wanted to stop by the house and see me. He said he wanted to talk to me.”

“Did he tell you what he wanted to talk to you about?” Heather asked.

“No, he did not. I figured it was probably about his father’s money.”

“Why?”

“Because their father, Bill, pretty much cut Bob, his brother Adam and sister Hailey out of his Will a few months before he died. Even though I had no idea he did it, they never believed me. They believe I pressured their dad into it or somehow got him to change his Will. I didn’t and the lawyer who changed the Will has told the kids this, but they still don’t believe it.”

“All right, please go on.”

“I agreed to see him at the Crocus Hill house and he came by shortly after 7:00.”

“When you spoke to him on the phone at 4:00, did he sound angry or upset?” Heather asked.

“No, he didn’t.”

“Okay, please continue.”

“I led him into the living room. I sat down on a sofa and he took a chair facing me, next to the fireplace.”

“There was a fire going in the fireplace. Why?” Detective Finney asked.

“Because it was a rainy, chilly day and I didn’t want to turn on the furnace. It was a little chilly in the house and the fire felt good. I told you this last night,” Mackenzie politely reminded the detective.

“After the two of you sat down, what happened next?” Heather asked.

Mackenzie took a deep breath then said, "He started right in again. Once again accusing me of manipulating their father against the three kids to get him to change his Will and cut them out. We had been over this many times and I was getting tired of it."

"Where did the gun come from that you used to shoot him?" Heather Anderson abruptly asked hoping to catch Mackenzie off guard.

"It was Bill's gun…" Mackenzie started to say, a little confused at the sudden change of direction.

"No, what I meant was where did you have it while you were talking?"

"Oh, I see. I had it in the right-hand pocket of my skirt," Mackenzie replied.

"Do you always carry…?" Heather started to ask.

"What do you say we let her finish then you can try to catch her with 'gotcha' questions," Marc interjected. "By the time she's done you'll likely know everything."

"Please continue," Heather Anderson said a touch of annoyance in her voice.

"Where was I?" Mackenzie rhetorically asked, "Oh, yes, I remember. He accused me of manipulating their dad to cut them out of his Will. I reminded him again, the lawyer who made the new Will told them Bill verified I knew nothing about it. Then I told him the real reason his dad changed his Will was because he was not pleased with them."

"How so?" Marc asked.

Mackenzie looked at Marc then turned back to the camera.

"Bill thought Bob, the oldest, was a total wimp. His wife, Paige, whom Bill despised, led him around by the nose. Hailey and Adam were worse. Hailey had been the apple of her dad's eye before she became, and these are Bill's words, not mine, 'a cheap slut who didn't have any sense of morality or values at all.' Adam was the worst of the three of them. Drugs, booze, fast cars and bimbos were his passion. Again, those were Bill's words, but I agree with him. Could I get a glass of water?" Mackenzie asked Marc.

While Marc was pouring her a glass of water, she continued.

"At that point, he got down to the real reason he came to see me. He accused me, again, of murdering Bill. I denied it again, then he said he was going to have Bill's body dug up and a new autopsy performed.

"I didn't know what to say to that. Of course, I didn't want that done. It sounded ghoulish. Let the poor man rest in peace next to Elizabeth, his first wife and the kids' mother. So, I told him I was against that, but he said he had talked to a lawyer and the lawyer, I believe he saw Simon Kane, told him it wouldn't be a problem.

"I said I would oppose it and then Bob told me he would let the whole thing go if I paid the three of them each ten percent of what the company was sold for. Somehow he knew how much that was and he wanted two point seven million for each of them."

"What did you say to that?" Heather asked.

"I was absolutely appalled. I thought about throwing him out but instead I said something like, 'Let me see if I understand you. You believe I murdered your father but you're willing to let that slide if I pay the three of you eight point one million dollars. Is that what you're saying?'"

"Then he said: 'The old tyrant is dead. We just want what we had coming before you screwed us.'"

"By then I had had enough, and I told him to get out. I told him they didn't deserve anything, and I wasn't going to pay blackmail.

"He got really angry. I could see it in his eyes and face. He stood up, grabbed the fireplace poker, waved it at me and yelled something like, 'you fucking bitch, I'll make you pay for what you did' and he took a step toward me.

"The next thing I remember, he was lying by the fireplace and I was holding the gun. I remember going into the dining room and calling 9-1-1. My hands were shaking so bad I could barely punch the numbers. I remember talking to a woman, but I can't really recall everything I said. I must have told her I shot someone. I'm sure I did.

"Then I was sitting at the dining room table and a couple minutes later I thought to call Marc. I found his card, called him and he told me to stay where I was and not talk to the police until he got there.

"I remember it seemed like an hour but was probably only a few minutes. Then all of a sudden, there were people all over the place.

"After a little while Marc and Ms. Rivers arrived, we talked and well, here we are," Mackenzie concluded. She picked up the glass of water and as her hand trembled slightly, took a large drink.

"What happened to the gun? After you shot Robert Sutherland, what did you do with the gun?" Detective Finney asked. "You didn't mention it."

"The gun? Um, I'm not sure. I think I dropped it or maybe tossed it away in the living room. Why? Didn't you find it?" Mackenzie answered.

"Yes, they found it," Marc answered her. "In the living room right where you dropped it."

"Why did you have a gun in your pocket in the first place?" Finney asked.

Mackenzie looked at Marc who said, "Go ahead, tell them."

"Because Bob had threatened me several times. I'm not sure I was afraid of him, but I was worried. I thought if he threatened me again, I'd scare him with the gun," she said.

"Can anyone verify this?" Heather Anderson asked.

"Yes," Mackenzie said. "The lawyer who handled the estate and the sale of the company, Cooper Thomas. Bob threatened me in his conference room when they were told about Bill's estate and the sale of the company. The other two Sutherland kids were there too but they'll lie.

"There was someone else there," Mackenzie continued as if she just now remembered. "Cooper had a security man in the room because he was worried about how the three of them would react to the news about the money. In fact, when Bob threatened me, he stood up behind Bob to protect me. I don't know his name. Cooper will have it."

Mackenzie took Cooper's card from her purse and handed it to Heather Anderson. She wrote down the information then gave it to Finney who did the same thing.

"Will you call Mr. Thomas and give him permission to talk to the detectives?" Heather asked.

"Oh sure, certainly," Mackenzie answered.

Marc waited a few seconds then asked, "Mrs. Sutherland, describe your feelings when Robert Sutherland waved the fireplace poker at you."

"I was really scared. I'd never seen Bob so mad. Usually he's kind of passive but the look in his eyes and on his face was terrible. I truly believed he was going to kill me. I remember standing up, he took a step toward me then I shot him."

"To be clear, are you saying you were in fear of your life at that moment?" Marc asked.

"Yes, absolutely," Mackenzie answered him.

For the next half-hour, the authorities asked her questions, mostly going over the same ground. It was obvious they were trying to trip her up, unsuccessfully. Mackenzie handled the questioning and Marc finally called a halt to it.

"Since she is telling the truth you're not going to poke holes in her story. I think we've done enough for today," Marc said. "Now what?" he asked Anderson.

"Now, we'll complete our investigation and let you know," she said.

"I want a copy of the 9-1-1 tape," Marc said. "Have you listened to it?"

"Yes, I have," Anderson said.

"And?"

“It’s corroborative,” Anderson admitted.

“Don’t sound so disappointed,” Marc said. “People do have the right to defend themselves, especially in their homes.”

“I know, Marc,” she agreed. “I didn’t mean to sound disappointed.”

“I want a copy of this video also,” Marc said. “Can you convert it to DVD?”

“Sure, no problem. I’ll messenger both to your office probably today or first thing tomorrow,” Anderson promised him.

As the three of them were getting ready to leave, the police lieutenant shut off the camera and asked, “Are you willing to take a lie detector…”

“Yes,” Mackenzie quickly answered.

“…test?” Evans finished.

“No,” Marc emphatically said. “Not a chance,” he continued looking at Anderson.

“Why not?” the cop asked.

Marc looked at Evans then said, “Because there’s no such thing as a lie detector test and you know it.”

“I don’t mind,” Mackenzie said.

“Listen to your lawyer,” Maddy quietly told Mackenzie. Both women were standing and Maddy gently took Mackenzie’s arm to lead her away.

“You will listen to your lawyer on this,” Marc sternly said to Mackenzie with a serious look in his eye. “I’ll explain why when we leave.”

Marc turned his head back to the people across the table and repeated, “No polygraph and I better not read about her refusing it in the papers.”

When the three of them were back in Marc’s car and driving toward downtown to take Mackenzie to the hotel, Mackenzie asked Marc about the lie detector test.

“First of all, there is no such thing as a lie detector machine,” Marc began. “It measures body functions; skin temperature, heart rate, breathing that kind of thing. They are not reliable.”

Marc looked in the mirror at Maddy in the backseat and said, “Hey, ex-cop, tell her what cops think when someone passes the test.”

“They figure you found a way to beat the machine,” Maddy said.

“And if you failed it, I guarantee the media would be reporting it before we left the building,” Marc added.

“So, they’d figure I cheated if I passed the test and try to use it against me if I didn’t,” Mackenzie said.

“That’s right,” Marc and Madeline said together.

EIGHT

The three police detectives and both prosecutors were about to watch a replay of the video when the interrogation room door opened. A handsome black man with the build, moves and grace of a natural athlete, entered. He took the chair that Maddy Rivers used to join the group.

"What did you think, Max?" the detective lieutenant asked him.

"She's lying," Detective Max Coolidge replied. "She's good at it but I told you, I've known Bob Sutherland for twenty-five years. He's a helluva nice guy who wouldn't do what she claims. I'm not buying it."

"Let's watch the video, then we'll talk," Heather Anderson said.

The six of them silently reviewed Mackenzie's entire statement. When it ended all six of them quietly waited for someone else to say something.

"Make sure we get a copy of that to her lawyer," Anderson broke the silence and told the other prosecutor, Wade Keenan.

"Will do," he answered.

"She agreed to take a lie detector test," Finney said to Coolidge.

"She knew her lawyer would say no," Coolidge replied.

"Max…" Evans started to say.

"Look," Anderson interrupted him, "the forensics and the scene at the house match her story. His fingerprints are on the handle of the fireplace poker…"

"He wasn't in the chair. He must have stood up and grabbed the poker before she shot him," Finney interjected. "It matches her story."

"The 9-1-1 call sounds legitimate and if this other lawyer, Cooper Thomas, verifies that Sutherland threatened her…" Anderson said.

"That will do it," Evans finished.

"So, we'll just take the easy way out and let her walk. It's at least manslaughter," Max almost pleaded. "Take it to a grand jury."

"She has the right to defend herself in her own home," Finney reminded him.

"I told you I talked to Bob at his dad's funeral. All three kids said she was a manipulative bitch," Max started to say.

"A beautiful, younger woman marries a rich widower and the kids resent it. That's hardly a news flash. If this other lawyer verifies that he threatened her…." Evans repeated.

"And I'm sure both he and the security guy who was there will or she wouldn't have told us about it," Finney added.

"Then it's a solid self-defense case that we can't win, and the county attorney's office won't bring," Anderson said.

Silence descended on the small room again. The five people seated across the table from him all patiently waited for Coolidge, informally known as Max Cool, to say something.

A full minute went by, then Coolidge looked at his boss, the lieutenant, and asked, "You mind if I dig around myself?"

"Yes, I do mind, but I know it's pointless to argue with you," Evans replied.

"I don't like him looking over my shoulder and second-guessing me," Finney's partner, Dale Kubik, said obviously annoyed.

"Relax, Dale. He's not second-guessing anything. Besides, the family still needs to be interviewed. He knows them, let him do it," Finney told him.

"I still don't like it," Kubik said.

"I'll do it on my own time. Paige, Bob's wife, asked me to. I've known her since before they were married. I watched their kids grow up. If I check it out and don't find anything, she'll probably be more willing to accept what happened."

"You be very careful around Mackenzie Sutherland," Anderson sternly told him. "You don't ask her anything without her lawyer. I know him. He won't sit still for it."

"I'll only talk to her if I find something and you guys agree to bring her in for more questioning. Okay?"

"All right," Evans told him.

The two lawyers from the county attorney's office and the lieutenant waited for the detectives to leave. When they were gone Anderson turned to Wade Keenan, himself an experienced prosecutor.

"What do you think, Wade?" she asked.

"If the lawyer, Cooper Thomas, corroborates her claim that Sutherland threatened her, there's no way we convict her of anything," Keenan answered her.

"Manslaughter?" Evans asked the two lawyers.

"Maybe," Anderson said. "But she has a good lawyer and the physical evidence backs up a self-defense claim."

"What about the gun?" Keenan asked.

"It's legal," Evans replied. "We ran the serial number and it was purchased by a William Sutherland almost eight years ago. What about the fact she had a gun in her pocket?"

Anderson shrugged then said, "Nothing illegal about carrying a gun around inside your own home. And she has a plausible explanation."

"You know," Keenan said, "she could be telling the truth. This could be a legitimate case of self-defense."

"Even if it isn't, what do we do about motive? Why would she shoot him? She got everything," Anderson said.

"To prevent the second autopsy," Keenan answered him. "But that's thin. What about Coolidge?" Keenan said to Evans.

"He can be a bulldog," Evans told him. "I say we quietly let him go and see what he comes up with."

The two lawyers looked at each other than Anderson said, "I'm okay with it. We'll see what he finds."

Marc and Madeline came through the office's exterior door at almost precisely noon. The office TV set was on and everyone was gathered around it. The local noon news was coming on.

"Hey, you two," Connie Mickelson, Marc's landlady said. "You've been on the radio, so we figured…"

"Ssssh, here it is," Carolyn told Connie.

Marc and Maddy joined the group in front of the TV as the male anchor started reading the story.

"Mackenzie Sutherland was questioned at the headquarters of the St. Paul police this morning about the shooting death of her stepson, Robert Sutherland."

He then went on to remind the viewers who the Sutherlands were, and that Mackenzie had shot Robert in her home the previous evening. He tossed in the noise about a dispute over the estate then handed the story off to his female co-anchor.

Her name was Faith Peterson and she was about as Minnesota Swedish as a woman could be. A pretty, girl-next-door type with perfect teeth, hair and diction and was a bookend for the blow-dried male anchor. The female of the duo informed the audience about Mackenzie's claim at self-defense.

"Mrs. Sutherland was represented by local high-priced attorney Marc Kadella."

Everyone turned to look at Marc and Barry Cline another lawyer in the office asked him, "When did you become high-priced?"

"Right this minute," Marc replied which caused a round of laughs.

"It has also been confirmed," the perky blonde continued, "that the police requested that Mrs. Sutherland take a lie detector test and her lawyer adamantly refused to let her."

"Goddamnit, I told them…" Marc said steaming.

"They're not always accurate," Dalton said.

"That's true," Faith agreed.

"That's the most sensible thought to ever come out of his tiny little head," Marc said, still annoyed about the leak regarding the polygraph test.

"Do you know him?" Sandy asked.

"Yeah, I've met him," Marc admitted.

"He's gorgeous," Sandy told him.

"Good thing, too," Marc answered her. "That is his gift to the world. He looks good and can read a teleprompter. There isn't much between those ears. This reminds me," Marc said looking at Maddy, "I meant to ask Mac if I should go on Gabriella's show."

"You have a couple messages from Gabriella," Carolyn said.

"Hello, Mr. Kadella," Gabriella's producer, Cordelia Davis greeted Marc.

He was seated in the reception room of the Channel 8 TV station. Marc had called Mackenzie and received permission to do the show. Mackenzie even suggested that she go on as well. Marc made her realize it would look unseemly the day after the shooting and Mackenzie agreed.

Maddy was unofficially assigned to babysit Mackenzie. For now, that meant helping her get more clothing and personal items out of the house. It was still considered a crime scene and was taped off with yellow crime-scene tape. Marc spoke to Heather Anderson and got permission for Mackenzie and Maddy to go into the house as long as a cop was present. After leaving Marc's office, Maddy drove back to St. Paul and the two women went to do that while Marc was taping the show.

"You're never going to call me Marc are you?" he smiled while shaking Cordelia's hand. "Mr. Kadella makes me think you either don't like me or I'm getting old."

"Both," Cordelia said suppressing a smile.

"Now that's cold," Marc laughed.

"Okay, Marc," she said. "We'll get you to make up and then to the studio."

Gabriella and Marc were seated at the 'casual set'. It had two comfortable living-room chairs and a small, round table between them. When the director told Gabriella they were ready, she looked into the camera to begin taping.

"We're fortunate to have as a guest today, criminal defense attorney Marc Kadella. Mr. Kadella has agreed to come on and discuss last night's shooting of Robert Sutherland."

Gabriella turned to face Marc and started to say, "Mr. Kadella…"

"What happened to the short skirt you promised to wear? She has great legs folks," Marc said into the camera while everyone in the room started laughing.

"Stop!" Gabriella yelled while laughing herself. She regained control and said to Marc. "Is this what we're going to do?"

"Hey, you promised," Marc said in mock protest.

"Very funny," Gabriella said. "We'll start over and you," she continued pointing a stern finger at Marc, "will behave yourself. I need twelve to thirteen minutes and I don't want it to take two hours to get it!"

"Okay, Mom," Marc insincerely replied. "I'll be good. I promise."

Having had his fun at Gabriella's expense, Marc settled down. The interview took less than thirty minutes with only a few stops to get a question or answer straight.

Marc was able to communicate that Mackenzie had a strong self-defense claim without giving too many details. He also made it clear why he would not allow Mackenzie or any client to take a polygraph test. Gabriella did her best to get the juicy, gossipy information out of him about the family squabbles. Marc pled ignorance of this using the excuse that he was a criminal lawyer and not privy to any of that. When pressed he simply fell back on the fact that other lawyers, whom he refused to name, handled William Sutherland's estate. When they finally called a halt to it, Gabriella did not look happy.

"I might be able to get twelve minutes out of that," she told Marc. "You used me to get out that self-defense story."

"Yes, I did," Marc admitted looking her directly in the eye. "Your station reported that I wouldn't let Mackenzie take a lie detector and said nothing about self-defense. Is that fair?"

"No," Gabriella reluctantly admitted.

"So I set the record straight. And you got an exclusive so what's the big deal?"

"You owe me…" Gabriella started to say but couldn't suppress a smile.

"Great! Here we go with that 'you owe me' line again," Marc said.

Gabriella laughed, threw her arms around his neck, kissed him on the cheek and said, "Why aren't you about ten years younger?"

Marc returned her embrace, ignored the question and said, "Next time, wear the short skirt."

NINE

Max Coolidge was at his desk reading through a file about an East Side street gang. Starting in the mid-eighties the east side of St. Paul, for decades a predominantly working-class area of the city started to see an influx of street gangs. It was an equal opportunity, diverse collection of white, black, Latino and Asians. The predominantly liberal Democrats that ran the city wanted to treat them as, at worst, indiscreet up and coming urban entrepreneurs. The cops had the archaic attitude that the drug trade should be treated as crime. At the street level, the cops held sway and mostly kept a lid on the worst of the violence.

Occasionally there would be an act of violence that even the city council and media could not ignore. Not too long ago there was a vicious gang beating of an innocent man whose sole offense was walking down the sidewalk. The victim was left with brain damage and was barely able to walk. A half-dozen of these street corner capitalists were arrested amid cries of: "How could this happen in our city?" A few of the miscreants were even sentenced to, what the cops believed, mild prison terms.

Max, a detective in the intelligence unit was one of those whose job it was to keep his finger in the dyke and make sure this particular sewer did not back up into certain other, nicer neighborhoods.

The file he was perusing was one concerning a Hmong gang called the East Side Hmong Boys. Max was reading over a report he did for the intelligence unit about an uptick in heroin in the Cities. Max worked with another cop, an Asian undercover, who was convinced this gang was responsible. They had made a connection with an Asian gang in Los Angeles a few months back and now had a steady supply. Of course, the local hospitals were seeing a concomitant increase in heroin overdoses along with several deaths. Apparently the local geniuses in this particular group of Asian entrepreneurs were not too adept at cutting the quality down. The dope was cheaper than crack and too potent and deadly.

Having trouble concentrating on his report, Max finally got through it and placed his hard copy in the physical file. Satisfied with its content, he emailed copies from his computer to the appropriate people.

Max Coolidge was christened by his parents as Eugene Maximillian Coolidge forty years ago. He was named by his mother, Harriet, after her father and a favorite uncle. Born in St. Paul, his mother was a fairly devout Baptist. His father, Alfred, was just religious enough to satisfy Harriet and keep the peace.

Max grew up in the predominately black Selby Dale area of St. Paul. When he was around eight or nine, one of his friends came up with the nickname Max Cool and it stuck. An athletic kid, Max helped St.

Paul Central's basketball team to the state tournament twice. High school was where he met Bob Sutherland. During their senior year, Bob got Max a job working with him at the *Sutherland's* grocery store in the Midway area. Max was well on his way to a solid career in the company when an event occurred that changed his life forever.

When Max was growing up, a younger smaller kid lived down the street from him. He was a very smart, bookish youngster that Max took under his wing for protection. Max was a tough kid in whom his parents instilled proper values. He wanted nothing to do with gangs, drugs or crime.

One day, a year or so after he graduated from high school, Max was at work. His little pal, Jimmy Jefferson, while innocently walking down a street was caught up in a drive-by shooting and took a bullet in the head, killing him instantly. A promising young life was gone forever. It was that act that sent Max to school to become a police officer. It was also the Sutherland family who helped him financially the way his bus driver father could not.

Finished with his report, he took a few minutes to think about the interview of Mackenzie Sutherland. Knowing Bob for twenty-five years, Max simply could not believe Bob Sutherland would grab a fireplace poker and threaten her with it.

"Hey, what do you think?" Max heard a voice alongside him ask.

Having been deep in thought, literally staring off at nothing, Max had not noticed Anna Finney walk up. He swiveled in his chair as she sat down next to his desk.

"Hi, Anna," he said to her. "Where's Sherlock Holmes?" he asked referring to her partner, Dale Kubik.

"Off dealing with his bookie. He doesn't think I know but he's got a couple of problems and sooner or later they will catch up with him," Finney replied.

"Don't let it rub off on you."

"I work with him. That's it. I spend no time with him outside of the office. Anyway, what do you think about this morning?"

"I'm not buying it," Max said.

"Why?"

"I've known Bob Sutherland since high school. I just don't see it."

"How much time have you spent with him lately? How well do you know him now?"

Max thought about this for a moment before answering. "Not much, to be honest. We get together for lunch once or twice a year. I was at both funerals of his parents. I knew them pretty well."

"How was he at his dad's funeral?"

“Angry,” Max admitted. “All three kids were. When I talked to him he even said he believed Mackenzie killed the old man.”

Finney gave him a serious look then said, “Jesus Christ, Max. You didn’t think that was relevant enough to tell me?”

“I didn’t think he would or even could do something…” Max started to explain.

“I don’t give a shit,” Finney whispered so as not to be overheard by other cops in the room. She took out her case notebook, flipped it open to a blank page and while holding a pen said, “I want it all, every word. What did he say?”

“Okay,” he began. “Out at the cemetery, after the graveside service, I found Bob to say hello. We gave each other a little hug. Then he said, ‘I know that bitch murdered him’. Then I asked him, ‘Do you have any evidence to back that up?’ or words to that effect. He admitted he didn’t. Then I told him to be careful about throwing accusations like that around.”

“Did anyone else hear the two of you?” Finney asked him.

“No, I don’t think so. We were off by ourselves and it was raining so everyone was in a hurry to get out of there.”

Finney made a few more notes then looked at Max and said, “What about the other two kids? Did you talk to them?”

“No,” Max said shaking his head. “To tell the truth, I can’t stand either one of them. Hailey was okay when she was a kid, but Adam was always an arrogant asshole. They’re both pretty useless.”

Dale Kubik, Anna’s partner, appeared. He said a brief hello to Max then said to Anna, “Look, ah, something’s come up. I need to take some personal time. You can handle the interview with the lawyer can’t you?”

“Sure, no problem,” Anna said inwardly relieved she would not have Kubik hanging around today.

“Great. Well, I’ll ah, see you tomorrow,” Kubik said as he quickly backed away then turned and fled.

“What’s that about?” Max asked.

Finney leaned closer to him and quietly said, “Just between me and you, I think he’s got a little nose candy problem.”

“Really?”

“I’m not sure but the signs are there. Hey, you busy? You want to go talk to this lawyer, this Cooper Thomas guy? The guy who wrote the new Will for old man Sutherland?”

“Sure,” Max said. “When?”

“We have an appointment with him right after lunch. He said he’d have the security guard who was in the room there also.”

Max looked at the wall clock and said, “You up for lunch?”

“Sure. You buying?”

"Nope," Max replied as they stood. "Let's go."

Two hours later they thanked Cooper Thomas and the security agent for their cooperation. Thomas politely escorted the two detectives to the elevators and waited with them until their car arrived.

"Well, what do you think?" Finney asked Max while the two of them rode down in the otherwise empty car.

"It didn't sound as bad as she made it out to be," Max replied.

"I think you're right, but it doesn't matter how it sounds to a trained police officer. What matters is how it sounded to Mackenzie Sutherland. Was it reasonable for her to take it is a legitimate threat?"

Max thought about this until they reached the ground floor. As the doors began to open he admitted, "A jury could easily believe it was."

"Exactly," Finney agreed. As they were walking toward the exit doors she continued by saying, "Let's go interview the widow. I'm glad you're with me since you know her."

"Yeah, I know her," he said without enthusiasm.

"What does that mean?"

"You'll see. She's no princess," Max replied.

The elevator doors had barely closed when Cooper Thomas turned to hurry back to his office. Seated on the expensive, leather couch in his office waiting for him was the security guard, Rod Partlow, who was also interviewed by the police. When Cooper entered the office Partlow stood up.

"Do you need me for anything else, Mr. Thomas?" he asked.

"Yes, please sit down, Rod. I want you to tell me exactly what you told the detectives."

Partlow sat back down on the sofa and Cooper sat in a client chair. In less than five minutes the security man went over the interview. Cooper asked a few questions to clarify a point or bring out more detail.

"Thank you, Rod," Cooper said when he finished. "I appreciate you coming by. Tell the agency to bill us for your time."

"No problem, Mr. Thomas," Partlow replied as Cooper led him to his office door.

"Will she be okay? She seemed like a nice lady and..."

"We'll see," Thomas shrugged. "She has a good criminal lawyer. It's up to the authorities now. Thanks again," he finished as the two men shook hands.

Thomas was on the phone within seconds of ushering the security man out. It rang twice, and Mackenzie answered her cell.

"They just left," Thomas said.

"Tell me," Mackenzie curtly ordered.

Thomas gave her a verbatim account of his interview and as much as he could of Rod Partlow's.

"What do you think?" she asked.

"Mine helped you but the security guy, maybe not so much. He made Bob sound like a wimp and the other two kids like the whiney brats they are. But he also said he wasn't surprised that Bob threatened you with the fireplace poker. Mackenzie, have you been watching the news?"

"Not really," she replied. "Why?"

"They're not being kind to you."

"Marc Kadella went on that afternoon show on Channel 8 yesterday," Mackenzie said. "I watched it and he did great. Marc comes across very well. He made the self-defense case just fine," Mackenzie said.

"You might want to consider hiring a PR firm…" Thomas started to say.

"Don't be ridiculous! How would that look? No, Kadella knows what he's doing. I'll leave it up to him."

"It's just as well. I worry about you and…"

"That's sweet, Cooper. Maybe when this is all over, we'll see," she said knowing that would keep the lawyer on a string. "I'll talk to you soon."

After Mackenzie finished her call from Cooper Thomas, she dialed another number by memory. A man answered, and Mackenzie identified herself.

"Yes, Mrs. Sutherland, I've been expecting your call," Larry Cunningham said to her.

"Has my request been fulfilled?" Mackenzie asked.

"Yes, ma'am. All six million anonymously sent, two million to each of them as you requested. I'm just sorry you didn't do it in a way that was tax advantageous for you," he replied.

"Larry, we've been over this several times," Mackenzie reminded the financial advisor, her impatience showing. "I don't care about the taxes. Have the recipients been informed?"

"Yes, Mrs. Sutherland. A company representative met with each of them separately. They were obviously quite surprised."

"That's why I want to make sure it remains anonymous," Mackenzie said. "And I'll remind you, if my name leaks out…"

"To be blunt, ma'am, you'll have my ass," Cunningham said to let her know he understood.

"Exactly. Thank you, Larry. I'll be in touch."

TEN

Max Coolidge and Anna Finney parked their department issued Crown Vic on the street at the Sutherland's. There was another vehicle, a Chevy van, parked ahead of them with a TV transmission antenna attached. The two detectives stopped in the driveway and took a hard look at the Channel 6 station logo on the van's side panel, neither one of them at all pleased to see it.

The Sutherland's lived in the moderately upscale neighborhood of Highland Park in St. Paul. Their house was on Mississippi River Boulevard with a view of the river and Fort Snelling on its south bank.

"Nice place," Finney remarked as they walked up the driveway.

"Yeah," Max agreed. "Every time I saw Bob he complained about 'the bitch's palace' and the mortgage. I think it was over his head, but it was Paige's idea and he didn't have the balls to say no to her," Max replied.

"You don't like her," Finney flatly said, a statement not a question.

"Not much, no," Max answered. "And the feeling was mutual. She never liked me much either."

"Is she a racist?" Anna asked.

Max considered the question for a second then said, "Maybe, but I think it's more about me being a cop and don't come from money. She does. Her family's got plenty." He stopped, looked at Finney and quietly said, "Don't let her con you, and she'll probably try, about how destitute she will be because of Bob's death. She and the kids will be fine."

The house was to their left with an unattached two-car garage to its right. There was a gap of twenty feet between the house and garage with a small sidewalk from the driveway to a back door and splitting off to the fence. A six-foot cedar privacy fence ran between the buildings with a gate in the middle. The two cops reached the gate and could hear voices coming from the backyard. The gate was unlocked, and Max pushed it open.

"There is no way that Bob threatened that woman with a fireplace poker," Paige Sutherland was saying to the reporter. "It just was not in him. And we all know she manipulated Bill Sutherland into changing his Will. Bill loved his children, all of them. He would've never cut them out."

Max and Anna stepped through the gate and stood on the lawn watching. At first, no one noticed them while the two of them surveyed the scene.

The interview was taking place on the large, granite stone patio. The TV station had sent a camera operator, a sound tech and the reporter.

Unknown to Max, Paige had contacted the station and offered to do the interview.

They watched the interview for more than a minute before anyone noticed them. Paige was seated in a padded, wrought iron lawn chair with the three kids seated around her. It was the youngest, Katie, age seven, who saw them.

"Uncle Max!" the little girl yelled as she took off toward them.

All three Sutherland kids were spoiled brats as far as Max was concerned. Mouthy, obnoxious and entitled but they were affectionate to him, probably to annoy their mother.

Their presence having been discovered caused a break in the interview. Max was one of the cops who broke the news to the family about Bob. Despite this, the kids still acted like they had not seen him for months. Even Paige gave him a firm, tearful hug as the camera recorded the scene.

While he returned Paige's embrace, Max whispered, "What the hell is wrong with you? Don't do this to the kids."

Paige stepped back, looked up at the taller man, put on a forced smile and quietly replied so only Max could hear her, "People need to see what that bitch did to us."

They all walked back toward the patio area. Max held up his badge and firmly told the cameraman to stop filming, which he did. Paige introduced them to the TV people then told the children to go inside.

"We'd love to get an interview with the two of you," the reporter, an attractive young woman said to Max and Anna.

"Sorry, no comment," Finney quickly said.

"The investigation is still ongoing," Max interjected. "We have nothing to say. We need to talk to Mrs. Sutherland, so we must insist you wrap this up and leave, please."

"That's up to her," the reporter said looking at Paige

"That's enough for now. I'll be available for more later," Paige smiled and said.

While the TV crew packed up to leave, Max, Anna and Paige pulled up chairs around the patio table. When they left, Paige pulled a pack of cigarettes from her skirt pocket and lit one.

"Okay," she said blowing a long trail of smoke into the air. "What the fuck do you want, Max?"

"That's the Paige I've always known," Max replied.

"Hey, asshole, that bitch murdered my husband and she's still walking free. What do you expect?"

"Stop!" Finney forcefully told her. "We're doing our job and…"

"So go arrest her, honey," Paige said taking another long drag on her cigarette. "Do your job."

"We'll be back when you're calmer and in a better frame of mind," Max said as he stood to leave.

"Put that murdering, thieving whore in jail. That will put me in a better mood. Until then, fuck you!"

When they were back in the car, Finney asked, "What the hell was that?"

Max swung the car around in a U-turn to go back downtown. As he did this he said, "That was Paige the Princess being Paige the Princess."

"Max, this is shaping up to be a legitimate self-defense case. What is she going to do if the county attorney refuses to prosecute her?"

Max said, "She can try suing her for wrongful death I guess. She probably will anyway."

Marc Kadella dropped his briefcase by his apartment's front door. He stepped into the living room, picked up the TV remote from the glass coffee table and clicked on the set. Before sitting in his recliner to watch the local news, he removed his suit coat and tossed it on the couch.

Marc had barely sat down to watch Channel 8 when his phone went off. He grumbled at having to retrieve it from his coat pocket then frowned when he saw the caller ID.

"Hi, how are you?" he asked Margaret Tennant.

"I'm okay," she replied. "Um, Marc…" she paused.

"Yeah," he said as if he didn't know what was coming.

"I think we need to talk," she said.

"Yeah, me too."

"Can you come over this evening?"

"Sure," he replied with more enthusiasm than he felt. "What time?"

"Anytime. I'll be here all evening."

"Okay. I just got home. Let me grab something to eat and I'll be along around 7:30. Is that okay?"

"Sure, see you then," Margaret replied.

When the call ended he quietly said out loud to himself, "So, we need to have the 'we need to talk' talk. I guess it's time."

Marc's phone rang again but this time he smiled at the caller ID.

"Hey, kid, what's up?" he asked.

"Are you watching the news?" Maddy Rivers asked. "Turn to Channel 6," she said without waiting for him to answer.

"Why?" Marc asked as he reached for the remote.

"They have an interview with Paige Sutherland. They're going to run after the commercials," Maddy said.

"I should call Mackenzie," Marc commented as he changed the channel.

"I already did," Maddy said. "What's wrong? You sound down."

"I just got a call from Margaret," Marc admitted. He told Maddy about the call.

"That's too bad," Maddy said. "You two were good together."

"Yeah, well, she didn't seem to think so as much lately. We'll see. It's coming on. I'll talk to you later," Marc replied.

The female anchor, whom Marc knew a little and avoided like the plague, read the interview's introduction. The screen then filled with the camera on Paige and the three kids on the patio.

The actual interview itself had taken almost an hour to set up and conduct. When it was over, the station had at least a half hour of film. During the afternoon, Channel 6 had run at least a dozen promos to boost the audience which the next day ratings would prove to be excellent.

They ran over six minutes of the interview which for a twenty-two-minute broadcast is significant. Poor little Paige Sutherland put on a great show. With the kids as a backdrop, the audience would be overwhelmingly sympathetic. The gist of it was that Mackenzie had brutally murdered Paige's husband and stolen the family fortune after poisoning Paige's beloved father-in-law, Mackenzie's husband, Bill Sutherland. Now she was using that very same money to buy her way out of answering for her crimes.

The interview ended, and the screen showed the station general manager, Gibson Stewart, seated at a desk, solemnly staring at the camera. His name and the words 'Station Editorial' were shown along the bottom of the screen. Stewart piously prattled on about justice for the rich and justice for everyone else. How the authorities must do a thorough, transparent investigation and not be allowed to sweep this case under some invisible rug. And of course, the paragons of the Fourth Estate, meaning of course, himself and his station would see to it that they did.

When it was over, Marc did not know if he wanted to vomit or throw something through his TV. Within seconds his phone rang. He answered without bothering to check the ID.

"Hi, Mac, I saw it too," he said.

"I should sue that lying, nasty, vile, foul-mouthed bitch for everything she has. And that station too," Mackenzie steamed. "I am so angry..."

"Hey, calm down," Marc soothingly said. "Take a deep breath. I don't think suing the widow of the man you shot is a good idea. At least not yet."

"I know," Mackenzie quietly said. "I just had to vent. She is a vile, foul-mouthed bitch, though. I've heard her curse at her kids using words that would make a sailor blush. Let me tell you something, the

Sutherlands always portrayed an image of being a model family. They were about as dysfunctional as everyone else. And between you and me, Bill was no prince. There was virtually no physical involvement between us for the last two years. He liked his hookers a little too much and I was afraid he would bring something home with him, an STD of some kind. We slept in separate bedrooms. The kids didn't know this about their beloved father. And he couldn't stand any of his kids."

"Interesting in a gossipy kind of way but keep it in mind. If any of this ever goes to trial, that could come in handy," Marc replied.

"Really?" Mackenzie asked. "I'll tell you what, I have plenty more on all of them. Marc, could I see you tonight?"

"No, sorry, I have to go see Margaret. She called. We need to have the 'we need to talk' talk," he said.

"Oh, sorry," Mackenzie said. "And I mean that."

"It's okay. It's been coming for a while. Probably for the best," Marc said.

"Call me tomorrow?" she sweetly asked.

"Sure, I'll talk to you tomorrow."

ELEVEN

The next day, both the St. Paul and Minneapolis papers included lengthy editorials about the Sutherlands. The theme of both articles was the moral dilemma claiming that there is one set of rules for the rich and one for everyone else. Both papers were also filled with letters to the editor from 'outraged' citizens expressing the same sentiment. Unknown to the public were the large number of letters that non-outraged citizens sent to the papers. These expressed the common sense, reasonable belief that judgment should be withheld until the investigation was complete and all of the facts were known. Not surprisingly, none of these were printed by either paper.

Heather Anderson arrived at her office before 7:30 A.M. Waiting for her was a message on her computer to see her boss, Shayla Parker, ASAP. Parker was the Ramsey County attorney and a summons from her this early was not a good way to start the day.

Heather grabbed a legal pad and pen and walked quickly down the hall to Parker's corner office. She lightly knocked on the frosted glass of the office door and opened it while Parker was responding.

"Have you seen the papers this morning?" Parker calmly asked.

"No, but I heard about it on the radio driving in. How bad are they?" Heather answered Parker as she took a chair in front of her boss' desk.

"Not good. Where are we with the investigation?" Parker asked.

"I have a meeting with the cops this morning. I got preliminary reports late yesterday from them," Anderson said. "Mackenzie Sutherland has a solid self-defense claim."

"I'm thinking about presenting it to a grand jury," Parker said.

"A little CYA?" Heather asked.

"A lot of CYA," Parker agreed. "Whether we like it or not, this is a political office and we answer to the voters. Could we get a first or second-degree murder indictment?"

Heather contemplated the question for a moment then said, "I'm not sure I want to. We'll slander this woman and lose at trial."

"Get the indictment, make a plea offer for minimal jail time," Parker suggested.

"Her lawyer would never take it. Plus, do we really want to do something that cynical? At best it is borderline ethical bringing a criminal case we don't believe in. We're supposed to believe we have sufficient evidence to prove guilt beyond a reasonable doubt. I don't think we have it here. And we will ruin this woman's life."

Parker looked at her subordinate over her glasses then said, "This is the real world, Heather. Besides, she has money. She'll get over it."

"Shayla, I understand that but…"

"Go talk to the cops. Maybe they can come up with more evidence for at least a manslaughter indictment. Think about the grand jury. I think we should do it. If the grand jury returns a 'no bill', so be it. I'd be okay with that," Parker said.

"You think that would cover our asses?"

"An indictment would be better. Even if we lose at trial we did our job," Parker said. "See what you can do."

"Yes, ma'am," Anderson said rising to leave knowing her boss had just ordered her to present the case to a grand jury and get an indictment for something.

"I'm going to release a statement to the press today that we're going to present it to the grand jury."

Heather turned her head back toward her boss as she opened the door, shrugged her shoulders and said, "Yes, ma'am. I'll see what I can do."

Marc Kadella's intercom buzzed and when he answered it, he heard Carolyn say, "You may want to come out here."

When Marc went into the common area the other three lawyers were all coming out of their offices. Everyone gathered around the TV and watched an interview taking place on a local station. The anchor was talking to a man identified on the screen as a former federal prosecutor. They were discussing the news being leaked that Ramsey County was going to present the Sutherland shooting to a grand jury.

"Did you know about this?" Barry Cline asked Marc.

"No, but I figured they might try this. The media heat is turning up and they have nothing to lose. If they get an indictment…" Marc said.

"They'll offer you a great deal for a plea," Barry interjected.

"And if they 'no bill' the case, Shayla Parker's ass is covered either way," Marc added.

"They'll try to get first and second-degree murder," Barry said. "Then offer her a sweet deal for first or second-degree manslaughter."

"Yep," Marc agreed. "I don't see how they can claim first degree anything."

"They'll try to convince the grand jury that she lured him to her house because of the family feud over the money. Then offer manslaughter with some minimal time."

"I won't let her take it. We'll go to trial if we have to."

"Anything new?" Heather Anderson said to the group seated around the conference room table. In attendance were Heather, Wade Keenan, Anna Finney, Dale Kubik and Max Coolidge.

"Yeah," Max said. "I saw Paige Sutherland last night," he continued looking at Finney. "She called me, said she wanted my advice about something and asked me to stop by."

"What did she want?" Heather asked.

"She asked me about digging up Bill Sutherland and having another autopsy performed," Max answered.

"Why?" Keenan asked.

"They're convinced Mackenzie poisoned the old man; gave him something to cause his heart attack."

"Do they have any evidence of this? A bottle of the drug she used? Something to back it up?" Keenan asked him.

"Not that I'm aware of and I'm sure she would have told me."

"Unless Mackenzie agrees to it…" Heather started to say.

"She already said no, and she would fight it," Max said.

"…it probably won't happen."

"What if we join her?" Keenan asked Heather.

"Same thing," she said. "What grounds do we have? Do we have probable cause or even a reasonable suspicion other than bitter, resentful children?" Heather answered him.

"She's going to do it," Max said. "She hired a lawyer and he's putting a motion together to get a court order. A guy named Simon Kane."

"You know him?" Heather asked Keenan.

"No," he answered.

"He's a corporate guy. Handled the business stuff for Sutherland's grocery store company," Max told them.

"Maybe we should join them," Keenan said. "That might lend some credibility to the attempt."

Anderson said, "I don't think so. Let her try it and see what happens. If she gets an okay to do it then she can pay for it. If she gets turned down and we come up with some grounds later we can ask for it then. If we join her now we might not get another crack at it later." She then turned to Finney and asked, "Anything else?"

"You have the reports of the interviews," Anna said. "Is it true, are you taking this to a grand jury?"

"Yes, I am. I'll let you know when I do. It will probably be next week. They don't meet again until then. I'll want all three of you to testify. Anything else?" she asked again.

"No," all three detectives answered in turn.

"Okay, I'll be in touch."

"Marc," Marc Kadella heard Sandy say over the intercom, "there's a Heather Anderson on the phone for you from Ramsey…"

"Put her through Sandy, thanks."

A few seconds later he heard Anderson's voice. "Hello, Marc. This is a courtesy call about Mackenzie Sutherland."

Hearing this from a prosecutor, Marc's defense lawyer antennae went up. "Okay," he cautiously replied.

"You'll find out later anyway so here it is. We're taking her case to the grand jury..."

"I know," Marc said. "It was leaked to the media already and was on TV a while ago. What are you asking for?"

"Murder one," Anderson flatly stated.

"You can't be serious..."

"She lured him into her house, pulled a gun and shot him dead. We think we can make a case for premeditation. Murder two at least."

Remaining calm Marc said, "Bull. You can't make that case at trial and you know it."

"Maybe, maybe not but we..."

"Need to get the media and political heat off so you're going to hide behind the grand jury," Marc finished for her.

"No comment," Heather said.

"My client wants to testify before the grand jury..." Marc started to say.

"I don't think so," Heather said.

"She has a constitutional right to testify," Marc sputtered.

"Not before the grand jury she doesn't," Heather calmly replied.

Knowing she was probably right, Marc hesitated, silently trying to think of something to say.

"Are you still there?" Heather asked.

"Yeah, I am. I'm going to go before Doug Feller and ask for an injunction to stop you from preventing her from testifying," Marc said referring to Chief Judge Douglas Feller, head of the Ramsey County courts.

"You won't get it. He has no jurisdiction about what goes on before the grand jury," Heather said with more certainty than she felt.

"Then I'll go on Gabriella Shirqui's show every day for the next month. When are you presenting this to the grand jury?"

"They don't meet again until next Wednesday," she told him.

"Heather, I mean it, I'm going to call Feller right now and ask for an emergency hearing. I'll have the pleadings to you this afternoon. What's your e-mail address?

Anderson gave him her email address then Marc's door opened. Carolyn stuck her head in and told him Mackenzie was calling.

"My client's on the phone. I need to talk to her. I'll be in touch."

Marc hit the button with the blinking light on the phone and he was barely able to say hello before Mackenzie started.

"Marc, it's all over the TV that they're taking this to a grand jury to ask for a first-degree murder indictment," she said almost in a panic. "What are we going to do? Can you stop this?"

"Calm down, Mackenzie…"

"Easy for you to say! They want to charge me with…"

"Take a deep breath. Relax. I just got off the phone with Heather Anderson…"

"The woman at the interview when they taped me," Mackenzie said trying to breathe easier.

"Yes. It's a political thing. The media…"

"Assholes," Mackenzie muttered.

"Yes, they are," Marc agreed "The county attorney is doing this for political ass covering. I'm going to try to head it off before they get an indictment."

"How?"

Marc went over his phone call with Anderson and his strategy for the grand jury. When he finished, he waited for her to speak. She was silent for a few seconds apparently thinking about what Marc told her.

"What do you think? Will this judge make her let me testify?"

"I don't think he can. I don't believe he has the authority. It's pretty much up to the prosecutor to decide what the grand jury hears. I'm hoping he can persuade her to let you do it. Feller's a good guy; a fair judge. It's at least worth a shot."

"I want to be there," Mackenzie said.

"Sure, no problem," Marc replied. "I'll call the judge's clerk and set up a time for the hearing right now."

"I'm having lunch with Madeline. Please join us," Mackenzie said. She told him where and when and Marc agreed to meet them.

Marc called Judge Feller's clerk and scheduled the hearing for the coming Friday. When he finished the call, Barry Cline knocked on his door and told him the local media was hyping the grand jury story. The two lawyers chatted for a minute then Marc went to work preparing his paperwork for Friday's motion.

"I haven't been here in years," Mackenzie said to Maddy while Marc placed their order.

"Cossetta's has the best pizza anywhere and I'm from Chicago and have had a lot of pizza in both Chicago and New York," Maddy said.

"New York pizza sucks," Marc said as he set the tray with their drinks on the table. He sat down next to Mackenzie and added, "New Yorkers love to brag about their pizza but compared to Cossetta's, it's like eating a soggy piece of bread covered with processed cheese and ketchup."

Marc held up his glass of Coke for a toast and said, "To Cossetta's pizza."

The three of them clicked their plastic glasses filled with soda, took a drink and shared a laugh.

"That's the first real laugh I've had since…" Mackenzie said.

Maddy reached over to her, took her left hand and said, "Relax, we'll get you through this."

Mackenzie turned up the corners of her mouth in a slight smile and said, "Thanks."

Marc was looking up at a TV set mounted on the wall a few feet away. "Excuse me, miss," he said to a server walking past their table. "Could you turn that up, please?"

"Sure," she answered. The young girl reached up and turned the volume knob, looked at Marc who nodded and mouthed the word thanks.

"What?" Maddy asked as she turned in her chair to see the TV.

"Shayla Parker," Marc said.

"Who is she?" Mackenzie asked. When she said this, the words 'Ramsey County Attorney' appeared at the bottom of the screen along with Parker's name.

The three of them watched while Parker conducted a live press conference. It was entirely about Mackenzie, whose picture appeared on-screen twice, and the grand jury. The main point of it was that Parker and the police were confident there was sufficient evidence for an indictment. They believed Mackenzie lured Robert Sutherland to her home to murder him over a family dispute about the Sutherland money.

"Then why isn't she under arrest now?" a reporter asked.

"Her lawyer assured us she would surrender herself if we obtained an indictment," Parker claimed.

"I did?" Marc asked. "That's news to me."

They continued to silently watch for several more minutes. Parker only took three or four questions then held up a hand to quiet the reporters.

"There is only one set of laws for the State of Minnesota and it will be applied equally. There will be no favoritism in Ramsey County as long as I am county attorney. Mackenzie Sutherland, like everyone else, will answer for any crime she commits."

With that comment, Parker flashed a big smile and stepped away from the podium. She then turned her back to them and fled while the reporters continued to shout questions at her. The last question to go out live over the air was one from a female TV reporter asking about Mackenzie's self-defense claim.

"That bitch!" Maddy snarled as she turned back toward Marc and Mackenzie. "Not a word about Mackenzie's self-defense statement."

The server arrived and placed their pizza on the table. When she left, all three of them silently stared at it for several seconds, no longer as hungry.

"Well, I'm still hungry," Marc finally said as he slapped two slices on his plate. He did the same thing for Mackenzie.

"I'm not hungry," Mackenzie quietly said.

"Don't worry about this B.S.," Marc said referring to the press conference.

"Oh, god, this is good!" Maddy said while chewing a bite.

Mackenzie smiled, picked up a slice and started in.

Just as Marc was about to join them, his phone rang. He looked at the ID, smiled, answered it and said, "What time do you want us, Gabriella?"

Marc and Mackenzie went on the *Court Reporter* with Gabriella Shriqui live the same afternoon as Shayla Parker's press conference. Mackenzie was able to tell her story to at least somewhat offset the damage done by Parker's appearance before the media.

On the drive back to St. Paul, Marc took a call from Heather Anderson.

"This isn't my idea," Anderson made clear up front. "Shayla told me to tell you any more TV appearances like you just did and we'll go to court to get a gag order."

Marc's face became almost beet red which caused both Maddy and Mackenzie to sit up.

"You tell Her Majesty from me: fuck you!" he almost yelled. "It's okay for her to hold a press conference but not okay for my client to exercise her first amendment right. Who the hell does she think she is? Tell her to go ahead and take her best shot."

"I told her not to threaten you," Heather politely said.

Marc more calmly said into the phone, "I'll see you Friday morning." He ended the call without waiting for a response.

For the next three days, Marc and Mackenzie did three more on camera interviews and a couple for radio talk shows. In addition, Marc returned every phone call from print journalists and politely answered all of their questions.

Marc did not hear another word from Shayla Parker and by Friday morning was wondering if that wasn't her plan all along; to let Marc get the word out about the self-defense claim. That way if the grand jury did not indict, Parker's ass would still be covered. Marc found himself wondering if the woman was really that clever and politically shrewd.

TWELVE

Marc and Mackenzie with Maddy trailing behind were led into the chambers of Chief Judge Douglas Feller. Already present was Heather Anderson.

Marc, having never met the judge, introduced himself, his client and his assistant, Madeline Rivers.

"Is it all right if Ms. Rivers sits in, your Honor?" Marc asked.

Feller, being a male with a pulse, looked over Maddy and with his best smile assured her she was welcome in his courtroom any time.

Maddy flashed the older gent a smile and took a seat on his couch. Marc and Mackenzie each took a chair in front of his desk, Marc next to Heather Anderson.

"Mr. Kadella, I assume you want a record made of this hearing?" Feller asked, referring to the stenographer.

"Yes, your Honor, thank you."

The judge made a brief statement for the record what the case was about and the names of those present.

Addressing Marc, Feller began, "I have read your pleadings and you want me to issue an injunction enjoining the county attorney from preventing your client from testifying before the grand jury, is that correct, Mr. Kadella?"

"Yes, your Honor."

"Do you have any case law on point that allows me to do this?"

"Well, no your Honor, but the Minnesota federal courts allow a defendant to testify and..."

"I know that," Feller said. "What about it, Ms. Anderson? What's your position?"

"We see no reason to allow the defendant to testify, your Honor," Anderson said. "She is going to assert self-defense. As you know that is an affirmative defense, one she has to prove. It is simply more appropriate to bring it at trial than before the grand jury. All we are obligated to do before the grand jury is establish probable cause that a crime has been committed and the defendant did it."

"Mr. Kadella?" Feller said to Marc who was patiently waiting for his turn.

"Judge, they're trying to get a first-degree murder indictment. And let's be grownups about this. They're doing it as an ass covering exercise. I'm sure your Honor is aware of the negative publicity this matter has already generated..."

"I've seen the papers," Feller acknowledged.

"A first-degree indictment will ruin my client's reputation. The media is already crucifying her. I have no doubt we'll get an acquittal at trial but who will believe she is innocent? The media is already on a campaign of 'one set of laws for the rich' and 'one set for everyone else'. An acquittal will just feed that narrative."

"He has an excellent point," Feller said turning back to Anderson.

"That's not our problem, your Honor."

Feller gave Anderson a stern look of disapproval and said, "It should be. People need to have faith in the judiciary." The judge looked at Marc again and continued, "I can't make her. But," he turned back to Anderson as he told the court reporter to go off the record, "you have to practice in these courtrooms," he told Anderson, a not so veiled threat.

Marc retrieved the DVD of Mackenzie's statement from his briefcase. He held it up and said, "This is a copy of my client's videotaped statement. How about if she plays this to the grand jury?"

"Let's take a look," Feller said.

There was a television with both tape and DVD player attached in a corner of his chambers. Feller placed the disk in it and they all watched Mackenzie's statement.

When it was over, Feller turned again to Anderson and said, "Seems pretty exculpatory to me. The forensics match Mrs. Sutherland's version of what happened?"

"Substantially, your Honor," Anderson reluctantly agreed.

"How about it? How about at least showing the statement to the grand jury?" Feller asked Heather.

"We have no obligation to…" she began.

"How about in the interest of justice?" Marc interrupted. "How about because the county attorney is supposed to be in business to find justice and not just political ass-covering!"

"Mr. Kadella," Feller quietly said stopping him. "He has a point," the judge said to Anderson.

Anderson noticeably sighed then said, "Let me call my boss. I'll be right back." With that, she stood up and started to leave.

"Tell Shayla I would take it as a personal favor," Feller said before she opened the door.

While pacing up and down the back hallway, Anderson gave Shayla Parker a quick rundown of the hearing.

"What do you think?" Parker asked her when she finished.

"I'm inclined to agree to it," Anderson said. "We get the same political coverage if they refuse to indict. Plus, we can leak it to the media that the Sutherland woman does have a strong self-defense case."

"We can even leak some of the facts to support that," Parker agreed.

"And there's still a chance that they'll indict her for something," Anderson said.

"You think so?"

"No, but stranger things have happened. Even if they do indict, her lawyer will push it to trial. She has plenty of money for it and unless we can come up with something else, no way we can prove much of anything beyond a reasonable doubt. Kadella will never let her take a plea."

"I just wish I hadn't been so adamant about murder one at the press conference," Parker said.

"Kadella's been all over TV. No one will be surprised about the grand jury buying her self-defense story. Besides, you can act mad at the grand jury when you make the announcement."

"If they fail to indict, you'll make the announcement," Parker informed her. "Okay, play the DVD for them."

"The family is still going to try to exhume the old man. Who knows, maybe they'll get it done and find something. I'll talk to you later."

Anderson went back to the judge's chambers and announced their decision. They would show the DVD to the grand jury.

"I want to be in the room," Marc said.

"No," Anderson answered.

"Why? I have the right to protect my client's interest..."

"Not in front of the grand jury you don't," Anderson said.

"Look," Marc softened, "I'll sit there and not say a word. You don't even have to tell them who I am. I just want to make sure they see an unedited version of..."

"What are you accusing me of?"

"Nothing, Heather, relax," Marc said.

"I don't see why that should not be allowed," Feller said. "He sits there and says nothing. If there is a problem, the two of you can leave the room to discuss it."

Anderson mulled it over then said to Marc, "Not a peep out of you."

"The soul of discretion," Marc said, a statement that elicited a hearty laugh from Maddy Rivers.

The four of them, including Heather Anderson, went out into the main hallway. As they headed toward the elevators, a plain looking man who was standing in the hall walked up to them from behind. He was holding a letter-size manila envelope in one hand.

"Are you Mackenzie Sutherland?" he asked.

When she heard this, Madeline went into a "protect and serve" mode. She grabbed the man's left wrist, pinned his arm behind his back, spun him around and slammed him up against the wall.

"Maddy, wait!" Marc almost yelled. "What do you have?"

Maddy had the intruder's left arm bent behind him and his face flattened against the wall, her right hand on the back of his head. He held up the envelope in his right hand and muttered something that sounded like the word 'process'.

"Let him go," Marc quietly said while Anderson and Mackenzie stood back watching the show.

The man turned around and handed the envelope to Marc. While the process server rubbed his left shoulder and looked Madeline up and down, Marc told him he was Mackenzie's lawyer, gave the man his name and said he would accept service for her.

While Marc looked over the papers, Maddy mumbled an insincere apology to the man.

"That's okay. In fact, any time. I got a great story to tell," he said as he hurried toward the elevators.

"Did you know about this?" Marc asked Heather.

"I may have heard something about it," she replied.

"May have? You didn't even ask me what it is. How did he know to find her here?"

"Give me a break, Marc. It's not my problem. See you next Wednesday," Heather said then turned and left.

"What is it?" Mackenzie asked.

"A motion to get a court order to allow them to exhume Bill Sutherland. They want another autopsy done."

"Can they do that? Will they get it?" Maddy asked.

"I don't know. I don't know what the law is on it. I'll have to do a little research. What do you think?" Marc asked Mackenzie.

"I think it's grotesque," she said with obvious annoyance. "That petty, vindictive bitch makes me sick. Let this poor man rest in peace."

"What petty vindictive bitch?" Maddy asked.

"Paige Sutherland," Mackenzie said almost spitting out the name.

"What about offering her a settlement?" Marc asked.

"I did not kill Bill Sutherland and I'm not going to say I did by paying off Paige the Witch. It's the principle of..."

"There's no such thing," Marc interrupted her. "That word 'principle' is an emotional word that grownups should not use. Usually what it means is: 'I am going to do something stupid because I am acting like a petulant child.' Nine times out of ten it will cost you more than you gain."

More calmly, Mackenzie said, "I didn't do anything wrong and I shouldn't have to reward her for it."

"Besides," Maddy said, "even if she settles with her what's to stop her from exhuming the body anyway?"

Marc considered the question then said, "That's a really good point. Probably nothing."

"Then," Mackenzie said, "Excuse my language, but fuck her. We'll fight it."

Marc was seated on a bench in the hallway on the seventeenth floor of the Ramsey County Courthouse. He was outside the grand jury room waiting for the grand jury's decision. The showing of Mackenzie's interview had caused a noticeable stir among the twenty-two jurors. When it was over, several of them had questions about the legal definition of self-defense. Marc stayed long enough to hear Anderson's explanation. He then slipped out while Heather was giving the grand jury their final instructions.

In the hallway, he was immediately accosted by a small herd of media types. Almost all of them were hitting him with questions at the same time. Marc held up a hand for quiet then told them he had no news for them. That statement stopped them for about four seconds before starting in again.

"No comment, no news, no nothing," he repeated several times until they finally gave up.

Milling about the hallway were four more prosecutors waiting to present cases to the grand jury. Marc said hello to a couple of them that he casually knew then sat down on the bench to wait. About ten minutes later Heather Anderson came out and she was subjected to the same media attack. Fifteen minutes after she left the room a deputy came out and informed her the jurors had voted.

Marc watched her re-enter the jury room. Despite how well he believed the jurors received the video, he still felt a serious lump in his throat. Barely a minute later Anderson was back wearing her best poker face. She indicated to Marc to follow her into a side room.

"They voted no bill. No indictment," Anderson told him. "I'm going to announce it to the media, but I wanted to let you know first. I'm going to act really pissed off about it."

A relieved Marc Kadella laughed at her last statement and said, "Do what you gotta do, Heather. I'll let you go first then I'll just say, 'I knew my client was innocent. She acted totally in self-defense and the grand jury vindicated her.'"

"Okay," Heather said. "I hate dealing with the press. Parker should do this but…"

"She would look like an idiot after her press conference," Marc finished for her.

THIRTEEN

Mackenzie took the last bite of her chocolate croissant along with a swallow of her morning coffee. She was seated at the breakfast bar in the kitchen of the Crocus Hill house. Mackenzie blankly stared out of the kitchen window at a rare sighting of a Baltimore Oriole flitting about the backyard. While she watched the beautiful bird, she was clicking her perfectly manicured nails on the granite table top as she contemplated two problems: *What should she do about Paige Sutherland? And what to do about the feelings she was having for Marc Kadella?*

Mackenzie had moved back into the house over the weekend. On that Saturday night, Marc had taken her to dinner at the Lexington on Grand Avenue in St. Paul. They had a wonderful meal and the most pleasant time Mackenzie enjoyed since she could not remember when.

Toward the end of the evening they discussed her moving back home. Marc was concerned that living in the house where she shot Bob Sutherland would be too disturbing. Mackenzie assured him she would be all right. In fact, although she did not tell him this, she knew it wouldn't bother her in the least bit.

Marc drove her back to the hotel and the two of them went into the bar for a nightcap. Mackenzie invited him up to her suite for the drink, but Marc declined. He admitted that he was very attracted to her but had to go slow. Marc explained that there are serious ethical problems getting involved with a client. In fact, he could even be disbarred for it. The next morning Mackenzie woke up and the first thing she thought of was Marc. The thought was a very pleasant one and the feeling she was having Mackenzie had not experienced for a long time.

The Oriole flew off and Mackenzie's thoughts returned to the present. It was Monday morning, a few days before the court date to exhume Bill's body. She looked down at the morning paper she had pushed aside and frowned at her picture in it. Ever since the Ramsey County Grand Jury refused to indict her, a debate had raged through the media. The topic of the debate was whether or not the judicial system should be completely overhauled to avoid such a travesty in the future. Apparently the talking heads on TV and the newspaper editorialists had tried and convicted her.

Judges, lawyers, law professors and other qualified experts had weighed in and were unanimously on the side of no, the system worked fairly well. On the other side of the issue were those with the biggest mouths, egos and audiences, especially on radio talk shows and local TV. One of the local TV stations even did an hour-long focus group discussion which drew significant ratings. Of course, the members of the focus group were all lay people whose biases are fed by the same media talking heads.

Marc Kadella was interviewed at least a dozen times. In addition, Marc and Mackenzie made another appearance on the *Court Reporter* with Gabriella Shriqui. Afterwards, Gabriella was very positive that they were extremely convincing about Mackenzie's claim of self-defense.

A few days ago, the media frenzy, having wrung this story dry or so Mackenzie believed, had died down. Another celebrity show business divorce, a rock star and his supermodel wife, were sadly ending their three-month-old marriage and the nation's attention span had shifted to that latest headline grabber.

Mackenzie picked up the newspaper and read the story about her again. A new round of gossip and speculation was about to begin. The news of the coming exhumation hearing was the topic this time. Paige Sutherland was quoted several times carefully accusing Mackenzie, without actually saying it, of murdering Bill Sutherland. Marc was quoted once explaining that an autopsy was performed, and Bill died of a heart attack, pure and simple. There was no evidence to the contrary and Paige Sutherland was acting out of spite, vindictiveness and greed.

Mackenzie finished the story, folded the paper, set it aside and smiled. Despite the scared, concerned act she was able to portray, the truth was Mackenzie was not the least bit concerned. Mackenzie endured a lot worse from the media in Chicago. She was a little surprised that the Chicago media had not picked up the story, except in Chicago she was not known as Mackenzie Cartwright. There she had used the name Frances, and changed it back to Mackenzie, her real name, when she came home to St. Paul. Along with changing her appearance with glasses, makeup and hairstyles it would take an expert to connect the two women as being the same person.

Mackenzie refilled her coffee cup, returned to her seat at the breakfast bar and continued contemplating Paige Sutherland. Mackenzie's instinct was to do something to shut her down. The question was: What should she do? Obviously putting Paige in the ground next to her husband was out of the question, however desirable. Even her kids would be better off without the malevolent witch.

Mackenzie finished her coffee, rinsed the cup in the kitchen sink and quietly said out loud to herself, "Oh well, don't worry, something will come up."

"Before we get started, you should know I have read your pleadings and briefs and I must tell you, Mr. Kane, I haven't seen anything to persuade me to grant your motion," Judge Gabriel Sendejo told Paige's lawyer, Simon Kane. "I'll let you present your case and I hope you have more than what I've seen so far. You may proceed."

Marc and Mackenzie were seated at one of the tables in the well of courtroom 1427 in the downtown St Paul courthouse and City Hall. Marc had been involved in hundreds of court proceedings of various kinds over the years. When the presiding judge opens by telling one of the lawyers what Sendejo just told Kane, the deal was pretty much sealed before it started. Simon Kane, being a very experienced lawyer himself, knew it too.

Sitting in the gallery in the front row directly behind the table where Kane and Paige were seated was Heather Anderson, Max Coolidge and Anna Finney. Also, in the gallery were at least a dozen media members. The rest of the seats were filled with curious citizens and regular court watchers.

Simon Kane thanked the judge, stood and for the next fifteen minutes basically reiterated what was in the paperwork he had submitted. Marc listened carefully, looking for anything that might be new. He also watched the judge who appeared to be patiently following Kane's argument. When Kane was about half-way through his monologue, Madeline Rivers made her entrance. She walked up the center aisle to a reserved seat in the front row and smiled at Mackenzie. While she was doing this, Judge Sendejo was obviously distracted.

"May I call a witness?" Kane asked when he finished.

"Certainly," Sendejo indulgently said.

Kane called Paige Sutherland who was sworn and seated.

Paige, with Kane expertly moving her along, testified about every aspect of life with the Sutherlands. What a wonderful man the poor, deceased father-in-law was, how close he was to his adoring children and the certainty that Mackenzie had turned the old man against his family. All of this was totally irrelevant, and Marc objected to it twice. Both times Sendejo gave him a bored look, agreed it was irrelevant then made the point that there was no jury involved, so he would allow it.

Without actually using the words, what the judge was really saying was, "I don't care, let her prattle on. It won't affect my decision." Both times, even though he was overruled, Marc had to suppress a smile.

When she finished, Kane turned Paige over to Marc for cross-examination.

"I have only one question, your Honor," Marc said from his chair.

"Go ahead," Sendejo told him.

"Mrs. Sutherland, isn't it true that you have absolutely no evidence of any kind to present to this court that William Sutherland died from anything other than natural causes; by that, I mean a heart attack?"

Paige paused and gave both Marc and Mackenzie a look indicating she would like to drive a stake through each of them. Unfortunately for her Sendejo also saw this.

"Answer the question, Mrs. Sutherland," Sendejo sternly ordered.

"No, I don't," she admitted.

Paige was dismissed and Sendejo asked Kane if he had anything else. Kane said he did not, then rested.

"Mr. Kadella, you may proceed," Sendejo told Marc.

Originally Marc was prepared to make an argument and put Mackenzie on the stand. Something in the back of his mind told him having her testify under oath could possibly come back to haunt her. Anything she said could be used against her in any future court proceeding. Plus, Sendejo made it clear he was unimpressed with Paige's case.

"No, your Honor. Everything is covered in my pleadings and clearly there was nothing presented to grant the Petitioner's request."

"I agree," Sendejo began to say.

"Your Honor, may I address the court?" Heather Anderson said as she stood behind the bar.

"No, Ms. Anderson, you may not. The county attorney's office is not a party to this case. If you want to get involved, bring your own request. Before you do let me warn you I will make sure it will be assigned to me and you better have more than I've been presented with today."

Anderson meekly sat down and Sendejo turned to Kane and Paige. "The evidence presented in court and counsel's pleadings makes it clear to the court that the reason we are here is mostly because of spite, anger and grief. These are hardly sufficient grounds to grant the Petitioner's request. There is a valid, thorough autopsy report setting out the cause of death of William Sutherland as a heart attack."

Sendejo picked up the autopsy report and began to read from it. "It reads: the heart attack was most likely brought on by many years of overwork, stress and poor diet." He looked up at the courtroom and continued. "It goes on to indicate a toxicology screening was done and no evidence of foul play was found."

"Your Honor," Kane interrupted, "there are drugs that would not necessarily be found in a routine autopsy."

"You had a perfectly good opportunity to present any evidence of this and failed miserably, Mr. Kane," Sendejo said obviously annoyed at the interruption. "Petitioner's request is denied."

"She murdered my father-in-law and my husband and—"

"Mr. Kane, get control of your client!" Sendejo boomed out.

Kane grabbed Paige's arm and pulled her back into her chair. As he did this, she took one more shot.

"She shot and murdered my husband and you're letting her get away with it!"

"Not another word, Mr. Kane."

"Yes, your Honor," Kane said to the judge. He then put an arm around Paige whose face was covered in tears.

Sendejo looked down at Paige, sighed slightly, then quietly said, "I am aware of the recent death of your husband and I am sorry for your loss. However, his tragic death has no bearing on today's hearing and Mackenzie Sutherland has been exonerated for it."

While this exchange was taking place, the reporters in the gallery were furiously scribbling in their notebooks. Mackenzie took a pen and piece of paper and wrote Marc a note: 'Those tears are so phony I don't know whether to laugh or be sick.'

Marc folded the note, leaned over to Mackenzie and quietly whispered, "Don't start laughing. We're winning."

"Mr. Kadella has requested attorney fees in the amount of seven thousand five hundred dollars to be paid by the Petitioner. I'm going to split it, Mr. Kane. Your firm will pay half and your client will pay the other half. Don't waste my time like this again Simon, you should know better. We're adjourned."

Marc had all he could do to not burst out laughing. Marc and Mackenzie remained seated as Paige stormed out through the gate. Simon Kane looked at Marc as he walked past, shrugged his shoulders and rolled his eyes. He then held the gate for Maddy as she stepped through it to join Marc and Mackenzie.

"That went great," Mackenzie gushed. "It's too bad Paige doesn't have to pay all of your fees herself."

"Trust me," Marc laughed. "By the time she gets Kane's bill the fees will be hidden in it somewhere and she'll have to pay."

As the three of them were exiting through the courtroom doors, a young man walked up to Mackenzie holding a large manila envelope.

Marc saw him coming and quickly said, "Maddy take it easy. He's just doing his job. Don't throw him on the floor."

Both women laughed, the process server stopped and Maddy said, "You take away all my fun."

"I'll take it," Marc said to the worried looking man who quickly handed it to Marc. Marc opened it, read the caption on the Summons and Complaint then noticed Paige and Simon Kane watching by the elevators. An elevator arrived, and Paige flashed a disingenuous smile and stuck out the middle finger on her left hand. She then turned and entered the elevator car.

"What is it?" Mackenzie asked.

"It's a wrongful death lawsuit Paige is bringing against you," Marc answered her as he watched the elevator doors close. "Let's go to my office. I have someone there I want you to meet."

While Maddy ran around the office hugging everyone except the two male lawyers, Barry Cline and Chris Grafton, Marc introduced Mackenzie to them. On the way back to Minneapolis from downtown St. Paul, Marc called ahead to make sure his landlady, Connie Mickelson, had time for them. After introductions were completed, Connie brought all three of them into her office. Mackenzie and Maddy took the two client chairs forcing Marc to fetch a chair from the common area.

"How do you get all of these good-looking broads to come after you?" was the first thing Connie said to Marc.

Marc leaned forward and while Mackenzie and Maddy laughed, sternly said to Connie, "Good looking what?"

"Oh, I'm sorry, Mr. P.C. I meant attractive women," Connie replied.

Marc paused for a moment then said, "My obvious good looks and charm."

"No, that's not it," Mackenzie quickly said joining in. "Good luck with that."

Marc reached behind him, opened the door and yelled out, "Help me! They're ganging up on me."

Carolyn yelled back, "Good. Make a recording. We'll want to listen to it."

"Thanks, that's helpful," Marc yelled back as he closed the door.

"Okay," Marc continued looking at Connie, "You've had your fun."

"Not yet," Connie said.

Marc had given her the Summons and Complaint for the wrongful death suit served on Mackenzie. Connie took a few minutes to scan the document. When she finished, she placed it on her desk.

"Have you read it?" Connie asked Marc.

"Not completely, no."

Connie looked at Mackenzie and continued. "Here's the deal. You're being sued for intentionally and/or negligently causing the death of Robert Sutherland. I assume Paige is the widow?" she asked Marc who nodded in agreement.

Mackenzie had been threatened with this by angry survivors three times before. This was the first time anyone acted on it. She put on a convincing façade of being confused, uncertain and even a little frightened. The reality was she wasn't the least bit concerned. Over the years, Mackenzie had learned enough about the law to believe Paige's case was weak, at best.

"She is suing on behalf of her husband's estate for a whole list of things," Connie continued.

Mackenzie had read the document in the car on the way back from court. She understood what it was about but did have one question. "What is loss of consortium?" she asked.

"Means Paige's not getting laid regularly," Connie answered her.

"It's a little more than that," Marc interjected. "It means loss of love and affection, companionship, stuff like that."

"Mostly she's not getting laid regularly," Connie said again.

"Join the club," Maddy chimed in. Connie looked at Maddy and said, "If you're not getting laid regularly, it's because the entire male population of the Cities has turned gay."

"How can she sue me if the grand jury had already found me innocent?" Mackenzie asked.

"Good question," Connie acknowledged. "It's because that was criminal, and this is civil. In a criminal case, they have to find you guilty beyond a reasonable doubt. That's the highest, most difficult standard in the law. In a civil suit, they only need to find you liable. That's not the same as guilty or not guilty. They have to find you intentionally or negligently liable for Robert's death by a preponderance of the evidence. That's the lowest standard. In lay terms it means the evidence of wrongdoing needs to only slightly outweigh the evidence that you did nothing wrong by, for example fifty-one percent to forty-nine percent."

"What about self-defense?" Mackenzie asked.

"That is, of course, as good a defense in a civil case as it is in a criminal case," Connie answered her.

"So, if we show I shot him in self-defense, I win?" Mackenzie asked.

"Well, yes, you should," Connie answered.

"What do you mean I should?" Mackenzie asked with concern in her voice.

"You never know what a jury will do," Connie said.

"What about a motion for summary judgment?" Marc asked Connie.

"That's probably our best bet," Connie said.

"What's that?" Mackenzie asked.

"We bring a motion to dismiss the lawsuit. Basically, we go before the judge and tell him that the facts of the case are not in dispute. You acted in self-defense. Because it is clearly self-defense, the law is that there is no valid claim and the suit should be dismissed."

"Great, let's do that," Mackenzie said.

“First things first,” Connie said. “I’m usually on the other side of these things representing the plaintiff. Most of the time an insurance company has the responsibility to represent you. We can try to get your homeowner’s insurance company involved but they’d claim this was not an accident and they have no responsibility here. I can handle your case, but you’ll have to pay my fees. We’ll ask for attorney fees but don’t count on it.”

“Money’s not a problem,” Mackenzie said. “If Marc thinks you can handle this, that’s good enough for me.”

Connie looked at Marc, raised her eyebrows and said, “Good looks and charm, huh?”

“Never fails me,” Marc grinned.

“The male ego strikes again,” Maddy said.

Connie filled out a retainer agreement and handed it to Mackenzie. She tried to give it to Marc who told her to read it. Mackenzie signed it without reading it, handed it back to Connie and took out her checkbook.

Mackenzie handed Connie a check for her retainer and emphatically said, “I won’t settle with her. We’ll win this thing.”

FOURTEEN

Paige Sutherland was in a hurry. She was seated at her bedroom vanity applying the final touches of makeup and primping her hair to make it look the best that she could. Paige put down her hair brush, satisfied with the results. She almost laughed knowing her hair and makeup would be a mess before much longer anyway. The thought of what she was up to made her inner thighs warm and sent a slight shiver through her in anticipation. Her children had finally gone to sleep and would be out until morning. Paige had seen to this by slipping each of them a crushed sleeping pill in a glass of lemonade. The man who was her lover for over two years would be along any minute. Paige swiveled around in her chair and glanced out the bedroom window. Almost dark enough she realized.

When Max Coolidge had arrived and gave her the news that Bob was dead Paige was mildly surprised at her own reaction. She actually felt a certain level of sadness about it. Genuine sorrow if not grief. After Max explained how it happened her first thought was: *now that bitch is going to go to prison and I'll get at the Sutherland money.*

Max tried to gently explain to her that it looked like self-defense, but Paige was barely listening. To Max and the other cop, she appeared numbed by the news. If Max had known what she was really thinking about, well, she did not want to think about that.

This evening, still waiting for her lover, Paige went over what he said at their last tryst. The idiot had actually told her he was going to divorce his wife so the two of them could get married. Fortunately, Paige had the presence of mind to quickly remind him she would have to play the grief-stricken widow role for a while. That settled him down.

Staring at herself in the mirror, she again contemplated marriage to him. At thirty-seven, Paige was a fairly attractive woman. Sure, she could stand to drop a few pounds but was she ready for marriage again? Did she love him? The answer to that was an emphatic no. He was better in bed than Bob, especially orally she smiled, but then who wasn't better than Bob?

At that moment she saw the light from a car's headlights flash through her window. This can only happen when a car turns into her driveway. Paige stood up, straightened her skirt, checked herself in the mirror and went out to answer the door.

Directly across Mississippi Boulevard from where Paige was anticipating the evening's bedroom wrestling match, was the bluff above the Big Muddy. Running along that side of the street was an asphalt pathway. In the evenings, with the view of the river and Fort Snelling on the south side, it was a favorite route for bikers, joggers and walkers.

A woman in a black hoodie was among them this cool, summer evening, indistinguishable from the many others who traversed the pathway. Only this woman had gone past the Sutherland home from each direction several times. Now, just as darkness settled over the city, she was back among the trees at the edge of the drop to the water below.

While she watched the house she again wondered why she was here. What did she expect to find? The mysterious jogger only knew that some irresistible force within her had brought her here. She needed to think and come up with an idea, a plan of some kind. Being here watching across the street would hopefully cause something to trigger in her mind.

She had been watching the house for fifteen minutes. Standing among the trees she was almost invisible in her dark clothing with the hood covering her head and most of her face. She decided to give it another few minutes then try again tomorrow night. Just then a car slowed and turned into the driveway and drove up almost to the garage before stopping.

The driver got out, went to the back door and stood waiting for it to open. A few seconds later the light above the door came on and she could see that the visitor was obviously a man. The door opened, Paige stepped out and the two of them embraced and passionately kissed. The woman watching from the shadows realized that this was no casual acquaintance.

"What have we here?" she whispered to herself. "Paige the Ice Cube has herself a boyfriend. This might be something."

She waited until the light in the backyard went out. Before coming out of the shadows she looked up and down the dark street and around the neighboring houses. She started to jog across Mississippi Boulevard when she noticed a light come back on in what she knew was Paige's bedroom.

"That was quick Paige, you horny little slut," she quietly said with a smile realizing this tawdry affair must have started long before Bob's death.

She quickly and silently trotted up to the man's car to check it out. In the ambient light she was able to read the license plate number and the make and model of the car; a Mercedes E350 sedan. It was too dark to tell the car's color, but it was obviously black or dark blue.

Comfortable that she had the license plate memorized at least enough to get to her car and write it down, Mackenzie walked out of the driveway to head home.

"Hi," Mackenzie said to Maddy the next day as she opened the front door for her. "Come in, I need to talk to you about something."

It was the morning after Mackenzie's vigil at Paige Sutherland's. She had called Maddy, not too early, and asked her to come to the house.

"Okay," a puzzled Maddy said. "That's what you told me but…"

"I didn't want to talk about it over the phone," Mackenzie said.

The two women went into the kitchen. Maddy took a seat at the breakfast bar while Mackenzie poured coffee.

"What's up?" Maddy asked as she took a sip from her cup.

"Okay," Mackenzie began, "I need a private investigator and I would like you to do something for me," she paused.

"But?"

"For now, at least, I want to keep it from Marc."

"Oh, oh," Maddy said with a worried look.

"It's nothing illegal," Mackenzie quickly added, holding her hands up, palms out to reassure her friend. "And I will probably tell Marc myself, depending on what I find out. It's just, for now, I want to do this without him knowing. I'm afraid he'll try to talk me out of it. You know how lawyers are."

"True enough," Maddy laughed.

"Can you do it?"

Madeline thought it over then said, "I work for you, but I also work for Marc. Ethically I could probably do it but I'm not comfortable with it."

"Okay, I'll find someone else," a disappointed Mackenzie said.

"I know someone," Maddy said. "He's very good and very discreet. He knows Marc. In fact, he introduced me to Marc. If you tell him not to tell Marc, he won't. Let me call him."

"Oh, great, thanks," Mackenzie said.

A minute later Maddy said into her phone, "Hey, paisan, I got a job for you."

Maddy listened for a moment then said, "No, it's not for Marc and yes, she'll pay you." Maddy held the phone away from her face and asked Mackenzie, "Do you want him to come here? He has time this morning."

"Yes, that would be great, thanks,"

Maddy went back to her phone, gave the man Mackenzie's address and told him she would wait for him to introduce them.

"He's on the way. His name is Tony Carvelli and you'll like him. At first he'll probably seem a little rough around the edges but he's really a sweetie. He's a good friend and I adore him."

"That's good enough for me," Mackenzie smiled.

Twenty minutes later the front doorbell chimed, and the two women went to answer it. Maddy opened the door and a slightly Italian looking man was there. He was dressed in five-hundred-dollar loafers, expensive gray wool slacks, a light, tan leather jacket and a white, silk shirt with two open buttons.

"Hello, beautiful," Carvelli said as he stepped inside and gave Maddy a hug and peck on the cheek.

Maddy introduced him to Mackenzie and the three of them walked back to the kitchen. Mackenzie poured coffee for Carvelli while Maddy picked up her shoulder bag.

"I'm taking off. I don't know what she wants and at this point, I don't want to know," Maddy told Carvelli.

Carvelli's eyebrows went up and Maddy quickly assured him by saying, "It's nothing illegal and you'll understand why I don't want to know what's up yet."

Maddy turned to Mackenzie and said, "You can tell him everything about me, Marc, what you want, everything."

"I will," Mackenzie said.

Maddy gave Carvelli a quick kiss on the cheek and said to both of them, "See you later."

FIFTEEN

Tony Carvelli left the Crocus Hill house without having committed to working for Mackenzie. What she wanted, although not illegal, was not something Carvelli would normally do.

Tony Carvelli was in his early fifties and due to his years on the streets of Minneapolis he looked it but could still make most women check him out. He had a touch of the bad boy look they couldn't resist plus a flat stomach and a full head of thick black hair touched with gray highlights; a genetic bequest from his Italian father.

Carvelli was an ex-Minneapolis detective with the reputation of being a street predator, which was well deserved. He looked and acted the part as well. Dressed as he was today, he could easily pass for a Mafia wiseguy. Growing up in Chicago, he had known a few of them and could have become one himself and very likely, a successful one. Instead, after his family moved to Minnesota, he became a cop.

He was retired from the Minneapolis P.D. with a twenty-year pension and became a private investigator. Over the years he was able to build a nice, successful business doing mostly corporate security and investigations.

When he had driven his two-year-old Camaro a couple of blocks from Mackenzie's house, he tapped a number on his phone. The first ring did not finish before it was answered.

"So, are you going to help her?" Maddy Rivers asked without saying hello.

"I left it up in the air," Carvelli answered her. "It's not something I normally take on."

"I figured that," Maddy said. "I was hoping I could get you to do me a favor. I'd do it but I'm working for Marc on Mackenzie's legal problems…"

"…and she doesn't want him to know about this yet. Tell me what you can about her legal difficulties."

"The shooting of Bob Sutherland was self-defense. No doubt about it. The scene, the forensics, the background, everything backs that up. The rest of it is about kids pissed off that dad's second wife is getting the money, pure and simple."

"You're comfortable with that?" Carvelli asked her. Tony had known Madeline since she moved to Minneapolis several years ago. They were good friends and he trusted her opinion.

"Absolutely," Maddy answered him.

"Okay, I'll do this for her. Plus, she told me she would tell Marc what I find out. I don't like keeping things from her lawyer, especially one I know."

"She told me that too. She will tell him. I'm not sure but I think it may have something to do with the wrongful death lawsuit Bob Sutherland's widow brought against her."

"Okay," Carvelli said again. "For you, I'll do this. Talk to you later, sweetheart."

"Thanks, Tony."

Mackenzie hurried to the front door after hearing the doorbell chime. While she walked toward the door she checked the time on a wall clock and saw that her guest was right on time, 4:30. She opened the door, pleasantly smiled and greeted the man.

"Hello, Mrs. Sutherland," Carvelli said. Tony called Mackenzie about a half an hour ago to let her know he had some information and wanted to stop by. Impressed with Carvelli's prompt service she told him to come right over.

"Please don't call me that. It's Mackenzie," she said. "Come in," she continued.

Tony followed her into the living room and sat in the same chair Bob Sutherland had while Mackenzie sat on the sofa.

"What do you have?" she asked.

"The car is owned by a Simon Kane," Tony began

"Seriously?" Mackenzie said with an astonished look. "Simon Kane? I wouldn't have thought he had it in him," she laughed.

"You know him," Carvelli said.

"Yes, indeed. He was the corporate lawyer for the Sutherland's grocery store company. Simon Kane and Paige the Bitch," she said with a large smile. "Talk about an odd couple. Of course, I can't imagine anyone with Paige."

"Mackenzie, I have a lot of background information on him I can write up for you," Tony said. "This is starting to sound a little too personal for me."

"I'm sorry. I know we talked about this before but it's more than personal. If it was just a personal catfight, I wouldn't do it. But Paige Sutherland is suing me for the death of her husband. It was self-defense; you can ask Maddy or Marc. I need all of the ammunition I can get."

"Who's representing you?"

"Woman in Marc's office..."

"Connie?"

"Yes, do you know her?"

"Sure," Tony said. "She's good."

"Simon Kane is Paige's lawyer and he's screwing his client, and not just for his bill," Mackenzie laughed.

"Tell you what," Tony said. "Since this isn't a personal thing, but legal business and I know Connie would want all of the dirt she can get, I'll keep digging. I'll try to find out how long this has been going on. How long Kane has been servicing his client outside of the office."

The last part of the statement brought a hearty laugh from Mackenzie.

"I know for a fact because Marc told me, Kane could get in a lot of trouble, ethically, for being involved with a client," Mackenzie said.

"And I know Connie," Tony said. "She'd love to have that information. Let me dig around for a day or two and see what I can find out before you say anything to Connie or Marc or Maddy. I'll need to hire this computer geek I know to do some digging about on our Mr. Kane also, you okay with the expense?"

"No problem. While you're at it, check out Paige Sutherland too please."

"Sure," Tony said.

Mackenzie looked at Tony with a look as if she ate something bad then said, "It's a little sleazy, isn't it? Distasteful."

"A little," Tony agreed. "What the hell," he shrugged. "I haven't done any of this since I stopped doing divorce work. A little sleaze won't hurt me."

"If she wasn't suing me, I wouldn't be doing this. I actually don't give a damn who Paige is screwing."

"I get to be there when you tell Connie," Tony said. "I'll want to see her reaction. She'll love this."

"I think I like her," Mackenzie said.

"I definitely do," Tony added.

At 9:00 the next morning, Carvelli drove up to the home of someone who did computer geek work for him. He was standing on the front steps and tried knocking on the door for the third time. His patience was getting a little thin and his knocking was more like hammering with his fist. Tony had called ahead so he knew the young man was home which made his irritation a little more inflamed. *At least he'd better be home*, Carvelli thought.

Carvelli was standing on the front steps of a small, eighty-year-old, two story brick house in South Minneapolis. The owner was a computer whiz Carvelli had caught hacking one of Carvelli's business clients. Instead of turning him over to the Feds or Minneapolis cops, Tony had scared ten years off of the young man's life. He also had him in his pocket to do certain clandestine searches whenever Carvelli needed it.

A second before he hammered the door for the fourth time, the home's occupant opened it. The bearded, disheveled younger man opened the door wearing a confused look while Carvelli stepped inside and brushed past him.

"Oh, that's right, I forgot you called," he said.

"I called ten minutes ago, Paul," Tony said. "Jesus Christ, Paul, open a window once in a while. It smells like a *Grateful Dead* concert in here."

"Hey, Carvelli, do I tell you how many olives to put in your martinis?"

Carvelli gave him his best angry cop stare then said, "I have some business for you. I'll pay you a grand, cash."

"You got it. What do you need, dude?"

Carvelli gave him the information he had about Simon Kane and Paige Sutherland.

"I'll get on it right away," Paul said. "I should have it this afternoon. What are you looking for?"

"Everything you can get. Go back to the big night when mommy and daddy bounced around in the back seat of the car and made him."

"You got it, dude."

"Thanks, Pavel," Carvelli smiled using his real name. "I'll call you later."

Paul Baker, christened Pavel Bykowski by his devout Roman Catholic mother, was a world class hacker. Whatever there was to know about someone, Paul could dig it out of the internet.

Baker's office was the entire second floor of his mortgage-free home; mortgage free because Paul had hacked the lender and wiped the debt clean. There were two bedrooms upstairs and the wall separating them was gone creating sufficient space for his setup. Unknown, but certainly suspected by Tony Carvelli, Baker had at least a dozen more cash clients, including two FBI agents. It was enough to keep Paul Baker supplied with the latest equipment and all the best weed he desired.

Around 3:00 P.M. Carvelli called him and Paul told him to come by. His magic keyboards had done their work and he was ready for Tony.

Carvelli arrived and this time, Paul let him in right away. They went into the living room where Paul showed him a small stack of papers.

"Looks like your two love birds have been doing the horizontal two-step for at least a couple of years," Paul said. "I got hotel charges, sometimes three times a week, for No-Tell motels and hotels all over the Cities."

"What else?" Carvelli asked.

"I'm surprised at you, Tony. I didn't think you did this kind of stuff."

"I'm doing a favor for a friend," Carvelli absently said as he looked over the copies Baker made for him. "Not that it's any of your business. What's this?"

"That's a summary I typed up for you. Not much about Paige Sutherland. Some minor bullshit in the society pages of the local papers. Crap like that. A lot of stuff on this Kane dude. He some kind of hotshot lawyer?"

"I guess," Tony shrugged. "Downtown corporate lawyer type."

"He did a lot of work for the Sutherlands," Paul said. "Including servicing Paige quite a bit."

"How do you know it's her he was seeing?" Tony asked becoming very serious.

"Well, ah," Baker started to answer a little nervously. "You wanted to know about her too so, I just assumed..."

"Bullshit. You have video of them and don't lie to me," Tony said stepping up to the taller, younger man and poking a finger in his chest.

"Yeah, okay. I found some..."

"I want it, all of it. What do you think you're going to do, blackmail somebody?"

"No, well, maybe. I don't know," Paul stammered stepping away from Tony.

"You idiot," Tony calmly said. "You'd trip over your own dick trying something like that. You email all of the videos to me and then forget about it. Am I clear?"

"Yeah, sure, you got it."

Tony took an envelope from his inside jacket pocket and handed it to the hacker.

"Here's your money. Thanks. Now send me the video and I'll talk to you later."

"Okay, Tony. Thanks."

Carvelli drove directly to the Crocus Hill house to meet with Mackenzie. On the way, he called ahead to be sure she was home and she assured him she would be there.

The two of them spent an hour going through all of the information Paul Baker obtained for them. Most of it was mundane, trivial minutiae that makes up the details of everyone's life. The information about the long-running affair, while a little tawdry both agreed, might be worth having to fend off the lawsuit.

"You know something," Mackenzie said when they were finished, "I know Simon Kane and he is not a very likeable person. In fact, I always thought he was an arrogant, little prick; the smartest guy in the room type. After going through all of this," she continued waving her hand at the documents, "there's nothing special about this guy at all. Probably a decent lawyer. I think Bill, my dearly departed husband, liked the way Simon sucked up to him and kissed his ass."

"That's pretty much what corporate lawyers do," Tony said. He took out his phone and speed dialed a number.

"Hi, Carolyn, it's Tony. I'm with Mackenzie Sutherland and she needs an appointment with..." he paused. "No love, Connie. But Marc can be there." He put his hand over the phone, looked at Mackenzie who was shaking her head at the mention of Marc's name and said, "You can't keep this from him and you shouldn't."

Mackenzie frowned then said, "Okay, you're right. Have him there."

"What, dear?" Tony said into the phone to Carolyn. "Yeah, that should be okay." He looked at Mackenzie again and said, "Ten o'clock tomorrow morning?"

"Yes, that's fine," she agreed.

"Okay, hon. Ten tomorrow. See you then."

"Madeline asked me to meet with Mrs. Sutherland," Carvelli said to begin the meeting the next day. Tony and Mackenzie were seated in the client chairs in Connie Mickelson's office. Marc Kadella was standing along the wall to their right, leaning on a tall bookcase. Connie was sitting behind her desk.

"Maddy told me she had a job for a P.I. and asked me to do it as a favor. I met with Mackenzie and she wanted me to find out who the owner of a particular car was. Maddy could've done this but Mackenzie asked me to keep it from Marc for now."

"Oh?" Marc said looking directly at his client.

"I wanted to wait until we found out who it was before telling you to be sure it was something. It is," Mackenzie said.

"Okay, go on," Connie told Tony.

"It's a Mercedes belonging to a lawyer of your acquaintance: Simon Kane."

"Please don't tell me you're trailing Simon Kane?" Marc said. "I can't count the ethical violations for that."

"No, we're not," Tony told him.

"Why did you want to know whose car this was?" Connie quietly asked Mackenzie.

Mackenzie hesitated for a moment then said, "I saw it parked in Paige Sutherland's driveway late one night. He was obviously not there to give her legal advice. It was a little late, all of the lights were out, and she was apparently having a friend spend the night."

"I then had a guy do a search online," Tony continued, "and found out Paige and Kane have been involved for at least two years. We have credit card receipts and video of the two of them at various hotels and motels around town. And Kane has been using his law firm's credit card to pay for it."

"To keep it from his wife," Connie said.

"I'm surprised you did this," Marc said to Tony.

"It was a favor for Maddy," he shrugged. "Nobody can say no to her, including you."

"I know this is kind of sleazy..." Mackenzie started to say.

"Which is why I like it," Connie interjected and wiggled her eyebrows three or four times. "I want it all, Tony. All of the paper and the videos."

Tony handed her a large envelope and said, "Here it is. DVDs and credit card receipts. I spent last night going through it all and matching receipts with the videos. They're all date and time stamped. There's a list in there for you."

"What else did you find?" Marc asked.

"The usual stuff, nothing damaging. Do you want it?" Carvelli asked Connie.

"Yeah, get me all of it."

"I'd like to talk to Connie for a minute. Would you wait in the waiting area please?" Marc asked.

When Tony and Mackenzie had left, Marc took Tony's chair and said, "What are you going to do with this?"

"Find an appropriate moment then shove it up Simon's ass. Why?"

"This is more than a little sleazy," Marc said.

"Hey, Boy Scout. They started this. She's suing our client for millions of dollars. This is no bullshit litigation," Connie said.

"Yeah, okay," Marc agreed. "I guess I'm okay with it if it can help Mac beat this suit. Don't we have an obligation to report this?"

"Not that I'm aware of," Connie coyly answered him.

"What Kane is up to is a clear violation of the ethical canons and..."

"If we don't know we're supposed to report it then..."

"We're supposed to know," Marc reminded her. "We're officers of the court."

"Yeah, I heard that somewhere, way back in law school which was a long time ago. My memory isn't what it should be. Besides, I hate these fucking asshole, downtown lawyers. All they care about is billable hours. They don't give a shit about their clients."

"I think Simon Kane has more than a passing interest in Paige Sutherland," Marc said.

"And when I get the chance, I'll make him regret it," Connie added.

SIXTEEN

Max Coolidge was slowly cruising eastbound on Grand Avenue in St. Paul. A beautiful, sunny, summer day, he was driving his summer car; a 1969 black Pontiac GTO, a Motorhead's wet dream that Max had picked up for a song ten years ago. The classic car was in rough shape at the time having been in the backyard of a Latino drug dealer for years. The cops had confiscated it as the fruit of a criminal enterprise and Max, with department cooperation, got it as soon as it became available. An ex-con Max knew with a gift for cars, which is why he had done time, did the work to refurbish the car and turned it back into a thing of beauty.

It was mid-afternoon a few days after the hearing to exhume Bill Sutherland. Ever since then Max had been in a foul mood. Something about the Sutherlands and this entire affair still nagged at him. An itch he could not scratch.

Max was looking for a snitch that was supposed to be on a street corner three blocks back and twenty minutes ago. Max had grown tired of waiting for him and his irritation was growing, he was now driving down the busy avenue booking for the skel.

Stuck at a light on Victoria behind two cars Max looked down the street and saw the young man a block away turn south on a side street. Really irritated knowing his snitch was deliberately avoiding him, the instant the light turned green he slammed his right hand down on the horn. The driver ahead of him, a man, looked in his mirror and flipped him off; the gesture adding fuel to his anger.

Instead of chasing down Grand, Max made a quick right on Victoria, pushed the accelerator to the floor and the 400 cubic inch engine roared. Barely two seconds later he was at the next corner braking and spinning to his left.

Unnoticed by Max, a St. Paul patrol car was behind him on Grand and the cops saw him take off. Not knowing who was driving the classic muscle car, they decided to follow him. The two cops in the squad car turned on Victoria just in time to see Max squeal around the corner a block away. The rack of lights on the roof went on and the patrol cops went after him.

Max flew down the street to the next corner and whipped into another left to make that turn. As soon as he did, he saw his junkie snitch slowly coming up the sidewalk on his right walking toward him. Less than ten feet before the man got to the alley dividing the block, Max screeched to a stop, half in and half out of the alley's entrance. The car had not stopped rocking before Max was out of it and on top of his quarry.

"Come here you little asshole!" Max yelled, his eyes almost shooting flames.

"Hey, Max, dude. I was just looking for you."

His foul mood, the chase, the adrenaline and the lie sent Max, normally a very calm, controlled person, over the edge.

"Marvin you son-of-a-bitch, don't you lie to me!" Max practically screamed. He grabbed the scrawny, street hustler and then really lost it. Max slapped him once, twice, three times then threw him on the sidewalk and stood over him.

As Max was grabbing Marvin by the front of his shirt, the patrol car slid to a stop behind his Pontiac. The two cops jumped out leaving their doors open and ran toward Max pulling their night sticks. One of the cops, an older black sergeant, recognized Coolidge as he ran toward him.

"When I tell you to be somewhere, you be there!" Max yelled down at the terrified Marvin.

"Jesus Christ, Coolidge," the sergeant said as he held up a hand to stop his partner. He grabbed Max by the arm and spun him around. When he did this, Max looked at the cop with a confused expression then back at his snitch still lying on the sidewalk.

"What are you doing? What the hell happened here?"

"Hey, uh, Cleveland," Max quietly said to the cop. "I ah, ah. Sorry," he said looking down at Marvin. "Jesus Marvin, I'm really sorry," he continued as he reached down to help him up.

"Are you okay?" the sergeant asked Marvin.

"Yeah, yeah, I'm okay. No problem."

"Do you want to press charges against Detective Coolidge?" Cleveland asked.

Marvin silently shook his head and said, "No, no. For what? No, it's all good."

"Sarge," his younger white partner said. "We got a bigger problem."

"What?" Cleveland asked.

"Across the street," the cop said tilting his head in that direction.

Cleveland looked where his partner indicated, saw what he meant and said, "Oh, shit, I hate those goddamn phones."

Standing across the street were two boys in their late teens. Both were watching the scene, and each was holding a smartphone filming the entire episode. What they saw and filmed made it obvious that the patrol cops knew that Max would be identified later by whichever TV station paid the most to the two teens who sold them the film.

"Let me try to talk to them," Cleveland said. As soon as he started across the street walking toward the boys, they bolted and ran. With the thirty extra pounds Cleveland had accumulated around his waist, there was no way he would catch these two sprinters.

An hour later Max was at his desk waiting for the summons from his captain. He could see into the captain's office and Roy Cleveland was in there telling McCarthy what happened.

"Max," he heard McCarthy's voice boom across the room.

Coolidge raised his right hand to indicate he heard the captain as he pushed his chair back. He made his way through the squad room while McCarthy patiently waited for him at his door.

When he entered the office he looked at Cleveland, smiled slightly as Cleveland said, "Sorry, man. I had…"

"Don't worry about it, Roy. I did it, I own it, and I'll take it. You had no choice and we're cool."

The two men shook hands and Cleveland closed the door as he left.

"Sit down, Max," McCarthy calmly said indicating a chair in front of his desk.

"I'm really sorry, Dave," Coolidge started. "For the life of me, I don't know what came over me. I just lost control; no excuses."

"You've been going around here snapping and growling at everybody for two weeks. What's up?"

Coolidge didn't answer right away. Instead, he turned his head to his left and stared out the window thinking about the question.

"It's this Sutherland thing," he said looking back at his boss. "I'm having a little trouble letting it go, I guess."

"That's not like you," McCarthy said.

"I know," Coolidge nodded his head. "I guess it's because I'm not sure I'd be here today if it wasn't for that family. My life could've taken a very different turn."

"Bullshit," McCarthy said. "They may have helped you get started but you are where you are because of who you are and nothing else.

"Let me tell you something," McCarthy continued. "You don't know dick about that family and you don't owe them a thing. You know this: what goes on in somebody else's home is not something you know unless you live it. You may not know this, but old man Sutherland was a drunk and a whore chaser. Yeah, that's right," he said when he saw the surprised look on Coolidge's face. "He was connected to politicians downtown and his partying ways got brushed aside plenty. Hell, I caught him with hookers a couple of times myself. So, don't get all weepy over the Sutherlands. Their 'Leave it to Beaver' image was bullshit."

McCarthy stood up, walked around his desk and took the chair next to Max. In a friendly way, he brushed some unseen lint off of Max's knee then said, "There's going to be a shit storm around here for a few days after that film hits the TV."

"I know, sorry," Max quietly agreed.

"Don't worry about it. We'll handle it and it will blow over. You slapped a junkie around. So what? We'll leak out something to soften the whole thing. But I want you to take a few days off. I got a job I need somebody to do."

"What?"

"Chicago P.D. is holding Rodrigo Barnes for us. Remember him?"

"Yeah, he's wanted for that drive-by a few months ago that killed that six-year-old girl over in Frogtown," Max said. "You want me to go get him?"

"Yeah, take a couple days…."

"I'm not a cab driver," he started to protest.

"You're not driving there, you'll fly, and this isn't really a request. Go to Chicago, take a couple days, relax, go to a club or two, hell, do you some good to get laid. I want you out of here for the next couple of days. Understood?"

Max sighed, shrugged his shoulders and said, "Yes, Captain."

Two years ago, Max was involved with a gangbanger drug deal and homicide case that involved the Chicago P.D. The case lasted more than six months and Max became friends with several CPD cops and detectives, two in particular.

They were a salt and pepper pair of homicide detectives named Sean Flaherty and Luther Cole. Flaherty was a forty-eight-year-old with twenty-two years on the force. Cole was thirty-three and had nine years on the job. They called each other, in private only, Klan and Panther. In reality, they were good friends and had the highest clearance rate in the department. Before leaving for Chicago, Max called them, talked to both men and let them know he was coming.

There are flights between Minneapolis/St. Paul and Chicago every day approximately once an hour. Catching a flight to Chicago was nothing. Max strolled up the passenger ramp into O'Hare and saw the two detectives waiting for him in the passenger waiting area. Max had a black leather bag with a shoulder strap slung over his left shoulder. As he approached the two men, each acknowledged him with a slight nod and serious look.

Max shook hands with both then said, "I don't think I've ever seen two guys who look more like cops than you two. Did you even have to show TSA your badges to get through security?"

"No wonder they have this guy working intelligence in St. Paul. Nothing gets by him," Flaherty said to his partner.

Cole smiled and said, "We were wondering, has that place thawed out yet?"

"Almost," Max replied. "We get our two weeks of summer in August."

The three of them made the long walk to the main terminal. When they exited the building Max immediately spotted their department-issued car.

"You left your flashers on?" Max asked.

"Gets us great parking and nobody fucks with the car," Flaherty laughed.

The detectives got in front and Max tossed his bag on the back seat and climbed in after it. As they pulled away from the terminal Max placed his shield up against the window.

"What are you doing?" Flaherty asked from the passenger seat.

"I know it's extremely rare for a black man to be sitting in the back seat of cop car in this town," Max said with obvious sarcasm. "I just want people to know you guys are my chauffeurs."

The three of them made cop banter on the ride to the CPD homicide division. About halfway there, Flaherty turned in his seat to look at Max.

"So, you're here for the popular Rodrigo Barnes."

"Yeah, you guys know him?" Max replied.

"Oh, yeah," Luther chimed in. "Mr. Barnes got his start here."

"You guys got a good case against him?" Flaherty asked."

"So, I'm told," Max answered. "I don't know much about it. Drive by that got a six-year-old little girl killed. Would be nice if these gangbanger assholes would learn how to shoot."

"You ever meet him?" Luther asked.

"No," Max admitted.

"He's a no-doubt-about-it bad ass, Max. I'm surprised they only sent one guy for him," Flaherty said.

"Why did they send you?" Luther asked.

"My boss thought I needed a vacation," Max told them.

For the rest of the drive Max told them his story about the Sutherlands. He told them everything with special emphasis on the shooting of Bob Sutherland and the family's suspicions about the death of the old man, Bill Sutherland.

"So, what do you think will come of it?" Luther asked.

"Nothing," Max answered. "The grand jury refused to indict her for shooting Bob and the court ruled there were no grounds to dig up the old man for a second autopsy."

"She good looking?" Flaherty asked.

"Who?" Max said.

"The Sutherland woman. The one that shot your friend," Flaherty said.

"Yeah, actually, she is," Max said. "Very good looking. Close to beautiful."

"She married the old man, the kids resent it, she inherits the money and one of them confronts her about it, gets pissed when she tells him to go pound sand, threatens to kill her in her house and she shoots him. Could've happened exactly the way she said. Probably no love lost on either side of this deal," Flaherty said.

"Could be," Max reluctantly agreed.

A few minutes later, just before they reached their destination, Luther said, "You remember that case we looked at up on the North Side a few years back? The same kind of thing."

"No, I don't," Flaherty said.

"Sure you do," Luther insisted.

"Okay, fine, you're right I do. But maybe you can refresh my memory for me," Flaherty cracked wise.

"See what I have to deal with Max? Early onset Alzheimers. That rich guy, what was his name?" Luther continued. "Cooper, Cartwheel…"

"Cartwright," Flaherty said.

"Yeah," Luther said snapping his fingers. "That's it."

"I remember now, she was wife number four or five," Flaherty said. "He was an old drunk, womanizer. Coroner said he was a heart attack waiting to happen. There was no case there."

"I know, Klan," Luther said. "I'm just saying it sounds like the same deal. You remember, real good-looking younger wife. She gets all the dough and the ex-wives and a couple of kids get squat."

While Luther parked the car Flaherty said, "They were all a bunch of worthless assholes anyway." He turned to Max and said, "They made a bunch of accusations but had no evidence. The M.E. ruled it a heart attack."

"Was an autopsy performed?" Max asked.

The two CPD detectives looked at each other, shrugged and Luther said, "I don't remember. Probably not. The guy smoked like a chimney and drank like a fish. Liked the nose candy a little too much as I remember."

"Maybe I'll take a look at it anyway," Max said. "You guys have case notes?"

"Sure," Flaherty said. "No charges were filed but the notes would have gone into storage."

"Plus, it was all over the news for at least a couple weeks. There should be plenty about it on the internet," Luther added.

Max left his bag in the car and the three of them went into the building. Flaherty introduced Max to the desk sergeant who reviewed the extradition paperwork Max had with him.

The sergeant typed on his computer and shortly afterward said, "He's still at Cook County. When do you want him?"

"How long will it take you to get him?" Max asked.

"Better give us at least a four-hour heads up," the man answered.

"Okay, will do. Thanks, Sarge," Max answered.

SEVENTEEN

Sean Flaherty checked with his captain, explained to her why Max wanted their Cartwright file and got her okay to let him see it.

Flaherty retrieved the file from the basement storage area then found a desk for Max to use. Fortunately for Max, the desk came equipped with a PC on it. In less than fifteen minutes, Max was standing at Flaherty's desk.

"Is this it?" he asked holding up the Cartwright file.

"Yeah," Flaherty said. "I warned you there wasn't much in it. Is there an autopsy in it?"

"Yeah, it's here. Heart attack was the C.O.D.," Max said. "Why did you get involved in the first place?"

By this time Luther Cole was listening and said, "Rich, white people."

"Heavy contributors to the Democrats," Flaherty added. "Plus, the grieving relatives were raising hell with the Party demanding an investigation, screaming that the merry widow had murdered the old man and robbed them. So, as the old saying goes, 'shit rolls downhill' kicked in and it landed on us."

"We interviewed all of the grief-stricken relatives and it was pretty obvious they were a lot more grief-stricken about the money than the old man," Luther added.

"I got that from your notes," Max told him. "Was there a lot of stuff in the media about it?"

"Oh, yeah," Flaherty nodded. "They even started referring to the wife, what was her name?" he asked Luther.

"Frances," Max said.

"Right, Frances. Anyway, they are starting to refer to her as a possible — they always use the word possible — Black Widow," Flaherty said.

"It didn't stick, though," Luther said. "The whole thing lasted maybe two weeks then died down."

"I heard she moved somewhere. New York or Arizona, I don't remember."

"How about Minnesota?" Max asked.

Flaherty looked at Luther, both men shook their heads then Flaherty said, "No, never heard that one."

"Says here the body was cremated?" Max asked.

"If that's what it says," Flaherty said. "There was nothing there, Max. The old man was a drunk, a womanizer — I love that word — and partier. Lived a fast life and his heart gave out."

"We did a thorough investigation and didn't find anything other than broke, bitter ex-wives and a couple of worthless kids," Luther said, a touch of annoyance in his voice at being questioned.

"I believe you, Luther. I'm just grasping at straws because of the Sutherlands," Max almost apologized. "Maybe I'll check online for news stories and see if I can come up with a picture of her."

"Knock yourself out," Flaherty said with a smile. "You are joining us for lunch?"

"Since you're buying, absolutely," Max replied.

Max sat down at the desk he was using and fired up the computer. There was quite a bit of material about the death of Wendell Cartwright and he read through all of it. The basic story was exactly what the two CPD detectives told him. Cartwright had died of a heart attack after a lifetime of good living. There was even a story that claimed he had inherited one hundred million dollars and had blown sixty of it on fast women, slow horses and unsuccessful marriages.

In one of the stories by the *Chicago Tribune*, there was a picture of the grieving but lucky widow. Max studied it for a minute looking for any resemblance to Mackenzie Sutherland. The features were similar, but her hair was a natural blonde cut in a style that framed her face, her eyes were a bright blue and she wore very stylish black glasses. Also, according to the articles in the news, Frances Cartwright was eight or nine years younger than Mackenzie would have been.

Max continued his search, but the picture kept creeping back into his head. He went back to it twice and the second time an idea came to him. Max took out his phone and made a call.

"Anna Finney," he heard the St. Paul detective say.

"Hey, it's Max Coolidge," Max told her. "Do you have a clear picture of Mackenzie Sutherland?"

"What are you up to Max?"

He quickly told her where he was and what he was doing.

"You think this Cartwright woman might be Mackenzie?" Anna asked.

"I don't know," Max answered. "No, probably not but it's worth checking out. I need to get a picture of each of them to compare side-by-side."

"You know there's software that can do that, too," Anna said.

"Do we have her picture?"

"I don't think so, but I know a guy at the *Pioneer Press*. They must have one. She's been in their paper a few times. It'll cost you."

"How much?"

"Probably a hundred."

"Okay, do it. Call me back," Max said.

"Sean," Max quietly said as he approached Flaherty's desk. The Chicago detective was reviewing a file when Max spoke to him.

"What's up?" Flaherty asked.

"You know anybody at the *Tribune* who can get me a copy of a photo of Frances Cartwright?"

"Sure, it will cost you a c-note," Flaherty said.

"What is it with these people?"

"It's a two-way street, Max. You know that. When do you want it?"

"Now," Max shrugged.

"Let me give her a call," Flaherty said. He found the woman's number, called her and chatted her up for a couple of minutes. He got down to business and she agreed to get him a clear copy of Frances' photo.

"We'll pick it up at lunch," he said to Max.

At that moment, Max's phone rang, and he took the call. It was Anna Finney calling him back.

Max listened for a minute then said, "Can he email it to me?"

After Anna assured him the man could, Max looked at Flaherty and said. "Give me your email address."

Flaherty told him what it was, and Max relayed it to Anna.

"Thanks, Anna, I owe you one. Tell your guy I'll pay him when I get back."

"I'll have to pay him now," Anna told him.

"Good, take it out of petty cash."

"Yeah, right. There's usually six or seven dollars in there," Anna said.

"I'll pay you back," Max promised.

"Yes, you will."

When the three detectives returned from lunch, Max had the photo of Frances Cartwright and the one of Mackenzie Sutherland had arrived via email. Flaherty got a tech guy to make a clear print of Mackenzie on photo paper.

"What do you guys think?" Max asked the two CPD detectives. All three of them had carefully compared both photos.

"I don't know," Flaherty said. "Maybe, but I wouldn't swear to it in court."

"I think there's a definite resemblance," Luther told Max. "Look at the facial features; the nose, cheekbones, chin. If either of them was smiling, the teeth would give it away."

The tech guy who made the copy of Mackenzie's print was looking over Max's shoulder and said, "I can run a facial comparison through our computers for you."

"You can?" Max asked.

"Sure, it will take a while. But I have to warn you, it's not perfect."

"Go ahead," Max said, and he handed the two photos to the young man.

As the techie walked away to compare the photos, Max asked the two detectives, "Would you guys mind it if I re-interviewed the family members?"

Flaherty and Cole looked at each other, shrugged their shoulders and shook their heads.

"No, not at all. In fact," Flaherty continued turning back to Luther, "we got nothing going, you want to go with him?"

"Sure, why not? Maybe the Sherlock Holmes of Minnesota could teach us something," Luther replied.

"Probably," Flaherty added.

"No doubt," Max said.

Two hours later the three detectives were back at the CPD homicide division. Of the four ex-wives of Wendell Cartwright, they were able to interview only three. Even though Wendell had died several years ago, the passage of time had done nothing to diminish their bitterness. All three were convinced wife number five, Frances, had murdered him. Of course, there was absolutely no evidence to support this except for their anger over the money.

When Wendell was alive each ex-wife and Wendell's two adult children were all receiving monthly payments to live on. The payments were all coming from the trust Wendell received through his family. Because the terms of the trust prohibited Wendell from taking large lump-sum amounts to pay off each wife and be done with it, millions to each of them, the monthly payments were the best he could do. All four ex-wives and the two progenies were receiving twenty-thousand-dollar per month payments, tax-free.

No more monthly payments and no insurance to make them up. Since they all lived well off of Wendell's trust none of them had saved or invested much for the future. Because of this, they were all looking at a serious lifestyle downgrade. The happiest person involved was, of course, Mackenzie Frances Cartwright, who went by her middle name, Frances.

Waiting for Sean Flaherty was a note from the techie asking him to call. While he did this, Max wheeled a chair up to the desks of the two

CPD cops. Flaherty made the call to their techie as Max sat down next to Luther Cole.

"I remember when we interviewed them the first time, they were all living in nice houses or luxury condos," Luther told Max. "Now they're in one-bedroom apartments. Quite a comedown."

"He'll be here in a minute," Flaherty said after hanging up the phone.

"What did he come up with?" Max asked.

"He wouldn't tell me over the phone."

"What do you mean 'he wouldn't tell you over the phone', why not?" Max asked.

"He wouldn't tell me," Flaherty shrugged. "Wants to come up and tell us in person. Techies, they're a strange breed."

"I ran the photos through two different software programs," the young man announced when he got there. He was holding the two photos as if the detectives did not know what he was referring to. "Both came up with a similar finding. One had them an eighty-seven percent match and the other an eighty-five. I ran them twice just to be sure and the scores were the same."

"Thanks, Aaron," Flaherty said as he was handed the photos. "You can go back to your world now."

"Hey, detective," Aaron said. He bent down and poked a finger into Flaherty's soft midsection. "Have another doughnut. I bought stock in Krispy Kreme just because of you."

"Nice shot!" Luther said while he and Max burst into laughter.

When the jocularity died down and Aaron had left, Max said. "Eighty-seven percent."

"It's her," Flaherty said.

"Probably," Max answered him. "But is eighty-seven percent good enough in court?"

"So what?" Luther asked. "So what if it's her? Cartwright died of a heart attack because of his lifestyle. Your guy in Minnesota, same thing. She hit the lottery twice. Lucky her. You see a crime here?"

"He has a point," Flaherty said.

"We're cynical cops," Max reminded them. "You guys think this is a coincidence?"

Luther and Flaherty looked at each other then back at Max and both said at the same time, "No."

"It might be enough to exhume the bodies…" Max started to say.

"Cartwright was cremated," Luther reminded him.

"Oh, shit, that's right," Max said. "Sutherland wasn't. Maybe this is enough to dig him up and do a more detailed tox screen."

"To find what?" Flaherty asked.

"To find out if he was drugged or poisoned and see if that's what caused the heart attack."

Max looked at a clock on the wall and absently said, "I was hoping to hear back from the son, Phillip. I'm flying back tomorrow morning and I'd like to talk to him first."

Flaherty's intercom buzzed, he answered it and said, "Thanks, Cheryl. Send him back." He put the receiver in its cradle and said, "Speak of the devil."

The three men looked toward the front of the room and Phillip Cartwright came in. Flaherty waved at him and he headed toward them. To the three streetwise police detectives, it was obvious that Phillip had a drug problem, probably a serious one. Phillip Cartwright, who was almost forty, sported long, stringy hair, an unshaven face and was wearing an open, green flannel shirt, a red T-shirt, jeans with holes and beat-up sneakers.

Introductions were made, and the three cops took him into an interview room. They all took chairs around the cheap table.

"So, you want to talk to me about my cheap-ass, old man? Did that bitch that killed him decide to give up some of the money she stole?"

The interview went downhill from there. For the next twenty minutes, while Max tried to get whatever useful information he could from him, all Phillip wanted to talk about was how bad he got screwed by his "cheap-ass, old man and the bitch that murdered him." This was followed by a whining session about how tough his life was and whose fault it was; certainly not his.

Finally, fed up with his poor, poor me, sad story, Max asked, "Don't you have a college degree?"

"Yeah," Phillip answered. "So what?"

"Where did you go to school?"

"Macalester College," he answered."

"In St. Paul?" Max asked a little surprised.

"Yeah, that's right. My mother went there. Again, so what?"

"What was your major?"

"Partying," Phillip answered with a grin showing off his bad teeth. "English lit," he said.

"Maybe you could stoop to getting a job and working to support yourself," Luther sarcastically added.

"Kind of a warm day for a long sleeve shirt," Flaherty said believing Phillip was covering needle tracks.

Phillip nervously looked the three men over then said, "What is this? I haven't done anything. I'm out of here." He stood up knocking the cheap plastic chair over and went to the door.

"Throw that bitch in prison and get my old man's money. I deserve it, she doesn't." He slammed the door when he left.

"Meth," Max said when Phillip was gone.

"And heroin," Luther added.

"He's dealing, too. That's how he's supporting himself. Worthless little shit," Flaherty said.

"Can you have Rodrigo here in the morning? I booked a flight out at ten oh five."

"Sure, no problem," Flaherty said. "You want a ride to the airport?"

"That would be great, yeah. Thanks."

EIGHTEEN

Anna Finney placed the documents she was reading back into the file folder on her desk. She stared off into space thinking about what she had seen.

"What do you think?" Coolidge asked her.

Max returned from Chicago with his prisoner in tow the day before. After turning Rodrigo Barnes over to the Ramsey County jail, Max spent the remainder of the day once again combing through every word in the file he received from the Chicago cops and the news stories he had printed off concerning the death of Wendell Cartwright. This morning he sought out Finney to get a second opinion. Max was seated next to her desk while she went through everything.

Before she answered, Anna picked up the photos of Mackenzie Sutherland and Frances Cartwright. She held them next to each other comparing them for the fourth time.

"It's her," she said. "I absolutely believe it."

"Me, too," Max agreed. "What about the file?"

"His medical records show he had an EKG two years before he died. It came out well within the normal range. No history of heart problems in his family except an aunt that died of heart disease. He dies of a massive heart attack and the grieving widow conveniently had him cremated. What happened to the ashes?"

"Lake Michigan," Max said.

"Is that legal?" Anna asked.

"I don't know, probably not. You want to try to get her for polluting Lake Michigan? It's probably a fine," Max said.

"What do you want to do?" Anna asked.

"Dig up Bill Sutherland. This is too much of a coincidence."

"You think this is enough?"

"Let's talk to McCarthy. See what he thinks," Max said referring to their captain.

Max knocked on the glass portion of Captain McCarthy's door. Without waiting for a reply, the two detectives walked in.

"Where's Kubik?" McCarthy asked Anna Finney.

"Called in sick," she replied. "Which reminds me," she continued. "I'd like a new partner."

McCarthy ignored her request, looked at the file Max was handing him and said, "What's this?"

Max and Anna took the two chairs and Max gave the captain a summary of why they wanted to see him.

"Don't you two have enough to do without continuing to flog this dead horse? What do *you* think?" he said looking at Anna.

"Look at the photos, they're right on top," Anna said pointing at the file.

McCarthy held up the two photos, looked them over carefully and said, "Okay, they're very similar."

"The Chicago PD tech ran them through two different facial comparison programs. The report is in the file. Eighty-seven percent match."

"Not enough for a conviction," McCarthy said.

"I'm not looking for a conviction," Max said. "I want to get Bill Sutherland's body dug up and another autopsy performed."

"Why?"

"There are drugs, chemicals that can cause a heart attack and would not show up on a routine autopsy," Anna answered him.

"This woman is wrong, Dave," Max said leaning forward, his hands on the captain's desk. "I can feel it in my bones. I think she murdered both Bill Sutherland and this Cartwright guy for their money."

"And if she did that," Anna said, "how much of a stretch is it that she set up Bob Sutherland and murdered him, too?"

"Okay, let's say you get a court order to dig up old man Sutherland, then what? You got any evidence she drugged him?"

"If his heart attack was drug induced, she did it and we'll find out how. We'll tear her life apart and we'll find it," Max said.

McCarthy thought it over then quietly said, mostly to himself, "Three possible homicides." He looked at the two detectives and said, "Okay, take it to the prosecutor's office and see what they think."

"We'll go talk to Heather Anderson. She knows more about this than anyone else," Max told him.

"We'll end up back in front of Gabe Sendejo on this," Heather said to Max and Anna, "and he won't be happy to see us."

The three of them were sitting in Anderson's office in downtown St. Paul. Max and Anna had waited patiently for a half-hour while she reviewed the Cartwright file. Before bringing their case to her, Max had a St. Paul police tech run the photos for a computer comparison. His program came back with an eighty-eight percent match.

"Three homicides, Heather," Anna reminded her.

"Maybe," Heather said. She paused for a few seconds, sighed and said, "Oh, what the hell. I haven't taken a flyer for a while. What do you say we give it a shot?"

"That's my girl!" Max said with a big grin.

"Tell you what," Anderson continued, "today's Friday. Let me keep this over the weekend," she said pointing at the file. "I'll review it, go online and check out the news stories from here and Chicago and I'll talk to you two on Monday, okay?"

"You won't regret it," Max said as the two detectives stood to leave.

"We'll see about that," Anderson replied.

Later that same day, in mid-afternoon, Mackenzie received a phone call on a private phone that very few people knew about. Before answering it she looked at the number, a Chicago area code and hesitantly answered it.

"Mrs. Sutherland," she heard a familiar man's voice say, "it's Lou Travis," the man said.

"Yes, Lou," Mackenzie said. "Do you have something for me?"

"Yes ma'am," the man said.

Lou Travis was a private investigator that Mackenzie had retained to keep her informed of any developments in Chicago. So far the man had proven himself to be competent, reliable and discreet. Because of this, Mackenzie always paid him promptly and with an added bonus. She also did so by money order which allowed Travis the option of keeping the IRS out of it.

"What is it?" Mackenzie asked.

"There was a St. Paul detective in town for a couple days. He was here to transport a prisoner that the Chicago cops were holding back to Minnesota."

"His name?" Mackenzie asked although she was certain she knew who it was.

"Guy by the name of Max Coolidge. He and a couple CPD detectives, I know both of them, went around town interviewing your dead husband's ex-wives. They also had Phillip into the homicide division for a little chat. I heard he was pretty uncooperative."

"And how is Phillip doing?" Mackenzie asked.

"Not so good," Travis answered her. "He's got a pretty good drug problem still; meth, crack and I think he's moved up to heroin."

"And the women, the ex-wives?" Mackenzie asked.

"Not much better. A couple of them are drunks and they're all living off of social security disability scams and what little they managed to save."

"They should have invested and saved more when they were sponging off of Wendell," Mackenzie said.

"Mrs. Sutherland," Travis continued, "There's something else. My source told me this Coolidge guy has a picture of you from Chicago and one from St. Paul. I don't know what he knows or what he'll do with it, but I thought you would want to know."

"I see, yes, that is interesting," Mackenzie said. "Anything else?"

"No, ma'am. That's all I have. I'll keep my eyes and ears open and let you know if anything comes up."

"Should I send the usual amount?" Mackenzie asked.

"That would be very kind, very generous," Travis answered.

"Thank you, Lou," Mackenzie said and ended the call.

Mackenzie placed the small flip phone back in her purse. Thinking about the phone call she went into the kitchen, poured herself a glass of ice water and took a seat at the breakfast bar. While she sipped the water, she stared out the kitchen window wondering what she could do.

"Probably not much you can do about it," she quietly said to herself.

Mackenzie picked up her iPhone from the countertop and dialed a number. It was answered before the second ring.

"Hi," Marc said. "Everything okay?"

"Yeah," Mackenzie answered. "Why wouldn't it be?"

"Because people don't call lawyers unless they have a problem."

"You're right," she said playfully. "I do have a problem. I want someone, you, to take me to dinner."

"Okay, I can do that."

"I want a cheeseburger and fries. And I want a pitcher of beer. I'd kill for a good burger. You know a place? I haven't had a good, greasy cheeseburger in years."

"Yeah," Marc said with a laugh. "I know a place."

"And I'm wearing jeans and sneakers," Mackenzie said.

"No top?" Marc asked.

Mackenzie laughed and said, "You think they'd serve us if I was showing off the girls?"

"It's okay with me. I'll pick you up at 6:00."

Mackenzie set the phone down and a warm glow went through her. It was something she had not felt in many years and caused her to smile.

"God, I feel like I'm a teenager getting ready for a first date with a boy I really like."

Marc arrived promptly at 6:00 and drove the two of them to a locally owned restaurant in South Minneapolis. It was located on Lyndale a couple blocks south of Lake Street. It was also within walking distance of Marc's office. Because it was a Friday evening, the place was very busy, mostly for the bar area. The wait for a table was less than ten minutes. The college-age waitress, a pretty blonde, was at the table in less than a minute and took their orders.

"Why is she wearing a Green Bay Packer shirt?" Mackenzie asked.

Marc leaned on the table and said, "Look around, they're all wearing Packer shirts. During football season, this is a Packer bar."

"I hate the Packers," Mackenzie said. "I've always been a Vikings fan."

"That's because you're a sensible person and do not need therapy," Marc said. "Last year, during the playoffs, I was in here with a couple of friends who are Packer fans watching them play Seattle. The Seahawks did everything they could to lose that game…"

"I remember, I saw it," Mackenzie said.

"This place was jammed to the walls. Because we're so close to Wisconsin, there are a lot of Packer fans in the Cities.

"Anyway, the place was going nuts. They all thought Green Bay was going to the Super Bowl and win it. Then the Seahawks started kicking their ass and came back and won."

"In overtime," Mackenzie added. "I jumped up and cheered."

"Yeah, it was great. The place went dead quiet. I had all I could do not to rub it in. Of course, I would have been taking my life in my hands, but it was enjoyable watching the place go from crazy to dead quiet."

The waitress brought a pitcher of house beer that Marc warned Mackenzie about. It was barely drinkable, but they were having such a nice time neither cared.

Between eating their burgers and drinking the beer, they had a pleasant evening talking about anything and everything except Mackenzie's legal situation. A few minutes before 10:00, Mackenzie reached across the table and took Marc's hand.

"Since I don't have any legal problems you're handling, what do you say we go back to my place?"

"I suppose technically I'm not your lawyer so, yeah, sounds like a plan."

The next morning Marc was sitting at the kitchen's breakfast bar in a T-shirt and jeans. Mackenzie, wrapped in a fluffy white, terry cloth robe poured them each more coffee and handed Marc's cup to him.

"I could always claim you drugged me and took advantage of me," Marc said.

"You were pretty cooperative," Mackenzie said with a laugh.

"I like your laugh. You need to laugh more."

"I will," Mackenzie said turning serious. "When I get through all of this and put it behind me. Will you help me do that?"

"My pleasure," Marc said.

NINETEEN

"Judge Sendejo is on vacation for the entire month of July?" Heather Anderson incredulously said into her office telephone. "Must be nice."

It was almost 11:00 Monday morning and she was talking to a clerk in the Ramsey County Clerk's office. Sendejo had made it clear that any motion to exhume Bill Sutherland would be assigned to him. Anderson was calling the clerk's office to schedule a hearing toward the end of July. It occurred to her that, since Sendejo was going to be gone, she could schedule it with a different judge. If Sendejo found out when he came back, she would deal with that then.

"How about Miriam Nagel? Is she available the week of July twenty-seventh?"

"Let me check," the clerk said.

Heather could hear the keyboard clicking while the clerk did her search. Someone knocked on her door. Anna Finney's head appeared through it and Heather silently motioned Anna and Max to come in.

"How about Monday, the twenty-seventh?" Anderson said while holding her right index finger to her guests while they say down. "Ten o'clock? That's fine," Heather said. "Block out two hours for us."

She listened for a moment then said, "Thanks, Carol."

Heather ended the call then turned her attention to Anna and Max.

"Thanks for coming. I've talked to my boss and she okayed taking a shot at exhuming old man Sutherland," Heather told them.

"Yes," Max said with a slight fist pump.

"The twenty-seventh? Why wait until then?" Anna asked.

"We have to serve the paperwork on Mackenzie Sutherland this week to give her time to respond. I'll have them delivered to her lawyer at the same time."

"Do you want me to do it?" Max eagerly asked.

"No, I'll have our process servers do it. This weekend is the Fourth. I'll be gone Friday the third through Monday the sixth. I'll have them served on Friday. That way Kadella won't be able to get a hold of me until Tuesday. It will give him a few days to calm down." *Plus, I'll have it leaked to the media for the Tuesday morning news,* Heather thought.

"Or make him madder because he can't find you right away," Anna said.

"What, so you care how mad he gets?" Max asked.

"I don't. I'm just going to jerk his chain a little bit," Heather said.

"Do we have enough?" Anna asked.

"Maybe," Heather shrugged. "We'll see. Judge Sendejo is on vacation so I scheduled it in front of a more prosecutor friendly judge,

Miriam Nagel. That won't hurt. In the meantime, if you can find anything else..."

"How about a search warrant?" Max asked.

"We aren't even close to having grounds for that," Heather replied. "One step at a time."

Mackenzie drove her BMW 750 into the garage and parked it. Before getting out, she pushed the button to lower the garage door. While driving up the street she noticed an older model Ford parked across from her house. The car looked clearly out of place which is why it caught her attention.

Mackenzie was returning from an hour at the hair salon having her hair done, a manicure and pedicure. Having money was a lot nicer than not having money she liked to remind herself.

It was almost 11:00 A.M. Friday morning and she was almost school-girl-giddy at the prospect of a long weekend with Marc. Between the death of Bill Sutherland and the reunion with Marc, she was beginning to think a normal life might be available to her after all.

The front doorbell chimed and somehow she got the sense that this was not good news. Mackenzie opened the door to find a young man there dressed in slacks, a white shirt and cheap, hideous tie.

"Mackenzie Sutherland?" he asked.

It was the way he asked it, almost formally, that made Mackenzie realize what was coming.

"Yes," she said as she put out her right hand.

"This is for you," he said and handed her the envelope.

For a brief moment, Mackenzie thought about saying something rude. Realizing he was only doing his job, she smiled weakly and thanked him instead.

Back in the kitchen she opened the envelope and removed the documents. She tipped it upside down and two photos fell out onto the counter. Staring back at her were the two pictures of her; one from Chicago and one from St. Paul.

Mackenzie spent the next ten minutes browsing through the papers. When she finished she picked up her phone and made a call.

"I'm sorry, Mrs. Sutherland, Marc's in trial this morning. He thought he would be done by noon," she heard Sandy tell her.

"Ask him to call me as soon as he gets back, please," Mackenzie politely said.

After ending the call Mackenzie quietly said to herself, "That's something I need to talk to Marc about. I need to get my name changed. I hate being called Sutherland."

Less than an hour after Mackenzie left a message for Marc to call, just before noon, her phone rang. She looked at the ID and with a feeling of dread, answered it.

"Hi," she nervously said.

"So, I got back from court and an envelope was waiting for me with some very interesting things in it," Marc said.

"They served you, too?"

"Yeah, she did. I think we need to talk. Have you had lunch?"

"No, I'm not hungry."

"You need to eat. I'll pick you up in twenty minutes."

"Okay. Marc?" she said.

"Yeah?"

"Are you mad at me?"

"No," he sincerely lied. "Besides, I'm a lawyer. We're not allowed to get mad at their clients."

"Is that what I am now, a client?"

"Mac," Marc softly said. "Relax. I'll see you in a little bit. We'll talk then."

While Mackenzie waited for him, she reflected on their conversation. She was genuinely upset and concerned that Marc would be angry. It was a feeling Mackenzie had not had for a very long time; worried about what someone else felt.

The two of them ordered lunch in a chain restaurant, seafood place. It was located in a suburb east of St. Paul and for a Friday lunch, it was not very busy. They had a booth in the back out of earshot of the other patrons. Marc had decided to wait until they were at the restaurant before talking about Mackenzie's latest problem. The drive, a little awkward because of that, was made mostly in silence. Mackenzie felt like a little kid in school waiting to be scolded.

"I scanned over the motion pleadings and got the general idea of what's going on," Marc calmly began. "Have you read through them?"

"Yes," Mackenzie quietly replied.

Marc removed the two photos from his inside coat pocket, placed them side-by-side on the table facing Mackenzie and said, "Mackenzie, I have to know the truth: Is that you?"

She hesitated for a moment then said, "Yes, that's me when I was living in Chicago. It was years ago and yes, I was married to Wendell Cartwright and he also died of a heart attack. Forty-five years of drugs, booze, women and partying can do that. I did not kill him, and I did not kill Bill Sutherland. If nothing else," she continued as she reached across the table, took both of Marc's hands in hers and with a pleading sincere look, said, "I want you to believe that, please."

Without hesitation, Marc looked her in the eye, squeezed her hands and said, "Don't worry, I do."

Relieved, Mackenzie sat back, visibly sighed and quietly said, "Thank you."

"Why Frances? Why were you using the name Frances?" Marc asked.

"It's my middle name and my mom's name. Did you know she died?"

"No."

"When I was nineteen; breast cancer. I was very close to her. My dad was a bit of a drunk actually. He got a lot worse after mom died. We didn't get along and I finally moved to Chicago. I met Wendell at a party and to be honest, I found out he was rich, and I was tired of struggling. I know this sounds awful and makes me out to be a gold-digging slut, but I went after him. He was pleasant and charming and very nice to me. He really loved me as much as Wendell could. No one, and I do mean no one, was surprised when his heart gave out."

"What about the money? Did you know he had left everything to you?"

"Of course," Mackenzie answered him. "I honestly did not know Bill Sutherland did, but I knew Wendell had. He had no use for his children. If you ever meet them you'll know why, and it delighted him to know he was going to stick it to his ex-wives.

"When I met Bill Sutherland, I had more money than he did. Where's my motive? Why did I kill Bill? I could have easily divorced him, and we would just go our separate ways."

"Why didn't you tell me this before?"

"I wasn't especially proud of myself," she shrugged and looked down at the table top. "Wendell was actually a sweet man. He was just weak. He died and made me rich. If anyone had a motive to kill Bill it was his kids. They ought to look at Paige. That greedy, conniving bitch could do it."

"Okay," Marc said. "What about this motion to exhume Bill Sutherland?"

"I don't know," Mackenzie shrugged. "Part of me wants to say, 'screw it' and let them do it. But I'm more inclined to fight it. I hate the thought of giving Paige what she wants."

"This has become a little personal between the two of you."

"There was no love lost, that's for sure. From what I was told there was no love lost between her and Bill's first wife, Bob's mother, Elizabeth.

"I'm serious about looking at Paige for killing Bill, if he was killed. They were living far beyond Bob's means and she comes from money. I'm sure she'd love to get her hands on the Sutherland money."

"I tried calling Heather Anderson," Marc said, "the lawyer handling this. She's out until Tuesday which is why she served you on the Friday before the Fourth."

Mackenzie leaned forward again, took Marc's hand and with her best seductress look asked, "Does this mean our weekend is off now that you're my lawyer again?"

Marc smiled, rolled his eyes up toward the ceiling and replied, "Well, we haven't really established that yet. So, what do you say we wait with that until Tuesday?"

TWENTY

"Come in," Heather Anderson loudly said in response to a knock on her office door. Her guest entered and took a chair in front of her desk. It was the Tuesday morning after the Fourth of July weekend. Her visitor, Justin Baker, was a lawyer in the county attorney's civil division. Justin also fancied himself quite the ladies' man and any day he expected Heather to let him into her bed. This made Justin easy for Heather to manipulate.

"How did it go?" Heather asked.

"No problem," Justin said. "I met that chick from Channel 10, Cindy Amundson, and leaked it to her. She's a little hot for me so, no problem."

Heather inwardly bristled a bit when he referred to a professional woman as a chick. When he made the comment about her being hot for him she thought: *tell me again how you made it through law school.*

"Why didn't we get it out on Friday?" Justin asked.

"It's a holiday weekend," Heather answered. "People don't pay much attention to the news on holiday weekends. It will get a lot more air time and attention during the week, especially in the summer. What did this Amundson woman say when you gave it to her?"

"She was hot for it," Justin replied. "She begged me to go on camera with her, but I wouldn't."

"You made sure you told her she couldn't use your name, didn't you?"

"Yeah, yeah, no problem. She said she would say a source close to the investigation."

"Good, now we should see a little media heat on Mackenzie Sutherland," Heather said.

Marc Kadella heard Carolyn call his name through his open office door. Curious, he went into the office's common area to find out what she wanted. When he got there he saw both secretaries, Sandy and Carolyn and the paralegal, Jeff Modell, huddled around the radio behind their desks.

"What?" Marc asked.

Carolyn held up her left index finger to quiet him then used it to indicate he should join them. When he got there whatever they were listening to was finished. All three of the office staff turned to him.

"The guy on the radio just reported that Channel 10 had the story about Mackenzie and old man Sutherland," Carolyn told him. "The phone will probably start ringing any minute."

While Carolyn was telling Marc this, Sandy used the remote to turn on the television. She quickly changed the channel to 10. A promo was being aired giving viewers a hint of the breaking story about the investigation into Bill Sutherland's death. The hook was that the authorities have reason to believe he was poisoned and are going to exhume the body for a more thorough autopsy. Before the thirty second promo ended, the phone rang.

"I'm sorry," Marc heard Carolyn say, "He's in a meeting. May I take a message?" Carolyn covered the mouthpiece and quietly said the word "reporter" to him.

"Thank you," Carolyn told the caller, "I'll be sure he gets the message," even though she had not written it down.

Connie Mickelson came through the exterior door, looked around at the staff, Marc and the TV and asked, "What's going on?"

"We need to talk," Marc said.

"Okay, come in," Connie told him.

Sandy answered the phone and told Marc Maddy was calling.

"Tell her I'll call her back. I need to talk to Connie."

Fifteen minutes later, Marc was back at his desk after bringing Connie up to date. The first call he made was to Mackenzie.

"How did they get this?" she asked referring to the media report.

"Heather Anderson leaked it to them. Or, more likely, had someone else leak it. Probably a cop. Standard operating procedure. They like to get their side out to the public to try to taint any potential jurors."

"Jurors! What jurors? For what?" Mackenzie asked a bit startled.

"Mackenzie," Marc calmly said, "they're not digging up your former husband for their amusement. They're looking to find something. And the media will be reporting the death of Wendell Cartwright today, too."

"Oh, sure, okay," Mackenzie said obviously more relaxed. "Well, I don't know what they think they're going to find."

"One step at a time," Marc said. "They don't have permission to dig him up yet."

"I've been thinking," Mackenzie said. "Maybe I should agree to it. Show them I have nothing to hide. What do you think?"

After a long pause Marc said, "As a defense lawyer my inclination is to never agree to help them with anything." Marc was sitting at his desk holding the phone with his left hand, his elbow on the desktop. He drummed the fingers of his right hand on the desk while he silently thought for a moment then said, "But you may have a point."

"You think so?"

"Yeah. Plus, this judge has a bit of a reputation as a prosecutor's judge. She will likely think this isn't a big deal and let them do it anyway. We may as well get out ahead of it."

Sandy quietly opened his door, looked in and whispered "Maddy" to him while she held up two fingers to indicate line two. Marc nodded his head in acknowledgement and Sandy quietly closed the door.

"Call her up, tell her I'll agree to it," Mackenzie said.

"Then I'll tell the media that you did it because you have nothing to hide."

"Exactly," Mackenzie said.

"Maddy's on hold," Marc told her. "I need to talk to her. I'll call Anderson and tell her your decision. I'll call you back afterwards."

Marc took Maddy's call and quickly told her what was going on. While he was doing this, Connie came into his office and sat in one of his client chairs. When he finished talking to Madeline, he turned to Connie.

"How's the beauty queen?" Connie asked.

"She's good," Marc said. "You know this judge in St. Paul, Miriam Nagel?"

"Yeah, I know her," Connie said. "She's okay except she likes prosecutors a lot more than defense lawyers."

"How did she get on the bench in Ramsey County? Don't you have to be a card-carrying member of the Bleeding Hearts Club?"

"Not if you're a female," Connie said. "You'll likely lose your motion to dig up Sutherland."

"That's why we're going to agree to it," Marc said.

"Probably a good idea," Connie agreed. "Will make it look like your gal has nothing to hide. You banging her yet?"

"Why, Ms. Mickelson," Marc said feigning indignation. "That would be unethical."

"Don't get caught like this horny idiot Simon Kane."

"What's going on there, with the civil suit?" Marc asked.

"We swapped discovery requests. Once those are done we'll schedule depositions. I'm thinking by the end of July. After that I'll set it for a summary judgment motion and see if I can't make it go away. We got a pretty clear self-defense case. I don't see it going anywhere."

"When are you going to drop the hammer on Simon for his extra special servicing of his client?" Marc asked.

"You remember my husband number three?" Connie asked. Connie had been involved in a half-dozen successful marriages. Or, as she liked to point out, successful divorces.

"No," Marc said. "I can't keep track of all of your ex-husbands. I'm surprised you can."

"Very funny, asshole. You remember, Isaac Bergman," she said.

"Yeah, okay. I remember Isaac. He's a professor at the U law school. Teaches..."

"Ethics," Connie said, "and he's on the board of the Office of Professional responsibility. I've already set something up with him. It's a little shady but I'll get our Mr. Kane when the time is right."

"So, you and your ex-husband, the ethics professor..."

"He teaches constitutional law, too."

"...are doing something that is likely unethical to win a civil suit because the other lawyer is doing something unethical."

"Sounds about right," Connie agreed.

"Do you see a problem here?" Marc asked.

Connie put on her best, innocent face, batted her eyelids several times and said, "Nope, I don't."

"Do I want to know what you promised Isaac to get him to go along with this?"

Still wearing the same expression Connie said, "Nope, you don't."

Marc shook his head then said, "I have to call Heather Anderson. You'll have to excuse me, so you don't drag me into whatever it is you're up to."

"See you later," Connie said as she stood to leave while Marc opened Mackenzie's file to find Anderson's phone number.

Marc picked up the phone and a second before he punched a button for a line to call Heather Anderson, his intercom buzzed.

"Yeah," he said into the phone.

"You should come out here. We just heard another radio news report..." Carolyn started to say.

"About Mackenzie," Marc finished.

"Yep, and it's not good."

Marc leaned against the back of Carolyn's desk, his arms folded across his chest. Carolyn was in her chair next to him while the other office members gathered around. They were all intently listening to a different radio station reporting the story that Channel 10 was promoting for its noon news.

The radio blabber mouth had very few facts to report. Something about Mackenzie Sutherland and the death of her husband William, the founder of *Sutherland's* grocery store chain. They also reported a rumor that she was involved in the same thing in Chicago with a previous husband who died, as they put it, suddenly and mysteriously. The reporter mentioned that Mackenzie was using the name Frances at the time. Supposedly she inherited a fortune from his death just as she did from the death of William Sutherland.

Of course, not having all of the factual information had never been a deterrent before. The announcers, three of them doing a talk show, spent the next fifteen minutes pompously speculating about the news leaks that Ramsey County was going to exhume old man Sutherland. This allowed them to walk right up to the line of accusing Mackenzie of murder. Why else would the county attorney do this?

Marc, having been through this before with prosecutors, was not even angry about it. He went back to his office and called Heather Anderson. Not surprisingly, she didn't answer so he left a message in her voice mailbox.

When noon came, everyone in the office was gathered in front of the TV. Marc had called Mackenzie and Maddy to let them know about it also.

It was the lead story and was worse than Marc feared. They had all of it: the news about the exhumation hearing and the death of Wendell Cartwright. While the anchor, a man whom Marc did not know, interviewed their reporter Cindy Amundson about Cartwright and Chicago, the two photos of Mackenzie appeared on the screen. The story took almost seven minutes and at the end of it, the anchor looked at the camera and made the comment that Mackenzie appeared to be a Black Widow.

"There it is," Marc said. "I knew someone would get around to calling her that."

"What are you going to do?" Barry Cline asked him.

While everyone silently watched him waiting for an answer, Marc thought about what to do.

"Call Gabriella Shriqui and see if she'll let me on her show today," he finally replied.

"Let you? She'll send a limo for you," Connie said.

"I better call Mackenzie," Marc said to no one in particular. He then looked at Sandy and Carolyn and said, "If Heather Anderson calls back, I'm not in."

"Okay," they replied in unison.

The office phone rang and Jeff Modell, the paralegal answered it.

"Just a minute," he told the caller. "Speak of the devil," he said to Marc.

"Heather?"

"No, Gabriella," Jeff replied.

TWENTY-ONE

Marc arrived at the Channel 8 building shortly before 1:00 P.M. Gabriella herself came out to the reception area to get him. Being good friends, they greeted each other with an affectionate hug. Gabriella looped her arm through his and began leading him back to her studio.

"I thought you were a big shot TV star who had servants to come out front for me," Marc teased.

"I do but every once in a while I like to come out and mingle with the peasants, smartass," she said as she slapped him on the shoulder. "Let's go back to my office and talk about this first."

"We're taping it, right?"

"Yes, but I want to hear what's going on first to prepare," she said.

Gabriella closed the door behind them and joined Marc on her sofa. "So, tell me what's going on."

"We're still off the record?"

"Yes."

"Are there any listening devices in here?"

"Marc!"

"Okay," he said.

Having discussed this with Mackenzie, Marc knew exactly what he wanted to say. He very carefully gave Gabriella just enough information to bring her up to date without making any admissions.

"Is Mackenzie this woman, Frances, from Chicago?"

Marc admitted she was, explained why she used the name Frances and how she met Wendell Cartwright. He also told her there had been an autopsy, an investigation of Wendell's death and no wrongdoing was found. Another twenty minutes and Gabriella was satisfied she had enough for the interview.

"What about this hearing to exhume Sutherland?" she asked.

"Ask me about it during the interview," Marc coyly replied.

"What does that mean?"

"It means ask me about it during the interview," Marc repeated.

Gabriella arched her eyebrows and gave him an inquisitive look. Marc silently responded with a mischievous smile. There was a knock on the door and Gabriella said, "Come in."

Cordelia Davis, Gabriella's producer looked in and said, "We're all set. We need to get Marc to makeup."

Gabriella stood up and Marc said, "I need to make a quick phone call. Give me two minutes."

When the two women were gone, Marc called Mackenzie.

"I'm going in for the interview now," Marc said. "Last chance, are you sure you want to agree to exhume Bill's body?"

"Yes," Mackenzie said. "We both agreed we need to counteract the bad publicity. I have nothing to hide."

"Okay," Marc said.

"I still think I should be there to tell my side. I feel like I'm hiding behind my lawyer," Mackenzie told him.

"They're already referring to you as a Black Widow. It's best for you to keep a low profile for now. You'll get plenty of opportunities to tell your side if need be," Marc reminded her.

"Okay," Mackenzie sighed.

"I'll call you when it's done."

"We're delighted to have the well-known local defense attorney, Marc Kadella with us today," Gabriella began the taping by speaking directly into the camera and announcing. "Mr. Kadella is the lawyer for Mackenzie Sutherland the widow of William Sutherland, the late founder of Sutherland's grocery store chain.

"Hello, Marc and welcome back," she said turning to him.

"My pleasure, Gabriella," Marc replied.

Gabriella turned back to the camera and continued. "For those of you who may not have heard, it was reported by our colleagues at Channel 10 that the Ramsey County attorney is going to ask for a court order to exhume William Sutherland's remains for a second autopsy. They also reported that Mackenzie Sutherland was previously married to another wealthy man, Wendell Cartwright under the name Frances while she lived in Chicago several years ago. Wendell Cartwright, again this is what was reported, died of a mysterious heart attack and Frances inherited a large estate."

"Gabriella," Marc interrupted, "there was no mystery about Wendell Cartwright's death. The man had a heart attack after almost fifty years of fast living and inattention to his health."

"Marc, I'm simply stating what Channel 10 reported earlier. They said it was a mysterious heart attack, not me."

And you couldn't resist taking a shot at a competitor's loose reporting, Marc thought.

"That's why I'm here, Gabriella. They got their information leaked to them behind my client's back by the Ramsey County attorney's office. It's standard procedure for prosecutors to leak news to try to make someone look guilty of something. There's also a lot of politics involved."

"Is Mackenzie Sutherland the same person as Frances Cartwright?"

"Yes, she is," Marc admitted. "She was living in Chicago and using her middle name, Frances. It is also her mother's name. She was very close to her mom who died of breast cancer. She was using the name

Frances to honor her mother. She was lonely and met Wendell Cartwright. He was charming and rich, and Mackenzie married him. He was quite a bit older than her and after a couple of years he had a heart attack and died. It happens. I've seen the autopsy report of Wendell's death and the medical examiner ruled it a natural death. It was also thoroughly investigated by the Chicago police. They found no evidence of foul play: case closed."

"What do you think the Ramsey County attorney expects to find?"

"Ask them," Marc said. "There was an autopsy done of William Sutherland and he also had a heart attack. We lose hundreds of thousands of people to heart attacks every year. It's hardly unusual and certainly not rare. In my opinion, this entire matter is being driven by Paige Sutherland, Robert Sutherland's widow."

"The man Mackenzie shot and killed who attacked her in her home."

"Yes. Mackenzie acted in self-defense and the grand jury exonerated her. Paige is still after the Sutherland money. That's what this is all about."

"Will the county attorney get an order to exhume William Sutherland for another autopsy?" Gabriella asked.

"They won't have to. Mrs. Sutherland told me she will not oppose their request. She will agree to exhume the remains and let them conduct their autopsy."

A slightly startled Gabriella asked the perfect question. "Why would she do that?"

Having Gabriella toss him a softball, Marc did not miss it. "Obviously because she has nothing to hide."

Marc trudged up the creaky back stairs of the Reardon Building to the second-floor suite of offices. At the top, he again vowed to find more time to exercise and get in better shape. It was almost 5:00 and Gabriella's show had aired but Marc had not seen it.

"Hey, everybody," Sandy yelled when Marc came through the door. "Our TV star is back."

Marc looked at the twenty-something girl and scratched his nose with the middle finger of his right hand. Both Sandy and Carolyn laughed at the gesture as the other lawyers came out to join them.

"How was it?" Marc asked.

"Good," Carolyn said while handing him a dozen messages.

"I think you did your client some good. That line about her having nothing to hide came across well," Barry added.

"Let's hope she doesn't," Connie chimed in.

"That's not a thought I want to have," Marc said to her. "Besides, why would you say that? Do you know something…?"

"No, not all. Just being a cynical, old lawyer."

The phone messages waiting for Marc after Gabriella's show were from various TV and print reporters. He dialed Mackenzie's phone while reading through them.

Mackenzie answered, and they chatted for a few minutes about the TV appearance. Marc told her that he had other requests for interviews. He then suggested that the two of them do one or two more TV interviews together to get her story out. While they talked there was a knock-on Marc's door and Connie came in without waiting for a response from Marc.

"You talking to our girl Mackenzie?"

"Yeah, why?" Marc asked.

"Can I talk to her?" Connie asked and sat in one of the client chairs.

Marc told Mackenzie and handed the phone to Connie.

"Hey," Connie said. "I scheduled your deposition for the civil suit for three weeks from now, July thirtieth. Is that okay?"

"Sure," Mackenzie replied. "What time?"

"9:00 A.M. here in our office. I'm not going downtown. They can come here. We'll do Paige Sutherland at the same time."

"Kind of quick isn't it? You trying to push this thing along?" Marc asked.

Connie covered the mouthpiece of the phone with her hand and said, "Yeah, I'll tell you why in a minute." She went back to Mackenzie and asked, "So, you're good with that?"

"Sure, let me talk to Marc again, please."

Connie handed the phone back to Marc and listened while they agreed to do two TV interviews. Marc would set those up and call the reporters for both the St. Paul and Minneapolis papers to do a phone interview by himself. When they finished, Marc hung up the phone and looked at Connie.

"I'm pushing it because they don't have much of a case. It was clearly self-defense or, at least, they can't prove otherwise. I've been over all of the police reports, the autopsy and court records. The sooner we get discovery done, the sooner I can get this before a judge on a motion for summary judgment."

"What about mandatory mediation?" Marc asked.

"We'll do that if we lose the summary judgment motion," Connie said.

Connie stood up to leave and as she did she said, "Oh, and one more thing. Now that I've decided what to do about Simon Kane, I don't want to know if you're banging Mackenzie Sutherland."

Marc started to speak but Connie cut him off. "I don't want to know. Just keep a low profile."

A week later Max, Anna Finney and Heather Anderson met in Heather's office.

"What are we waiting for?" Max asked looking at Heather. "Why aren't we at the cemetery digging up Bill Sutherland?"

"I'm thinking we should let the whole thing cool down for a while," Heather said. "Kadella threw us a pretty good curve ball, if you'll excuse the metaphor. The widow agreeing to it, then going on TV to complain about the unwarranted, so she claims, persecution had played pretty well with the public. Have you been watching the letters to the editor published in the papers?"

"No," Max said. "Whenever I read those things they all sound like morons."

"Yeah, well, those 'morons' are siding entirely with the poor widow," Heather said.

"And if we go to all of this trouble and don't come up with anything then who looks like the morons?" Anna interjected.

"Exactly what my boss, Shayla Parker, the Ramsey County attorney, remember her, said?" Heather told Max.

"And if we do find something?" Max asked.

"I'm not saying we won't do it. We will. Bill Sutherland isn't going anywhere. I think we should give it some time. Let it cool down."

"Yeah, okay," Max agreed. "How long?"

Heather shrugged and said, "I don't know. Three, four weeks."

"The media and the public have the attention span of your average six-year-old," Anna added.

"We'll go get him," Heather assured Max.

TWENTY-TWO

Returning from court Marc came through the office's exterior door to find the suite devoid of the usual chatter. Carolyn, Sandy and Jeff Modell were at their respective desks, their heads down quietly working. None of them even looked up to greet him when he came in. The doors to the lawyer's offices, including his own, were all closed; a very unusual sight.

The common area where the staff worked was fairly large, but it was also mostly open space. Marc saw three people seated in the client chairs, two women and one man. All sat quietly with sullen, almost annoyed facial expressions. He recognized one of them as Paige Sutherland. He looked at the wall clock and noted the time was 10:35, five minutes past the time of Paige's scheduled deposition. The blinds covering the windows to the conference room were closed so Marc assumed Mackenzie was still being deposed inside.

"I have a couple messages for you," Carolyn said. While she handed Marc the message slips Carolyn quietly told him the other two people were Adam and Hailey Sutherland.

Marc looked down at her with a puzzled expression as if to say, "Why are they here?" Carolyn, understanding what he meant, merely shrugged.

"Hello, I'm Marc Kadella," he said to Paige as he extended his hand to her.

She barely shook it and muttered her name with fire in her eyes.

He turned to the surly looking man, offered his hand and said, "Marc Kadella."

Adam shook it with what Marc believed was the weakest handshake he had ever received. Without standing or barely making eye contact, Adam said, "You're that fucking bitch's lawyer, I guess."

Momentarily taken aback by the vitriol from this worthless man-child, Marc looked down at him and politely smiled. He then leaned down to look directly into Adam's eyes who visibly slumped down in his chair. Marc stared at him for three or four long seconds then quietly, firmly said, "If you ever speak like that about somebody in this office again, I will personally drag your ass out the door, down the stairs and throw you out into the parking lot. You got it?"

A terrified Adam muttered a barely audible "Yeah, I guess."

Marc, still glaring at him said, "I didn't hear you."

"Yes, I ah, I got it. Sorry."

Marc retreated to his office and left the door open. Ten minutes later he heard the people in the conference room come out. Within seconds, Mackenzie, without bothering to knock, was in his office closing the door behind her.

"Why are they here?" she snarled at Marc.

"Hi, Mac, how did it go?" he asked in return, ignoring her question.

There was a knock on the door and Connie opened it and stepped in.

"Hi, Marc," Mackenzie said. "Why are they here?" she repeated.

"Paige has to do her deposition and…"

"I know that," Mackenzie said. "I meant those two worthless brats."

Marc looked at Connie for an answer who merely held up her hands with an uncertain expression. "I'll find out," Connie said and left.

While she was gone, Marc and Mackenzie chatted. According to Mackenzie, the deposition went almost precisely the same as the taped statement she had given to the cops.

Connie came back and told them Adam and Hailey were here in case anyone had questions for them. They were also to provide moral support for the grieving widow, Paige.

"Isn't Simon Kane providing enough moral support for her?" Mackenzie sarcastically asked. "Besides, that's BS," she continued. "I know these two. Daddy was paying their extravagant lifestyle and I'll bet they're both about to run out of money. They're hanging around looking for a payday."

"Carolyn told me you threatened to throw Adam out on his ass. Good for you," Connie laughed.

"What? What happened?" Mackenzie asked.

"Nothing, he said something rude about you and…"

"He called you a fucking bitch and Marc told him if he did it again he'd drag him downstairs and throw his ass out," Connie said.

"My hero!" Mackenzie said fluttering her eyes at him. "Seriously," she continued, "thanks. Although, no offense, any one of us could throw the little snot's ass out of here." She turned to Connie and asked, "Now what?"

"Now, you're done. You can take off. They're using the conference for a minute to confer. When they're ready, I'll take Paige's deposition," Connie answered her.

"Paige is about to get her ass lopped off and handed to her. I've seen Connie do this. She's very good at it," Marc said. He looked at Connie and asked, "How did Mackenzie do?"

"Great," Connie said. "It was pretty much a repeat of her statement to the cops. Self-defense."

"Are you going to win a summary judgment motion?"

“I think so,” Connie said. “The facts are not really in dispute and the law’s clear. Where’s the liability? Plus, I still got an ace up my sleeve; Kane and Paige dancing between the sheets for two years.”

“We’ll go get lunch and be back. How long do you think it will take?” Marc asked.

“Not long. Hour, hour and a half. We’ll see. Kane’s trying to make a big deal out of old man Sutherland changing his Will,” Connie said.

“You got an affidavit from the lawyer swearing Mackenzie knew nothing about it. Besides, what does that have to do with this case?” Marc asked.

“He’s trying to claim Bob was provoked into threatening Mackenzie because of the Will.”

“Will that work?” Mackenzie asked.

“No,” Connie said. “How can you provoke someone about something you had nothing to do with? He should be angry at his old man, not you.”

There was a knock on the door and Sandy stuck her head in, looked at Connie and said, “They’re ready.”

“We’ll go across the street and get some lunch,” Marc told Connie. “Talk to you when we get back.”

Kitty-corner across Lake Street from Marc’s building was a small, popular diner. Marc and Mackenzie were early enough to beat the lunch crowd and took a booth toward the back. The waitress, a woman in her early fifties whom Marc knew, came to their table. After a minute or so of good-natured banter between the waitress and Marc, she took their order and left.

“Come here often?” Mackenzie asked Marc when the waitress left.

“Yeah,” Marc smiled. “At least two or three times a week. It’s convenient and the food’s good.”

“I’ve been meaning to ask you,” Mackenzie said turning serious, “What’s taking them so long to dig up Bill?”

“Not sure,” Marc replied. “I haven’t talked to Heather Anderson lately.”

“It’s been three weeks since I signed the authorization form. I’d like to get it over with.”

“I think it maybe they’re letting it cool down. They were a little surprised when you agreed to the exhumation. Letting the media go on to something else. The Vikings are in training camp now. That will give the public something else to distract them.”

“You think they might not do it; might let it slide if they believe I have nothing to hide?” Mackenzie asked.

Marc thought about the question for a moment then said, "Maybe, but I doubt it. It's not cheap. Probably cost the taxpayers fifteen to twenty grand. But sooner or later the media will start asking questions."

The waitress brought their meals, a salad for Mackenzie and a turkey club for Marc. They started to eat, and Marc said, "I made sure Anderson is to call me and let me know when they dig him up. I want to be there."

"I don't," Mackenzie said.

"You don't have to."

Mackenzie laid her fork down and said, "This civil suit with Paige, do you think I should make her an offer to settle it?"

"It's your money," Marc said through a mouthful of sandwich.

"I'm tired of having it and this business with Ramsey County hanging over my head."

"I think you should let Connie handle it and see if she gets it dismissed. You can always try to settle it after that. Let them make the first offer."

"I suppose you're right," she sighed.

"Be a little patient, you'll get through this. So, what are you doing this weekend?"

"Sneaking around with my lawyer so he doesn't get caught fooling around with a client."

"Sounds like a plan," Marc smiled.

When they returned to Marc's office, Adam and Hailey were gone and Paige's deposition was wrapping up. Marc grabbed the morning newspaper and they retreated to his office. Marc took the sports section and Mackenzie the A section to read the news. Twenty minutes later Connie knocked on Marc's door, walked in and sat next to Mackenzie.

Connie looked at Mackenzie and said, "She's lovely. She is a lovely woman. I'll bet holidays were fun with her around."

Mackenzie laughed then said, "Oh yeah. You have no idea how many times I thought about dumping a bucket of water on her just to see if she'd melt."

"I'd pay good money to see that. '*I'm melting, I'm melting*'" Connie said mimicking the witch in the Wizard of Oz. "Anyway," she continued, "the depo went fine. She basically admitted they have no case other than emotional loss. Their problem is liability. Kane made a settlement offer."

"Which is?" Mackenzie asked.

"Three million each for her, Adam and Hailey. They figure that's how much they should have received from the sale of the business."

"That's pretty ballsy," Marc said. "What did you tell him?"

"I told him I'd put it to my client."

"What do you think?" Mackenzie asked Connie.

"I think it's your money and if you want this to go away we can agree or counteroffer. Me, I'd tell them to go pound sand. I wouldn't give that miserable…"

"Connie!" Marc said to stop her, knowing the kind of nouns she was capable of using.

Connie looked at him with an innocent expression and said, "I was going to say, not a nice person."

"Yeah," Marc said. "I'm sure that's what you were going to call her." He looked at Mackenzie and added, "Connie can out cuss most sailors."

"She probably wouldn't have called her anything I haven't," Mackenzie said. "Marc and I talked about this a little at lunch. I've decided I don't want to reward them," *especially Adam,* she thought, "so, no deal."

"Atta girl," Connie gleefully said. "I was hoping you'd say that."

"Now what?" Mackenzie asked.

"I'll call the judge and schedule a hearing," Connie said. "I'll bring a motion to see if we can get this dismissed."

"Who's the judge?" Marc asked.

"Hubert Farley," Connie said.

"Farley? Is he still on the bench? He looked old ten years ago," Marc said.

"He's headed toward retirement and that probably helps us," Connie replied.

"Why would that help?" Mackenzie asked.

"Because he likely won't want this thing dragging on for another year or more than going to trial," Marc answered her.

Later that same afternoon Mackenzie was in the kitchen enjoying a small glass of wine. She was seated at the breakfast bar going through the mail she had ignored for several days. Her purse was on the counter by the refrigerator and she heard the private burner phone she kept for special use start ringing. She retrieved it from her purse and saw the call was from area code 414, Milwaukee, Wisconsin.

"Hello," she answered believing she knew who it was.

"Mrs. Hayes," she heard a man's voice say. "This is Byron Stewart, from Milwaukee."

"Yes, Mr. Stewart, I thought I recognized your number," she politely said. "Do you have something to report?"

"Yes ma'am. Thought you might like a quick update. One of the girls, your stepdaughter Faye, is getting divorced. Seems her husband got some pictures of her with her boyfriend at a motel sent to him, anonymously, of course."

"Thank you for that," Mackenzie said. "What about Junior?" she asked referring to her second husband's son, Kenneth Hayes, Jr.

"He's still the night manager at that Motel 6 on the edge of town. Still has the drinking problem.

"Mrs. Hayes," he continued, "or should I call you Mrs. Cartwright or Mrs. Sutherland? I'm a little uncertain."

Using her other names had set off an alarm bell in her head. He had never done so before and as far as she knew, this private investigator was unaware of her subsequent marriages.

"I'm sorry, what did you call me?" Mackenzie asked.

"Mrs. Sutherland," he continued. "I'm not going to play games. I grew up in St. Paul and still follow the news there. I know what's going on. Your disguise while living in Milwaukee was good, but I know you're the Sutherland woman and the widow of Wendell Cartwright. Don't insult my intelligence by denying it."

"What do you want?"

"That's better. Let's keep this a simple business deal. I want a half a million bucks. Small bills, non-sequential. Nothing bigger than a fifty."

"Why would I agree to this blatant attempt at extortion."

"Because if you don't, I go to the St. Paul cops with another dead husband from a heart attack story."

Mackenzie knew this was what he would say. It was something she feared all along. She had believed it would come from the man in Chicago since he was smarter than the other two. She should have known it would be Stewart since he was the least reputable.

"It will take at least a week to come up with the money. That much cash will take a few days and tomorrow's Friday."

"That's better," Stewart said. "I knew it would take a couple days. I'm a patient man. Next week will be fine. I'll be in touch." He hung up without waiting for a reply.

Mackenzie drew a deep breath, looked through the kitchen window into the backyard, then down at the phone still in her hand. Her face flushed a bright red as the anger rose in her. For a brief moment she felt like throwing the phone through the window. She took a couple of deep breaths and calmly set the phone down. She had known for some time that something like this was possible. Mackenzie had put it out of her mind believing she would deal with it when and if it ever came up. Now, here it was. What to do?

Mackenzie thought about paying him. Obtaining the cash would not be much of a problem. The drive time to Milwaukee from St. Paul was roughly five hours. She could be there and back before anyone knew she was gone. Would paying him off put an end to it? Highly unlikely. More likely it would just encourage him to go for more.

She had hired Byron Stewart because he had been recommended by a woman she knew, an acquaintance, who used the private investigator to catch her cheating husband. Mackenzie had developed some misgivings about the man; too late to do anything about it.

Mackenzie stood up, walked to the refrigerator and refilled her wine glass. She returned to her seat, took a large drink, then admitted to herself what must be done.

"I've come too far to let this sleazy, amoral ex-cop stop me," she quietly said to herself.

TWENTY-THREE

Byron Stewart was in a great mood. He was shooting pool and winning in his favorite tavern, Hanlon's, a friendly, neighborhood joint six blocks from his office. Stew, as he preferred to be called hating the name Byron, won his fourth straight game of eight ball and pocketed his opponent's twenty-dollar bill.

Normally Stewart was, at best, a moderately competent pool player. Of course, he thought of himself as a hustler, but usually went home with a lighter wallet for his effort. Tonight, for some inexplicable reason, he was on a can't miss roll on the backroom table, which made the normally annoying ex-cop even more obnoxious than usual.

Stewart played one more game and the alcohol he consumed was taking effect. That and the man he played was a lot better which was the real reason he lost. He had tried to con Stew into a hundred-dollar game which the usually cocky P.I. sensibly and out of character turned down.

Stew paid the man the twenty, drained his glass of Miller, strolled to the bar and took a seat. The bartender brought him another shot of bourbon — the cheap stuff — and a glass of beer. Before the bartender could retreat, Stew tossed down the shot and started to speak. "Great day today, Paulie," he said to the bartender. "I'm tellin' ya', my ship is about to dock."

Paul, and most of the bar's regulars, had heard this or similar versions of it numerous times. "That's great, Stew," the man said as he tried to back away.

Stew looked at his twenty-dollar watch and said, "I'm feeling so good. I think I'll go get laid. Give some lucky lady a good time tonight."

"Have a good time, Stew," Paul said while thinking: d*on't forget to take enough cash to pay her.*

Byron Stewart was a forty-eight-year-old retired Milwaukee police detective. His original plan when he joined the department, was to put in thirty years, retire with a full pension then get a gravy gig doing corporate security. By the time the first twenty years were up his superiors let it be known they wanted him out, now.

Corporate security jobs did not beat a path to his door, so he became a P.I. Two years later, wife number two was gone which left Stew alone with his drinking problem. Between the amount of his pension that the ex-wives did not get and the money he hustled as a P.I., Byron Stewart got by, barely. And then he saw the news from St. Paul.

A slow afternoon in his rundown office left him with time on his hands to check up on the news from his hometown. It was the same day that the story came out about Mackenzie Sutherland and Frances Cartwright. Their pictures were staring back at him from his computer and they looked very familiar. An hour of online research led him to the conclusion that Donna Hayes, a client of his, was the same person. Byron Stewart, while seated at his desk, looked heavenward and thanked his lucky stars. Keeping an eye on the Hayes kids was the easiest gig he ever scored, and it was about to become far more lucrative than it already was.

The conversation he had with her a few days ago confirmed that his ship was, indeed, about to come in. Donna Hayes would be back in Milwaukee tomorrow with a suitcase full of cash. And if she thought that would be the end of it, she would have to be taught that Byron Stewart was nobody's fool. He was going to live a very long and comfortable life on her money.

"Paul, I'll see you later," Stew yelled out to the bartender. He slid off of the barstool, hitched his belt up under his over-hanging gut, looked at his watch again and went through the front door.

When he reached the sidewalk, he stood for a minute looking up at the sky. He knew he had a little too much to drink so he took in several deep breaths to clear his head. Stew turned to his right to go to his car parked half a block away. As he did this, he removed his phone from the inside pocket of his cheap sport coat. He stood under a street light and dialed the number of the prostitute he wanted to see. She answered on the second ring. They made their business arrangement and Stew replaced the phone and continued down the street.

As he approached his car he noticed a medium sized person in a dark, gray hoodie walking toward him. *Probably some punk, black kid acting like a tough guy*, Stew thought.

He reached his car at the same time the hooded stranger got to him. Stew looked at the hazy yet familiar face and opened his mouth to speak.

Mackenzie pulled a small, .22 caliber revolver from the pocket of the sweatshirt. She leveled it at the P.I. took one step closer and from barely three feet away shot him once in the face. The bullet entered his head at the corner of his right eye a quarter inch from his nose. It traveled upward into his brain and being a soft-lead, hollow point, mushroomed and ripped his brain apart.

Her victim dropped like a rock onto his back. Although already brain dead, the body had not yet received the news. For another five or six seconds his mouth opened and closed like a fish, his hands fluttered, and feet twitched.

Mackenzie quickly knelt down next to him and removed his watch, wallet and phone. She also unclipped the holster from his belt with the 9 mm automatic in it. She quickly ran her hands over him, especially his ankles, looking for any more weapons. Mackenzie stood up, slightly crouched over and quickly walked back in the direction she had come from. She would be in her car, the hoodie removed and in a plastic shopping bag, within one minute.

"You hear that?" Artie asked his neighbor, Franklin Carver. Franklin was out walking his dog and Artie had been on his front steps enjoying the pleasant night. Franklin lived two doors down and both men, widowers each, lived across and down the street from Hanlon's. The noise Artie referred to was the gunshot that had killed Byron Stewart.

"Yeah, sounded like a gunshot," Franklin said. "There he is." He was referring to the dark figure who had stood up at that moment and was walking away from the scene. There was just enough light from the streetlights to illuminate the person but not enough to see clearly who it could be.

"Goddamn little black-ass, sonsobitchin', gangbangers comin' around ruinin' our neighborhood…"

"Franklin," Artie said. "You're black."

"So what?" Franklin angrily replied. "Am I supposed to like these worthless little assholes?"

"Should we go check it out?" Artie asked.

Both men looked around to see if anyone else had heard or seen anything. They saw no one else on the street and no one coming out of Hanlon's.

"Yeah, he's gone. You think he shot someone?" Franklin said as the two men and the dog began cautiously walking across the street.

When they found Byron's body, Artie said, "You want to wait here, and I'll go call?"

"Hell, no. What if he comes back? I'll go with you and we'll both wait for the police."

The two detectives parked across the street from where Byron Stewart was lying. There were two Milwaukee PD squad cars, an ambulance and an M.E. rep already on site.

"What do you have?" the older detective, Norm Bleeker asked a uniformed cop, a sergeant who had taken charge.

"One DOA. White male; probably late forties early fifties. A GSW to the face. No wallet, watch or phone," the cop told him.

"Robbery?" Bleeker asked.

"Looks like."

The sergeant led the two detectives to the body. The M.E. rep was leaning over him examining the wound with a small pen light. The second detective, a younger woman, Justine Carver, shined her flashlight on the victim's face. There was only a small trickle of blood from the wound, barely enough to see where the bullet had entered.

"Holy shit," Bleeker quietly said when he saw the man's face. "It finally happened and why am I not surprised?"

"You know him," Carver said to her partner.

"Don't you recognize him, Sarge?" Bleeker asked the uniformed cop.

"No, should I?"

"Yeah, maybe," Bleeker said. "It's Byron Stewart," he told him as he leaned down for a closer look. "Hey, Doc, what do you have?" he asked the M.E.

"Looks like a single shot. Hit him in the corner of the eye probably directly into the brain. Would have killed him almost instantly."

"We got a couple of witnesses, Norm," the sergeant said.

Bleeker stood up and he and Carver walked over to the two men standing by with another uniformed officer. The detectives introduced themselves to the two men and heard their story.

"You're sure it was a young, black man?" Carver asked when they finished.

"Yes, ma'am," Franklin told her. "Dark hoodie them gangbangers like to wear."

"We didn't actually see his face but in this neighborhood…" Artie added.

"We canvassed the people in Hanlon's. He was there but the bartender said he left alone. Nobody in there heard a shot," the sergeant told them.

"Was he carrying a gun?" Bleeker asked.

"Don't think so. We didn't find a holster."

"Odd that he wouldn't be carrying," Bleeker commented. "He had a P.I. license. I'll bet he had a gun and the killer got that, too."

"Would we have a record of it?"

"Sure," Bleeker said. "If our gangbanger uses it, we'll find him."

Mackenzie had left St. Paul that same morning and arrived in Milwaukee in mid-afternoon. She drove her dead husband's eight-year-old Tahoe SUV believing she would blend in a little better with that than her new BMW.

After receiving the call from Byron Stewart a few days ago she quickly made up her mind what to do. She also decided on the simplest way to do it. Look for an opportunity and don't hesitate.

Mackenzie had followed Stewart to the bar he frequented. Believing he would be there are at least a couple of hours, she drove back to his office. It was an old three-story brick building from the 40s and the lock on his office door probably came with it when it was built. Using a credit card the way she had seen on TV, she was inside the office in ten seconds. Mackenzie went to his file cabinet and much to her relief, found it unlocked. She quickly found the file for Donna Hayes and removed it. As she was about to leave she noticed the P.C. next to Stewart's desk. Did he have a file of her in the computer? She thought about removing the hard drive but knew she didn't know how and now was no time to learn. For a brief moment she considered unplugging the computer and taking the entire box. Believing Stewart was probably not the most computer savvy guy she decided to take the chance that he did not have client information on it and quickly left.

When she got back to Hanlon's, she checked to be sure Stewart's car was still there. Mackenzie then spent another ten minutes driving around the neighborhood looking for something specific.

After finding what she wanted, she drove back to the bar and parked around the corner from the local tavern and waited. From where she was parked, she had a clear line of sight of the front of the bar and a good getaway route. There was a light above the bar's entryway which clearly illuminated anyone coming out. She could also see Stewart's car and could easily get to it before he did.

She watched as Stewart exited the bar and stood in front of it for a few seconds. Mackenzie pulled up the hood on her sweatshirt and went after him. She was wearing surgical gloves and in her right-hand pocket she had a small, cheap .22 caliber revolver. Totally untraceable, Mackenzie purchased the gun for protection over twenty years ago. While loading it that morning, she was careful not to touch any part of it or any of the bullets without wearing the gloves.

Within less than a minute she was back in the SUV and driving down the street after doing the deed. Another minute later, she stopped at the street corner she had found earlier. She lowered her window and tossed the handgun she had taken from Stewart onto the sidewalk. One of the four young black men standing on the corner heard it land and before he retrieved it, Mackenzie was gone. If he was ever caught with the gun he would have a difficult time convincing the cops it wasn't him that popped Byron Stewart.

Having planned ahead, Mackenzie headed out of town but made two quick stops on the way. One was at an office building with a dumpster in back. She removed the hoodie in the plastic grocery bag and shoved it into the dumpster under several larger garbage bags.

Her next stop was after crossing a bridge over the Fox River. She got out of the truck and hurried down to the riverbank. This was the most dangerous part. If a cop came along and caught her she would be looking at life in prison without parole. Still wearing the gloves, as soon as she was close enough, Mackenzie took the small pistol out and threw it fifty feet into the water.

Mackenzie had a small, muslin bag with draw strings. She placed the gloves, wallet and watch in the bag. She then removed the battery from Stewart's cell phone, tossed the battery into the river and put the phone in the bag also. She found two good sized rocks and for weight placed them in the bag. She tied the drawstrings and threw it into the river as far as she could.

Within five minutes she drove down the westbound ramp onto I-94 and took the first relaxed breath she had since pulling the trigger. Looking at the car's clock she figured to be home by 5:00 A.M. While she drove away from Milwaukee she ran down a mental checklist. Get rid of the clothes she was wearing, everything including shoes and underwear and run the contents of the file she stole through a shredder was all she had left to do. All of that would go out with the garbage to be picked up around 7:00 tomorrow morning.

Mackenzie took a few minutes to think about Byron Stewart. Feeling a bit remorseful, she rationalized it by reminding herself he had brought it on himself. It was his idea to try to blackmail her and Mackenzie was certain the payments would never end.

TWENTY-FOUR

Marc parked his Buick SUV on the street in the cemetery near the Sutherland's plot. It was easy enough to find. There were four TV news vans from local stations and several cars already parked along the same street. A black hearse from the Medical Examiner's office was parked on the grass near the grave and a backhoe was working on the project. In addition, there were about two dozen people, including reporters and camera operators, watching the excavation crew.

Marc put his phone in his pants' pocket, left his suit coat on the front seat and headed toward the crowd. It was a beautiful, warm, sunny mid-August day and Marc was thinking how odd it was for him to be where he was. *At least you get to bill your client for it*, he thought.

One of the reporters, a young woman from Channel 6 spotted him and made a beeline for him, her cameraman in tow. All of the others noticed this and quickly followed suit. Marc held a mini-press conference which amounted to him telling them he was there only as an observer.

"What's the matter, don't you trust us?" Heather Anderson asked him with a smirk. Marc had spotted her standing with Max Coolidge and Anna Finney then walked over to them. Marc said hello to all three of them before answering Heather's question.

"No, to be honest, I don't. Should I? You don't exactly have my client's best interest at heart, do you?"

The four of them stood together silently watching the backhoe operate. It took about ten minutes to get down to the casket. At that point, the operator backed it away from the gravesite. As soon as the backhoe's bucket was clear of the hole two men with small shovels carefully climbed down to finish the job.

When this occurred, Marc turned to watch the media members. The four local TV stations represented were all filming the entire process. As he watched the two men climbing into the grave, the woman from Channel 6 strolled over to him without her microphone.

"Are you really going to put this on the air?" Marc asked.

"It's going out live now," she said.

"Seriously? This is on TV now?"

"It's not my idea," she shrugged.

Marc was talking to her with his head turned toward the street and the line of parked cars. He saw a black BMW 750 pull up and a well-dressed woman exit the car. He immediately began stalking off in her direction to get to her before the media saw her. Unfortunately, they noticed this and were in force right behind him.

"I'm sorry," Mackenzie said when Marc reached her. He stopped in front of her and gave her his best angry dad look. "I couldn't stay away. It's like watching a car accident. I had to see for myself if they were really going to do this."

"The big sunglasses aren't much of a disguise," Marc said just before the reporters started hurling questions at her.

Marc held up both hands gesturing for quiet. He noticed Heather and the two detectives were now barely twenty feet away and watching.

The reporters fell silent and with Mackenzie standing slightly behind him, Marc addressed them. "My client has no comment to make. She is here as a spectator watching the authorities who, for no worthwhile reason, are desecrating her husband's final resting place. She will not be making a statement."

Undeterred, two or three of the reporters shoved recording devices at the two of them and shouted questions. The questions were mostly along the lines of: was she afraid of what would be found?

Marc held up his hands again and they took a minute to settle down. Marc looked them over as an adult would speaking to a group of unruly, simpleminded children.

"Okay, here it is," he finally said. "Here's your quote. If she was afraid of what they might find, would she have agreed to this in the first place? Thank you and that's it."

Marc led Mackenzie through the gaggle of reporters who still persisted in shouting questions.

"How do they always know when to show up for things like this?" Mackenzie asked Marc.

"They have sources in the police departments and prosecutor's offices around the Cities. Many of them even pay for the tips. They'll slip a cop fifty bucks for a juicy piece of news. Stuff like that. There's nothing illegal about it. It just seems a little sleazy, but it really isn't. They're just looking for information; for stories."

When they reached the gravesite, Marc and Mackenzie stood apart from everyone else.

"Hi," she smiled and said to Marc when no else could hear her. "I've missed you."

"Hello, to you," he smiled back. "Are you getting a little itch?"

"Yeah, I think so," she quietly, seductively said. "Can you do something about it?

"I just might be able to fix that," he whispered while hiding a smile.

Marc's phone went off, he pulled it from his pocket, read the ID and a wave of relief come over him.

"Hey, thanks for calling, Jason," Marc said without preamble. "Give me some good news."

"He'll be there next Monday. I just got off the phone with him and the trial he testified at finished late yesterday."

"Great, thanks, Jason," Marc said.

"He's excellent, Marc. A bit eccentric but juries take to him."

Mackenzie was watching him with an inquisitive expression. Marc lowered the phone away from his mouth and said, "Good news."

"What? Who are you talking to?" the caller asked.

"My client," Marc said into the phone. "We're at the cemetery right now. They're hooking up the casket to pull it out."

"Ghastly business. Well, if you need anything else, let me know," Jason said.

"I will and thanks again, Jason. I'll be in touch," Marc said.

While Marc put the phone back in his pants' pocket Mackenzie asked, "Who was that?"

"His name is Jason Briggs and he's a criminalist I have used in the past. He's like a private CSI guy. Very good, very professional. He's sending an independent pathologist to watch the autopsy and do our own toxicology tests. He's not cheap, but..."

"If you think we need him, money isn't a problem," Mackenzie said.

"We need him," Marc said.

"Then don't worry about it."

"Wait here and do not talk to the media. I'll be right back."

"No chance, buster. I'm coming with you."

They walked over to where Heather and the detectives were standing.

"I told you I was getting a pathologist to observe the autopsy. He'll be here on Monday," Marc told Heather.

"We don't want to wait that long," she replied.

"Tough shit. You've waited this long, a few more days won't matter," Marc responded, obviously annoyed.

Heather looked at the casket which was out of the hole and being swept to remove the dirt. Standing next to it was a bald man in a white coat supervising.

"Hey, Alfredo!" Heather called out to the man. He turned to look, and Heather waved him over.

She introduced the man to Marc as Dr. Alfredo Nunez, the Ramsey County Medical Examiner. They shook hands and Marc explained to the doctor that he hired a pathologist to observe the autopsy.

"Who?" Nunez asked.

"Dr. Oscar Johnson," Marc said.

"Oh, good," Nunez sincerely said. "I know Oscar. He's a good guy. Very good pathologist. When will he be here?"

"I just found out he can't make it till Monday."

"No problem," Nunez said. "We'll get to it first thing next week. In fact, I'll give him a call when I get back to the office and set it up."

TWENTY-FIVE

The hand clamped down on Mackenzie's mouth muffling her screams of protest. She tried raising her hands to ward off her attacker; to no avail. Her arms and legs were pinned down, completely immobilizing her. Mackenzie tried to look at the face of the man who straddled her abdomen, but it was too dark to see it. She tried to struggle to free herself, but her head wouldn't move, her arms felt like concrete and her legs were devoid of feeling as if they were gone.

Using all of her willpower, strength and determination Mackenzie put forth one last, final, massive effort to break fee. In an instant, it was over, and she found herself sitting up in her bed, gasping for air. The comforter and sheet were on the floor where she had thrown them. The dream was gone, and she was alone in her bedroom.

Mackenzie reached behind herself and propped up two pillows on the bed's headboard. She retrieved the plastic bottle of water from the nightstand then leaned back against the pillows. By this time her breathing had normalized, and her mind had cleared. She sipped the water and the thought about the dream.

"Where the hell did that come from?" She quietly said to herself comforted by the fact it was only a bad dream.

She glanced at the alarm clock next to the bed which read 6:27. Normally she would have stayed in bed until 7:00 but the dream had frightened her awake. *Might as well get up*, she thought.

Ten minutes later she was sipping her first cup of coffee at the breakfast bar. Having dismissed the dream, she again found herself thinking about Marc. Wondering if it was possible that, after everything she had been through and done, could she have a normal life, a normal relationship? The life she had led was so far outside the scope of "normal" Mackenzie wasn't sure if she could even recognize what normal would be.

It was the Tuesday morning after Labor Day. Summer was unofficially over even though the day's weather promised to be gorgeous.

The two of them had taken off early Friday morning to spend a quiet weekend together. Four days in a four-star resort on the North Shore of Lake Superior. The first real getaway with someone she may actually be in love with since…

"I can't remember if I've ever done that before," Mackenzie softly said to herself.

While she poured herself a second cup she looked at her phone. It was still set in the charger; exactly where she had placed it Thursday night. Mackenzie picked up the phone and carried it back to the breakfast bar. She took a minute to scan through the calls and messages, deleting the ones she would not bother with.

She saw four calls from Cooper Thomas, the lawyer who handled the estate and sale of the business for her.

Cooper had made no effort to hide his feelings for her. Since the funeral and the confrontation in his office with the Sutherland children, he had called at least once a week. Because of his knowledge of Bill Sutherland's Will and the business sale, Mackenzie believed she had little choice but to string him along for now.

It was too early to call him at his office. Mackenzie had his personal cell number and she thought about calling him on it at home. *Getting him in hot water with his wife would serve him right*, she thought with a bit of an evil grin.

She decided to wait a while to call him. Maybe a discreet lunch meeting would keep him calmed down. Instead, Mackenzie hurried upstairs, changed into her workout clothes and headed to the Life Time Fitness club on Ford Parkway.

Two hours later she was back home standing in the shower letting the hot water pound on her sore muscles. Mackenzie had overdone the workout a bit and would be a little sore later because of it.

After showering, Mackenzie sat at her bedroom vanity wrapped in her bathrobe. She held her phone in one hand, looked at the number to call, took a deep breath and pressed the call indicator.

"Cooper Thomas," she heard him say.

"Cooper, it's Mackenzie. How are you, dear?" she asked.

"Fine," he said with clear delight. "Thank you for calling. I'm sorry I called so many times, but my wife was out of town and I hoped we might get together."

"I'm sorry. I was out of town," she answered him. Mackenzie knew he was dying to ask who she was with. It was none of his business and as a way of exhibiting control, she was determined not to tell him. "We should meet for lunch."

"Yes, lunch. When and where?" he quickly agreed.

"There's a place at the Mall of America. It's called the Cadillac Ranch. It's on the south side, third floor. I want to go somewhere that we can hide in the crowd. I still need to keep a low profile. You understand, don't you?"

"Certainly, Mackenzie. I'll call and make a reservation in my secretary's name. I'll see you at noon."

A half hour later she was downstairs and checking her burner phone for calls. She had received one on Friday afternoon from area code 727 which she recognized as St. Petersburg, Florida. A feeling of dread came over her. *Was she about to have a repeat of Milwaukee,* she wondered? She listened to the innocuous message then, not one to put off potentially bad news, she quickly re-dialed the number to find out what the man wanted.

"Ernie Harper," Mackenzie heard the man say.

"Mr. Harper," she said, "this is Donna Bauer. You left a message on Friday. Sorry, I've been gone all weekend."

"That's okay, Mrs. Bauer. I got some news for you I thought you'd want," Harper answered her.

Ernesto Harper was the son of a Cuban mother and Anglo father. He was a private investigator working in the Tampa-St. Pete area. Basically, he was doing the same thing as Lou Travis in Chicago and the late Byron Stewart in Milwaukee. He was keeping an eye on Mackenzie's dead husband's children and ex-wife.

"I have it from various reliable sources that your former stepson, David, got his hands on his mother's money, invested it in various things and lost every dime," Harper said.

"Are you sure?" Mackenzie asked suppressing her glee.

"Yes, ma'am. It's solid. That's not all. This dummy tried to get it back by going into the drug trade. He was busted in a sting trying to broker a deal for fifty kilos of cocaine."

"When?"

"Thursday night. I did some checking with a DEA guy I know. They think the bust is solid and little David is sitting in jail unable to make bail. His partners are Cubans and DEA is trying to get him to flip on them. So far, he isn't cooperating which is probably good. These Cuban guys would kill him if he did," Harper told her.

Mackenzie remained quiet for almost thirty seconds taking in the news. The fact that her former husband's idiot son, David, had blown his mother's divorce settlement was the best news. But the drug bust almost made her laugh.

"Are you still there?" Ernie asked.

"Yes, yes," she said. "Sorry. I was just thinking. Wow! David Bauer. I'm a little surprised, but not entirely. They spoiled him rotten. Anything else?"

"No, ma'am. That's it for now. I'll keep an eye on it for you. Do you want me to do anything else?"

"No, Ernesto, thank you and I'll send you some money this week for sure," Mackenzie said.

The call ended, and Mackenzie spent the next five minutes walking around the living room, alternately laughing and shaking her head.

Mackenzie parked her Beamer in the East ramp at the big mall. This was only the second time she had been here and when she got inside the size and scope of the place still amazed her. Mackenzie's number one thought upon entering the place was how thankful she was that she could afford to shop elsewhere. While she made her way to the restaurant, she was delighted to see that with the exception of a couple of admiring males, no one paid the slightest bit of attention to her.

Mackenzie stood in the entryway and looked over the restaurant's crowd. Before the hostess had a chance to speak to her, she spotted Cooper at a table along the wall.

"Thank you," Mackenzie said to him as he held the chair for her.

Cooper sat down opposite her, reached across the table to take her hand and said, "I'm very happy to see you."

"So am I," Mackenzie lied with a slight smile. "But we have to be very careful. This whole thing is such a dark cloud hanging over me."

Cooper let go of her hand, crossed his arms, leaned on the table and whispered, "A lawyer from the Ramsey County attorney's office called just before I left to come here."

"Really? Who?" Mackenzie calmly asked.

"A woman. She said her name was Heather Anderson."

"What did she want?"

"She asked me about William's Will and the sale of the company," Cooper replied.

"And what did you say?"

"I told her that was privileged information and refused to answer her questions. I reminded her I submitted an affidavit swearing the new Will was Bill's idea. Then I told her I was not at liberty to discuss any other matters with her. She makes me nervous, though."

"Why? Relax, she's fishing. Whatever happens, I have complete confidence in Marc Kadella to handle it," Mackenzie said.

"Are you sleeping with him?" Cooper abruptly asked.

Mackenzie leaned forward, looked him in the eye and said, "That would be unethical from what I understand."

Cooper opened his mouth to speak and ask another question then thought better of it. She did not say no, she wasn't sleeping with Marc and Cooper decided he did not want to know anyway.

The two of them made a little small talk while they ate, mostly about the gossip surrounding Mackenzie. Cooper had been calling her once or twice a week ever since the meeting with the Sutherland kids in his office. Without expressly stating it, he made it obvious he was totally smitten by her. For her part, until the legal issues hanging over her head were resolved, Mackenzie would keep him on a string. The problem for her was that the longer it went on and the more he mooned over her like a lovesick puppy, the less respect she had for him.

When the waiter had cleared their empty dishes and left, Cooper started in again.

"I can't help it, this woman from Ramsey County worries me," he said.

"For God's sake, act like a man, Cooper!" Mackenzie ripped into him.

Being so abruptly chastised by her, the sensitive lawyer had the look of a hurt puppy on his face. He seemed on the verge of tears.

Realizing she had gone a little too far, she calmly said, "I'm sorry, Cooper. I shouldn't have been so sharp with you." She patted his hand and continued, "There's nothing going on. Besides, you're a lawyer. Attorney-client privilege precludes you from even being questioned by them. It's Paige Sutherland. I'll bet she calls her lawyer every day and he calls the county attorney. Her case is about to be thrown out of court."

The touch of her hand on his was enough to make his heart skip and calm him down. He reached over with his other hand and held hers in both of his.

"Be a little patient, my dear," Mackenzie said with a sincere smile. "It will be over before you know it."

"When do you go to court on Paige's lawsuit?"

Mackenzie leaned back and pulled her hand out of his grasp. "Day after tomorrow. Connie is pretty confident the judge will dismiss it."

"I wish you had let me handle it for you," he said.

"Better we keep a little distance," Mackenzie reminded him. *And I wanted a lawyer who wouldn't wet himself at the sight of a courtroom*, she thought.

TWENTY- SIX

Connie Mickelson barely waited for the elevator doors to open before elbowing her way through the crowd. Connie was in her mid-sixties; an old school feminist who did not wait for anyone or anything. Her attitude had always been: if you want something, get off your ass, roll-up your sleeves and earn it. Connie made her own way in life.

She turned to her left towards the courtroom of Judge Farley. Connie noticed Simon Kane and Paige standing together along one wall opposite the courtroom doors. Looking at Connie with a relieved half smile was her client, Mackenzie Sutherland.

"I told you that you didn't have to be here for this," Connie said to her.

"I decided to come anyway," Mackenzie replied as she watched a casually dressed young man walking toward them.

Connie turned her head toward the young man very slightly, nodded at him and discreetly pointed a finger at Simon Kane.

Mackenzie noticed this and whispered "Connie, what's going on?"

"Watch," Connie told her trying not to smile. "Watch Kane and Paige."

The young man walked up to Simon Kane and said something that Connie and Mackenzie could not hear. While nodding his head, Simon said something in reply. The process server handed him a letter size manila envelope and without another word, turned and walked back to the elevators.

"What is that?" Mackenzie asked.

"Sssssh, watch," Connie said.

While the two women watched him and with Paige looking over his shoulder, Kane removed the contents of the envelope. With his lips moving, Kane began reading the document. His eyes widened, his lips moved faster, and his hands began to tremble.

Connie and Mackenzie continued to watch, and they heard Paige ask him what was in the document. He ignored her and after roughly fifteen seconds the color completely drained from his face. Kane stopped reading and after quickly flipping through the remaining pages, held the document at his side and looked up at the hallway ceiling.

Barely able to contain her laughter Connie walked over to him while Paige repeated her question to find out what was in the document.

"Why, Simon," Connie said when she reached him. "You look like someone just walked over your grave. Are you all right?"

Gathering himself he held up the document and angrily asked Connie, "What do you know about this?"

"Me?" Connie innocently asked. "I'm not sure what you mean."

"I don't believe you," he snarled.

"Well, Simon, I'll say this," Connie said. She tapped the pages with an index finger and continued. "This will be Defense Exhibit A if this case goes to trial. We'll use it to refute the claim that the poor, suffering widow is destitute without the companionship of her late husband."

"Why you bitch! If you were a man I'd punch you," he almost yelled.

Connie laughed and replied, "Simon, if you were a man, you could."

At that moment a court deputy unlocked the courtroom door. Connie said, "See you inside," turned and led Mackenzie inside.

"What is going on?" Mackenzie tried to ask as they walked up to the gate.

"I'll tell you later," Connie said.

The two women took the table to the left facing the judge's bench. It was almost two minutes before Kane and Paige followed them in. As they passed through the gate Connie turned her head enough to peek at them. Kane still looked like he had seen a ghost, but Paige glared at her. Kane must have told her what he had received and if Paige had a gun, Connie and Mackenzie would be in serious trouble. Of course, the look on Paige's face caused Connie to smile and wink at her knowing it would twist the figurative knife she had stabbed her with a little deeper.

"All rise," the deputy intoned the traditional order to commence court. Judge Farley came out, took his seat and told the four of them, the only ones in the courtroom, to be seated. His clerk was to his left and the court reporter set up his equipment in front of the judge. The clerk read the case information into the record and the lawyers identified themselves.

"You're here on a motion for summary judgment?" the judge asked while looking at Connie.

"That is correct, your Honor," Connie answered.

Farley nodded toward the podium situated in-between and a few feet forward of the tables and said, "You may proceed, Ms. Mickelson."

Connie took her place at the podium and for the next fifteen minutes spoke directly at the judge to make her case. She started with the background of Mackenzie's marriage; the difficulties with William's children and their attitude toward Mackenzie, the threats upon her life by Bob Sutherland and the shooting. Connie laid out the investigation by the police for him and the refusal of the grand jury to indict her.

"Obviously, your Honor, this is a case of self-defense. Their claim that she negligently and/or intentionally inflicted harm on the Plaintiff is without merit. Robert Sutherland's death, while tragic, was brought on because he was going to attack my client with a fireplace poker.

"The facts of this case are not in dispute, your Honor. Mackenzie Sutherland acted in self-defense and they know it," Connie said pointing a finger at Kane and Paige.

"Finally, your Honor, it is obvious this lawsuit was brought for the sole purpose of harassing my client. It is vindictive, spiteful and without merit and they knew it. Not only should it be dismissed but costs and attorney fees awarded."

Connie removed two documents from the manila file on the podium and handed one to Kane. As she walked toward the judge she said, "I have an affidavit to go with my request for fees and costs, your Honor," She handed a copy to the judge.

"It totals eleven thousand eight hundred and forty-four dollars," she continued as she walked back to the podium.

"Did you include some time for this morning's hearing?" Farley asked her, a clear hint he was inclined to award them to her.

"Yes, I did, your Honor. In conclusion, the facts of this case are not in dispute and as a matter of law it must be dismissed. Thank you."

The entire time Connie made her argument Simon Kane sat staring straight ahead almost trancelike. He barely heard a word of what Connie had to say. All he could think about was the ton of bricks dropped on him in the hallway. At best, he would only be suspended and not be fired. The reality was he would likely be disbarred, fired and divorced.

"Mr. Kane?" the judge asked.

Kane remained motionless for three or four more seconds, then the judge said his name again.

"Simon!" Paige whispered in his ear.

"Oh, yes, your Honor," Kane finally said and looked up at the judge.

Farley held out his right hand toward the podium and said, "Would you like to present your argument?"

"Yes, your Honor," Kane stammered as he gathered his notes, stood and took Connie's place.

Connie, while watching this debacle, almost felt a slight twinge of sympathy for him. Then she realized again he had brought it on himself. Having a two-year affair with a married client, the wife of another client, was his choice. He had some serious explaining to do.

Kane started out by trying to claim there was a factual dispute to present at trial. He barely got the words out before Farley interrupted him.

"You have some facts to present to refute what the police, county attorney and grand jury all found to be a self-defense homicide?" Farley asked.

"Um, well, we believe Mackenzie Sutherland set-up Robert Sutherland and murdered him," Kane said. "And..."

"Really? What evidence do you have to present and why haven't you turned it over to the police?"

"Well, your Honor, we believe with further investigation we will find it," Kane said.

"So, the answer to my question is, no, you don't have any facts or evidence to present, do you?" Farley asked.

"We believe there is enough of a factual dispute now to present to a jury, your Honor. Enough to convince you to dismiss this motion for summary judgment and allow the case to proceed to trial," Kane managed to calmly, confidently say.

"I see," Farley said nodding as if he agreed causing Connie to stir in her seat, "Well, Mr. Kane, with all due respect, I don't. Mackenzie Sutherland acted in self-defense. I have been through the pleadings including the police reports and findings by the grand jury and all of the evidence supports an act of self-defense. Therefore, I will grant Defendant's motion for summary judgment, but I will dismiss the case without prejudice. If you come up with new evidence, you can file again.

"I'm also going to make a finding that this case was without merit, brought for the purpose of harassment and award defendant's attorney fees and costs."

"What?" Paige practically screamed. "That bitch shot my husband and I have to pay her?"

"Get control of your client, Mr. Kane," Farley calmly said. Hubert Farley had been on the bench for over twenty-five years. Angry outbursts were nothing new and barely fazed him.

Mackenzie followed Connie from downtown St. Paul on westbound I-94 through downtown Minneapolis back to Connie's office. Mackenzie was relieved with the hearing's outcome but not as much as she should be or thought she would be. She knew why, too. The results of the second autopsy of William Sutherland should be known any day. And although she was able to fake her concern, Mackenzie knew what they might find.

When they reached Connie's building, they both parked in the back lot. Mackenzie, happy to see Marc's SUV, parked the BMW next to it.

"When are you going to tell me what happened before court in the hallway?" Mackenzie asked Connie as they strolled toward the back door.

"I'll tell you upstairs," Connie answered her with a big smile. "I want to fill-in Marc too."

They entered the suite of offices to find Marc's door closed. Connie pointed at it while looking at Carolyn with an inquisitive look on her face.

"He's on the phone," Carolyn said. "Oh, no he isn't," she added when the light went off on her phone. "He just got off."

Connie knocked on his door then turned the knob and pushed it open while Marc answered her.

"Hey," Marc said to the two women as they sat down in his client chairs. "So, how did it go?"

Connie told him the whole story starting with the hearing. Marc congratulated both of them for the result and expressed shock at the award of attorney fees.

"If that isn't a clear statement to old Simon that he doesn't have a case I don't know what is," Connie said.

"It ought to cool out Paige from pursuing this any further also," Marc added. "What about the complaint against Simon?"

Connie then told them what went on in the hallway before court.

"You should've seen him," Connie told Marc. "He looked like he had seen a ghost. He even threatened to punch me."

"Probably a good thing he didn't," Marc said. "Knowing you he'd still be looking for all of his teeth."

A slightly stunned Mackenzie, silent until now, said, "Simon Kane got served with a bar complaint just before court for his affair with Paige? You got him in trouble for the same thing Marc and I…"

"Stop! I don't want to hear it," Connie interrupted her.

"Besides, we could reasonably argue that our personal relationship started before I began to represent you," Marc said.

"It did?" Mackenzie asked looking puzzled.

"Close enough," Marc answered her. "I looked it up," Marc continued looking at Connie. "His firm could get jammed up for it as well."

"All for one and one for all," Connie said.

"Is he in a lot of trouble?" Mackenzie asked.

"He has some serious explaining to do. It could help him if Paige helps him out," Connie said. "He may be in bigger trouble with his firm for using their credit card for all of this."

Mackenzie thought for a moment then said, "Good, I never liked him, anyway. He was a total butt-kissing, suck-up to Bill."

They heard a knock on the door and Sandy poked her head in.

"You need to come out and hear this," she said to all three of them.

Sandy opened the door and all three of them filed out into the common area. Carolyn had the TV on and was checking the local channels. She came across one that was about to broadcast a news break.

"This just in," the female anchor began by saying, "It is being reported that the autopsy results on the late William Sutherland, the founder of *Sutherland's* grocery store chain, have been completed. A more thorough laboratory analysis has found trace amounts of the drug Interleukin-2. We are told that this is a cancer fighting drug that can induce a heart attack. To repeat, it is being reported…"

TWENTY-SEVEN

"What?" Mackenzie said looking over the crowd in front of the TV. "What is inter..., whatever she called it? Bill didn't have cancer. She said they found a cancer drug in him. I don't understand. Marc?"

"Let's go in my office," Marc calmly told her. He gently took her by the arm to guide her to his office.

Before they could get seated, after Marc closed the door, Mackenzie looking puzzled and confused said, "Did the autopsy show Bill had cancer? I don't understand why he would have taken a cancer drug."

As Marc was sitting down he calmly said, "Mac, sit down, please. As far as I know, there was no cancer found in the original autopsy. You tell me," he continued while carefully searching his client's face for a reaction, "why would he take a cancer drug?"

Mackenzie was sitting upright, her back stiffened and with a confused look, shook her head and said, "I told you, I have no idea. We need to talk to his doctor. Get his medical records. I want to find out what's going on, too."

"Okay," Marc said. "First, let me call our pathologist."

While Marc was dialing the phone he said, "I'm really tired of getting this kind of information from the news. The prosecutors always pull this crap. Hello, Dr. Johnson, please," Marc said into the phone before Mackenzie could respond to his statement. "Sure, I'll wait."

The pathologist came on the phone and Marc identified himself. Marc then explained why he was calling and what had been reported in the news. With his office in Madison, Wisconsin, unless the Ramsey County M.E. had called him, Johnson would not know about the cancer drug.

"What was the name of the drug?" Johnson asked him.

"Inter-luke 2, something," Marc replied.

"Interleukin-2?"

"Yeah, that's it," Marc said. "Do you know about it?"

"Sure, it's a member of the interleukin cytokine family of drugs. I think its primary use is for the immune system."

"What about cancer?"

"Yes, it can be used for certain types of cancers. William Sutherland did not have cancer," Johnson emphatically said.

"Could it cause heart failure?" Marc said.

"Among other things, yes," Johnson said. "A normal autopsy, especially of an older man with a history of hard living and a poor record of taking care of himself and has a heart attack would not reveal the drug's presence. The toxicology screen, whoever performs it, would have to be looking for it.

"Let me call the lab where I sent the tissue samples and check with them," Johnson said.

There was a knock on Marc's door, Sandy opened it and quietly told Marc, Heather Anderson was on line three for him. Marc nodded an acknowledgement to her.

"Call me back as soon as you know anything, please. I have the county attorney's office on hold."

"Will do," Johnson replied.

"Hello," Marc said to Heather Anderson.

"Marc, I just called to let you know our tox screen of William Sutherland found a suspicious drug in him. A drug that our experts tell me induced his heart attack and caused his death."

"I saw it on TV, Heather," Marc blandly replied. "It was nice of you to give me a heads-up after it was leaked to the media."

"Anyway," she continued. "I wanted to let you know what was found. Have you talked to your pathologist?"

"Yes, he's going to check on this. Was there anything else?"

"No, that's it. I'll try to keep you informed as much as possible."

Marc ended the call and told Mackenzie about the conversations with Dr. Johnson and Heather Anderson.

"Now what?" she asked obviously concerned.

"Now they're going to try to find out where this drug came from and how it got into Bill Sutherland. You can expect a search warrant, probably yet today. It won't take her long to find a friendly judge to sign one."

"Great. They're going to tear my house apart, aren't they?"

"Maybe, I don't know. Depends on what exactly they're trying to find," Marc said.

"Can you stop them?"

"From getting a search warrant? No. But if I'm there I may be able to keep the damage down."

"How?"

"By writing down everyone's name and badge number and threatening to sue every one of them."

There was another knock on his door and Connie Mickelson joined them. Marc told Connie about his phone calls then asked her if there had been any further news reported.

"No, just the bit about the drug found in the deceased," Connie said. "How are you holding up?" Connie asked Mackenzie.

Mackenzie sighed then said, "I don't know. I don't know what the hell to think. I just have no idea what's going on and now Marc tells me they're going to get a search warrant for my house…"

"And cars," Marc said.

"…looking for this drug, I guess."

Marc said, "It's almost noon. Let's watch the news and see if there is anything else. Then we'll get some lunch. I'm hungry, you want to come with?" Marc asked Connie.

"Please," Mackenzie added.

"Sure, where?" Connie said as the three of them started toward the door.

"We'll go across the street," Marc said.

"And you're buying," Connie told him.

"We have been told, by more than one source inside the investigation into the death of William Sutherland, that the drug found in his system definitely caused his heart attack," the male anchor on Channel 3 reported.

"Definitely caused his heart attack?" Barry Cline, one of the office lawyers asked.

The announcer continued reading the story off of the teleprompter while everyone silently watched. The only additional comment of substance was the fact that the authorities were still investigating. Toward the end of the three-minute story, Mackenzie's picture appeared on screen behind him. The photo itself was quite unflattering, obviously chosen for effect and stayed on screen while the anchor reminded the audience who she was. He wrapped up by reporting Mackenzie's previous husband's death by heart attack.

"Is this just a coincidence?" he looked at the camera and asked. "We report, you decide."

Carolyn shut off the TV. Before anyone said anything, Marc broke the silence by holding up his right hand and counting with his fingers, slowly said, "One, two, three…" and the phone rang.

Sandy went quickly back to her desk and answered the call.

"Just a second," she said while placing the caller on hold.

"Gabriella," Marc said.

"You got it," Sandy smiled.

"That's my girl," Marc said. "I'll take it in my office."

"Can I come with?" Mackenzie asked.

"Sure, come on. I think we'll go on TV this afternoon," Marc told her.

Two minutes later the two of them emerged from Marc's office. Connie was waiting for them.

"Maddy called," Carolyn said. "She saw the news and was wondering what was going on."

"I'll call her," Marc said. He looked at Connie and said, "We're going to the station to tape Gabriella's show."

"You gonna eat first?" Connie asked.

"Yeah, we need to be there around 1:30," Marc said.

While they ate lunch, Marc called Madeline back and told her what he knew. This was not much more than what was reported on TV.

"You're going on Gabriella's show?" Maddy asked. Gabriella and she had become good friends, "Mind if I meet you and watch?"

"No, not all," Marc said. "In fact, I just had an idea. Yeah, I get one about once a month, Miss Smartass. Anyway, I was thinking about going to Mackenzie's house and spending the day. I don't have much going on and I think Ramsey County is going to hit her with a search warrant today. I'd like to be there to keep an eye on things."

"Won't they call and tell you first?" Maddy asked.

"No, I doubt it. They should, but they don't have to. Want to come with us and hang out? Keep Mackenzie company?"

"Sure, I'll meet you at Channel 8 at 1:30. Oh and it's about time you took me and Gabriella to lunch again."

"Why not an expensive dinner?" Marc asked.

"Better still," Maddy agreed.

"Why do you want Maddy to hang out at Mackenzie's with you waiting for the warrant?" Connie asked.

Marc shrugged then said, "Her presence can't hurt, and she'll distract the male cops who do the search."

Mackenzie laughed then said, "You're a sexist pig."

"Thanks," Marc said.

The three of them, Gabriella, Marc and Mackenzie were seated on a casual, studio setting. The taping began with Gabriella introducing her two guests. She then spent almost two minutes explaining a little history of William Sutherland's death and Mackenzie's alleged involvement.

Gabriella played it straight and gave her two guests legitimate questions. She wasn't looking to fool them and get them to admit something they did not want to. First of all, Gabriella knew Marc well enough. She had interviewed him enough times to know he would be cautious, careful and deliberate in his answers. He also would be very careful about what his client would say. In fact, the two of them with Connie's input, had thoroughly prepared during lunch.

Gabriella was also savvy enough to know that if she treated them well, this interview was likely just the beginning. The cops and prosecutors were probably coming after Mackenzie.

The interview itself would get maybe fifteen minutes of air time during Gabriella's half-hour show which consisted of twenty-two minutes of air time. The taping took almost an hour, most of which would be cut.

When it was finished, Marc was quite satisfied. They were able to make several salient points. First, that Mackenzie knew nothing about any drugs that may have been found during the second autopsy. Second, Mackenzie had no idea how they got into her husband and from Marc, there is no way anyone could say definitely that Sutherland's heart attack was caused by this drug or was anything but a natural death.

Gabriella's boss, Hunter Osgood the station's news director, sat in and watched the interview next to Maddy Rivers. When they finished he personally assured Marc the 6:00 and 10:00 P.M. newscasts would lead with their denials. Not because he believed them, but because it would scoop their competitors.

"Heather, it's Marc Kadella," Marc said into his cell phone. He was driving east on I-94 with Mackenzie and Maddy following in Maddy's car.

"What can I do for you, Marc?" she politely asked.

"I'm just wondering when the search warrant is going to be served on Mackenzie Sutherland."

"What makes you think…"

"Give me a break, Heather. We both know, you're getting one now," Marc said.

Heather hesitated for a couple of seconds before saying, "How did you find that out?"

"I didn't, I was bluffing. But it seemed reasonable," Marc said.

"I don't have to tell you about a search warrant or when we choose to execute it," Heather told him, annoyed he had outfoxed her a little bit.

"Heather, let's stop this. Do you have a search warrant, yes or no?"

"Yes, Marc. We just got it a few minutes ago," she admitted.

"Okay," Marc continued. "I'm on my way to the Sutherland house now. Mackenzie is with me. We'll be there in ten minutes. Why don't you and your guys meet us there and we'll get this over with?"

"We don't have to do this at your convenience," Heather said immediately regretting her testy tone.

"Heather, if your guys show up in the middle of the night I'll hold a press conference, tell them about this conversation and make you look like the Gestapo."

"Yeah, okay. I'll get some people together and see you in about an hour."

"You going to be there?" Marc asked.

"Yeah, I think I will. It will give me an excuse to get out to the office."

Marc parked his SUV in Mackenzie's driveway and Maddy pulled up next to him. As he was shutting off the engine, his phone rang. Marc looked at the ID and took the call while sitting in the car.

"Marc, it's Oscar Johnson."

"Tell me something good," Marc told his pathologist.

"Sorry, no can do. I called the lab and told them about the IL-2 found by Ramsey County. They rushed the test and found it also."

"I guess I expected that," Marc said.

"There's something else," Johnson continued. "I went over the original autopsy report and there was no mention of needle marks."

"So?"

"IL-2 is normally administered intravenously; by a shot or IV drip. There was no indication of that."

"What does that mean?" Marc asked looking through his windshield at the two women and holding up an index finger to them indicating they should wait.

"To bring on a heart attack, especially one that causes death a single dosage would have to be fairly large. There is no indication of that here. It looks like the drug was ingested probably through food or drink, in small amounts over time."

"Shit," Marc quietly said.

"Yeah, shit," Johnson agreed. "Now, I don't have to put any of this in a report or even testify to it as a medical certainty."

"Okay," Marc said.

"Between you and me it looks like the deceased was poisoned with small amounts over time and the cumulative effect brought on the heart attack. The good news is: they're going to have a tough time proving that beyond a reasonable doubt."

"Or who did it," Marc added.

TWENTY-EIGHT

Marc, Mackenzie and Maddy were seated at the dining room table. Marc told them about the call to Heather Anderson and the soon to be served search warrant. He also told them a little about the call from Dr. Johnson; basically, limiting what he told them to the fact that he, too, found IL-2 in William's tissue samples. For now, he decided to keep the news about the poisoning himself.

A half-hour later, Heather Anderson arrived with six St. Paul police, including detectives, Max Coolidge and Anna Finney. While Mackenzie and Maddy remained in the dining room, Marc went to the door.

"Hi, Heather. Come in," Marc said. "Here's your copy," she told him and handed Marc a copy of the warrant.

While Marc and Heather stood in the foyer Marc read over the one-page document. As he did this, the four uniformed officers, led by an overweight, surly-looking sergeant tried to muscle their way past into the house.

"Hold it, just hold on a minute," Marc said to them.

The sergeant turned to him and said, "Don't interfere or try to tell us what to do, lawyer."

When the cop said this, Heather visibly cringed, knowing what was coming.

"Oh, you must be the tough guy. The one that thinks he's in charge and can intimidate me," Marc said taking one step toward the man. When he did this, the cop, being used to bullying people, took an involuntary step back.

"I want everyone's name, rank and badge number," Marc said as he continued staring at the sergeant. "You will get cooperation, but if you guys think you're going to go through here and tear the place apart, guess again. Any of that kind of nonsense and I'll sue every one of you."

"You can't win that suit," Heather weakly said.

"Maybe, but I can make their lives a living hell for three or four years," Marc answered her while still staring at the cop.

He pointed toward the living room and said, "My assistant has a pad of paper. She will take down the information."

While Marc did this, Max Coolidge was watching with a large smile. He knew the uniformed sergeant and despised the man. Max knew he was a bully and a closet racist as well.

"Sergeant Collins," Max said to the man. "Why don't you wait outside while we do this?"

"Good idea," Heather chimed in.

The chastened sergeant angrily left. As Max walked past Marc he winked at him and whispered, "Nicely done, counselor."

Marc finished reading the search warrant while Heather watched.

"You're taking her car and her husband's SUV? Why?"

"To look for evidence. She'll have them back in a day or two, unless we find something," Heather told him.

"What do you expect to find in the cars?"

Something to put your client away for life, Heather thought. "Don't know. We'll see."

For the next hour and a half, while Marc and Maddy kept watch, the five cops carefully went over every inch of the house. Maddy, as Marc expected, served as a distraction for two of the younger men who paid more attention to her than their work.

While this went on, Mackenzie moved Marc's SUV and Maddy's Acura out of her driveway. Two tow trucks arrived and took the Beamer and Tahoe to the downtown police department.

When they finished, the only things they removed were the personal computer from William's den and Mackenzie's laptop. Marc almost asked why these were being removed before realizing why. The police techies were going to look for internet searches for drugs that can cause heart attacks.

"Thanks for being here," Mackenzie said to Marc and Maddy when the cops were gone. "At least they didn't make a mess."

"They kind of like to do that," Maddy acknowledged.

"I need a car," Mackenzie said. "I guess I'll rent one, somewhere."

"Can you help her with that?" Marc asked Maddy. "I need to stop back at the office and check on things."

"Sure, no problem," Maddy said.

"Then you'll take us both to dinner. Some place nice," Mackenzie said.

"Yeah, none of this Arby's or KFC stuff," Maddy added.

Marc looked as if he was going to protest but the look he got from both women stopped him cold. Instead, he said, "Yes, I was going to suggest the same thing."

"And you're not going to do what most downtown big-firm lawyers would do and bill her for it," Maddy added.

Two days after the search of Mackenzie's house, there was a meeting in Heather Anderson's office. Max Coolidge, Anna Finney and Heather's boss, Shayla Parker were in attendance.

"I heard back from the tech guys. They went through William Sutherland's computer and found something interesting. Beginning about four months before his death, someone was on his computer searching for drugs that can cause heart attacks. There were twelve general searches and three specifically for the drug they found in him."

"Let's arrest her, now," Max said.

"It's not enough," Shayla Parker spoke up. "It's not even her computer."

"Do you think Bill Sutherland did this to himself?" Max asked Shayla.

"Of course not," Heather answered for her. "But Shayla's right. It is a piece of evidence but not enough. We're a little weak on motive…"

"The money," Anna Finney said. "She stood to inherit the whole thing."

"She claims she didn't know that," Heather said. "And the lawyer who wrote the new Will backs her up."

"I've been thinking about him," Max said. "What if he's lying to help her out? When I was at Bill Sutherland's funeral, I noticed them together.

"I watched them a little bit and he, the lawyer, this Cooper Thomas guy, followed her around like a puppy. Like a teenage boy with a crush on a teacher. It looked a little strange."

"You're a cynical cop," Heather said with a smile.

"I'm paid to be a cynical cop. What if he lied for her because he's smitten with her? He doesn't look like the toughest guy in town. He's a corporate lawyer not a litigator. Maybe we could take a run at him."

"How?" Shayla asked. "He could claim attorney-client and not say a word."

The four of them sat silently thinking this over for almost a full minute.

"What do you know about him?" Anna asked Max. "Is he married? His wife might find a little gossip about her husband interesting."

"I don't know," Max said. "Probably. No, wait. I remember he was wearing a ring. I specifically looked when I saw him with Mackenzie."

"I've heard enough," Parker said. She stood to leave then said, "I don't want to know the details but if you can get to him, it's worth taking a shot."

"He signed an affidavit," Heather blurted out. "He signed an affidavit swearing that William Sutherland had him change the Will and Mackenzie knew nothing about it. I have it in the file," she said as she started looking for the document. "Here it is!"

"Perjury, if he wasn't telling the truth," Parker said. "I'm leaving. Do what you have to do to bring this woman down, but don't tell me about it." With that she left.

"How do we do this?" Heather asked.

Max and Anna looked at each other then Max said, "We could go interview him again. You know, just tell him we're doing routine follow up because of the second autopsy."

"Then during the interview, we can ask him about the affidavit; he'll say it's accurate. Then I'll ask him if lying on an affidavit is perjury. Make it sound like I'm just curious," Anna said.

"Then in a few days, I could bring him in here and put the fear of God into him. Tell him if I find out he's lying I'll prosecute his ass. He'll also get disbarred and fired," Heather said.

"Better yet," Max said, "We bring him downtown and interrogate him in one of our rooms. Let him look at a holding cell to see what is in store for him if he doesn't cooperate."

"And the wife and kids will be gone," Anna added.

"We'll go see him now, just before lunch. Then we'll sit on him and see if he goes to Mackenzie," Max said.

"Good," Heather said. "It probably won't work but we might shake something loose."

The two detectives stood to leave, and Heather asked Anna, "What happened to your other partner, Kubik?"

"He's ah, got some personal issues to deal with."

Heather touched the tip of her nose and sniffed loudly indicating a cocaine problem.

"Among other things," Anna said.

"Do you have an appointment to see Mr. Thomas?" the law firm receptionist asked them.

"We're the cops," Anna reminded her. "We don't make appointments."

Totally intimidated, the young woman called back to Cooper and told him there were detectives to see him. He assured her he would be right out.

Cooper Thomas replaced the phone in its cradle then stared at the wall in front of his desk. He could feel a bead of sweat break out at his hairline. He took three or four deep breaths then quietly said to himself, "This is why I went into corporate law."

Cooper Thomas was a fair corporate lawyer. A partner in a fourteen-lawyer firm in downtown St. Paul, he made an excellent living with a healthy list of mid-size corporate clients.

While in law school at Michigan, he spent a summer clerking for a trial judge. This experience was enough to let him know, if he didn't know it already, that litigation was not in his future; especially criminal litigation.

Now he sat staring at a wall while two detectives were waiting in the reception area. Cooper had little doubt who they were and why they were here. The black man, Max something-or-other, intimidated him without even trying.

Another couple of deep breaths and he went out to fetch the two detectives.

Twenty minutes later, Max and Anna left his office and found their own way out. Cooper was thankful he did not have to show them to the exit. His knees were so weak after their questioning he was barely able to stand to shake their hands.

The conversation itself did not go into anything the police did not already know. They said they were doing a little more investigation because of the second autopsy and wanted to make sure all of their T's were crossed and I's dotted.

Cooper calmly dealt with most of it because he had been through it before. They again asked about Bill Sutherland's Will and the sale of the company. Some of it he acknowledged; some of it he covered with attorney-client privilege. On the whole, he handled it well and just when he thought they were finished, the woman asked him about affidavits and perjury.

Cooper had always been a terrible poker player. In college, his fraternity brothers liked playing with him because he was always good for losing a lot. When Detective Finney asked him the perjury question, he felt his face give it away. They knew the affidavit was a lie. And sooner or later, even though neither of them said a word, they were going to come for him.

TWENTY-NINE

Ten minutes after the two detectives left, Cooper Thomas was barely beginning to breathe normally again. *They knew*, he thought. Their questions about an affidavit containing false statements being perjury was not a guess. They knew. They were not fishing.

Using his personal iPhone, he punched a number and put it to his ear. On the third ring, she answered.

"Hello, Cooper. I was just thinking about you," Mackenzie lied.

"Can you meet with me? I need to talk to you," he managed to calmly say.

"Well, I guess so. What's wrong? What happened?"

"The police were just here. Those two detectives, the black man and the white woman. They came to my office. To my office, Mackenzie! I'm surprised the managing partner hasn't called me to her office."

"Calm down, Cooper. I'll meet you at the restaurant we met before. Do you remember?"

"Yeah, sure. I'll leave now. I'll be there in thirty minutes."

Ten minutes later he was in the parking ramp attached to his office building on Sixth Street. As calmly as possible he walked to his car, got in, backed it out of his reserved spot and headed toward the exit on Cedar.

"He just pulled out and he's headed toward the exit on Cedar. You should pick him up in a minute," the handheld radio Ann Finney was holding informed them.

"Roger, that," she replied. "Are you following him?"

"Yes, I'm one car behind him," the rookie cop answered her. His name was Bret Jurgens. He was barely old enough to shave and Max liked to tease Anna about having a cougar crush on him. They had tapped him to watch Cooper's car. In plain clothes and driving his own car he was delighted to get the chance to help the two detectives.

Not being a professional crook, Cooper was quite easy for them to follow. Barely fifteen minutes after leaving his office, he entered the ramp on the east end of the Mall of America. After parking their cars, the three cops, Bret included, followed Cooper into the huge shopping mall.

"God, I hate this place," Anna said as they strolled along with the shoppers and mall walkers.

"If we don't have a terrorist attack here, it will be a miracle," Max said.

"I'm surprised it hasn't happened already what with Minneapolis being the number one terrorist recruiting center in America."

"I just realized something," Max said. "If he's meeting Mackenzie…"

"She knows the two of us and may spot us. Bret, you stay with him. Use your radio to let us know where he goes," Anna added.

"Yes, ma'am," the young patrolman said and hurried off.

Max and Anna found a bench and sat down. Anna was looking down at her shoes.

"What's wrong?" Max asked.

"He just called me ma'am," she said. "How much does that suck?"

Max laughed and said, "Could be worse."

"Yeah, how?"

"I don't know. I'm just trying to say something to cheer you up."

Less than two minutes later, Anna's radio burped, and she answered it.

"He's in a restaurant sitting with a woman," Brett said.

"Describe her," Anna replied.

He did and when he finished Anna said to Max, "He's with Mackenzie."

"Tell him to stay with him."

Anna relayed that to Bret and he responded with, "Yes, ma'am."

"Bret, please don't call me that."

He hesitated for a couple of seconds then said, "Yes, ma'am," which caused her to cringe again.

"Hello, Cooper," Mackenzie pleasantly said as he sat down. "Are you all right?"

The waiter took their drink order before Cooper could reply. As the young man was walking away Cooper could reply. "I'm better now. I just don't deal well with the police."

"I don't understand," Mackenzie said. "What did they want?" As she said this she casually turned her head sideways to look out into the mall. Without looking directly at him, she spotted a young man, early twenties, seated alone on a bench. He was looking right at them and held what appeared to be a two-way radio. *Cop*, she thought.

"They claimed they were doing some follow-up on the investigation of Bill's death. But I don't think that's why they were there," Cooper said.

"Oh, why do you say that?"

"Because they asked me about perjury and affidavits. Mackenzie, they know," he whispered.

"Know what? I don't understand," she said.

"They know about the affidavit I wrote and signed, swearing Bill Sutherland came to me to write a new Will and you know nothing about it."

"I still don't understand," Mackenzie replied with an innocent look.

The waiter brought their drinks, a lemonade for Mackenzie and a vodka martini for Cooper. The waiter took their lunch order and left.

"Mackenzie," Cooper said as if speaking to a child. "Bill told me you were pressuring him to change his Will."

"He did? Cooper, I didn't know anything about it."

Cooper leaned back and with a puzzled, distraught look said, "He told me you were insisting on it because he had violated the terms of the prenup. The no infidelity clause."

"Bill told you that?"

"Yes," Cooper said leaning forward again. "I told you this. In fact, now that I think about it, you told me about it which is why he came to me and not his lawyer, Simon Kane."

Calmly, while sipping her drink, Mackenzie said, "Cooper, I don't remember doing any such thing. The first I knew anything about it was after Bill's heart attack and death. Since I really don't know anything about Bill changing his Will, how could you have perjured yourself by signing that affidavit?"

Cooper Thomas was actually a very smart man. Not necessarily street smart, but certainly no dummy. His problem was dealing with pressure. It took until Mackenzie made this last statement for it to finally sink in where she was going with her denials. Unless Mackenzie herself said otherwise it would be almost impossible to prove he committed perjury.

The waiter brought their meals, a salad for each of them, and they quietly ate for several minutes.

"Have you calmed down?" Mackenzie asked.

"Yes, you're right. I was mistaken you didn't know anything about Bill changing his Will. You had nothing to do with it."

They finished their lunch, during which Mackenzie noticed the young cop still watching. When they left the restaurant, she walked right past the young man. The radio was no longer visible, and he was doing a poor job of trying to casually ignore her.

Mackenzie headed toward Macy's and the west and parking lot. As she strolled along she suddenly stopped in front of a jewelry store to look in the window. While pretending to window shop she checked for the young man and saw him following Cooper.

Before arriving for this impromptu lunch date, Mackenzie wondered if Cooper would be wearing a wire. Since he told her the police had been at his office asking questions, she doubted he would be wired. He would not have told her about the two detectives. But she was almost certain the next time they met, he would be wearing one. Cooper Thomas, she knew, was simply too weak to stand up to the authorities.

What to do about Cooper? she wondered. Getting rid of him permanently was too risky and he did not really deserve it.

"But," she quietly said to herself as she opened her car door, "the next time I see him he'll be wearing that wire."

Max had called ahead and talked to Heather Anderson. He knew she was in her office and waiting for them so when he knocked he did not wait for her to answer. Instead the two detectives went right in.

"So, what happened?" Heather asked while the detectives sat down.

"I think Max may have guessed right," Anna said. "He went running scared right to her."

Max told her the entire story through following him out to the Mall of America and back to his office.

"He was lying to us," Max concluded. "We could see it in his eyes when we brought up the question about sworn affidavits and perjury. For a lawyer, he's a damn poor liar."

"So, your little fishing trip paid off," Heather said ignoring the insult about lawyers. "Why didn't one of you follow Mackenzie?"

"We couldn't," Anna said. "We were parked on the wrong end of the mall. The best we could've done was have Bret follow her back to her car. That would've been pointless."

"So far," Heather continued, "we have means and opportunity. We have the heart attack drug in William Sutherland's body. We have the searches for the drug done on his computer. We have statements from the Sutherland survivors that the old man's heart was fine. We'll get his medical records if we can show some probable cause for them."

"Why can't we get them now?" Anna asked.

"We don't have enough to take to a judge. Maybe, but it would have to be a very friendly judge," Heather said.

"Would be nice if we could connect her to the drug that killed him," Max said.

"Do we even have the M.E. willing to say it was the drug that did it?" Anna asked.

"He says if what the kids say about their dad's heart is true, then he can testify that it was the drug. But if he had a bad heart we would have a problem," Heather answered her. "We'll see what his medical records say."

"Even then, her lawyer will bring in his own expert to claim it wasn't the drug and try to create reasonable doubt," Max said.

"Yes, he will. That's why we need to nail down motive. Right now, motive is a little weak. We have no way to argue she was after his money. Plus, she has money of her own. If we can show this lawyer Cooper Thomas is lying and Mackenzie knew all along, or better still, had the old man change his Will, then we have a case to take to a grand jury."

"Pretty circumstantial," Anna said.

"There are a lot of people sitting in prison because of weaker circumstantial cases than this," Heather said. "Besides the media will salivate over this. They will turn her into a greedy, gold digging Black Window."

"What about the husband in Chicago? Can we get that into evidence?" Max asked.

"Not unless we can show he died the same way; a heart attack brought on by a drug somehow introduced into him," Heather said. "You might want to take a closer look at that, but…"

"His ashes are somewhere in Lake Michigan," Max said.

"Exactly," Heather agreed.

"Now what?" Anna asked.

"We need to get Cooper Thomas off his story. We need to find a way to get him to admit the Will being changed was at least known by Mackenzie. If we can get that then maybe we can come up with the reason for why the old man did it. Even without that we can at least show she lied about it."

There was a moment of silence among the three of them while they each thought about this situation. It was Max who spoke first.

"We investigate the life of Cooper Thomas," he said.

"Carefully," Heather interjected. "The courts take a dim view of investigating lawyers unless we have a good reason. I'm not sure we do, yet."

"This guy won't stand up to much direct scrutiny. We find a reason to bring him in and question him…" Anna began.

"…he'll fold like a cheap suit," Max finished the thought.

"But he'll bring a lawyer with him," Heather said. "He's smart enough to do that."

"He's at least vulnerable because of this school-boy crush he has on Mackenzie Sutherland. A divorce for a guy like that could get messy and very expensive," Max said

"It's a place to start," Anna said. "We find out what's going on at home. Find a weakness and exploit it."

"Are we sure about this?" Max asked.

"Sure, about what?" Heather said. "That Mackenzie Sutherland murdered her husband and probably another man in Chicago? Yes, I am."

"Okay," Max said. "Let's go get her."

THIRTY

When Mackenzie drove out of the parking ramp she turned right on Killebrew Drive, named for the Minnesota Twins Hall of Fame slugger. The Mall itself was situated on the exact same spot where the old Met Stadium stood. Hence the homage to one of the Twins' all-time favorite players.

Mackenzie took the ramp to Cedar Ave to get to I-494. Instead of going east back to St. Paul, she went west to go to Minneapolis. While she drove, she retrieved her phone from her purse and called Marc.

"I'm sorry, Mrs. Sutherland," Sandy said. "Marc is at lunch. Can I take a message?"

"When do you expect him back?"

"Anytime, now," Sandy told her.

"Do you think it would be okay if I dropped in? Is he available?"

"Yeah, he's open all afternoon. He was supposed to be in trial, but they settled it, Mrs. Sutherland."

"Please, Sandy, call me Mackenzie," she said while thinking, *I have to get that name change done.* "I'm in my car. I'll be there in about fifteen minutes. Would that be okay?"

"Sure, that shouldn't be a problem. He'll probably be back by then."

Sandy was wrong about Marc's return time. It was almost an hour before Marc along with Barry Cline and Chris Grafton returned. In the meantime, Mackenzie got to know the office staff.

Carolyn Lucas, the office manager and secretary, chatted with her quite a bit. Mackenzie was still in the news. In fact, she had been the main feature of the Channel 3 noon news. Even though there was nothing new to report, they reported it anyway.

"Hey," Marc said looking at Mackenzie when the three lawyers came into the office, "What's up? Why didn't you call?"

"I tried your phone; you didn't answer," she replied.

"Oh, yeah," Marc said. "That's because it's in my desk drawer."

"Nice job," Mackenzie said as she rose to greet him. "Must be nice to have a job where you can take a two-hour lunch if you feel like it."

"When's our turn?" Carolyn asked.

"Talk to the boss," Marc said pointing at Connie's office. "I barely work here. Come on in," Marc said to Mackenzie.

They went into Marc's office and he sat next to her in a client chair. Gently taking her hand he asked, "What's wrong? You look stressed."

Mackenzie took a deep breath and said, "I think the police are following me." She then went on to tell Marc most of the details about her lunch meeting with Cooper Thomas. Mackenzie was careful not to get into the part about whether or not she knew Bill Sutherland had changed his Will.

"So, you saw a guy you think was watching the two of you and he had a radio with him?"

"Yes, I'm certain he was watching us. He sat there the entire time. And he was still there when I left. I walked right past him. He pretended not to notice me, but when I walked a little way past I turned and saw him. He was walking in the same direction as Cooper and talking into his radio."

"You say he was a young man?"

"Yes, early twenties."

"A rookie. Not very good at surveillance. He was following Cooper when he left?"

"Yes."

"It was Cooper they were following. What the hell's the matter with him? If the cops came into my office asking questions about a client I'd throw them out in a heartbeat. He's a lawyer, tell him to act like one."

"Cooper's a good corporate and contract lawyer," Mackenzie said. "He's not the – how shall I put this – toughest man I've ever met."

"He's a weenie," Marc said.

"Well, yes, a bit," Mackenzie smiled.

Marc sat quietly thinking for a moment then said, "They're entitled to investigate. I can't do anything about it, yet. They are not entitled to harass you. If it comes to that, I can try to stop it.

"As for Cooper Thomas, you might want to call him up and tell him to grow a pair. He should use attorney-client privilege and tell them to pound sand."

"I'll do that," Mackenzie smiled. "Marc, let me take you to dinner tonight. I'll call and make a reservation for, what, seven?"

"Seven's fine. Put it in my name. We don't need some maitre'd picking up a few bucks by calling the media to get pictures of you. I'll pick you up at 6:45."

"Do you like sushi?" Mackenzie asked.

"I tried it once. Didn't care for it. Tasted too much like raw fish," Marc said.

"Too bad," Mackenzie said, "I want sushi. I'll make a reservation at a place downtown. The Akagi Sushi bar. You can try it again."

"Okay, but we may drive through a Burger King afterwards."

Upon returning home from Marc's office Mackenzie checked the burner phone she kept for private calls. There was a number showing as having called. It was a Chicago area code and she recognized the number.

The private investigator she was using called but did not leave a message. Mackenzie called the number back while wondering what he wanted.

"Mrs. Sutherland, thank you for calling back," Lou Travis said.

The use of her current married name by the man made her cringe and she flashed on the P.I. in Milwaukee. As calmly as she could, Mackenzie said, "Yes, Lou, what do you have for me?"

"First of all, Mrs. Sutherland, I have been following the news from Minnesota about your husband's death. I want you to know, no matter what, I'm in your corner. If there's anything I can do for you, do not hesitate to ask. I'm not sure what that could possibly be, but I wanted to let you know that."

"Well, thank you, Lou," A relieved Mackenzie said. "I appreciate that. Everything will be fine, don't worry. I'm innocent and that will protect me. There is one thing you can do."

"Name it," Travis said.

"Please call me Mackenzie. I've told you this before."

"Yes, ma'am," he laughed. "I'll try. Anyway, the reason I called. Phillip Cartwright was found in an alley next to a dumpster this morning. Dead from an apparent overdose of drugs, Probably heroin."

"Oh my god!" Mackenzie said, genuinely startled but not upset. "Are you sure?"

"Yeah, he was identified by his mother. I got word from a cop friend about an hour or so ago. The cause of death had not been definitely determined. But he was found with his pants down and a drug syringe sticking out of his thigh. Drug overdose is a pretty good guess."

"Yes, seems to be. How's Louise, his mother?"

"None of the ex-wives are doing well. Between you and me, they're a pretty useless bunch. I don't feel the least bit sorry for them. I'm sure they deserve everything they got."

"You have no idea," Mackenzie said. "Check on Louise for me now that her little angel has killed himself. I'll put a money order in the mail tomorrow. And thank you, Lou."

"You're welcome Mrs… sorry, Mackenzie. I'm not sure I'll get used to that. I'll wait a couple days, then check on Louise. Thank you, Mackenzie."

Mackenzie replaced the phone into her bag. She poured herself a glass of ice water while thinking about the news. *Rest in peace, Phillip, you worthless, despicable scum,* she thought with a knowing cunning smile.

"Stop stabbing it with your chopstick," Mackenzie laughed. "Do you want a fork?"

“No, that’s okay,” Marc said as he picked up the piece of raw salmon with his fingers and put it in his mouth. “See,” he said after swallowing it whole, “nothing to it.”

Mackenzie covered her mouth with her left hand to stifle a laugh. She shook her head and said, “I can’t take you anywhere.”

There was another couple, a few years younger, seated next to them. The man saw Marc eat the fish with his fingers then said, “So that’s how it’s done.” He then followed Marc’s example by plucking something whitish-pink from his plate and shoved it in.

“Don’t!” The woman he was with said trying to stop him. She looked at Mackenzie, Mackenzie looked back at her and Mackenzie said, “Is it too late to switch tables? Put these two Neanderthals together and we’ll enjoy the food.”

The four of them introduced themselves and for the next hour bantered back and forth while eating. The women were thoroughly enjoying it while Marc and the other man, Tom, did their best.

The bill came, and the waitress handed it to Marc. Mackenzie tried to snatch it away from him before he could read it.

“A hundred and sixty-five bucks for this? For raw fish? Are they serious?” Marc said.

“How much?” Tom asked.

“Give me that,” Mackenzie said as she took the bill from him. “Never mind,” Mackenzie said to the younger couple. “It’s worth every penny.”

She leaned forward and whispered to Marc, “Be a good boy and I’ll let you spend the night.”

Marc whispered back, “Do I want to spend the night? Does this stuff make you, you know, gassy?”

Mackenzie gave him a sneer and said, “You’re pushing your luck, buddy.”

The next morning, wearing a robe Mackenzie had bought for him, Marc brought in the St. Paul paper. Mackenzie was still upstairs in the bathroom while Marc sat at the kitchen island counter sipping coffee and reading the paper. He had the Sports section lying open in front of him when Mackenzie came in.

“Hi,” she sweetly said and kissed him on the cheek.

“Good morning,” Marc replied without moving his head to look at her.

“Anything in the paper?” she asked as she set down her cup of coffee and pulled up a chair opposite him.

“Twins won,” Marc said.

Mackenzie opened the local news section and on page three saw it. In the upper right-hand corner was a clear, one-eighth page photo of the two of them leaving the restaurant. Mackenzie's left arm was looped through Marc's right and they were adoringly looking at each other.

Mackenzie quickly read the caption and the short, three paragraphs that accompanied the picture. When she finished she looked across the island at Marc.

"What?" he asked when he noticed her.

"Oops," she said.

"What?"

She handed him the paper; he looked at the photo, read the story then looked back at Mackenzie and said, "Oops."

THIRTY-ONE

While Marc and Mackenzie were making plans for dinner, Anna and Max were making plans for Cooper Thomas.

"So where do we begin?" Anna asked.

Max and Anna were in Max's department issued Chevy. They had left Heather Anderson's office and were on their way back to police headquarters.

"First thing we do is identify this lawyer's weakness; his vulnerability," Max said.

"I know that," Anna said. "I meant where do you want to start digging through his life?"

"I'll drop you off. Find that kid, what's-his-name, that you wanted to cougar-up," Max said with a big grin.

Anna playfully punched him on the shoulder and said, "I did not want to 'cougar-up' to him as you put it. He's just, kind of, you know, a little hot is all," she sheepishly added. "Besides, how old do you think I am? I'm barely thirty."

"You're thirty-six which makes you biologically old enough to be his mother."

Anna slumped down, sighed and said, "Yeah, I know. It kind of sucks."

"No, it doesn't. I just turned forty. It's a great age. You're not a kid and you're not old. If I could, I'd stay this age forever. Besides, what would you do with him? Play video games?"

"I can play video games," Anna said.

"Twelve hours a day?"

"No, you're right. He is easy on the eyes, though," she added.

"I thought women didn't care about that. They're always claiming that men are superficial pigs and women care about the inner person."

"Oh, um, yeah that's true," Anna said rolling her eyes and looking away.

"Uh huh," Max smiled. "Anyway, find him and put him back in the parking ramp on the lawyer's car. You hang out outside. If he goes anywhere, you tail him and call me."

"Where are you going?"

"I know a guy, a hacker. I'll go see him and put him on Cooper Thomas. He can find out more online in a couple hours than we can find in a month."

"What's his name?"

"I can't share that, sorry. Not yet at least. He's very paranoid and..."

"Of course, he is. He's a tech guy. Have you ever met one that got along with humans?" Anna asked.

"Good point. Anyway, I'll drop you off. You find the kid…"

"Bret Jurgens."

"Whatever. I'll go see this guy while you two sit on the lawyer."

"How do you know this hacker?"

"An FBI guy I know put me on to him," Max said.

"Do the Feebs use him?" Anna asked.

"Off the books. At least a few of them do. What this guy does isn't strictly legal, but he cuts through a lot of BS and gets good information."

A half-hour after dropping Anna off at her car, Max parked in front of the same eighty-year-old house that Tony Carvelli had. Max was in South Minneapolis, definitely not in his jurisdiction.

Paul Baker, Pavel Bykowski, opened the door before Max had a chance to knock. Max went inside and took a seat on the cheap, worn, living room sofa.

"Paul, you really need to air this place out. It's making my eyes water. And if I get stopped by a cop I'll reek of dope and they'll make me piss in a cup."

"What can I do for you, Detective Max Cool?" Baker asked ignoring the critique and using Max's street name.

There was a beat-up coffee table in front of Max and Baker sat in a chair opposite his guest, the coffee table between them. Max took a piece of paper from his inside coat pocket and handed it to him.

Baker unfolded it, read the names and information listed on it and said, "So, we have Cooper and Bethany and their three adorable girls, Kristi, Sophie and Abby." He looked at Max and said, "Please tell me the 'Beaver Cleaver' family here isn't as boring as I imagine."

"Probably worse," Max said.

Baker went back to the paper and read the note Max had made. "He's a corporate lawyer, she's a Stepford Wife and the three girls will all run screaming from them to become doper-hookers as soon as they find out what a nightmare they're living."

"And I thought cops were cynical," Max said.

"What do you need?" Baker asked.

"Everything you can get on them."

"Do you have social security numbers?"

"No."

"Okay. I'll get them from somewhere else. I'll need them to get at his tax records."

"Do what you gotta do," Max said. "The main focus is him. Everything you can get about the wife too, but mainly him."

"I'll need some money."

"How much?"

"Five," Baker said.

"No problem," Max said. He pulled out his wallet, took out a five-dollar bill and held it out to him.

"Ha, ha. Very funny. Five hundred."

"Two hundred," Max said.

"Five," Baker repeated.

"Three."

"Five. I have to eat," Baker said. "Be thankful you're not the Feds. I get a grand from them."

"Hang on," Max said. He pulled out his phone and dialed a number. It was answered immediately.

"Hey, Heather. I got a guy here who can cut to the chase and get us all the information we need on that guy we're checking on."

"Do I want to know how?" Heather said.

"No. He needs five hundred bucks. Can you get it?"

Heather went silent for a moment thinking it over then said, "Yeah, I'll get it. Can you pay him, and I'll reimburse you?"

"Okay, will do. Thanks." Max pulled two one hundred-dollar bills from his wallet and set them on the coffee table. "Get going. I'll find a TCF ATM and be back with the rest. How long will it take?"

"How soon do you want it?"

"An hour ago," Max said.

Baker shrugged and said, "As boring as the people sound, it shouldn't take more than a couple hours. That is unless he's in the CIA or something."

"No, nothing like that," Max said. "What you see is what you get. Get going and I'll be back."

Less than two hours later, Max slid into the passenger seat of Anna's car. They were parked on the street across from the parking ramp Cooper used. In Max's hand was a large, manila envelope with the printouts of what Paul Baker had come up with on the Thomas family.

Max looked at his watch and said, "Almost five. Let's hope he's not one of these workaholics who stay until nine every night. Is the kid still on station?"

"Yeah, he is," Anna said. She then used her handheld radio to check with Bret. He was still there and sounded as excited as a puppy as well.

"What did your guy come up with?" Anna asked. "Did you read it all?"

"No, I just scanned it over then came here," Max answered as he removed the pages.

For the next twenty minutes the two detectives read through the life of Cooper Thomas and his family. Max would read each document first then pass it to Anna.

"These people are so boring they make watching paint dry sound like a good time," Max remarked when he finished.

"Makes a damn good living," Anna said looking over his tax returns for the past three years.

"No kidding. Six hundred and fifty grand a year. I could get by on that," Max agreed.

Anna's radio beeped then they heard Bret say, "He's almost at his car. Probably leaving for the day."

"Roger that," Anna said. "We'll pick him up when he comes out. You can take off. We'll stay with him."

"Are you sure? I'll be happy to help out," the young cop volunteered.

"It's okay. He's probably headed home. We'll take it. Thanks," Anna said.

While this conversation took place, Max gathered up the documents and placed them back in the envelope. He got out of Anna's car and made it back to his sedan just as Cooper Thomas drove out of the parking ramp. It was a one-way street, so he had to drive past them as he left.

Alternating positions and keeping cars between themselves and Cooper, they followed him home. By the direction he was heading, it was obvious where he was going. The detectives had his address but had never been to the house itself.

Cooper had a home in Sunfish Lake, a very upscale suburb southeast of St. Paul. With a population of less than five hundred and fifty people, Sunfish Lake is one of the wealthiest communities in America. When they arrived, Anna got into the car with Max and hoped they looked inconspicuous.

"We're sticking out like a sore thumb in this neighborhood," Anna said.

"What do you figure that place costs?" Max asked. "Gotta be at least a million."

"A million five," Anna said. "Three and a half acres, two hundred feet of shoreline. It was in the papers. Didn't you see it?"

"I must have missed it," Max said.

Max looked at his watch and said, "What do you think the over/under is for how long till a cop shows up wanting to know why a black man and a white woman are sitting here?"

Anna laughed then said, "Five, six minutes maybe. Just for laughs, let's find out."

It was a beautiful, sunny, late-afternoon day. They were parked under two large oak trees and believed they were sheltered from the houses scattered around the area. Despite being as unobtrusive as possible, Anna's guess was off by barely fifteen minutes.

"Here we go," Max said with a smile as he looked in his rearview mirror. Anna's car was behind them and Max saw the roof lights of the car that pulled up behind her. The sheriff's deputy turned on the lights as he got out of his car to walk toward them, his hand on the butt of his handgun.

"Good afternoon, Deputy," Max politely said through the open window. He smiled at the Dakota County deputy sheriff and handed the younger man his shield and credentials. The deputy carefully scrutinized Max's then looked over Anna's while Max held them up for him.

"What are you doing here?" he asked.

"We're on the job," Max said smiling.

"Yeah, but what are you doing here?" he repeated.

"We're on the job," Max said more seriously, the smile gone. "If you have a problem with that have your boss call the Ramsey County Attorney."

"Max," Anna said bringing his attention to the Thomas' driveway. Cooper Thomas, with his wife and three daughters, was driving away in his wife's Mercedes Benz S550 SUV. Fortunately, Cooper paid no attention to the scene on the street. Instead, he turned right, away from Max, Anna and the deputy.

"Gotta go," Max said as he snatched his shield away from the deputy.

"Hold on," he tried to command them. "I want to know…."

Anna leaned over the front seat and snarled, "If you blew our cover, I'm gonna have your balls. Now beat it." Anna got out and hurried back to her car as Max pulled away to go after the Mercedes.

For the next hour they continued to follow the Thomas family. What they hoped to find neither detective could explain. First, they went to a local Perkins restaurant for dinner. When they finished there, the detectives followed the family to a very nice, obviously successful, Lutheran Church.

Max and Anna parked in the street alongside the church. After the Thomas' went inside, Max walked over to Anna and leaned down to talk to her.

"Following this guy around us pointless. He's not going anywhere or doing anything. Besides, I think I know how to go at him."

"And I have a date," Anna said.

"Don't tell me," Max said. "You're not really going to cougar that kid."

"It's just a little dinner thing," she sheepishly answered. "Besides, I'm not that old and he's not that young."

"If he asks you to go into a liquor store and buy him some beer, you better get out of there," Max laughed.

"Very funny."

"I'll see you tomorrow. Don't wear the kid out. We may need to use him some more."

THIRTY-TWO

"Good morning," Max said to Anna as she dropped her purse on her desk. When they became partners, Anna moved her things to the desk opposite Max's.

"Don't say a word, I don't want to hear it," she admonished him.

"Relax," Max smiled. "I wasn't going to."

"Good!" she severely said. Then more softly, she added, "So, where are we?"

"I called Heather at home last night while you were out trying to commit child abuse…"

"I'm warning you!"

"How did it go?" Max politely asked, quietly laughing.

"I don't see it happening again. He's pretty and a really nice guy, but we have nothing in common," she admitted. "What did Heather have to say?"

"We're to meet with her at ten o'clock. Here, I made a copy of everything we have on Cooper Thomas and family," Max said as he tossed an envelope over to her. "I made a copy for Heather, too."

"When are you going to tell me who this guy is, the guy who came up with this stuff?"

"We'll see," Max shrugged. "Trust me, it's not you, it's him. He doesn't play well with humans."

Max and Anna patiently waited while Heather Anderson read through the documents. Half-way through, without averting her eyes from the papers, she asked, "How did you get all of this so quickly or don't I want to know?"

"You don't want to know," Max said.

Heather looked at him over her glasses in a disapproving way and frowned.

She continued reading and a couple minutes later said, "Holy shit! Look at this house!"

"The photo doesn't do it justice. It's even nicer than that," Anna said.

"I have to get into private practice," Heather said looking up for a moment. "I have a two-bedroom, one bath condo I can barely afford."

"Yeah but look at how much fun it is to put assholes in prison," Max said.

"That almost makes up for it," Heather agreed while going back to the documents.

Ten minutes later she finished reading and placed the paperwork and her glasses on her desk. She looked at Max and said, "You're right.

I think I'll stay where I am; putting assholes in prison. Compared to these two," she continued tapping the documents with her index finger, "I lead a wild life.

"How do we go at him?" Heather asked.

"It's right there," Max said pointing at the papers. "It's his life, his lifestyle."

"How long do you think he'll hold out if we threaten to take it away from him?" Anna asked.

Heather thought about it for a moment then said, "Not long. But we don't have much leverage. We believe he falsified that affidavit about Mackenzie not knowing about the old man changing his Will. What if we're wrong? What if we confront him with it and he sticks to his story because it's true?"

"Nothing ventured, nothing gained," Max said.

"Bullshit!" Heather said. "It could be our collective butts if we aren't careful. This guy is an officer of the court, a lawyer in good standing and a partner in a prestigious firm. What we're trying to do is coerce him into breaking client confidentiality by threatening him, probably with prison time. If he gets a lawyer and tells us to shove it, we could be looking for jobs."

"Well sure, if you're gonna be negative and focus on just the dark side of things. But what could really be bad?" Anna said trying to lighten the mood.

Max and Heather both laughed a little then Max said, "I saw the look on his face when Anna asked him about perjury and affidavits."

"He did it," Anna interjected. "He lied when he signed it and he knows we know. His vanilla-bland, boring suburban life will look like a dream if he sees the image of himself picking up a bar of soap in a prison shower."

"Ah, what the hell," Heather said. "What's the worst that could happen?"

"We all end up standing on a street corner holding 'Will work for food' signs," Max said.

"See," Heather said, "We're worrying about nothing. How do you want to handle it?"

"We pick him up and bring him in for questioning," Max said.

"And if he doesn't want to come?"

"We arrest him for suspicion of conspiracy to commit fraud," Anna said.

Heather thought it over then said, "Okay, but pick him up on the street. Do not drag him out of his office. The place is full of lawyers. Catch him when he's alone, tomorrow morning when he arrives for work."

"We'll get him in the ramp. He has a reserved spot where he parks every day," Anna said.

"That way we'll have him all day, too," Max said.

"What if he asks for a lawyer?" Anna asked.

"Tell him we'll deal with that when you get to the department. Bring him there. That will scare him some more. Do not give him Miranda. Wait until we want to talk to him. I'll be at the police department waiting. Don't ask him anything. Tell him his questions will all be answered."

"He may ask for a lawyer, but I doubt it. I bet he doesn't say a word. He'll know why we picked him up and he'll be scared shitless," Anna said.

"Let's hope so," Heather answered her.

"Here he comes," Anna said, "right on time." Max and Anna were parked in the ramp three spaces away from Cooper's reserved spot. They had arrived before 7:30 expecting the anally punctual lawyer to show up just before 8:00.

Cooper parked his Mercedes and as he walked away, he pressed the car's key fob to lock the doors. As he did this, Max got out of Anna's car while she started the engine. They were parked between Cooper's spot and the elevators, so Cooper had to walk right up to them. When Max was roughly fifteen feet from him, Cooper recognized the detective and stopped walking; the color draining from his face.

"Mr. Thomas," Max said when he reached the spot where Cooper stood. Max opened his leather pouch and held up his shield. "We need you to come to the police department with us."

By this time Anna had pulled the car next to them and got out. She walked around the front of it to stand next to the obviously distraught Cooper Thomas. Max Coolidge, being the veteran that he was, could intimidate just about anyone without trying. Anna half expected Cooper's knees to buckle.

"Um, sorry, no," he managed to say. "I'm busy today. It will have to wait."

"Sorry," Max deadpanned, "we're doing this now."

Finding a little more testosterone Cooper said, "Am I under arrest?"

"No, not yet," Anna said emphasizing the word, yet. "But we will arrest you if necessary."

"We'd like you to come along and answer a few questions, voluntarily," Max said still staring directly into Cooper's eyes.

"Um, ah, okay," Cooper said looking back and forth at the two cops. "Can I, ah, call my office first?"

"We'll take care of that on the way to the department," Max said as he opened the backseat passenger door for him.

Cooper climbed in and Max followed him into the backseat. Anna got back behind the wheel. Fifteen minutes later they walked into the main department building northeast of downtown St. Paul.

"Have a seat, Mr. Thomas," Anna said pointing to one of the cheap, gray, padded metal government issued chairs.

They had taken him into one of the interrogation rooms; a room Cooper Thomas had never been in and in his worst nightmare never believed he would see. It was a 12 x 18 rectangle with one window with bars over it. The walls were gray painted cinderblock, stark and cold. In the middle of the room was a 3 x 8 feet table with a half-dozen cheap, government chairs around it exactly like the one Cooper was sitting on. To Cooper's left was a one-way mirror used to allow observers to see in and watch the proceedings. The piece of final stark décor was a cell in front of which Cooper had been intentionally seated so he had to look directly at it. It was a holding cell. It consisted of a totally empty space surrounded on three sides by steel bars with a small door. It was attached to the wall providing a graphic picture of what this place really is: a jail. Since sitting down, he had not taken his eyes off of it.

"You relax for a minute. We'll be right back," Max politely told him. "Can we get you anything? A cup of coffee, maybe?"

"No, um, thanks," Cooper croaked. He was still staring at the holding cell, his arms wrapped around the briefcase he had with him holding it on his lap against his chest.

Without another word, Max and Anna walked out and went into the observation room. Heather Anderson was watching Cooper through the mirror.

"I hope he doesn't wet himself," she said. "This is almost cruel."

"He'll be fine," Max assured her. "He needs a good look at what he might be facing," Max continued referring to the cell.

"Besides," Anna said, "I'm close to one hundred percent sure he did it. He's covering for her."

"Why do you think that?" Heather asked.

"He hasn't asked us one word about why he's here," Max said.

"He knows," Anna added.

The three of them stood silently watching Cooper for two more minutes; a long time when you're sitting alone in an interrogation room at a police station. Cooper actually calmed a bit. His breathing looked to be normal. He put the briefcase on the floor and mopped his brow with a handkerchief.

The three of them entered the room and Heather introduced herself to him.

"Did you give him his Miranda warning?" Heather asked.

"Not yet. We haven't asked him anything," Max said.

"Do it now, please," Heather pleasantly asked Max.

When Max finished reading from the laminated card he carried, Heather removed a single sheet of paper from the soft leather bag she had placed on the table. She had taken the chair opposite Cooper while Max and Anna leaned on the wall behind him.

"This is a document I need you to sign," Heather said smiling as she slid the paper with a pen over to Cooper. "It merely acknowledges that you were read your rights before you were asked any questions."

Cooper looked it over doing his best to act like a lawyer who knew all about these things. He picked up the pen, scrawled his signature where indicated then said, "I think I want a lawyer."

"You think you do but you're not sure?" Heather asked.

"I'm sure," he said. "I want to call a lawyer."

"Would you like to call someone from your firm?" Heather asked.

"Oh, god, no!" Cooper almost yelled.

Perfect answer, Heather thought. *He doesn't want them to know about this.*

"Look," Heather softly said putting the pen and signed acknowledgement into her briefcase. "Before you get a lawyer and turn this adversarial, let me explain some things. You can always get a lawyer at any time. Do you understand that? Hear me out then you can decide if you want to bring a lawyer into this. Okay?"

"All right," Cooper said relaxing a bit.

"Good. First of all, it's not you we're after and I think you know that, unless you are a co-conspirator in the murder of William Sutherland."

"Of course not!" Cooper yelled.

Heather ignored his outburst then said, "We are absolutely certain that Mackenzie Sutherland murdered her husband, William Sutherland."

Cooper started to protest again then stopped when Heather held up a hand to him.

"Please just listen. We believe she murdered the old man and his son, Robert and her prior husband when she lived in Chicago, a man named Wendell Cartwright. Don't bother to protest," she said when Cooper started to again.

"We are going to convict her. I believe we have enough evidence already, but we can always use more. The question for you is: are you so in love with her that you're willing to go down with her?"

By this point, Max had quietly moved around and was leaning on the cell bars. He wanted to be in position to see Cooper's reaction.

"I, ah, don't know what you're talking about," Cooper stammered unconvincingly.

"Please," Heather said with a sly smile. "Please don't insult our intelligence. She murdered old man Sutherland and the husband in Chicago for their money. I'll admit we can't prove the murder of the husband from Chicago. We will get her for William Sutherland and she set up Bob Sutherland and murdered him, too. The woman is a serial killer and you could be found to be an accomplice. You committed perjury when you submitted an affidavit in which you swore you changed William Sutherland's Will leaving everything to Mackenzie and she didn't know about it. According to the medical examiner, the timeline for it is perfect," Heather lied. "You changed the Will and she started to poison him shortly after. We know it and we'll prove it. Now is your one and only chance to get ahead of this and help yourself."

"Did she promise you that you would be together once things settled down?" Max asked him.

After a full minute had passed, a completely defeated Cooper Thomas whispered, "Yes."

A heavy silence filled the room as Heather and Max continued to stare at him, shocked by the admission. Anna took the chair at the head of the table to Cooper's right, folded her hands on the tabletop and added her unblinking look.

"I'm not going to play games with you," Heather said breaking the silence. "If you want to get a lawyer all bets are off and we come after you right along with her. You'll be charged as a co-conspirator."

"You're asking me to..." he said then paused.

"...break a client's confidence," Heather finished for him. "Here's the deal," Heather continued. "You cooperate and come clean, we grant you immunity and don't prosecute you for perjury and conspiracy. Maybe you get to keep your nice home on the lake, the country club, your partnership and your family. Don't cooperate and I guarantee you'll lose it all."

"You can't prove..." Cooper started to say.

"Really? Why didn't William Sutherland go to his own lawyer, Simon Kane? Why you? Because you were Mackenzie's lawyer, that's why. You didn't think we'd notice this? Don't underestimate us. You are so far over your head you can't see up."

Heather placed her right elbow on the table, raised her right hand and with her thumb pointed over her shoulder at the holding cell. "How's that looking to you right about now? Think about losing everything you have then spending the next thirty years in one. We're going to step out now and let you think about what you want to do with the rest of your life."

Heather and Anna stood up and Max went to the door. Before she walked away from the table, Heather placed both hands on it and leaned over to look directly at Cooper.

"In case you haven't figured it out yet, Mackenzie Sutherland is playing you for a fool."

THIRTY-THREE

Heather went through the door first followed by Anna then Max. By the time Max closed the door behind them Heather was bent over leaning against the opposite wall taking deep breaths.

"What's wrong? Are you okay?" Anna whispered.

Heather straightened up, looked at the two detectives and said, "We are on very thin ice here. If he goes for a lawyer, we're screwed, trying to coerce a lawyer to break the attorney-client privilege. I'll be lucky if I only get suspended."

Max smiled and said, "Relax. It'll be all right. He just admitted we're right when he said we're trying to get him to break a client's confidence." He then went into the observation room to watch Cooper.

"He'll go," Anna said. "You'll see. I can smell the fear and it's because we're right; he did commit perjury when he signed that affidavit."

"I hope you're right," Heather quietly said. "Well, we're up to our ass in alligators now. Might as well finish draining the swamp."

"Atta girl," Anna said. "Let's go watch. Oh, and you were really good in there. You had me convinced we can prove he did it."

The three of them stood silently behind the mirror watching the lawyer. He was obviously nervous. At one point he took out his phone and stared at it.

"Did he call his office to tell them he'd be delayed?" Heather asked.

"In the car on the way here," Max said.

"If he makes a call, it will be to a lawyer," Heather said.

Cooper held the phone in his hand trying to decide what to do. He turned his head to look at his side of the mirror probably realizing he was being watched. A minute or so after he took it from his coat pocket he put the phone back where it came from.

"He's ready, let's go," Max said.

"I want some assurance that you will help me with the Office of Professional Responsibility," was the first thing Cooper said to Heather even before she sat down.

"Absolutely," Heather quickly said. "Whatever I can do, I will. In fact, I'm willing to tell them your conscience got the better of you and you came forward voluntarily." Heather said this knowing it was probably a lie and would not help him anyway. The only promise she could keep would be not to prosecute him criminally. Whatever problems Cooper was going to have with the OPR, and they would be numerous and severe, were going to be his problems to deal with. Later, when she had taken the time to think about it, Heather would be mildly amused at how little she cared what would happen to Mackenzie's fallen lawyer.

"Here's the deal," Heather began as she took a legal pad and pen from her briefcase.

"I should still have a lawyer," Cooper said.

"It's up to you. Look, you can trust me, Cooper. It's not you we want. Mackenzie Sutherland is a cold, calculating, serial killer. She has to be stopped. You are being given complete immunity from prosecution for anything related to your representation of her and the crimes she has committed."

Heather pulled a sheet of paper from her briefcase and continued. "In fact, I'll write it up now." Which she did.

Cooper read over the grant of immunity and signed it. Heather assured him he would get a copy of it.

"The immunity is contingent on a couple of things. First, you will be one hundred percent cooperative. That includes testifying in front of the grand jury and at trial and anywhere else that becomes necessary. Second, and most importantly, you will be totally forthcoming, honest and truthful. Any lying or keeping things from us and the deal's off. Okay?"

"Okay," Cooper agreed. "I'll wait with the lawyer for now. The fewer people who know about this, the better."

"We're going to hear you out and go over your story. Then we'll do it a second time and videotape it.

"Tell us about William Sutherland's Will. Were you the one that drafted his Will approximately four months before his death?"

"Yes," Cooper began. "Mackenzie came to me about a month before this and told me she was thinking about a divorce. She said they barely spoke to each other and had no sexual relations for over a year. But she said he had violated the terms of their prenuptial agreement through numerous infidelities."

"They had a prenup?" Heather asked. He looked back and forth at Anna and Max and asked, "Why am I just now hearing about this?"

"No one knew," Cooper interjected. "They kept it secret."

"How do you know that?" Heather asked.

"I was Mackenzie's lawyer when it was written. They both wanted it. Mackenzie had a lot of money of her own before she married Bill. More than Bill had. In the event of a divorce, she had more to protect than he did."

"I'm not sure that's true," Heather said. "I don't know a lot about family law, but I do know her money would be considered pre-marital."

"True," Cooper agreed. "But that alone doesn't always protect it in a divorce. Especially if some of it gets commingled."

"Okay, tell us about the prenup," Heather said.

"Basically, it spelled out that in the event of a divorce, they shake hands and walk away. Whatever additional assets either of them acquired during the marriage would be considered the sole and exclusive property of the one who accumulated it. Unless..."

"One of them committed adultery," Heather said.

"Right. Mackenzie insisted on that clause because..."

"Bill Sutherland was a notorious womanizer," Max said finishing the thought.

"Exactly," Cooper said. "And Mackenzie had plenty of proof he had not been faithful."

"What happens if one of them cheats and they divorce?" Anna asked.

"The cheater, Bill, pays Mackenzie five million dollars."

"How much money did Mackenzie have before the marriage?" Heather asked.

"I don't know, exactly. At least forty million. I never saw her complete financials," Cooper shrugged.

"Don't they have to disclose this in the prenup?" Heather asked.

"Yeah, but they each signed an amendment to it that stated they both had received complete financials from each other and were satisfied that everything had been fully disclosed."

"Wait a minute, if Bill has to pay her five million in a divorce and she pays him nothing, isn't that more of a motive for Bill to kill her?" Max asked.

"Except, when she came to me about writing a new Will, she claimed they had decided to go to marriage counseling to save the marriage. This was Bill's idea. Bill even told me this. But Mackenzie used that as leverage to get him to change the Will. They also had me draft a postnuptial agreement voiding the prenup. In the event of a divorce, they walk away no matter if anyone cheats."

"Why didn't Bill get the divorce after that?" Heather asked.

"Bill was serious about saving the marriage," Cooper shrugged again. "He wasn't getting any younger. He had a young, beautiful wife and he realized he might not have another chance."

"Little did he know," Anna said.

"Did Mackenzie say anything to you about poisoning Bill?" Max asked.

"Of course not!" Cooper said. "I still don't believe she did it."

"Let me get this straight," Heather said. "William Southland changed his Will and cut out his kids to save his marriage. Is that what happened?"

"Bill hated his kids. They were a huge disappointment to him. Bob was an okay grocery store manager, the other two were worthless."

"Over the years," Max said, "there has been talk of the family having to bail Adam out of some legal scrapes. I never knew what because I always steered clear of it because of my personal relationship with the family. I heard a couple may have been pretty serious, prison time serious."

"Tell us about Bob's death. Did Mackenzie set him up?" Heather asked.

"No," Cooper shook his head. "At least not that I'm aware of. What I told you before about the kids hating her and Bob threatening her in my office was true. I believe her when she said he came at her with the fireplace poker."

"Let's get back to William's death. Whose idea was it to falsify the affidavit you signed claiming she knew nothing about the Will being changed?" Heather asked.

"Hers," Cooper reluctantly admitted. "She kind of hinted around about it and I understood what she wanted. So, I wrote it and signed it."

"Why?"

"Because you people were starting to investigate. You wanted to exhume the body. She insisted she had done nothing wrong, but you wouldn't believe her. You would want to use the new Will as motive."

"Which it obviously is," Anna said.

"Anything else?" Heather asked Max and Anna.

"No, that about covers it, for now. Let's go talk in the hall," Max said.

The three of them went back into the hallway and Max asked, "Do we have enough?"

"Certainly for an indictment. We can get old man Sutherland's medical records and find out about his heart. Did he have a heart condition? It would be nice if we could figure out how she got the drug that killed him," Heather said.

"What about the searches for it that were done on the old man's computer at home?" Anna asked.

"Good, circumstantial evidence and probably enough combined with everything else," Heather said.

"We'll keep digging," Max said. "He," Max continued referring to Cooper, "is gonna wear a wire and try to get her to admit something."

"She's too smart," Anna said.

"It's worth a shot," Heather interjected. "We'll make him do it. I can hold off on going to the grand jury. They don't meet again for a week anyway. Set up the wire for this week yet."

They went back into the interrogation room. While Anna called for a videographer to videotape Cooper's story Heather told him about the wire.

"I can't do that to her," he said emphatically shaking his head.

Max leaned forward, he was now sitting in a chair right next to Cooper and glared at him. He stayed this way intimidating Cooper until Cooper quietly asked, "What?"

"Get it through your head," Max patiently told him. "Your little fantasy about running off to romp on the beach and live happily ever after with Mackenzie Sutherland is over. It was never going to happen anyway."

"And if it did," Heather said, "you would likely be her next victim."

"I know," Cooper quietly agreed. "I just hate to…"

"Tough shit," Max said still staring at him. "We own you now. Until this thing is done you will do what we say."

"That's part of the 'you will cooperate' deal you made to stay out of prison," Heather reminded him.

"You're right," Cooper reluctantly agreed.

THIRTY-FOUR

"How long before we get a copy of the disk?" Heather asked the video tech. They had finished taping Cooper's statement and the man was gathering up his equipment.

"You in a hurry?" he asked.

"Yes," Heather answered, a touch of irritation in her voice.

"Give me a couple of hours," he indifferently answered. He knew he could have it done in thirty minutes or less but did not like being bossed around. "I'll see what I can do."

Max saw what was happening and when the video tech left, Max excused himself to follow him.

"Hey, my man," Max called out to the techie when he got into the hall. The techie turned around and Max hurried up to him.

"Hey," Max said to him when he caught up with him. "Sorry about that. She can be a bit of a ball buster." Max pulled a twenty-dollar bill from his pocket and handed it to him. "This is a murder investigation and we need the disk as soon as possible."

The techie looked around the hallway, took the bill and put it in his pocket.

"Give me an hour," he said.

Forty-five minutes later the four of them, including Cooper Thomas, were back in the interrogation room viewing the disk. When it was finished the two cops and Heather looked at Cooper.

"Is this an accurate portrayal of your statement?" Heather asked Cooper. "Is there anything you would like to add, delete or change?"

"No," Cooper said after thinking for a moment. "I think it's okay. You know," he continued, "it's almost a relief to have it over with. Now what?"

"Now you wear a wire and get Mackenzie Sutherland to verify your story," Max said.

"Is that really necessary? I hate the thought of doing that to her," Cooper said.

Anna was seated on Cooper's right, leaned over and said, "The deal is you cooperate. Remember? Figure it out Cooper. You're not going to run off and live happily ever after with Mackenzie. How many times do you have to be told this?"

"Cooper," Heather gently said. "It never was going to happen."

"I know," he sadly said. "I just, well, I know her a lot better than any of you and I don't believe she murdered Bill Sutherland and..."

"She did and we're going to prove it," Heather said. "Save yourself. Besides, you're already in too deep."

Heather turned to look at Max and asked, "The wire, when do we want to do it?"

"No time like the present," Max said.

"Don't you have enough to take to the grand jury now?" Cooper asked a little desperation in his voice.

"If we get an indictment before we get her on tape, she'll never do it. We have to go at her first," Heather said.

"Call her," Max said. "Use your phone and give her a call right now. Tell her we came to see you again and you're worried."

"You want to come to her house and meet with her. No restaurant this time," Anna said.

"Why? Wouldn't a public place be better?" Cooper asked.

"Too many people, too much background noise. With our equipment, if you are in a quiet environment, we can pick you up and record you up to a half a mile, easily," Anna said.

"When do you want to do this?" Cooper nervously asked while holding his phone.

"Right now. We can have you wired in a half-hour and be set up by the time you get there," Max answered him.

"Okay, I'll call her. But I still don't believe she had anything to do with Bill's death."

"Wait a minute," Heather stepped in and said. "Let's be clear. We're not looking to get her to admit to the murder. That would be nice, but it won't happen. We just need her to admit she knew about the Will being changed."

"Should we even have him bring the murder up?" Anna asked.

"I don't know," Max said. He looked at Cooper and said, "Play it by ear. Bring it up if it seems like an appropriate thing to do."

"Okay," Cooper quietly agreed. "God I hate this."

Less than an hour later, Mackenzie heard Cooper ringing the front door of the Crocus Hill house. Mackenzie agreed to see him when he called. In fact, she pretended to be somewhat eager to do so. Barely ten seconds into the conversation Mackenzie, through her phone, heard a chair scrape on a floor. This made her realize, or at least believe, Cooper had his phone on speaker. At least one other person and probably more, were listening in.

Cooper told her the police had been to see him again and make him quite anxious. For the benefit of the listening audience Mackenzie seemed totally baffled as to why they would bother Cooper and had no idea what they hoped to find.

When the conversation was done, and Mackenzie invited Cooper to come to the house she took a minute to think about it. Should she call

Marc Kadella? Absolutely convinced Cooper would be wearing a listening device, Mackenzie decided to leave Marc out of it. Instead, she would handle it herself and hopefully convince them she had nothing to do with William's death. Having her lawyer attend would just make her look guilty.

"Hello, dear," Mackenzie said when she opened the door. She offered a cheek for Cooper to kiss then led him into the living room.

"Can I fix you a drink?" she asked.

"Sure, scotch on the rocks," Cooper said.

Less than a block away, fifty feet past the corner of the street Mackenzie's house was on and across the street was a plain-looking Ford van. It was facing in the direction of Mackenzie's house and inside were Max, Anna and a sound tech. Each of them wore a headset and could clearly hear the conversation while it was being recorded.

"No, you idiot!" Max said. "No alcohol. We should've thought of that."

"Too late now," Anna said.

"Here you are," they heard Mackenzie say when she handed Cooper his drink. "Why are the police bothering you? I don't understand."

"They believe you not only knew about Bill changing his Will, but it was your idea," Cooper said. Obviously nervous, he took a large swallow of the scotch emptying the glass.

"Let me refill that for you," Mackenzie said.

When she returned with the drink, while the two of them sat on one of the couches, the trio in the van listened with decreasing hope. For the next half-hour, and a third scotch, Cooper tried his best to get some, even vague, admission from her. Instead, Mackenzie, acting like the blonde in dumb-blonde jokes, parried every attempt by Cooper. She steadfastly avoided any knowledge of anything. By the time she was done, Cooper was starting to wonder if he was wrong about the Will and it was Bill Sutherland's idea.

"She knows," Max quietly said. "She knows he's wired."

"Or at least believes he is," Anna said.

"Or she's innocent," the tech added.

Anna and Max looked at each other then the tech and simultaneously said, "No."

Cooper finished his third scotch in less than forty minutes. He was already starting to feel a pretty good buzz. Still sober enough to realize Mackenzie was not going to bite, he decided to give it up.

The two of them sat on the couch chatting for a few more minutes. Mostly Cooper trying to find a way, through his alcohol addled fog, to casually bring up the Will again. He finally gave up, looked at his watch and announced he had to leave. Mackenzie took his arm and walked him to the door. She lightly kissed his cheek then decided to give the cops one last shot.

"What's driving me crazy is this drug they found in Bill. The cancer drug they say caused his heart attack. I've been wracking my brain trying to figure that out; where it came from and how it got into his system," she said directly into Cooper's chest where she believed the microphone was.

"Huh," Cooper said. "I don't know. If I think of anything, I'll let you know."

"Oh, please do!" Mackenzie said. "It's been driving me crazy."

Mackenzie stood off to the side of the window facing her driveway. She watched Cooper get in his car, back out onto the street and drive off. Satisfied he was gone, she went into William's den and sat at his walnut desk. For the next fifteen minutes, as best as she could from memory, she wrote a verbatim transcript of the entire conversation.

The trio in the van heard them say good-bye and the door close behind Cooper. Anna and Max removed their headphones and Max disgustedly tossed his on the floor.

"That last bit – about the drug – that was a nice touch," Anna admitted.

"Get us a copy, Arnie," Max said to the tech.

"Just one?"

"Yeah, one's enough of this little drama. Let's go," Max said to Anna.

Max had been pacing up and down the hallway for over thirty minutes. He was on the seventeenth floor of the Ramsey County Courthouse in St. Paul. Occasionally he would take a seat on one of the benches, but it would rarely last a full minute. Then he would be up and pacing again, almost twenty years as a cop and never this nervous about an arrest or indictment. Every time he walked past the courtroom door he would slow down and look at it.

By now there were several lawyers hanging around, prosecutors waiting to present a case, defense lawyers hanging around for news on behalf of a client. Max knew most of them, including the defense lawyers. Even in a large metropolitan area the criminal bar was relatively small.

Cooper Thomas had been called about a half hour ago. He was the final witness to present. Max himself had testified and it was through him and the M.E. that most of the evidence was submitted.

Just as Max had reached the far point of his pacing the door opened, and Cooper came out. Max stopped and waited for Cooper to come to him.

"Well," Max asked.

"Went fine," Cooper said. He had the look of someone who had done something unpleasant and was glad it was over.

"Did the jurors ask you anything?"

"A couple did. Minor stuff just to clear up something," Cooper told him. "Can I take off?"

"I don't know. I guess so. Did Heather tell you anything different?"

"No," Cooper said.

"Then I guess you can go." Max said. "Oh and Mr. Thomas, thank you. I mean that."

Cooper turned back to him and angrily whispered, "I still don't believe she did it."

"We'll be in touch," Max quietly said.

Max watched Cooper walk to the elevators and after he was gone, turned back toward the courtroom doors. As he did so, Heather Anderson came out, saw Max and headed right for him.

"Got it," she smiled, holding up a sheet of paper. "First degree. Cooper leave?"

"Yeah, he did. When do I get to arrest her? Should we call her lawyer and have him surrender her?" Max asked.

"That would be the decent thing to do but we're not going to. People already believe rich people get all the breaks. Go sit on her house. Give it a while and if she leaves pull her over and slap the cuffs on her. Tow her car and bring her in the front."

"Where the TV cameras are waiting for her?" Max asked. Personally, he did not like pulling that stunt. It was for political points and Max had no interest in embarrassing anyone to help a politician.

"I'll have it set up. I'll call you when we're ready. If she hasn't left the house by then go knock on her door and get her."

Carolyn Lucas did not even bother to knock on Marc's door. Having heard about the arrest on the radio she immediately went to get him.

"You better get out here," Carolyn said.

"Why, what's going on?" Marc asked as he started to get up from his desk.

Carolyn didn't bother to answer him. She stood back as he went through the door and noticed Sandy turning on the TV. Within thirty seconds the entire office was crowded in front of the screen. They were treated to a continuous loop of Mackenzie Sutherland in handcuffs being led into the police department.

The phone rang. Marc beat Sandy to it and answered it himself.

"Yes, Heather. I'm watching it now," he said. She started to apologize but he cut her off.

"I'm not even mad about it. Getting mad at a prosecutor for pulling this stunt is like getting mad at a five-year-old for stealing cookies. They both know better but do it anyway. I'll be there in a half-hour. Nobody, and I mean nobody, says a word to her. And I want her arraigned this afternoon."

He listened for a moment then said, "I know you'll oppose bail, but the judge will set it anyway. I want my client out of there today!" and he hung up the phone.

Marc went back to his office, grabbed his suit coat and a briefcase. As he hurried toward the exit he said, "Carolyn, give Maddy a call and see if she can meet me at the downtown police department."

"Will do," Carolyn said.

"You want some help?" Barry Cline sincerely asked him.

Marc paused for a moment then said, "No, I can do this. But I'll let you know. I'll probably want some help with jury selection." Barry was a very good trial lawyer himself. He and Marc often worked on cases together.

"Let me know," Barry said as Marc left.

THIRTY-FIVE

At the time of her arrest, Mackenzie Sutherland was going to the Life Time Fitness center for a workout. She had an appointment with her personal trainer and was anxious to keep it, if for no other reason than to get out of the house for a while.

Mackenzie backed out of her driveway while opening the driver's side window. It was going to be a perfect mid-September, late-summer day and the fresh air pouring in felt good as she drove away from her house. She was barely a block from home when she saw the flashing lights of the unmarked police car in her rearview mirror. Mackenzie immediately realized who they were and what they wanted.

"Hello, Detective," Mackenzie said to Max Coolidge when he leaned down to talk to her through the open window.

"Good morning, Mrs. Sutherland," Max politely replied. "Ma'am, would you shut off the car please and step out?"

"Certainly," Mackenzie said and complied.

Anna Finney stepped forward, turned Mackenzie around, placed Mackenzie's hands on the BMW, then quickly frisked her for weapons. Anna then retrieved her gym bag and checked it also.

Max then told her about the warrant for her arrest for the murder of William Sutherland. He read her the Miranda warning and asked if she understood her rights.

"Yes, I do, and I have a lawyer..." she started to say.

"We know, ma'am," Max smiled. "You can call him when we get you downtown. Until then we will not ask you any questions and I suggest you keep quiet until you talk to Mr. Kadella."

With Mackenzie handcuffed in the backseat of their car, Max and Anna waited for the tow truck to impound the BMW. While they waited Max made a call to Heather Anderson to bring her up to speed. Heather informed him they were all set, and he could bring her in anytime.

When they reached the police department headquarters, instead of parking in the lot in back, they parked on Grove Street a half-block from the main entrance. Mackenzie could clearly see why they did this. Although inwardly furious about it, she was determined to maintain her dignity.

Max and Anna helped her out of the car into a phalanx of a half-dozen uniformed police officers. As they moved her slowly down the sidewalk toward the front door, a small mob of reporters and camera operators surrounded them. Mackenzie held her head up, her lips pursed tightly together and looked straight ahead while the herd surrounding her moved slowly toward the building. It took almost ten minutes to travel two hundred feet. All the while the cameras were whirring, and the reporters yelled questions that went unanswered. They finally got her inside as the cops held the reporters out. Waiting inside, barely able to contain the smirk on her face, was Heather Anderson.

Mackenzie looked her in the eyes and said, "So, that must be what you call a 'perp walk'. Did you enjoy it?"

Heather, slightly taken aback, said, "We're not here to accommodate you."

"That wasn't necessary, Ms. Anderson, and you know it. You could have called Mr. Kadella and I would have surrendered," Mackenzie coolly said. "I would appreciate the opportunity to call him now, please."

Although she would not admit it, even to herself, Heather felt a little ashamed of herself. Despite what they had just put her through, Mackenzie was acting far more dignified than the cops or the mob outside.

"We have to process you," Heather politely told her. "I believe we can remove the cuffs," she said to Max. "You won't try to make a break for it or attack a police officer?" she asked Mackenzie trying to lighten things up.

"Very unlikely," Mackenzie agreed while Anna unlocked the handcuffs and removed them.

By the time Mackenzie was finished being fingerprinted and photographed, Heather had spoken to Marc. After being told Marc was on his way, Mackenzie was escorted to a comfortable conference room to wait. Max brought her a small bottle of cold water and she was left alone. Barely ten minutes later, both Marc and Maddy Rivers entered the room.

Mackenzie was sitting at the table, on its opposite side away from the door. When the two of them entered the room a look of relief came over Mackenzie and the tension release caused her to sob three or four times.

Marc and Maddy took chairs on either side of her as she said, "I have never been so embarrassed in my life."

"Take a drink," Marc quietly said referring to the bottle of water.

Mackenzie did so and that helped calm her. Maddy took one of her hands as Mackenzie said, "Why was that necessary? I told that...bitch I would have surrendered..."

"There's an election next year. Your case is going to be a media sensation for months. Shayla Parker will try to get as much publicity out of this as she can. Sorry, Mac, but what happened today is just the beginning."

"What about bail?" Maddy asked before Mackenzie could.

"We'll get you arraigned yet today. I talked to Heather and she agreed to it. We'll waive reading the indictment. The judge will make sure you understand your rights. I'll ask for a speedy trial to get that clock started. Then we'll argue about bail."

"At some point the judge will ask you to enter a plea," Maddy said.

"Yeah, right," Marc said, realizing he forgot to mention that. "Just say not guilty."

"I am not guilty!" Mackenzie said.

"Mac, you don't have to convince us," Marc smiled.

"What about bail?" Maddy asked again.

"I'll make the argument that the case is entirely circumstantial. The evidence is thin, you're not a flight risk or a danger to the community. I think the judge will grant bail. He'll have no reason not to, but it will probably be pretty high."

"How high?" Mackenzie asked.

"I don't know," Marc admitted. "A couple million, maybe five."

"Okay," Mackenzie said. "I'll call my financial advisor and have him start working on it. Five I can do today. Anything more will take a little longer."

When she said this, Maddy gave Marc a look as if to say, "Five million. Must be nice."

At 2:15 the day's arraignment judge came back onto the bench. Since it was a middle-of-the-week afternoon, his calendar had been light. He had cleared all of the afternoon cases except Mackenzie's then had taken a short break at 2:00.

Without showing it, Marc's heart had sunk a bit when he heard who the presiding judge was. Otis Carr was a fifty-four-year-old black man with twelve years on the bench. He was a bald, six-foot-seven-inch one-time U of M basketball player with a gold stud in his left ear. His girth had grown significantly since his playing days due to a weakness for good food and a lack of exercise. It was also rumored that Otis, a still handsome man with a Barry White baritone voice, was having an affair with the County Attorney, Shayla Parker. Both of whom were married. Marc, having never appeared before the man until today, could only hope the rumors were exaggerated.

Marc, his client and Maddy were seated at the table to the judge's left. Maddy had retrieved appropriate clothing for Mackenzie and the ponytail and gym clothes were gone. Heather Anderson and a female lawyer Marc did not know were at the other table. Between the court watchers and the media there was not an empty seat in the gallery. There were even eight defense lawyers, most of whom Marc knew, seated in the jury box just to watch. The circus surrounding Mackenzie

Sutherland, already labeled the Black Widow or Ice Queen Case was about to begin.

The first thing Judge Carr did was to take a few minutes to sternly warn everyone in the courtroom to basically behave themselves. The judge read the case information into the record while the court reporter took it down. He then had the lawyers speak their appearance for the record. Heather also served Marc with a couple of discovery notices; a formality for the record.

Marc stood and told the judge he had received a copy of the indictment and his client waived the formality of reading it. He also told the judge she was ready to enter a plea. Carr courteously asked Mackenzie to stand. He then took a couple minutes to satisfy himself that she understood what was happening and then he read her the Miranda rights.

Mackenzie was charged with one count of first-degree premeditated murder and one count of second-degree intentional murder. The prosecution had decided to go for broke and not give the jury any lesser-included-offenses to fall back on. Carr elicited a quick and very firm "not guilty" to both counts. He then asked for bail applications.

Since Marc was already standing he beat Heather to it and made his bail request. "My client can put up a half a million dollars, cash, today, your Honor. She is not a flight risk, has strong ties to the community and is not a danger to anyone, including herself. Further, your Honor, the prosecution's case is not only a very thin circumstantial one, it is almost entirely speculative. It should not have gotten through the grand jury."

"Ms. Anderson?" Carr said.

"Your Honor, the defendant, in fact, has no ties to the community. She is quite wealthy and could be on a plane and out of here in an hour if she chooses..."

"I will not!" Mackenzie blurted out.

Before Carr could say anything, Marc bent his head down and whispered in her ear to settle her down. The reality was this was not a spontaneous outburst. Marc had prepared her for it and Mackenzie handled it perfectly.

"As I was saying, your Honor," Heather said a touch flustered from the interruption, "she has ample means to flee and bail should be denied."

Heather, knowing the rumors about Carr and Shayla Parker were in fact true, smugly sat down believing she had said enough.

Marc, still standing began to speak but was stopped when Carr held up a large hand and gestured for Marc to take his seat. This was a clear indication Carr had made his decision, probably before court even began.

"I'm going to set bail at two million dollars, cash or property, no bond. Plus, the defendant will surrender her passport and wear a monitoring device to be administered by court services," Carr ruled.

"Your Honor," a disappointed Heather Anderson said as she stood up.

"I'm not going to change my mind, Ms. Anderson. She's no longer a flight risk. I was also informed I have been assigned this case. Mr. Kadella, does your client waive her right to a speedy trial?"

"No, your Honor," Marc answered. "We may be persuaded later but for now I want the clock ticking."

"Very well. The omnibus hearing. My schedule is a little full for the next, couple of weeks. How about October fourteenth, 9:00 A.M?"

"Fine, your Honor," Marc said.

"That's fine, your Honor," Heather said from her chair. "There is one more thing."

"What's that?" Carr asked.

"The Sutherland estate, your Honor. Or more precisely the ill-gotten gains…"

"Objection," Marc said.

"Spare me the histrionics, Ms. Anderson. There's no jury here," Carr said.

"The money Mrs. Sutherland inherited. If she is found guilty of murdering her husband she'll have to forfeit all of it," Heather said.

"That is a maybe, on both points," Marc said. "It's at best speculative that she'll be found guilty and that does not automatically mean she'll forfeit the inheritance." Not being a probate lawyer Marc had no idea whether or not she would forfeit the money. In fact, he believed she probably would. He simply figured he had better make the argument.

"Oh, I believe she will forfeit the money," Carr said to Marc. "How much are we talking about?" he asked Heather.

"I have the final inventory here, you Honor," Heather said as she stood and stepped around the table. She dropped a copy on Marc's table then walked toward the judge. As she did this she loudly proclaimed for the audience. "Twenty-seven point four million dollars, total, your Honor."

A loud buzz and stirring went through the courtroom with this news.

"Knock it off!" Carr grimly thundered.

He took the document from Heather, set it aside and said, "What do you propose?"

"That she surrenders this sum to the court until its rightful ownership can be finally adjudicated," Heather said.

It was then that Marc noticed Paige Sutherland was seated in the first row behind the prosecution. Next to her sat both Adam and Hailey Sutherland. All three had nasty smirks on their faces.

"Your Honor," Marc said as he stood up again. "She is trying to deny my client her Constitutional right to select her own lawyer. She is trying to sequester funds my client has every legal right to and to use in her defense."

"She has plenty of other money she can use," Heather said with a trace of sarcasm. "Other money she made the old-fashioned way; inheriting it from a dead husband."

"Your honor…" Marc started to say.

"That's enough," Carr admonished Heather. He turned to Marc and Mackenzie and asked, "Is that true? She has other funds she can use?"

"Yes, your Honor," Marc had to admit.

"Then I'll give you thirty days to surrender the amount you inherited from William Sutherland to the court to be kept in escrow. That is in addition to the bail I set.

"Do we need a media gag order?" Carr asked the lawyers.

"No, your Honor," Heather said knowing Shayla Parker wanted to hold regular press conferences.

"No, your Honor," Marc agreed. "At least not yet. Plus, it would only apply to me. They would still leak whatever they want to the media."

When he said this, several members of that same media choked back laughs knowing Marc was right.

"Anything else?" Carr asked looking back and forth at the lawyers. "Okay, we're adjourned."

THIRTY-SIX

Winter's end was clearly in sight. Once January was behind them most Minnesotans felt a palpable sense of relief knowing the worst was probably over. February was a short month and March, even though normally the snowiest month of the year, normally brought milder temperatures. Also, when February rolled around baseball's spring training was about to begin and it had been a relatively mild winter at that. Only six days of sub-zero temps. Sufficient to send the East Coast into an Armageddon-expecting panic. It was hardly enough for the Upper Midwest to even notice.

The trial of the State of Minnesota vs. Mackenzie Sutherland was set to begin in less than a week Monday, February twenty-second. There had been three requests for continuances, all brought by the prosecution; the most recent one was barely a week ago. Judge Otis Carr, not necessarily the most patient of men, made it clear there would be no more of them. The twenty-second, he declared, was carved in stone.

Normally, with a case based on circumstantial evidence such as Mackenzie's, Marc would have pushed for an early trial date. Why give the prosecution more time to find more evidence? Having been previously involved in notorious, highly publicized trials, he decided it might be best to let this one cool down for a while.

For at least a month following Mackenzie's arrest, a day did not go by without a story about her on local media and even occasionally national news. Every story used the term *Black Widow.* Most of them even threw in the word poisoning, as in *Black Widow poisoning*.

To keep the story stirred up, Shayla Parker, with Heather Anderson at her side, gave two or three press conferences each month about the case. After the first month or so of this, attendance by media members began to dwindle. Also, it was about this time that a prominent state senator who was rumored to be a candidate for governor was caught cheating on his wife. The fact that he was a Republican only added fuel to the frenzy. The good news was that it pushed Mackenzie Sutherland out of the spotlight. Marc, by himself during this time made a couple of appearances on Gabriella Shriqui's show, *The Court Reporter*, to refute some of the worst of the prosecution's news leaks and propaganda. But he mostly kept a low profile.

Mackenzie, being electronically tethered to her home, was suffering from an acute bout of cabin fever. Between Marc and Maddy they managed to get permission to get her out of the house for short periods a couple times a week, but five months of house arrest was getting old.

The actual amount of evidence accumulated by the prosecution was not much. It came down to that it appeared William Sutherland was poisoned, and somebody did it. Who stood to gain and how much? Also, who had the access and opportunity to poison William Sutherland? The obvious answer to these questions was Mackenzie Sutherland.

"Butch Koll is here to see you," Sandy told Marc through the office intercom.

Marc thanked her and a moment later went into the common area. When he did, a man Sandy was practically drooling over, and the married Carolyn was sneaking peeks at stood up from a client chair to greet him.

Butch Koll was a former client of Marc's. For most of his adult life, Butch had made his living hanging around the fringes of the Cities' underworld. At six-feet-four and a solid two hundred forty pounds of weight-lifter muscle, Butch had earned his money as a physical intimidator and collector for various crooks. Mostly bookies and loan sharks, oftentimes one and the same person.

A couple years back, Butch was working for a Russian defector, the closest thing to organized crime the Twin Cities had. Marc represented Butch in a manslaughter-homicide case. Marc did a good job for Butch and it was Marc who helped find him legitimate employment afterward.

Butch and a friend of his, Andy Whitcomb, had done security work for Marc on a previous case. Unfortunately, Butch had been unintentionally shot providing that security then spent a month in the hospital.

"Hey, big guy," Marc genially said. "Thanks for coming by."

As the two men shook hands, Butch asked, "Should I have worn Kevlar?"

"You're never going to let me forget that, are you?"

Butch pressed his lips together, rolled his eyes up to the ceiling as if thinking over the question then said, "No."

"Come on back," Marc said.

Marc closed his office door behind him then said, "Want to earn some extra money?"

"Sure, what do you need?"

"Protection for a client. We'll get you a vest this time."

"Mackenzie Sutherland?" Butch asked.

"Yeah," Marc nodded. "We've received a lot of threats, nothing like Brittany Riley but enough to take them seriously," he continued referring to the young woman Butch had provided security for the first time.

"I still have nightmares..." Butch said.

"Me too," Marc quietly replied. "Can you get Andy Whitmore or somebody else?"

"Andy's available. To be honest, I'm a little surprised you want to use us."

"What happened wasn't your fault. There was a half-dozen deputy sheriffs there and it still happened. You can't stop crazy people," Marc reassured him.

"What I really want is for you guys to just be a presence. A couple of large, serious-looking men will keep most people in line. Mackenzie has plenty of money. Go find a couple top-of-the-line vests and she'll buy them for you. Don't go cheap. In fact, get one for her and me as well."

"You think people are that pissed off about her killing her husband..."

"She's presumed innocent," Marc said.

"Whatever. From what I've seen in the papers he was no prince. He probably had it coming. How much and for how long?" Butch asked.

"I'll have her pay you each two hundred bucks an hour, cash. What you tell the IRS is between you and them. As far as how long, the judge had blocked out two weeks, but I don't see it taking that long. I'll want you in court every day, all day."

"For two hundred an hour, you got me as long as you want me," Butch said, "What is she like?"

"Nice lady. You'll like her."

"As long as you're not married to her."

"You will not be on my jury," Marc laughed.

Shortly after 2:00 that afternoon, Carolyn called back to Marc and told him a messenger with a delivery was here. Marc went out front to find a pleasant looking, young African-American man waiting for him. He was dressed in slacks, a shirt and a tie.

Marc shook his hand and asked, "Are you clerking for Judge Carr?"

"Yes, sir," the young man said as he handed Marc a manila envelope.

"Where are you going to school?" Marc asked then turned his head to see Barry Cline come out of his office.

"William Mitchell, sir," the clerk said.

"Our Alma Mater," Barry said. "Won't be long before you're rich and famous."

"If you marry well," Marc said. "Is this the jury pool?"

"Yes, sir."

"Please stop calling me sir. It just reminds me I'm not getting any younger."

"Yes, sir. I mean Marc, sir."
"How many names on the list," Marc asked him.
"Um, I, ah, didn't look."
"Yes, you did," Marc laughed. "How many names?"
"A hundred," the young man smiled.
"Thanks for bringing it by," Marc said.

Along with the list of the one hundred prospective jurors, Marc received the juror questionnaires for each. When someone is summoned to jury duty they must fill out a juror questionnaire either online or by mail. It is an informational form to get basic personal data to be used to weed out biases, hardships and other reasons someone might be excused. Marc had Jeff Modell, the office paralegal, make several copies of all of this paperwork. While Jeff was making the copies, Connie Mickelson came out of her office.

"Did I see that yummy hunk of beef, Butch Koll, here a little while ago?" Connie asked.

Marc looked at Barry and said, "That's all they ever think about. I don't know about you, but I'm getting tired of being treated as a sex object."

Amid the laughter Barry replied, "I know what you mean. I wish they'd start appreciating us for our minds, sensitivity and inner beauty."

Connie looked at Carolyn groaned and said, "It's getting a little deep in here."

"I'd say," Carolyn replied.

"You got your jury list?" Connie asked.

"Yeah. Jeff's making copies. You got time to help?" Marc asked.

"Sure. What are you looking for?" Connie asked.

"I don't know. Twelve women married to assholes they'd like to kill would be good."

"So, just pick any twelve married women and you'll be all set," Carolyn said.

"Wow!" Marc said looking at Carolyn. "Where did that come from? Trouble in paradise? Should I call John and warn him to sleep with his gun handy and one eye open?"

"No, of course not. I didn't mean my Johnny," Carolyn said trying to look innocent.

For the remainder of the afternoon Marc, Barry and Connie, along with Maddy Rivers used the conference room to go through the list. While they did this, Jeff, Sandy and Carolyn used their computers to get what they could on each of the names. Jeff was a fair, amateur hacker who could get into some accounts and find out financial details of people. Of course, this was not strictly legal but...

Their intention was to come up with a spreadsheet categorizing each of the jurors as one of three things: a definite 'yes', a definite 'no' or a 'maybe'. For the 'maybes', they would further break them down with a number on a scale of one to ten. A one would be almost a definite 'no', a ten close to a definite 'yes'. Mostly what they were looking for were fairly well-educated people who would keep an open mind, not be influenced by pretrial publicity and follow the law.

Normally the staff would leave at 5:00 and the lawyers by around 6:00. During a trial as important as this one and to help Marc with the list, everyone agreed to stay late. At 6:00 they took a break to work on the pizza Marc had delivered.

They were all seated around the conference room table eating when Connie asked Marc, "I've been meaning to ask you, is Otis Carr still mad at you?"

"Nah, I don't think so," Marc said.

"Why would Carr be mad at you? What did you do?" Barry asked.

"I brought a motion requesting that he recuse himself," Marc said.

"On what grounds?" Barry asked.

Marc looked at Maddy and said, "Go ahead, tell him what you found."

"Marc had me check up on him," she began. "There were rumors that his Honor and the Ramsey County Attorney, Shayla Parker were very close friends."

"Oh, good, courthouse gossip. I like it," Barry said.

"Anyway, I have photos and other documentation that prove that the rumors are true," Maddy said.

"They're both married and not to each other," Connie chimed in with a big grin.

"Are you serious?" Barry said looking at Marc. "Does he realize how much trouble he could get into?"

"Otis is a smart guy. I'm sure he knows," Connie answered him.

"What did he say?" Barry asked.

"I didn't flat out accuse him, but I did tell him that there were rumors going around that the judge and Parker had a close, personal relationship. And in the interest of justice and to avoid the appearance of impropriety, blah, blah, blah, he should step aside.

"The good judge didn't take that very well," Marc said with mild sarcasm. "In fact, I thought he was going to come down off the bench and go after me. Needless to say, he didn't recuse himself. But to answer your question, he doesn't seem to be holding a grudge."

"And now you have grounds for an appeal, if you need it," Connie said.

"And likely reversible error," Barry added.

"Let's get back to work," Marc said.

By Saturday afternoon, with everyone's input, they had completed the list and were satisfied with the result of the hundred names. Seven were on the definite 'yes' list. All seven were college educated women with what appeared to be liberal leanings. Twenty-one were in the definite 'no' column. Nineteen men and two women who appeared to be conservative, law and order types. Of the remaining seventy-two, none were close to a 'no' categorized as a one or two. Those were already on the 'definite no' list. Also, none of the 'maybes' were a ten. There were a half-dozen nines but the bulk of the remainders were between three and seven.

Marc and Barry, who would be in court helping Marc with jury selection, were satisfied that they had a reasonable list to work with. Would any of this help? No one actually knew. The old belief that you could probably take the first twelve people through the door and do just as well was likely true this time. Except, no one had the balls to do it.

THIRTY-SEVEN

Marc placed his briefcase and laptop on the table nearest to the jury box. He hung up his overcoat on the coat rack along the wall by his table and removed his phone from the coat's pocket. It was five minutes past 8:00 A.M. on the first day of the trial. Surprised to find the courtroom empty, he sat down at his table to make a quick call.

"Yeah," he heard Butch Koll say.

"Hey," Marc said. "Bring her up and into the courtroom through the back way. There's a small mob of reporters in the hall. The deputies have the door locked so she can't get in that way. I'll have a deputy watch for you to let you in."

He listened for a moment and noticed the judge's clerk, the African-American law school student who had delivered the jury list. Marc lightly waved to him then said into the phone, "Okay, I'll see you in a while."

"Don't let the judge see you use a phone in his courtroom," the young man, Tyrone Carver, said smiling. "He wants you in his chambers," Tyrone continued. "The prosecution is already in there."

As Marc walked toward the door behind the bench he asked the clerk what was going on. Reluctant to tell him, he claimed he did not know. Marc's antennae went up and he had an uneasy feeling he was not going to like this.

"Have a seat, Marc," Carr's baritone voice boomed.

"Good morning, your Honor," Marc warily said as he sat down noticing the court reporter was not present. He turned to Heather and the younger woman next to her and asked, "Heather, what's up?"

"We're asking the judge to revisit his decision to exclude any testimony about your client's former husband, Wendell Cartwright…"

"Your Honor…" Marc started to say.

"Let her finish," Carr politely said.

"We've been in contact with the Chicago cops, the two detectives who did the investigation. Both are willing to come here, at their own expense, to testify. After we found the searches for heart attack inducing drugs on William Sutherland's computer, the Chicago P.D. went back into Cartwright's computer and found a half-dozen similar searches during the months preceding his death."

"Hold it," Marc said. "When did you find this out?"

"They got back to us yesterday."

"Sunday."

"Yes, Marc," Heather said, "Sunday." She handed him a document and continued. "This is an affidavit from the CPD computer tech who found the references on Cartwright's computer. He's willing to testify also." Heather turned to Judge Carr and continued, "We have now established a pattern, your Honor. The jury needs to know about this."

"Your Honor," Marc said, "This is so grossly prejudicial and lacking any probative value, if you allow this in it will likely be reversible error."

"We're not offering it as proof of the crimes alleged, your Honor," Heather said. "Only as evidence of a pattern. It is clearly admissible."

Carr sat forward, folded his big hands together and placed them on the desk blotter. He stared passed the three lawyers arranged before him with his best Solomon-like look on his face. Marc watched him while thinking: *The S.O.B. has already made up his mind and I'm about to get hosed.*

"I'm inclined to let this in but before I do I want to see in writing exactly what these three Chicago cops are going to say. You will put it in writing and get it to me before we have opening statements. It will also be provided to Mr. Kadella. We're going to be very careful with this.

"Also, if you want your own tech to search this computer get the name and address and Ms. Anderson will provide it by tomorrow. Understood?" he finished looking at Heather.

"Yes, your Honor," Heather solemnly said hiding her glee.

"Jason Briggs," a glum Marc said to her. As she wrote it down, he gave her the address.

"When you put the first of these witnesses from Chicago on the stand, Marc can repeat his objections for the record. I may even sustain them and disallow this. I reserve that right. For now, we'll go on the assumption I will allow it. Any questions? Good.

"Now, jury selection. I want this done by noon on Wednesday. Keep your questions short and to the point. Two weeks for this trial should be plenty and I don't like working weekends.

"I'll be out at 9:00 and we'll get this show on the road."

A disappointed Marc Kadella led the way into the courtroom. Aside from losing the judge's ruling to allow the jury to hear about Wendell Cartwright, something deeper was nagging at the back of his head.

Seated at the desk waiting for him was Barry Cline. Barry was an excellent trial lawyer in his own right and it had become almost habitual for Marc and Barry to help each with jury selection.

"What was that about?" Barry asked Marc referring to the in-chambers meeting.

"I just got royally sandbagged," Marc said. He told Barry what happened.

"And they just got this yesterday? These people lie really well," Barry said.

A doorway from the back hall into the courtroom opened and a Ramsey County deputy came through and held it open. In walked Madeline Rivers along with Mackenzie Sutherland and two rather large men, Butch Koll and Andy Whitmore, bringing up the rear.

"Maddy's here," Barry whispered. "Listen, why don't you move to the end of the table and let her have your chair."

"Next to you?"

"Well, yeah, that's the idea," Barry smiled.

They all greeted each other then Marc took Mackenzie into a conference room to bring her up-to-date. While he did this, she removed the Kevlar vest she was wearing.

"What does this mean?" she asked referring to the ruling about her ex, Wendell Cartwright.

"I don't know," Marc shrugged. "It means the jury will know about Wendell Cartwright."

"There's nothing to know," she started to protest.

"Wait," Marc said holding up a hand to stop her. "We'll deal with it when we get there. One step at a time. Let's go back and start picking a jury."

Because this was a first-degree murder case, by law, the jurors had to be questioned individually. This would slow down the process significantly. It would help a lot that the media coverage had died down to almost nothing until about a week ago. With little publicity for several months picking twelve jurors and four alternates who had not heard of the case would not be too difficult. It would also help that most Americans have the attention span of a four-year-old.

The judge's deadline of noon on Wednesday to have jury selection completed was pushing it. Questioning them one at a time is a naturally slow and tedious process.

Judge Carr had produced a list for the order in which they would be called. That person would be brought out and the judge would ask a few questions to get things started. He would then let the lawyers question the individual.

Marc, as the lawyer for the defense, would go first. What the lawyers are supposed to do is probe for biases. They would also use this opportunity to indoctrinate the juror. Marc would always inquire about the juror's ability to set aside any prejudice, to keep an open mind and decide the case solely on what was presented in court. Also, to make sure he or she understood what the presumption of innocence was and proof beyond a reasonable doubt. About the best Marc could hope for was jurors who claimed to understand these concepts and promise to be open-minded.

The first venireman called – the panel from which the jury is selected is called a venire, (pronounced vuh-near) – was a sixty-four-year-old retiree named William Stokes. Stokes was a stocky, balding, pleasant man who secretly wanted to be on the jury. Before arriving to do jury duty he had been coached by a lawyer who was a good friend. He was told not to look anxious to be on the jury, to be honest and promise to be open-minded.

Carr spent a few minutes asking about obvious bias due to the publicity. Stokes' friend had told him to admit he had heard about it but normally did not pay much attention to the media. They simply could not be trusted.

Marc introduced himself and Mackenzie then politely walked Stokes through his questions. He appeared open, honest and sincere. His promise to keep an open mind and decide the case based on the law and the facts certainly seemed genuine. Marc found the man acceptable and turned him over to Heather Anderson.

Heather spent barely five minutes with him before agreeing he could serve on the jury. Stokes was smiling as the deputy led him away to wait until the rest of the jury was selected. One down, eleven regular jurors and four alternates to go.

With short breaks in mid-morning and mid-afternoon and an hour for lunch, the process boringly crawled along until 5:00 P.M. By that time and only because Carr had pushed, a total of four jurors were selected.

"We'll adjourn for the day," Carr said as the most recent venireman, a twenty-eight-year-old, obviously liberal student who was attending college for a career and letting dad pay for it, was being led away. Despite the obvious lie he had told about not being biased against the 1%, the judge and prosecutor found him acceptable. Marc was forced to use one of his peremptory challenges to keep him off of the jury.

"Tomorrow morning, we are going to start at 8:00 and go until 6:00," Carr told the lawyers. "I meant what I said about having a jury impaneled by Wednesday afternoon."

As everyone was filing out, Marc, Barry, Mackenzie and Maddy chatted about the selections. The first juror, Bill Stokes, had originally been on Marc's list as a 'maybe' with a low score of four. One of the other three had been a 'yes' and the other two 'maybes' with high secondary scores. In addition to the last venireman questioned, the professional college student, Marc had used two other peremptory challenges to exclude people. All three of them had been on his list as a definite "no."

"What do you think?" Maddy asked Marc.

"We did okay," Marc replied. "In theory, we only need one to hold out."

"What do you think?" Maddy asked Barry.

"I think we did better than okay. That first one, Stokes, a working-man who would chew off his arm rather than vote for a Republican, seemed to be the worst of the four of them for our side and I got a good vibe from him. I think he'll be fair."

"You going back to the office?" Mackenzie asked.

"Oh, yeah," Marc said as he packed up. "Go over the list some more. See if Jeff and Sandy found anything else. Sleep is a luxury during a trial."

"Mind if I come with?" Mackenzie asked. Marc had received permission for her to travel to his office during the trial.

"Sure," Marc said. He looked at Mackenzie's bodyguards, Butch and Andy and asked. "How are you guys doing? Bored yet?"

"I think it's interesting," Andy said. "Makes me wish I'd gone to law school."

Marc looked at Barry and said, "The glamour. It's the glamour that is so appealing."

"Obviously," Barry said. "And the wealth and acclaim. The high esteem in which the public holds lawyers."

"Yeah, that too," Andy said totally getting the joke. "You mind if we come back to the office? We could help."

"Sure, why not?" Marc said.

THIRTY-EIGHT

True to his word, Judge Carr pushed hard on the second day of jury selection. He did so by limiting the questions the lawyers asked. If either of them wanted to delve into areas he had already covered, he was not shy about letting them know it was time to move on. By 6:00 P.M. they had selected nine more. This left them needing the twelfth and the four alternates.

"That might be the fastest murder one jury selection of all time," Barry Cline said to Marc.

It was not quite 11:30 A.M. on Wednesday morning, the third day of the trial. The twelve jurors and four alternates had been chosen, sworn and impaneled. Carr barely finished impaneling them, adjourned until 9:00 the next morning and fled the courtroom. The abruptness of it all caused Marc to look at Heather Anderson with his arms raised and palms up as if to ask her what was going on. She answered by shrugging her shoulders and shaking her head.

"Mr. Kadella, Ms. Anderson would you give me a minute, please?" Carr's clerk asked as he motioned them up to the bench.

"Hey, Tyrone," Marc said when the four lawyers got up to the clerk's desk. "I wanted to see the judge. I have a couple of issues to discuss with him."

"Sorry, he has a, ah, prior engagement. He wants me to tell you, be in chambers tomorrow morning at 8:00 for any last-minute motions." Tyrone looked at Heather and said, "He wants opening statements in the morning then be ready to call your first witness right away. Sorry," Tyrone continued, "I just work here."

As Marc and Barry were returning to the defense table, Marc loosely draped an arm around Barry's shoulders. "I think his Honor is a bit horny and Shayla Parker is on the lunch menu," Marc whispered in his ear.

"Don't say that! That's disgusting. The image of those two groping around is not something I want in my head," Barry said and shivered for effect.

Still whispering Marc said, "Think about it. Otis Carr bouncing around on…"

"Stop or I'll scream!" Barry said while Marc laughed.

When they reached the table Marc quietly told Mackenzie and Maddy what was going on.

"Are you sure?" Maddy asked.

"No, but the kid practically admitted it. I want you," he continued looking at Maddy, "to get downstairs and see if you can follow him. If you can, get some pictures. If he slips past you, meet us for lunch."

"Will do," Maddy said as she quickly grabbed her bag and coat and headed for the door.

On their way back to the office, Barry riding with Marc and Mackenzie with Butch and Andy following, Maddy called.

"Lost him. Sorry. Actually, I didn't see him come down."

"That's okay," Marc said. "Come over to the office and join us."

"Your Honor," Marc began, "I want to revisit a couple of issues."

The lawyers, absent Barry Cline, were seated in front of Carr's desk in the judge's chambers at 8:00 A.M. as ordered. The judge's court reporter was also present, at Marc's request, to make a record of this in-camera hearing.

Judge Carr was almost casually seated behind his desk. His robe hung up on a coat stand, his tie loose, wearing a pinstriped dress shirt and slacks. He also looked decidedly more relaxed than he had the day before.

"Your Honor," Heather started to protest.

Carr held up his left hand to stop her and said, "This is a first-degree murder trial, Ms. Anderson. We're going to be very careful here. Go ahead, Mr. Kadella, what's on your mind?"

"Wendell Cartwright, your Honor," Marc began. "I ask that the court review its decision. Judge, allowing in any testimony about his death is highly prejudicial, has no probative value and even the claim that it shows a pattern is very thin."

Carr listened patiently, looked at Heather and said, "Ms. Anderson?"

"The only reason there isn't more evidence is the defendant rushed to have the body cremated. His ex-wives are on our list. They will testify that Wendell Cartwright never said a word about wanting to be cremated."

Carr sighed and said to Heather, "What about that, the ex-wives? Can we limit it to one ex-wife?"

"If he'll stipulate that the others will say the same thing," Heather said.

"Not a chance," Marc said knowing they all had a serious financial stake and credibility problem. "They have no evidence that Wendell had any unusual drugs in his system and…"

"I'm going to allow it. You, I'm sure, will bring all of this out in front of the jury. I have this discretion and I think it will stand up on appeal. Anything else?"

"Yes, your Honor. I want Mrs. Sutherland's former lawyer excluded from testifying. She insists on invoking her rights under attorney-client privilege. Also, if he is to be believed, he is a co-conspirator and they have no independent corroborative evidence which is necessary to allow his testimony in."

"Again," Carr began using the word 'again' because they had been over this before, "he is not a co-conspirator. Your offer of proof that he was romantically smitten by Mrs. Sutherland does not make him one. A fool maybe, but not a co-conspirator. There is no evidence he stood to personally gain from William Sutherland's death. And your claim that he would have if he left his wife and married your client is too speculative. Do you have any evidence that this was going to happen?"

The only possible evidence of this would be testimony from Mackenzie and Marc had not decided if she was going to testify. In fact, at this point, he was leaning for not putting her on the stand.

"As for the attorney-client privilege and enjoining his testimony because of it, I'm afraid that ship has sailed. It's already been breached, with Mrs. Sutherland's permission, when he submitted the original affidavit in which he now claims to have perjured himself and made it public. Of course, Mr. Thomas will have to deal with the fallout from it, but I will allow him to testify.

"Anything else?" he asked of Marc first, then Heather. Both lawyers answered in the negative. Carr looked at the court reporter who understood what came next was off the record.

"I'll be out in…" Carr swiveled around to check the time from a clock on his credenza then swiveled back and continued saying, "twenty minutes, then we'll get going. Marc, you gonna make an opening now?"

"Yes, your Honor," Marc admitted even though he did not have to. As the defense, he had the option of waiting until the prosecution finished presenting their case and give his opening statement then. Because he already decided to give it now Marc saw no harm in admitting it.

"Very well," Carr said. "I'll see everyone out front in a few minutes."

"Greed, ladies and gentlemen," said Heather Anderson after again introducing herself to the jury and reminding them who she represented, 'the people of the State of Minnesota', to begin her opening statement.

"This trial is about one thing and one thing only: greed. That no matter how much money some people have, more is always better. It is about the estate of William Sutherland, twenty-seven million dollars, and who stood to inherit that estate. The evidence will show that only one person stood to gain, and that person was Mackenzie Sutherland, the wife of the late William Sutherland, the victim of her greed.

"You're going to hear a sordid tale about the death of a beloved father, grandfather, father-in-law and employer."

When Heather said this, Mackenzie, without being noticed, took a slip of paper, wrote a single word on it and slid it across to Marc: *Beloved!?* Unseen by the jury the corners of Marc's mouth twitched upward in a suppressed smile.

"A man who worked hard his entire life to build up a successful business. A chain of grocery stores, *Sutherland's*, that employed thousands of people, hundreds of whom attended this adored man's funeral.

"You will hear from the medical examiner that the cause of death was a heart attack," Heather continued slowly pacing in front of the jury box looking directly at each of the jurors while she spoke. "And that the heart attack was not from natural causes. It was brought on by someone introducing a drug, a cancer drug, which if administered improperly can induce a heart attack.

"To be completely candid and up front with you which you certainly deserve, we do not know how this drug was given to the victim. But the evidence will show there is only one person who could have done it. Only one person who had all of the elements necessary to prove guilt beyond a reasonable doubt. Mackenzie Sutherland, the allegedly grieving widow," she continued with barely concealed sarcasm which almost drew an objection from Marc, "is the only one with means, motive and opportunity.

"And then we come back to the word this trial is all about, greed.

"Mackenzie Sutherland had inherited a fortune from a husband who also died of a mysterious…"

"Objection to the use of the word mysterious, your Honor," Marc stood and said.

"Sustained," Carr said.

"Sorry, your Honor," Heather said knowing the damage was done. "I'll rephrase.

"Mackenzie Sutherland inherited a fortune, forty million dollars," – here the jurors snuck a peek at Mackenzie – "from a previous husband in Chicago, Wendell Cartwright. Mr. Cartwright also died of a heart attack. Despite having children and ex-wives to support, Mr. Cartwright changed his Will shortly before his death and left everything to Mackenzie Sutherland, who was using the name Frances at the time.

"You will also hear testimony from a former lawyer of Mrs. Sutherland that William Sutherland changed his Will shortly before his death. This witness will testify that William Sutherland did this, changed his Will and left everything to Mackenzie Sutherland, cutting out his children and grandchildren in an attempt to save his marriage. Or so he was led to believe.

"I'm going to be totally honest so there will be no surprise. Mackenzie Sutherland caught William cheating on her."

Heather then went on to explain the terms of the prenuptial agreement the Sutherlands had signed, and it was Mackenzie who pressured William into changing his Will. William went along with it because he truly loved her and was trying to save the marriage.

She then went on to explain in more detail the witnesses she would call, the testimony of each and the damage Mackenzie did to the family of William Sutherland.

When Heather was talking about the Sutherland family, Marc paid extra attention. If Heather even hinted that Mackenzie was in any way responsible for Robert's death, Carr had said he would call a mistrial. The shooting death of Robert Sutherland had been the subject of a lengthy and very acrimonious pretrial motion. The prosecution argued the jury should be told in detail about it because even if it was self-defense, it was Mackenzie who had driven Robert to it with her devious machinations and deceitful ways.

Marc won the argument because this act would be extremely prejudicial and offer nothing to prove who may have killed William Sutherland. In fact, the subject was so inflammatory that Judge Carr ordered that not a word of it was to be spoken in front of the jurors. The only time it would be brought up was during jury selection. The judge himself asked each juror if they knew or remembered hearing anything about Robert's death. The answer he received would be accepted at face value and was not explored further than that.

"At the conclusion of the trial, each side will make a final argument. At that time. I will bring all of the evidence together for you. I have no doubt that when you go back to deliberate and review the evidence and testimony, you will find the defendant guilty. Thank you, ladies and gentlemen."

When Heather returned to her seat Carr called for a break. Marc, Maddy and Mackenzie stayed at the defense table to confer.

"Even I don't like me right now," Mackenzie seriously said.

"Relax," Marc said with a smile. "We're just starting. I warned you she would paint you as a scheming murderer. Wait until the closing. It will be a lot worse. Opening statements are supposed to be an opportunity to lay out for the jury what the case is about and what evidence they'll see and testimony they'll hear. We have a long way to go. She held some things back that I thought she'd use. Like the computer searches. She must want to use these things for a surprise.

"Do you need to use the bathroom?" Marc asked her.

"Yes!" Mackenzie said. "I have to pee so bad it's starting to hurt but I don't want to go out in the hall."

"How about you?" Marc asked Maddy.

"Well, since you brought it up…"

"Come on, there's one in back you can use. Follow me and I'll show you," Marc said.

THIRTY-NINE

"Greed," Marc said beginning his opening statement. "Greed," he repeated. He was standing seven or eight feet in front of the jury box holding his hands together in front of himself slowly looking over the attentive jurors.

Without turning his head, using his left hand, he pointed at the prosecution table. "Greed is what Ms. Anderson wants you to believe this case is about," he said dropping his left arm. "That would be good for her because greed is an emotional word. It is a very negative, emotional word that most of us are taught is something to avoid. Greedy people are bad and should be punished. It's even one of the seven deadly sins. Apparently, you should go straight to hell if you are greedy," he said as he slowly started to pace while keeping eye contact with the jurors.

"The prosecutor wants you to punish my client and find her guilty of murder because Ms. Anderson has decided Mackenzie Sutherland is greedy."

Taking this approach was, at least, close to objectionable. Marc was making an argument which is supposed to be done during closing statements not during opening. But then, Heather Anderson had done the same thing during her opening. Was she able to provide any evidence that Mackenzie Sutherland was driven by greed to kill her husband? Only by inference.

"Well, ladies and gentlemen," he continued. "This isn't about greed or any other emotionally based word she will try to fool you with to distract you from what a trial is really about."

Marc stopped his pacing, turned and looked directly at the jury. "A trial is about evidence and not emotion. It's about the prosecution's duty to present sufficient factual evidence to prove the defendant guilty beyond a reasonable doubt. It's not about the prosecution tossing you a word," here Marc flicked his left hand at them as if tossing something, "that she knows you will find distasteful. Greed," he said again then paused to slowly look at each and every one of them. "Greed," he repeated. "She's greedy," he whispered pointing at Mackenzie. "She's not like you people. You're good because you're not greedy. She's bad because she is. Find her guilty because she's not like you. Find her guilty because I say she's greedy."

Marc straightened up, took a step back, folded his hands and again held them in front of himself. Shocked that he had not drawn an objection, he silently looked over the jurors again noticing that he had their rapt attention.

"First of all, ladies and gentlemen, you will not hear a single witness or see a single piece of evidence proving my client guilty of being greedy. And even if you did, being greedy is not one of the elements of the crime of murder that the prosecution must prove beyond a reasonable doubt for you to find my client, Mackenzie Sutherland, guilty of the crimes charged."

Over the next fifteen to twenty minutes Marc slowly paced and stopped, paced and stopped while he carefully, quietly spoke to the jury about the prosecution's case. Mostly what he did was to let them know that they would find out about flaws in the evidence. Without going over each individual piece of evidence and pointing out the flaws, he simply let the jurors know that there were flaws and he would show them to the jury.

He did this to keep from the prosecution what Marc would bring out during the actual testimony. Why tell the prosecution what he was going to do and give them a chance to fix it ahead of time?

Marc also, again, indoctrinated the jurors in the concepts of innocent until proven guilty, the prosecution's burden of proof and guilt beyond a reasonable doubt. "That is what this trial is about, ladies and gentlemen. Not some emotional word the prosecution has used to fool you."

As he went over each of these principles, he explained them and reminded each juror that he or she swore an oath to abide by them. He looked each juror in the eye and almost every one of them solemnly, silently nodded his or her head in agreement. Several of them even politely smiled.

Finally, Marc was trying to build an unspoken rapport with them. If this likeable, pleasant, well-spoken, nicely-dressed man believed his client is innocent, maybe she is. At the very least, the juror should do as promised and wait until everything has been presented.

"Keep an open mind, ladies and gentlemen. That's all I ask. Abide by your oath, wait to make a decision until you deliberate, and follow the law as the judge tells you. If you do those things, you will come back with a verdict of not guilty. Thank you."

When Marc finished, Judge Carr looked at the clock and decided to break for lunch.

As the jury was being led out, Mackenzie squeezed Marc's hand and whispered, "That was great. Thank you."

Max Coolidge, being the lead investigator from the beginning was the first witness called. Heather started out by having Max tell the jury about his position as a detective, years on the force and experience investigating homicides. Heather also had enough good sense to get out Max's personal relationship with the Sutherland family. Better for her to get it all out in a way she wanted to than leave it for Marc to do it. Admit it, discuss it, and move on.

Max explained to the jury that he was approached by the family and asked to look into William's death. Max claimed he was initially reluctant to do so since there was no evidence that William died other than by a natural heart attack.

"When did you decide to investigate Williams' death?" Heather asked.

"The children, Bob, Adam and Hailey told me about William changing his Will and leaving everything to his wife, Mackenzie, shortly before his death."

"Objection, assumes facts not in evidence. How did the Sutherland kids know when he changed his Will?" Marc said.

"We'll verify this later with another witness, your Honor," Heather replied.

"I'll overrule the objection, for now, subject to a later connection, but you'd better deliver, Ms. Anderson. You may continue, detective," Carr ruled.

"Changing his Will," Max continued, "made me a little curious, so I told them I would look into it. I talked to the medical examiner and read the autopsy report. Everything looked okay. Natural heart attack.

"Then Bob told me he wanted to exhume his dad's body for a more thorough autopsy and Mackenzie refused."

This statement was clearly hearsay and Marc considered objecting to it. Having already made one objection, an ill-advised one at that, he decided it was too early in the trial to look like he was trying to keep things from the jury. He had anticipated Max saying this and decided to let it go. Heather would be able to get it in some other way even if Carr sustained the objection.

"Then after Bob was shot and killed..."

"Your honor!" Marc practically yelled coming out of his seat.

"Stop right there," Carr angrily ordered Max. "We'll take a short recess. I'll see counsel in chambers. Detective, you stay right where you are." Carr indicated to the court reporter to come with and they all filed out back to the judge's chambers.

When the court reporter indicated she was ready Carr began the discussion.

"What did I tell you about this?" Carr asked. "Did I not make myself clear there would be no discussion about Bob Sutherland's death?"

"He just blurted it out, your Honor. It wasn't said as a result of my questions," Heather whined even though she was lying. The two of them had rehearsed this several times.

"Mr. Kadella?" Carr asked Marc.

"Mistrial, your Honor. Right now, every member of that jury is wondering how Robert died, who shot him and why we're keeping it from them. Unless one or two of them remembers reading about it in the news, we can't simply pretend it didn't happen."

While Marc was saying this, Heather was thinking: *Thank God Shayla took care of him yesterday afternoon or Carr would bite my ass for this.*

"Ms. Anderson?"

"An instruction to ignore it from you should be sufficient, your Honor."

Carr thought it over for a moment then said, "I'm not inclined to grant a mistrial this early."

"Then allow me to voir dire the witness. The jury now needs to be told what happened and I should be the one to do it."

"Granted," Carr quickly agreed.

"Your honor, that's hardly necessary," Heather tried to object.

"I've made my decision," Carr said. "Do you want a few minutes to prepare?" he said to Marc.

"No, I know what I want to do," Marc replied.

"Ladies and gentlemen," Carr began addressing the jury after the break. "You heard something from this witness that you should not have heard. I'm sure you are now curious about the death of Robert Sutherland. I'm going to allow Mr. Kadella to conduct a brief questioning of the witness to explain it."

While Carr was telling the jury this, a thought occurred to Marc that he might try.

"Mr. Kadella," Carr said to Marc.

"Thank you, your Honor. Detective Coolidge, let's get it out in the open, shall we? Mackenzie Sutherland shot and killed her stepson, Robert, didn't she?" Marc could almost feel the intake of air as each juror sat up straight and inhaled with this news.

"Yes," Max said.

"It was thoroughly investigated, was it not?"

"Yes," Max admitted.

"By you in fact?"

"Yes, I was the lead investigator."

"On the day of the shooting," Marc began not being specific about the exact date because he could not remember it. "He, Robert, called my client and asked to meet her at her home, is that correct?"

"Yes," Max said. "His phone records verified he called her that day."

For the next fifteen minutes, using short questions specifically designed to require only a yes or no answer, Marc walked Max through the details of the shooting and the day Robert threatened her at the lawyer's office. He paid special attention to the fact that Mackenzie was very cooperative with the police, tried to hide nothing and a video of her interrogation was made.

Max had little choice but to admit all of this was true.

"Isn't it true that when the investigation was completed, the determination was made that Mackenzie Sutherland acted in self-defense and the death of Robert Sutherland, while obviously tragic, was a justified shooting?"

"Not by me," Max defiantly answered.

Momentarily startled, Marc was not sure how to continue. He then asked,

"It wasn't your decision to make, was it, detective?"

"No, I thought it should have been presented to the grand jury right away."

"Because Robert Sutherland was a long-time, good friend wasn't he?"

"Objection, argumentative," Heather said.

"Overruled," Carr said. "You started this now we're going to finish it."

"In fact, it was eventually submitted to a grand jury, was it not?"

"Yes."

"It was presented to the grand jury not because the attorney handling the case thought it should be but for political purposes, isn't that true?"

"I don't recall," Max lied.

Marc looked at the judge and said, "Your Honor, I would like to continue my questioning regarding this subject by calling Heather Anderson."

All through Marc's exam of Max Coolidge, the entire courtroom had been quiet as a grave. When Marc asked to have Heather put on the stand, a buzz broke out loud enough to get the judge to gavel for silence. When everyone settled down, he listened to Heather vehemently object then called the lawyers up to the bench.

Carr looked at Marc who said, "The jury needs to hear from her that Rob's death was self-defense. The detective made it clear he had doubts. I want her under oath admitting she did not."

"Your Honor…" Heather started.

Carr held up a hand to stop her and said, "No, I'll put a stop to this right now. Return to your seats."

"Detective, I'll give you another chance to clear this up. Did Heather Anderson, the attorney for the state handling the case of the death of Robert Sutherland, express any doubts to you that his death was anything other than self-defense?"

"No, your Honor, she didn't," Max meekly admitted.

Carr addressed the jury and explained to them that the shooting of Robert Sutherland was self-defense. That he, the judge himself, had reviewed the case and was satisfied that Robert threatened her life, Mackenzie acted in self-defense and was, in fact, innocent. Finally, he ordered the jury to ignore Robert's death because it had no bearing on the present trial. When Carr finished, he ordered a short break.

Marc was left wondering how many of the jurors believed that Robert Sutherland threatened Mackenzie because Robert believed she killed his father. Would this have an influence on them?

FORTY

"Where were you with the investigation of William Sutherland's death at this point, detective?" Heather asked after the break.

"Nowhere," he replied. "In fact, there was no investigation. We didn't have enough evidence for a court order to exhume the body…"

"How do you know that?"

"We went to court, the judge turned us down and Mrs. Sutherland would not agree to it."

"What did you do next?"

"I received an assignment to go to Chicago and escort a fugitive back to Minnesota that the Chicago police were holding for us…"

Max went on to explain his trip to Chicago and meeting with two Chicago PD detectives. Max explained to the jury that he told the detectives about the Sutherland case. They then told him about a very similar case in Chicago a few years before. Max testified that, out of curiosity, he researched the Chicago case the detectives referred to him. He found many similarities and a picture of the deceased's widow who bore a distinct resemblance to Mackenzie Sutherland. Later, they would in fact verify that the two women, Frances Cartwright and Mackenzie Sutherland, were the same woman.

"How did you determine that they were the same person?"

"We ran a picture of each of them through several facial comparison computer programs. They came back with an eighty-five to eighty-eight percent likelihood of a match. Probably not enough for proof beyond a reasonable doubt but maybe enough to convince a judge to sign an order for a second autopsy of William Sutherland."

"What did you do next?"

"We were about to go to court to request the order to exhume William Sutherland but Mackenzie Sutherland agreed to it, so we no longer needed the court order."

"Let's back up, detective," Heather said. "What similarities did you find, if any, concerning the deaths of Mackenzie Sutherland's husbands?"

"Both were wealthy men in their sixties with no prior history of heart problems that we knew about. Both had families dependent on them for their financial well-being and both changed their Will leaving the entire estate to their current, much younger, wife," Max flatly said while looking directly at the jury.

While this was being said, Mackenzie, having been thoroughly prepared for this, sat impassively listening to the testimony. Marc had coached her about this on several occasions; to show as little emotion as possible. Of course, the media would misinterpret this. After today, she would not only be known as the Black Widow but also the Ice Queen.

"After the body was exhumed, what did you do next?" Heather asked.

Marc heard this and shifted his feet under his chair, so he could quickly stand. If the cop tried to testify about anything specifically that was found in the autopsy Marc would object to it. Coolidge was not a medical examiner. The testimony about what was found during the autopsy would have to come from the source. It may seem trivial, but reports can get lost, witnesses die or become unavailable. Anything can and has happened to prevent key evidence from being introduced at trial.

"Based on what we were told was found in the autopsy, we obtained a search warrant for the Sutherland home and cars," Max answered.

Apparently Heather had anticipated Marc's possible objection and had prepared Max for it. He told the jury, without saying what they found, that something significant was discovered during the autopsy. Without being prompted by a question from Heather, Max continued.

"We conducted the search of the house and impounded the car. We also took a laptop that we later were told belonged to Mackenzie Sutherland and a personal computer belonging to William.

"Based on what was found on William's computer, I believed we should immediately arrest Mrs. Sutherland for his death."

Marc could have objected since there was no testimony about what was found during the autopsy or the computer search. Marc believed Max would say this and decided ahead of time to let it go. He was an experienced police detective and his opinion would likely be allowed. Heather could easily get Max to testify that his opinion was based on his many years as a cop. Sooner or later this evidence was going to come in. At this stage of the trial, over something that was going to come in anyway, Marc did not want to look like he was trying to hide something from the jury.

"What did you do instead?"

"We continued to investigate and obtained more information about Mackenzie Sutherland. During the investigation into Robert's death we learned about William Sutherland changing his Will a short time before he died. He just about completely disinherited his two sons and his daughter and left almost everything, including the company, *Sutherland's* grocery store chain, to Mackenzie.

"She insisted, and the lawyer who wrote the new Will told us, that Mackenzie knew nothing about William changing his Will."

"Was this true?"

"We obtained information from the lawyer who wrote the new Will that it was Mackenzie who insisted William change his Will."

Up to this point, the jurors and spectators had been intently listening. This early in the trial everyone was still paying close attention. With the statement that Mackenzie had William change his Will, a significant buzz swept through the room and all heads turned toward Mackenzie. Again, having been prepared for this, she did not even flinch.

Judge Carr rapped his gavel a couple of times and order was quickly restored. In the second and third rows behind the prosecution's table, four different courtroom artists were seated. All four continued to watch the emotionless Mackenzie while drawing her profile. The pictures of the Ice Queen/Black Widow would be all over the news that night and in the papers the next day.

The remainder of Max's direct exam was spent on the arrest, another search of the Crocus Hill house and the mundane details of preparing the case. Max had made another trip to Chicago but had to admit he found no evidence of wrongdoing on Mackenzie's part for the death of Wendell Cartwright.

Max told the jury while he was in Chicago that he interviewed the ex-wives and children of Wendell Cartwright and what his death had done to them. During a pretrial motion hearing Marc had argued to keep this out. Since they were scheduled to testify themselves there was no need to have Max do so. Judge Carr ruled he would allow a little of it but would not allow Max to specifically quote any of the ex-wives, staying barely on the admissible side of the hearsay rule.

Heather had wanted the death of Wendell's son, Phillip, to be admitted. She hoped the jury would blame Mackenzie for driving Phillip to an overdose death. Judge Carr ruled that the information was too prejudicial and offered nothing to prove how William Sutherland died. The ex-wives were all on the prosecution's witness list and could tell their sad tale of destitution themselves. Would the whining of dilettante ex-wives find a sympathetic ear in the jury box? Marc was skeptical.

"How bad did we get hurt?" Maddy quietly asked Marc.

The direct exam of Max was over and Carr had called for a halt for the day. Marc would start first thing in the morning with his cross examination of Coolidge. Marc, Maddy and Mackenzie were still seated at the defense table.

Marc thought about Maddy's question for a moment before answering. He stared off into space, slightly nodded his head, looked at Maddy and said, "We got hurt. Especially that business about lying about William's Will."

When he said this the façade of the Ice Queen broke for a moment, Mackenzie cringed and softly said, "I'm really sorry."

"Sssssh," Marc quickly, seriously said. "Don't ever say that again. Besides, there's a long way to go. I'm looking forward to getting Cooper Thomas on the stand."

Gabriella Shriqui's show, *The Court Reporter,* was normally aired at 4:30 each weekday afternoon. The station decided during Mackenzie's trial to go live at 6:30 each evening following the 6:00 P.M. newscast then replay that show the next day during its normal 4:30 time slot.

During a production meeting for the show there had been a huge fight about whom Gabriella was to use as guest talking-head experts.

Gabriella's predecessor, Melinda Pace, had frequently used a former federal prosecutor and a criminal defense lawyer. The prosecutor, Steven Farben, would give his take on the day's trial news and the defense lawyer, Andrea Briscomb, would then give hers and normally in that order. The problem was these two knew each other, had tried cases against each other and they despised each other. They could barely stand to be in the same room at the same time.

Station management, the General Manager Madison Eyler and Gabriella's boss, Hunter Oswood, insisted that Gabriella use the two of them as her expert commentators. Gabriella, who knew both lawyers and wanted nothing to do with either of them, almost resigned over the issue. Management insisted on using them because the market research found the show's audience liked the adversarial interaction between them. The matter was resolved by the promise of a nice cash bonus for Gabriella based on the show's ratings.

A live show, of course, did not leave much room for error and no time for editing. If either of her guests took an inappropriate shot at the other — it had happened a few times before — it went out live. Probably one of the reasons why the audience liked these two overblown egos.

Gabriella introduced her guests and for the next half-hour, mediated their comments. Since all they had to analyze were opening statements and Max Coolidge's testimony, both were decidedly pro-prosecution. They spent most of the show dissecting the opening statements of both lawyers. Each "expert" explaining what he or she believed they did wrong and how much better they could have done it. They then talked about the damage done by Coolidge's direct exam and Marc's shortcomings, especially the times he missed an opportunity to object to a question. The last few minutes of air time were spent discussing Mackenzie's conduct.

"Ice Queen is right," Steve Farben said. "She practically gives off a wind chill factor." The second part of that comment Farben had thought up himself. Stroking his own significant ego, he was quite proud of himself for coming up with something so clever, or so he thought.

“I’m sure Kadella instructed her to be calm and impassive,” Andrea Briscomb said. “But I also think you’re right. She does seem to be that way naturally.”

“How much of a stretch is it to believe she is a Black Widow who can mate and kill?” Farben said.

What was not revealed to the audience was the fact that neither lawyer had spent even one minute actually sitting in the courtroom. They were basing their comments on notes, reports and drawings of others who had been in attendance.

The show ended on that note and, after her guests had left, Gabriella was in her office with the show’s producer, Cordelia Davis. Cordelia was a very efficient, African-American woman who had been with the show much longer than Gabriella. Cordelia went back to the days when Melinda Pace was the host and Gabriella was thankful every day to have her managing the show.

“This trial better not last much more than a couple of weeks,” Gabriella said to Cordelia. “I’m not sure how much of those two I can take.”

“We’ll see how the ratings are and what our bonuses will look like,” Cordelia said. “The extra money may be enough to make them a little more tolerable.”

FORTY-ONE

"Good morning, Detective Coolidge," Marc politely said while seated at the defense table. He introduced himself and continued by asking, "How long have you known the Sutherland family?"

"Oh, let's see," Max said, "More than twenty-five years now."

"You met Robert Sutherland while still in high school, didn't you?"

"Objection, relevance, your Honor," Heather stood up and said.

"Goes to bias and credibility, your Honor," Marc said.

"Overruled. Answer the question, detective," Carr said.

"Yes, that's correct," Max replied.

"In fact, Robert helped you get your first job in one of the *Sutherland* grocery stores didn't he?"

"Yes, he did."

"And William helped get you a job with the St. Paul police department?"

"Well, I'm not..."

"Yes or no, please, Detective Coolidge."

"Yes, I suppose he did," Max admitted.

For the next twenty minutes Marc asked a long series of short yes and no questions regarding his close friendship with the Sutherlands. In fact, Marc went a little too far. Some of this had been brought out by Heather during the direct-exam. The jury was getting a little bored with it and seemed to be thinking Marc had made his point and it was time to move on.

"Ms. Anderson did an excellent job of presenting your history as a police officer to the jury. You've had a fine career, haven't you?"

"Yes, I guess you could say that."

"And you owe William Sutherland a great debt for that, don't you?"

"Objection, argumentative," Heather said.

"Withdrawn, your Honor," Marc said.

"There was a court hearing to request an order to exhume the body of William Sutherland, isn't that true?"

"In fact, there were two," Max said.

"No, detective, there was only one. At first, Mackenzie refused to allow the body to be dug up and disturbed, the second did not take place because she agreed to it. Do you remember that?"

"Yes, sorry, you're right."

"And during the only actual hearing on the matter of the exhumation, after the prosecution requested William be exhumed, the judge turned them down, is that true?"

"Yes, that's correct."

"Were you in the courtroom then?"

"Yes."

"You were very angry with that ruling, weren't you, detective?"

"I wouldn't say that, no."

"Really?" Marc said to Max. Marc looked at the judge and asked for permission to approach the bench, which was granted. Heather and her associate, Danica Kyle joined him

"Your Honor, I have a tape I want to show the jury. It's a tape that was shown on TV news of the witness beating a man the day after the hearing…"

"There's no connection between the two events," Heather said.

"This was totally out of character for this police officer. The connection is obvious; he was angry about the result of the hearing."

"No," Carr said. "You can question him about it but no film."

"Let him deny it," Marc said taking one last shot at showing the film.

"No, and that's final."

"Detective, how many official reprimands have you had for the use of excessive force?"

"Objection, relevance."

"Overruled," Carr quickly said.

The question made Max slightly squirm in his chair and pause before answering. "Just once," he said.

"The day after the request to exhume William's body was denied, you met with a man named Marvin Gibbs, didn't you?"

"Yes, I did," Max calmly answered while thinking: *This is why cops hate lawyers.*

"You were supposed to meet with him and he failed to show up, isn't that true?"

"Yes."

"You saw him walking on Grand Avenue and then turn up a side street, isn't that true?

"Yes."

"And you chased him down, did you not?"

"I wouldn't say I chased him down," Max answered.

"I have the names of two police officers who witnessed this incident, Detective Coolidge. Would you like to change your answer?"

Squirming a bit and looking a little uncomfortable, Max said, "Okay, I suppose I took off to catch him and maybe drove a little too fast."

"And you did catch him, didn't you?"

"Yes," Max quietly answered.

"And according to your official reprimand, you, and I quote: hurried out of your car and slapped and punched Marvin Gibbs until he was laid out on the sidewalk, unquote," Marc said reading it off of a copy of the reprimand he had. "Is that what happened?"

Max leaned forward toward the microphone thinking about an explanation. After two or three seconds, he realized if he tried to explain it the lawyer could probably use that to make it sound even worse. Instead he simply said, "Yes," and sat back in the chair.

"Do you normally beat up people who miss a meeting with you?"

"Objection!" Heather yelled jumping to her feet.

"Of course not," Max defiantly added.

"Sustained," Carr said. He glared at Marc who was sitting with an innocent look on his face. "Watch yourself, Mr. Kadella."

Marc had gotten out of this line of questioning what he wanted. He could now argue in his closing statement that Max was inflamed by the adverse ruling disallowing the exhumation. This went to his bias toward the Sutherland family and against Mackenzie to the point that he closed his mind about other possible suspects.

"The next day you went to Chicago to escort a fugitive back to Minnesota, correct?" Marc continued.

"Yes, I believe it was the next day."

"Is this something detectives normally do, escort fugitives?"

"Sure, sometimes," Max said.

This answer was a lie and Marc decided to go fishing. He had a copy of the St. Paul police department's policy book in his briefcase. There is not a word in it about detectives performing this duty. Marc could easily impeach the witness with that policy book. He removed it from his briefcase and asked for permission to approach the witness. When he reached the witness stand he handed the book to Coolidge.

"Detective Coolidge, I have given you a book. It is the policy manual for the St. Paul Police Department. Do you have a copy of this manual?"

"Sure, somewhere," Max answered eliciting a laugh from the gallery.

"Is there anything in there about detectives escorting fugitives?"

"Probably not but that doesn't necessarily mean we don't do it."

"Really? And after you were promoted to detective, except for the trip to Chicago, how many times have you performed this duty?"

"Um, I can't remember," Max said.

"How about none?"

Max hesitated for a few seconds before conceding that this was a first.

Marc took the police manual back and returned to his seat.

"You went to Chicago because they wanted to get you out of town for a few days to let the beating of Marvin Gibbs die down, isn't that true?"

"Objection, argumentative and without foundation," Heather interjected.

"Sustained. Move on, Mr. Kadella."

"When you discovered Frances Cartwright might be Mackenzie Sutherland, you believed she used the name Frances to hide her identity, didn't you?"

This question broke the cardinal rule of not asking a question you do not know the answer to. Marc figured that the answer was obvious enough that the jury would believe Max did think this, even if he denied it.

"Yes, I suppose I did," Max agreed.

"Did you know her mother's name is Frances?"

"No, I did not."

"Did you know her mother died of cancer and Mackenzie was very close to her mother?"

"No, I didn't."

"Did you know Mackenzie's middle name is Frances and she used that name as a tribute to her mother?"

"No, I didn't."

"And isn't it true that your belief that she used the name Frances to hide her identity added to why you believed she was guilty?"

"Oh, I don't know, maybe…"

"Yes or no, detective," Marc said.

"Yes," Max admitted.

"When you discovered the cause of death of Wendell Cartwright, you suspected Mackenzie Sutherland of killing him didn't you?"

Max sat silently for ten or twelve uneasy seconds thinking about the question.

"Answer the question, detective," Carr said.

"Yes, I suppose I did."

"Did you think that if his death was not caused by a heart attack, that someone other than Mackenzie might have killed him?"

"No, I did not," Max claimed.

"So, if Wendell Cartwright's death was by other than a natural heart attack, you believed his death was caused by Mackenzie Sutherland, isn't that true?"

"Yes, I suppose so."

"It's safe to say that because Wendell Cartwright died of a heart attack, that is the reason you believed Mackenzie caused his death, isn't it?"

Max hesitated, shrugged his shoulders and conceded the point.

"May I approach, your Honor?" Marc asked.

Carr gave him permission to come up to the witness stand. Marc walked up to Max a second time, this time carrying a document and when he reached the witness stand he gave it to Max. For the trial record, Marc had to make a verbal identification of what he handed to the witness.

"Detective Coolidge, I've given you a document marked for identification as Defense Exhibit A. Do you recognize this document?"

"Yes."

"It's the official autopsy report for Wendell Cartwright, isn't it?"

"Yes, it is," Max agreed.

"Detective, please read the highlighted part in the box entitled Cause of Death."

"Acute myocardial infarction."

"Do you know what that means?"

"Objection," Heather said. "He's not a qualified medical expert."

"Do you know what a myocardial infarction is, detective?" Carr asked Max.

"It's a heart attack."

"Overruled," Carr said.

"Toward the bottom of the same page is another highlighted area. Please read the highlighted part, detective," Marc said.

"This sixty-four-year-old white male died as a result of an acute myocardial infarction brought on by his lifestyle. The examination shows signs of cirrhosis of the liver due to excess alcohol consumption. In addition, the muscles show signs of atrophy due to a lack of regular exercise and there are numerous signs of drug abuse. His toxicology screen (attached) shows traces of cocaine, heroin and methamphetamines."

"Thank you, detective," Marc said. He took the autopsy report and returned to his seat.

"Isn't it true, detective, despite the death of Wendell Cartwright having been investigated by the Chicago police and yourself, there was no physical evidence of any kind found to even hint that Wendell Cartwright died from anything other than a natural heart attack?"

"Yes, that's true," Max answered.

"After the body of William Sutherland was exhumed and a second autopsy performed, you focused all of your attention on Mackenzie Sutherland, isn't that true?"

"Well, I'm not sure I would say all of my attention on her." As soon as he said this, Max regretted it. Having testified in many trials, he knew exactly what the next question would be.

"Really? Tell me, detective, name one other person you considered to be a suspect in the death of William Sutherland, just one."

Max snuck a quick peek at Heather hoping to be rescued. Heather simply stared back, unable to think of a single objection that would not be overruled. After two or three quick seconds, Max realized he was cornered and decided to concede.

"Sorry, you're right, she was our only suspect because…"

"Nonresponsive, your Honor," Marc quickly said cutting off the explanation.

"Answer only the question asked," Carr reminded him.

"No, I can't think of anyone else."

Marc looked over his notes to decide if he wanted anything else from Max. After about twenty seconds Carr asked him if he had more questions.

"A moment, your Honor, please," he replied.

Marc decided he had gotten out of Max about all he needed to argue bias and a poor investigation. A significant point toward reasonable doubt.

"Just a couple more questions, your Honor. Detective, isn't it true that your investigation never came up with any bottles, syringes or other objects connected to the drug found in William Sutherland?"

"Yes, that's true," Max admitted.

"And you have no idea how it was taken by William Sutherland, do you?"

"No, we don't," Max agreed.

"I have nothing further at this time, your Honor. But the defense reserves the right to recall."

"Redirect, Ms. Anderson?"

"Yes, your Honor," she answered him.

"Detective Coolidge, after you found out the cause of death of Wendell Cartwright, why did you suspect Mackenzie Sutherland?"

"The similarities between his death and William Sutherland's seemed to be too much of a coincidence. Plus, we found out about both men changing their Wills shortly before their deaths."

"Why was Mackenzie Sutherland your only suspect?"

"Objection, your Honor" Marc said. "They had more than ample opportunity to thoroughly go over this during the direct examination."

Judge Carr thought it over then said, "I agree. The objection is sustained. Move on Ms. Anderson."

A shocked Marc Kadella stole a quick glance at Heather Anderson.

"I have nothing further, your Honor."

"Mr. Kadella, recross?"

Marc thought about going after him on the statement he made about the Wills of both men being changed. Marc decided he could do better with that issue with other witnesses still to come. "No, your Honor, but again, we reserve the right to recall this witness.

Carr excused Max and adjourned for the lunch recess.

FORTY-TWO

Alfredo Nunez, the Chief of Pathology of the Ramsey County Medical Examiner's Office was called to the stand. Dr. Nunez looked every bit the professional pathologist. A short, slender man, barely five-foot-seven and a hundred-thirty pounds with rocks in his pockets, he gave off an aura of total respectability. At fifty-seven, he still had a full head of coal-black hair and a neatly trimmed black mustache and goatee to go with it.

Nunez was an experienced witness who needed little preparation. In fact, he had testified so many times he could probably do his direct-exam by himself. The one flaw he had was a slight touch of insecurity that caused him to be a little too loquacious. At times, he could put a jury to sleep with his too detailed explanations. It seemed he had a need to show-off a little bit which could get a little boring.

Heather Anderson allowed her assistant Danica Kyle to conduct the exam. Danica was still in her first year with the prosecutor's office and handling an exam of someone as competent as Nunez would give her some experience with an expert witness.

The first part of his testimony, as is always the case with anyone to be qualified as an expert, is to let him tell the jury about his qualifications. With Alfredo, as much as he liked and needed to impress people, especially a jury, this took a while. Marc watched the jury's reaction and could tell the more Alfredo talked, the less impressed they were.

"Dr. Nunez," Kyle said to steer him toward the heart of the matter, "did you conduct the first autopsy of William Sutherland?"

"No, I did not. In fact, that was done at Regions Hospital by the deceased's attending physician. My office was not involved."

"Is this unusual?"

"No, not at all. When an elderly man in somewhat poor physical condition suffers an apparent heart attack, there would be no reason to involve the medical examiner's office. If there was no sign of foul play, we would not normally be called in."

"What if family members requested it?"

"They would have to convince the police or your office," Nunez said.

"Let's get to the second autopsy. Was there anything unusual found?"

"Yes, there certainly was."

"And what was that?"

"Trace amounts of a drug called Interleukin 2."

"And what is that, doctor?"

“It is a cytokine drug used in immunotherapy and cancer treatment.”

At this point, Ms. Kyle, having never done a direct exam of Dr. Nunez before made a mistake. Despite having been told by Heather Anderson to try to control him with short, specific questions she let him get away from her.

“Please explain to the jury what this is, doctor,” Kyle told him.

Explain to the jury was exactly what Nunez did. For at least a half-hour, Nunez treated the jury as if they were all third-year medical students preparing for an exam. Dr. Nunez had taken the time and effort to learn everything he could about IL-2. Whether they wanted it or not, the jury was going to get the full benefit of his research.

Kyle tried her best to get him to stop by mildly interrupting. She was silently begging Marc to object to something just to sidetrack him.

Nunez went over everything. From the research trials when the drug was first developed, through its chemical compound and how well it worked. This, of course, included comparing it to other drugs.

By the time he finished, Marc was ready to start laughing. Every eye in the courtroom was glazed over and probably no one, especially the jurors, had retained any of what the good doctor had just put them through.

Judge Carr, to everyone’s relief, called for a short recess to give everyone a chance to wake up.

During the break, Danica Kyle conferred with her witness and when court resumed, she reacquired control.

“Dr. Nunez,” she began after the break. “In your professional, expert opinion as a medical examiner with thirty-years-experience, what was the cause of death of William Sutherland?”

“Acute myocardial infarction brought on by being ingested with the drug Interleukin 2.”

“He had a heart attack and this drug…”

“Objection,” Marc interjected to stop her. “Asked and answered.”

Showing the savvy of a more veteran trial lawyer, Danica Kyle said, “I’ll withdraw and rephrase, your Honor. Doctor, in your expert medical opinion, would Mr. William Sutherland have died from a heart attack without having been given this drug, Interleukin 2?”

“No, he would not,” Nunez emphatically answered.

Oops, Marc thought to himself.

“I have no further questions, your Honor,” Kyle said with a tiny, smug smile on her face.

"Dr. Nunez, isn't it true that you have no idea how this drug was introduced into William Sutherland, do you?" Marc asked jumping right into the weakness of his examination of William's body and the doctor's testimony.

"Yes, that's true," he admitted, "except it was not through injections."

"Really? Given the amount of decomposition of the body by the time of the second autopsy small needle marks would have been almost impossible to find, isn't that true, doctor?" Marc knew this because his pathologist had told him this was so.

"Not necessarily..." Nunez started to say.

"Can you say to a medical certainty that the drug could not have been administered by injection, doctor?"

"No, I can't," Nunez quietly admitted.

"Isn't it true, doctor, you have no idea who may have introduced this drug into William Sutherland, do you?"

"No, I don't," Nunez said regaining his composure and sitting up straight.

"Could it have been a close friend?"

"I suppose."

"Someone at work?"

"Yes."

"One of his children?"

"Yes, I suppose if they had access."

"How about a doctor?"

"You've made your point, Mr. Kadella. Time to move on," Judge Carr said.

"One more your Honor," Marc said.

"Make it quick."

"How about a greedy daughter-in-law?"

"Objection!" Danica Kyle jumped up.

"Sustained. The jury will disregard that question," Carr said to the jury. He turned back to Marc and said, "Any more of that and I'll end this."

"Sorry, your Honor," Marc said but not meaning it in the least.

Marc picked up a document and asked for permission to approach the witness. As he did he handed a copy of the document to Danica Kyle and Carr.

"Dr. Nunez, I'm showing you a document marked Defense Exhibit B, have you seen this document before?" Marc said standing a few feet away from the witness stand. He would remain there until finished.

"Yes, I have."

"It's a report of an electrocardiogram administered on William Sutherland approximately a year before his death, isn't it?"

"Yes."

"Done during the course of a routine physical, was it not?"

"Yes, it was."

"Electrocardiogram is also known as an EKG, is that correct?

"Yes, it is."

"It's a test done to measure electrical activity of the heart. A test of the heart's strength, isn't it?"

"Yes, it is."

"William Sutherland's heart output was almost ten points below the standard deviation, was it not?"

"Yes, that is the result of the test but…."

"Isn't it true, doctor," Marc quickly said cutting him off, "this means William's heart was quite a bit below normal? Weaker than a normal heart?"

"I'm not sure I'd say that…"

"Doctor, should I bring in a cardiologist to answer that question? Someone more qualified than you as a heart specialist?"

Nunez sat silently, not wanting to answer the question that challenged his expertise.

"I'll ask again, doctor. Isn't it true William's heart was quite a bit weaker than normal when this EKG was administered?"

"Yes, I suppose you could say that."

Marc retreated to the defense table and picked up another document. He again handed a copy to Danica, one to Carr and one to Nunez.

"Dr. Nunez," Marc again said for the record. "I'm showing you a one-page document. It is a page from the physical performed on William Sutherland at the time of the EKG. It is marked for identification as Defense Exhibit C. Please read the highlighted portion at the bottom."

"It is recommended that the patient undertake major lifestyle changes. Specifically, he is to quit drinking alcohol entirely, smoking cigars, lose thirty to forty pounds and begin an exercise regimen."

"Based on your autopsy examination, did Mr. Sutherland do any of these things?" Marc asked.

"It did not appear so, no," Nunez said.

"In your medical opinion, doctor, do you believe his heart was stronger at the time of his death than when the EKG was administered?"

"Not likely," Nunez conceded.

"Your Honor," Marc began as he took the two documents from Nunez. "At this time, the defense requests that Defense Exhibits B and C be admitted into evidence."

"Objection, lack of foundation."

"May we approach the bench?" Marc asked.

Carr waved them up and Marc whispered, "Your Honor, they know these are valid. I was hoping they would stipulate to allowing them into evidence to save the bother of bringing in the doctor and technician who did the physical and EKG. The prosecution has these records."

"Ms. Anderson?" Carr looked at Heather.

"I'll stipulate, your Honor," Heather said.

The lawyers returned to their seats and Carr admitted the documents into evidence to be given to the jury.

Marc informed the court he was finished with Nunez. Danica Kyle had no questions for redirect and Carr ordered the lunch break.

The defense team, Marc, Maddy, the two bodyguards and Mackenzie went up Kellogg to Seventh to eat at Cossetta's. They were early enough to get a table and Butch Koll ordered two pizzas and drinks for everyone. During the lunch, Marc and the two guards bantered back and forth about the upcoming baseball season, the NHL hockey team – the Wild – and their playoff chances and another bad season by the Timberwolves. Guy stuff.

Normally Maddy had no problem joining in and contributing to the sports talk but not today. While Mackenzie added a little bit to the conversation, Maddy was unusually quiet.

"The state calls Jalen Wooten," Danica Kyle said. They were back following lunch and Carr had given her permission to call her first witness.

The exterior doors were opened by a deputy and a tall, slender, young man with frizzy hair and gold-rimmed glasses entered. He nervously walked up to the witness stand where a deputy swore him in. He took the stand and looked at Danica.

"Please state your name and occupation."

He leaned forward to speak into the microphone and said, "Jalen Wooten. I'm a computer technician with the Chicago Police Department."

Danica took a few minutes to go over his credentials, his education and experience. Wooten was the computer geek who had performed the search of the personal computer of Wendell Cartwright.

This testimony had been the subject of a very acrimonious hearing. Marc had fought tooth and nail to keep it out. The search had not been done until almost four years after Wendell's death. It was not until Max Coolidge had gone to Chicago and spoke to the Chicago cops that it even occurred to them to do it. There was no chain of custody – the computer was found in the basement of an ex-wife and the police could not prove it had not been tampered with during that time.

Judge Carr allowed it over Marc's objection for the limited purpose of showing a pattern. Marc believed this decision, because it was so blatantly prejudicial, was likely reversible error.

When Wooten finished giving his background, Danica began to ask him about Wendell's P.C.

"Your Honor," Marc said as he stood to address the court. "I renew my objection to this testimony in its entirety as being too prejudicial and without probative value. Also, there is a significant chain-of-custody problem," Marc objected, again to be sure it was on the record in case of an appeal.

"Overruled," Carr politely said. "I'm satisfied the chain-of-custody is not a problem and the computer was not tampered with."

It took Danica and the witness less than fifteen minutes to explain what Wooten did with Wendell's P.C. and what he found: six searches over a ten-day period for heart attack inducing drugs. These took place approximately four months before Wendell's death.

Danica took another ten minutes to have him explain how he knew the computer had not been tampered with by anyone. Most of this was techie gibberish but it got the point across.

Marc's cross-exam was limited to a couple of questions.

"Isn't it true, Mr. Wooten, you have no idea who conducted these searches do you?"

"That's true, I do not."

"In fact, for all you know, it could have been more than one person doing them?"

"Yes, certainly, that's also true," he answered effusively, happy that the questions were so easy.

"In fact, anyone who had access to that computer could have done them, isn't it true?"

"Yes, that is also true," he admitted.

"Did you find any searches for any specific drug?"

"Um, no, I did not. They were all general searches for…"

"Thank you, Mr. Wooten," Marc cut him off. "I have nothing further."

The next witness was one of the Chicago detectives, Sean Flaherty. Danica Kyle also conducted his direct-exam.

Flaherty, being a veteran detective and having testified many times, comfortably explained the reason they investigated Wendell's death. When politically connected rich people complained, the department listened.

He did his best to connect the similarities between Wendell Cartwright's death and William Sutherland's. What aroused their suspicions was the information received from St. Paul when Max Coolidge came to Chicago for a fugitive. It was all a little weak, but it did serve its purpose to show a pattern between the deaths of Mackenzie's two husbands.

"You didn't become suspicious of Wendell Cartwright's death until Detective Coolidge aroused those suspicions for you?" Mark began his cross-examination.

"I'm not sure I'd put it that way," Flaherty said.

"Wendell Cartwright died of a massive heart attack, didn't he?"

"Yes, he did."

"Isn't it true, detective, during your admittedly politically-motivated investigation, you discovered Wendell Cartwright had led the life of a pampered, dilettante, well known as an alcoholic, drug addicted womanizer?

"Well, I'm…"

"Yes or no, detective," Marc said.

"Yes," Flaherty admitted.

"You reviewed Mr. Cartwright's medical records, did you not?"

"Yes."

"Isn't it true that after reviewing his medical records, his lifestyle and the autopsy report you were satisfied the death of Wendell Cartwright was caused by a naturally occurring heart attack, yes or no, detective?"

"Yes."

"Isn't it also true that setting aside the coincidence of William Sutherland's death, you have obtained no evidence of any kind to indicate otherwise?"

"Yes, that's true."

The witness was returned to Danica Kyle for redirect.

"Detective Flaherty, what happened to the remains of Wendell Cartwright?"

"Objection, irrelevant," Marc jumped up and said.

"Overruled," Carr said, "You may answer."

"His body was cremated."

"And what happened to the ashes?"

"I was told by one of Mr. Cartwright's children that…"

"Objection, hearsay," Marc said.

Carr considered it for a moment then Heather Anderson said, "May we approach, your Honor?"

Carr waved them forward and as he always did, pushed the button to activate the white noise sound inhibitor so no one could hear the bench discussion.

"Your Honor, we have an ex-wife to testify. She will verify his answer."

The lawyers returned to their seats and Carr told Flaherty to answer the question.

"The ashes were thrown in Lake Michigan." He then added, "They could not be recovered."

The second part of his answer was clearly objectionable, but Marc decided to let it go. It was too late, anyway and fairly obvious that the remains could not be recovered.

Flaherty was excused and Carr ordered the afternoon break.

FORTY-THREE

The mid-afternoon break was over, and the courtroom was completely full again. There was a murmur of conversation because Carr, normally punctual for a judge, was not back on the bench.

"What's going on?" Mackenzie leaned over and whispered to Marc. Maddy, sitting to Mackenzie's left, also leaned in to hear Marc's answer.

"Don't know," he shrugged. "Maybe Shayla Parker's back there for a nooner."

Both women burst out laughing as Marc continued by saying, "At their age, this could take a while."

"Stop it," Mackenzie said trying to calm herself.

"No kidding," Maddy chimed in. "That's not an image I want to have. Besides, they're not much older than you."

"Oh, thanks for the reminder," Marc said.

Tyrone Carter, Carr's clerk came into court through the door behind the bench. He looked at the lawyers and motioned them to come forward.

"He's on the phone with another case. He wants you to come back for a minute."

The three lawyers followed Tyrone back and as they entered the judge's chambers Carr waved them forward. They took the chairs in front of his desk and tried not to listen while he finished the phone call.

"What do you have for this afternoon?" he asked Heather Anderson after hanging up the phone.

"A couple of ex-wives of Wendell Cartwright from Chicago," Heather said.

"Can you get them done in an hour? I have a motion I want to schedule for four o'clock on the case I was on the phone with."

"The direct won't take long," Heather said.

"Marc?' Carr asked.

"Should be okay," Marc said.

"Good, do your best. I know the lawyers for this other case. If I schedule them at four, I'll be lucky to be out of here by seven. Let's go," Carr said.

"State your full name and address for the record, please," Tyrone told the witness.

"Calista Cartwright," Wendell's first wife clearly stated along with her Chicago address.

Heather conducted the direct exam. The purpose of bringing this witness from Chicago, Wendell's first wife, was to establish that the two of them remained the best of friends, despite the divorce and the years apart. And her knowledge of Wendell's financial affairs.

Maddy had flown to Chicago and researched and interviewed all of the ex-wives and children, with the exception of wife number four. Her name was Ilse, a one-time exotic dancer/stripper who drove her Corvette, a parting gift from Wendell, into a bridge abutment. Drunk and loaded with crystal-meth, no one was surprised by her tragic demise.

What Maddy got out of Calista was the claim that Wendell was extremely unhappy with Mackenzie, who Calista still referred to as Frances. The report Maddy gave to Marc was Wendell was contemplating yet another divorce. This news had been argued before Carr who ruled not a word of it could be told to the jury. It was obviously hearsay and Carr would not allow it. One of the few victories Marc was able to get to suppress something overly inflammatory. Without this testimony being allowed, Marc was left wondering what she was being called for.

Heather spent the first twenty minutes having Calista testify about her relationship with Wendell, how much she still loved and cared for him and how devastating his death was. Heather walked her right up to the line of telling the jury about Wendell wanting to divorce Mackenzie/Frances.

"How did he seem to you in the last few months of his life?"

"Very unhappy," she started to say.

"Objection," Marc said to stop her.

"I'll allow it but be careful, Ms. Anderson," Carr ruled.

"I've known him forty years and I've never seen him so unhappy," she continued.

When she said this, Marc thought, *Great! My big mouth let her repeat it.*

"How was his health?"

"Objection. She's not a doctor."

"Overruled. She knew the man for forty years," Carr said.

"At times, not so good then other times he could be the fun, charming Wendell," she said.

"To your knowledge, did he ever have a heart…"

"Objection!" Marc said jumping up.

"Sustained. Don't go there," Carr said.

Heather asked for and received permission to approach the witness. She handed Calista a document, took three or four short steps back and said, "Mrs. Cartwright, I'm showing you a document marked for identification as State's Exhibit Seven, do you recognize it?"

"Yes."

"Read the title, please."

"Last Will and Testament of Wendell Martin Cartwright. This is the Will Wendell had made about six months after he married Frances, I mean, Mackenzie. Sorry."

"How do you know that?"

"Because he gave me a copy of it. I had copies of all of his Wills and most of his important documents," Calista testified.

"Is this the Will that was in place when he died?"

"No. I found out after he died that he had written a new one shortly before his death."

"Between the times he executed the Will you are holding, State's Exhibit Seven, and the Will he had at the time of his death, did he execute another one?"

"Objection, your Honor," Marc politely said. "I'm not quite sure where she's going but since Mrs. Sutherland is not on trial for the death of Wendell Cartwright, I submit this entire testimony is irrelevant."

"Come up," Carr said.

"Your Honor," Heather said when they reached the bench, "this goes to the pattern between the two deaths."

"She's made her point, judge," Marc said. "Anything more and we're getting into prejudicial grounds. She wants the witness to testify that there are funeral instructions in it that do not include cremation. She has no way of knowing, absent speculation, if Wendell changed his mind about cremation."

Carr turned back to Heather who said, "This witness knows he did not want to be cremated and..."

"Stop," Carr said. "Mr. Kadella is right. She's not on trial for Wendell Cartwright's death and any mention of where you're going would be too prejudicial and likely reversible error. Do you have anything else for this witness?"

"No, not really, your Honor," Heather answered him, disappointed Marc stopped her from bringing in disallowed testimony through a back door.

The lawyers returned to their seats and Heather passed the witness to Marc.

"Did you have access to your ex-husband's home?" Marc asked.

"Yes, I had a key and the code for the alarm system."

"Isn't it true that his second wife, Jeanne and her son by Wendell, Phillip Cartwright, also had access to Wendell's home?

"Yes, they did."

"Are you aware that Phillip struggled with drug addiction for over twenty years before dying of an overdose?"

The light went on in Heather's head as she realized where Marc was going with this line of questions.

"Objection, relevance," she said, the only thing she could think of to try to stop him.

"Your Honor," Marc began, delighted with the opportunity to explain it to the jury. "We've had testimony that there were six searches on Wendell Cartwright's computer for heart attack inducing drugs. The jury needs to know that there were a number of people with financial incentive and access to that computer other than my client."

"Overruled," Carr said.

"What was the question?" she asked.

Marc repeated his question about Phillip's drug addiction and Calista answered that she knew about his problem."

"Did he have money problems, too?"

"I'm not sure," she said.

"Isn't it true, he was living on the street when his father died?"

"I'm, ah, maybe. Yes, he was," she reluctantly admitted.

"You and the other ex-wives would have inherited several million dollars if Wendell had died without changing his Will, wouldn't you? You have a copy of it, you must have read it," Marc said.

"Yes, we would have," she answered.

"I have nothing further, your Honor," Marc said.

"Ms. Anderson?"

"No questions your Honor. I have no more witnesses for today," Heather said deciding she was not going to get much from the other ex-wife.

"We'll adjourn until 9:00 A.M. tomorrow," Carr said.

Butch and Andy came through the gate on the bar and joined Marc, Maddy and Mackenzie at the defense table. This was becoming habitual while they waited for the courtroom to empty. All of them, including the bodyguards, were tired of being accosted by media members.

The rule was, while in public even in the courtroom, no discussion about the trial. One never knew where a microphone may be hidden and pointed at them. An hour passed by and Marc decided it was probably okay to leave.

When they got outside onto Fourth Street, the weather hit them hard. Even though spring was on the way it was still February. The temperature was down in the mid-teens and the wind was whipping between the buildings on the narrow streets and biting the pedestrians on their uncovered faces.

Marc led the way up the street to the Victory parking ramp. Despite the cold and the fact most people on the street were in a hurry, they still received quite a few glances from people who recognized them. Fortunately, Butch and Andy's presence no doubt a contributing factor, they were not confronted by anyone and they made it to their cars unscathed.

Having called ahead to reserve a table, the hostess of Hennessey's Irish Pub had a table ready for them. The restaurant was in Minneapolis, across Lake Street and a block east of Marc's office and he and his officemates were semi-regulars.

During the next hour they had a nice comfort food meal. The conversation was light, sporadic and mostly between the men. Marc could not help noticing that Maddy and Mackenzie, seated next to each other, barely spoke. Mackenzie had a sleep-deprived stressed look and Maddy appeared to be distracted as if she was somewhere else.

"You sleeping okay?" Marc asked Mackenzie who was sitting to his left.

Mackenzie paused, smiled then said, "Not so much lately."

Maddy, to Mackenzie's left reached over and squeezed her hand.

"Hey," Marc whispered, "things are going okay. Trust me. Okay?"

In the parking lot they said their goodbyes, Maddy and Mackenzie affectionately hugging. Marc told the guys to get her home then he drove the block to his office. As he parked in the back lot he saw Maddy pull in next to him.

"You okay?" he asked her when they met outside their cars.

"Can we talk?" she quietly asked.

"Sure, come on up," Marc answered.

When they got upstairs they found the office empty except for Connie Mickelson who was still at her desk.

"How did things go today?" Connie asked.

"Okay," Marc told her.

Connie looked at Maddy and detected that something was not right. "What's wrong?" she asked Maddy.

"I need to talk to Marc. Would you join us?"

"Sure, hon," Connie said and followed them into Marc's office.

Maddy asked Marc, "Is Connie covered by attorney-client privilege?"

"For Mackenzie, yeah, she is. Why? What's the matter?"

"Marc," Maddy slowly said looking back and forth between the two lawyers. "I'm beginning to believe she's guilty. It's eating a hole in my heart. I..."

"Wait a minute," Marc stopped her. "The jury is the one who makes that decision, not you, me, Connie or anyone else. Besides, she's the same person you grew to like before all of this happened."

"Who else had access to both computers? Who else had motive? Who stood to gain? I can't avoid these questions," Maddy said.

"This is the risk of becoming emotionally attached to a client," Connie said reaching over from the client chair next to Maddy's and taking her hand. "We've been there. We've all had this happen. Believe it or not, there could be any number of people who had access to both computers."

Maddy gave Connie an inquisitive look and Connie said, "Hey, it's possible. It's also possible the computers were tampered with. Cops do that shit. Keep an open mind. Be a professional."

"How do you do that? How do you represent people you know are guilty?" Maddy asked Marc.

Marc hesitated for a moment then said, "I believe in the presumption of innocence and our Constitution. But you're right, sometimes it's not easy. Just so you know, I have more thoroughly studied the evidence and I believe Mackenzie is innocent. I've seen worse cases against people I knew were innocent."

"Brittany Riley," Maddy said.

"Yes, Brittany Riley."

"Okay," Maddy said obviously relieved. "I'll be okay. Thanks."

An hour after the meeting in Marc's office took place, Mackenzie Sutherland stepped out of the shower. A problem had been nagging at her for a couple of days that she had not been able to resolve. Mackenzie had stood under the shower letting the hot water pound away the tension she felt while she again contemplated her dilemma.

She toweled herself off, hung the towel up to dry then wrapped herself in her large, white, terry-cloth robe. Mackenzie brushed out her hair, scrutinized a couple of new lines around her eyes, shrugged, sighed and went downstairs.

She poured herself a half-glass of an excellent Burgundy then carried it into the living room. She sat down on the sofa closest to the television and curled her legs up on the couch underneath her. Mackenzie turned on the TV. She paid no attention to the noise coming from it or what the show was. She was withholding information from Marc that he should have, and she needed to figure out how to get it to him. Right now, it was likely true that everyone believed Mackenzie was the only one who may have had access to both Wendell's and William's computers. Who else could have done those searches for heart attack causing drugs? Mackenzie knew something that Marc could use to create reasonable doubt and she needed to think of a way to tell him.

"How do I tell Marc," Mackenzie said quietly out loud to herself, "that Adam Sutherland and Phillip Cartwright knew each other? How do I explain that I know that?"

FORTY-FOUR

Judge Carr had given the jury Wednesday off claiming he had other cases that required his attention. His appetite for Shayla Parker was the primary item on his personal menu.

First up Thursday morning was a lawyer from Chicago, Bennett Long. Long had been Wendell Cartwright's personal lawyer for many years. It was Long who had drafted the new Will.

Long was a long-time friend having been a fraternity brother of Wendell in college. Long had also handled Wendell's divorces and personal legal matters, which had been numerous, for forty years. Bennett Long had made a lot of money off of his friend over the years. More than he wanted to account for.

His appearance was essentially out of order. Carr had allowed testimony about the Will in place when Wendell died with the assurance that Long would verify it. For his part, Long wanted nothing to do with this trial and had tried to avoid it entirely. It was through Long that the prosecution hoped to establish that Mackenzie Sutherland, formerly Frances Cartwright, not only knew about Wendell's new Will, but forced Wendell to change it.

Marc had tried to prevent his testimony by claiming attorney-client privilege. Because Long was Wendell's lawyer and not Mackenzie's she had no standing to prevent him from testifying. Long also tried to claim attorney-client but Carr ruled it was waived upon Wendell's death because it concerned how he died. Plus, the privilege is for the benefit of the client only, not the lawyer.

Long was able to stall his testimony for a week claiming a scheduling conflict. That excuse was up, and he was now in court. His real problem was how he felt when he looked Mackenzie in the eye. Long had nurtured an infatuation with her that began even before she married Wendell.

Heather Anderson conducted the questioning and after the introduction and explanation of who the witness was, moved quickly to the main topic.

"Whose idea was it, Mr. Long, to change Wendell Cartwright's Will and leave his entire estate to the defendant?"

Long looked at Mackenzie who was staring back at him, shuffled uncomfortably on the witness stand then said, "I assume it was Wendell's decision. As far as I know. I don't know who else it could be."

Caught off guard by his answer, Heather hesitated a moment before asking, "Mr. Long, did you not tell Detective Coolidge, on October twenty-second of last year, during an interview in your office, that it was

Frances Cartwright's decision? The woman we know as Mackenzie Sutherland and you were certain of it?"

This caused a bit of a stir in the gallery and the jury box. Marc stole a quick peek at Mackenzie who was still staring, unblinking at the witness.

"The detective asked me if I believed Frances knew about it. I probably said yes, but…."

"And he asked you if you believed the defendant somehow coerced Mr. Cartwright into changing his Will and the beneficiary of his family trust to name her as sole beneficiary and according to Detective Coolidge's notes…."

"Objection, hearsay," Marc said referring to Heather using Coolidge's notes.

"Sustained," Carr ruled.

"You told Detective Coolidge that you were absolutely certain that not only did Frances, now Mackenzie, know Wendell changed the Will and Trust but that she manipulated him into it, did you not?"

Long again looked at Mackenzie who showed him a slight smile before he answered. "Look," he began, "you're asking me very specific questions. I'm under oath and have to be honest. I don't remember what caused Wendell to make those changes and I don't know if Fra…sorry, Mackenzie knew about it."

Danica Kyle handed Heather a document of several typed pages. Marc knew exactly what it was since he had a copy of it. He was going to object as soon as she started referring to it then decided to hold off.

"Mr. Long, I have a typed transcript of the interview you did with Detective Coolidge on October twenty-second. Did you receive a copy of this document?" Heather asked as she held it up.

"Possibly," Long answered. "I get a lot of documents. Is my signature on it?"

"On page four of the transcribed statement, you were asked…"

"Objection, your Honor," Marc said as he stood. "Asked and answered and now she is trying to testify from a document that has not been verified. The witness has answered her inquiry about whether or not Mrs. Sutherland knew about her former husband's Will."

"Sustained. Time to move on, Ms. Anderson," Carr told her.

A clearly annoyed Heather Anderson asked, "Why are you trying to protect…"

"Objection!" Marc said again jumping to his feet.

"Sustained. Watch yourself, Ms. Anderson."

"Request permission to treat the witness as hostile," Heather said. This is done so an uncooperative witness can be made to answer leading questions.

"Denied," Carr said. "I've seen nothing to convince me he's hostile. You just don't like his answers."

Heather picked up another document and asked for permission to approach the witness. It was granted, and Heather handed him the Will of Wendell Cartwright they had been discussing, State's Exhibit Seven. She curtly asked him a few questions to acknowledge this was the Will and the beneficiary change of the Trust. Once that was complete, Heather offered it into evidence, gave it to the clerk and returned to her seat.

"I have no further questions, your Honor."

"Mr. Kadella," Carr said.

Marc had prepared a series of questions to try to cast doubt on what Mackenzie knew about the new Will. These were premised on his belief that Long would testify Mackenzie knew about the new Will and it was probably her idea. This was the essence of the typed transcription of Long's interview with Coolidge. Since Long refuted it under oath and he never signed the transcription, Heather could not even use it to impeach his credibility and Long was a smart enough lawyer to know that. Without his signature on it, he could deny any knowledge of it. She would have to find a way to bring Coolidge back, but Marc could probably block that since she had said she was done with him.

Marc decided to ask just one question. "Isn't it true, Mr. Long, as far as you or anybody else knows, Mackenzie Sutherland, the woman you knew by her middle name Frances, had absolutely no knowledge about Wendell Cartwright's Will, State's Exhibit Seven?"

"Yes, that's true. At least not until after Wendell died."

Heather declined to redirect, the witness was excused and Carr ordered a break. When Bennett Long walked past the defense table to leave, he looked directly at Mackenzie with an almost pleading look in his eyes.

When Maddy and Mackenzie returned from the restroom during the break, Marc was still seated at the table. He led them into the adjacent conference room and asked Mackenzie, "What was that with Bennett Long?"

"A couple of things," Mackenzie said. "First of all, Bennett Long is a crook. He has made a career out of ripping off Wendell. I went through some of Wendell's bills from him once and told Wendell about it. He said he knew and didn't care, that Bennett was a good friend and blah, blah, blah. Basically, he put up with it.

"A couple weeks later, Bennett, who is on his third marriage, made a pass at me. Actually, it was more than a pass. He grabbed me, pushed me into a room at the home of a party we were attending. He came at me, tried to grope my boobs so I knee'd him in the balls and slapped his face.

I told him if he ever tried anything like that again I'd go to Wendell and audit every dime Wendell ever paid him.

"Two days later I get a card with a long letter. The sick twist liked it when I kicked him and fought back. Said he'd never been so much in love. And he left me no doubt he'd like to do a little S & M with me."

By this point Marc and Maddy had all they could do to contain their laughter.

"It's not funny," Mackenzie said. "Well, maybe a little," she added with a smile.

"Did you…" Maddy started to ask.

"No!" Mackenzie quickly said, "I shouldn't tell you this, but every time I saw him after that, whenever he could without someone hearing him, he called me Mistress Frances. When Wendell died I had to get a new phone number."

"I'm trying to picture you dressed up in leather with handcuffs and a whip," Marc smiled.

"Turns you on, doesn't it?" Mackenzie said arching her eyebrows at him.

"Have you spoken to Long since you left Chicago?" Marc asked.

"No, not a word. The first time I saw him was today. I was hoping he was over it."

"Okay, let's go back in," Marc said.

The remainder of the morning most of the attention was taken up by the St. Paul police computer technician. Her name was Bernie, short for Bernadette, Olson. A medium-height, slender brunette with her hair in a single braid down to the middle of her back, Bernie wore round, gold, wire-rimmed glasses and the only dress she owned.

Including the lunch break, Bernie took almost four hours to testify about the search of William Sutherland's personal computer. Apparently, whoever used William's computer to do the heart-attack-inducing drug search was a bit of geek who knew something about hiding searches and covering their tracks.

At times her testimony was somewhat interesting and at others painfully boring. Bernie did a professional job of explaining what she found and how she found the searches. Bernie had discovered twelve general searches for heart attack drugs and three specifically for the drug that was found in William Sutherland's body.

"Please tell the jury the date ranges of the searches you found. When was the first one and when was the last?"

"The first was December 14th and they went through until the last one was done on January 3rd, less than three months before William Sutherland died."

Bernie had also conducted a thorough internet search of Mackenzie Sutherland a/k/a Mackenzie Lange, Frances Lange and Frances Cartwright. What she found was a resumé done online by Mackenzie Lange over twenty years ago. Listed on the resumé were all the computer courses in which she claimed to have expertise. There were also two places of employment on it as references.

Max Coolidge and Anna Finney had searched for both of these companies. One had gone out of business but the second one was still active. It was a small tech support company located in Bloomington.

Fortunately for the prosecution, the owner, a now bald man in his late fifties, was extremely anal. The man never threw anything out. He was able to locate Mackenzie's personnel file in two minutes. Included in the file was the resumé Mackenzie had submitted as Mackenzie Lange. The only difference between it and the one Bernie had found was the company from whom they had been given the resumé, Stockton Tech Services, was not listed. Of course, it would not be since she had not worked there before submitting her resumé to them.

The owner, Kurt Stockton, even remembered her. She was in her mid-twenties and although attractive and pleasant enough, she was a bit quiet and kept to herself.

Max and Anna left with a copy of the resumé Stockton had in her file. They also served a subpoena on him in case he was needed to verify the resumé.

Mackenzie admitted to Marc that both resumés were hers but also said they were quite exaggerated. Since the document could be easily verified and Maddy had interviewed Kurt Stockton, Marc allowed it into evidence without an objection.

"In your opinion, Ms. Olson, would someone with that expertise be able to hide the searches for the drugs done on William Sutherland's computer the way you described it?"

"Sure, no problem. In fact, that is exactly what it would take."

With that Danica Kyle, who had conducted the direct exam, turned the witness over to Marc.

"Ms. Olson, would most individuals with a degree in computer science have the expertise to hide the searches the way you described it?" Marc asked. He knew the answer beforehand having gone over this with an expert of his own already. She was on Marc's witness list and would testify if needed.

"Well, um, I guess, probably. Maybe," she said. "I would have to know more specifics."

Marc received permission to approach, went to the witness stand and handed her a one-page document.

"Ms. Olson, I have handed you a copy of a resumé with the name redacted. This document is marked for identification as Defense Exhibit D. On this document are listed the areas this person claims to have computer expertise. Please take a minute to read those."

"Okay," Bernie said when she finished reading what Marc requested.

"Would this person have the requisite expertise to do the searches on William Sutherland's computer and hide them the way you described?"

"Oh, yes, for sure," she said.

Marc retrieved the document but stayed in front of the witness stand.

"Ms. Olson, isn't it true that you cannot say with any certainty who conducted the searches on William's personal computer?"

"Specifically, no," she admitted.

"When you were in your twenties and barely out of college, was it possible you might have exaggerated things on a resumé a bit to help you land a job?" This question broke the cardinal rule of never asking a question if you don't know the answer. Marc knew if she answered no, it would sound ridiculous since everyone does this at least a little bit.

"I suppose, sure," she admitted.

"One last question. If someone had these computer skills, the ones on Mrs. Sutherland's resumé from twenty years ago, but had not used those skills, that knowledge, for almost twenty years, isn't it true those skills would have faded over the years?" Another question that Marc could not know how she would answer except the answer was quite obvious.

"Yes, I suppose that would be true."

"I have no more questions," Marc said.

Danica Kyle declined to redirect and Carr adjourned until the next day, Friday, at 9:00 A.M.

FORTY-FIVE

Friday started more than an hour late because Carr was in chambers again with the lawyers listening to an argument on Mackenzie's case. Marc had correctly guessed that the state's case was about to wrap up. Heather was going to spend the last couple of days, today and probably Monday, with the Sutherland children and Paige Sutherland testifying about what a tragedy his death had been, how much it hurt them to lose his love and guidance as a father and a man they all considered to be a great friend. None of this would add anything to the question of guilt but Carr had previously ruled he would allow it. Marc was trying to have it excluded.

Marc assumed Monday would be the day to wrap up with Cooper Thomas convincing the jury Mackenzie not only knew about the new Will, but it was her idea.

Carr's court reporter was present making a record of the arguments. Also present was the defendant, Mackenzie Sutherland. There were four chairs in front of Carr's desk. The two prosecutors were to Marc's right and Mackenzie was to his left.

The more Heather Anderson painted the picture of the All-American family being devastated by the loss of its wise, loving patriarch, the more annoyed Mackenzie became. Eventually, she forgot about the court reporter and even though Marc had warned her, she reached her boiling point.

"This is such bullshit! Bill Sutherland was a…"

"Your Honor!" Heather almost yelled.

"…narcissistic drunk and whore-chaser who hated his kids and they hated him!"

"Mackenzie, stop!" Marc loudly said as he grabbed her arm to pull her back into her seat.

Judge Carr, who had known Bill Sutherland and knew that what Mackenzie said was true, almost started laughing. Instead, he sternly told Marc to control his client and ordered Mackenzie's outburst stricken from the record.

"If you want to make these allegations, you take the stand in court and subject yourself to cross-examination," he said to Mackenzie.

He looked at Marc and continued. "Unless you have something else, do you?"

"No, your Honor."

"Okay then. My ruling stands. I'll be out in a few minutes."

The first one called was the daughter, Hailey Sutherland. Danica Kyle conducted the exam. Danica had spent almost four hours with

Hailey preparing her testimony. There was nothing significant about it, nothing Hailey should have had difficulty with. Despite this, Danica would be happy when it was over.

Mackenzie almost laughed at the site of Hailey when she entered the courtroom. Gone were the purple and green highlights in her normally blonde hair. She had put on ten to fifteen pounds on her otherwise gaunt frame and looked healthier than Mackenzie had ever seen her. To top it off she was stylishly dressed for a woman her age having discarded the grunge band T-shirt, tattered jeans, boots and two pounds of metal spiked into various places.

At thirty-four-years-old, a month shy of thirty-five, Hailey Sutherland had the maturity of an average twelve-year-old. Mentally, and she had been tested a couple of times, she was well within the normal range of intelligence in spite of her alcohol and drug abuse. It wasn't that Hailey was a falling down drunk or useless junkie. The problem was her emotional maturity was still in high school, right where Daddy had allowed her to keep it, dependent on him. Hailey Sutherland was a spoiled Daddy's Girl. And up until his death, Daddy bailed her out of every jam she got into.

To William's credit, he had paid for several trips to rehab, a couple of years of college, gave her several soft managerial positions with *Sutherland's* and tried to straighten her out. There were even three or four almost abusive rants that he put her through which included threats to cut her off. One of these had taken place at the family Christmas dinner, the last one of his life before he died barely four months later. Hailey had withheld this information from the prosecution, but Mackenzie had told Marc every detail of it. Maddy had located and subpoenaed that month's idiot, loser boyfriend of Hailey who had also witnessed it.

In less than an hour, Danica had walked Hailey through her life as a daughter of the Sutherland's. If one did not know better, you would believe it was the most normal, All-American upbringing anyone could hope for.

There were admissions of drug and alcohol abuse. Danica knew better than to leave that to Marc to present. But it was so smoothed over and polished her story came across as mere blips on the road of life. And her dearly beloved Father was always there with a firm hand to help her through. She even sobbed when she testified about William's death and how much she would miss him.

Danica winced a bit at this, knowing it could come across as contrived. Because of that, Danica wrapped up her exam and gave the witness to Marc.

"It's your testimony that you had a very close relationship with your father?" Marc asked Hailey.

"Yes, I did."

"You were basically, and I mean this in the nicest way, Daddy's girl?"

"I suppose you could say that and I'm not ashamed of it."

"How many times did he pay for drug rehab for you?"

This question caused a minor stir.

"Um, ah," Hailey stammered, "Three, no, four, four times."

"The last time being almost two years ago, is that correct?"

"Objection, relevance," Danica said.

"Goes to her credibility, your Honor."

"Overruled."

"That sounds about right."

"Let me remind you, you're under oath. Are you still using drugs?"

"I'm trying to stay clean..."

"Is that a yes?" Marc asked.

Hailey lowered her head and admitted it was.

"Have you taken any drugs to make you high this morning?"

"Objection..."

"Overruled. The witness will answer."

"No, of course not," she said almost indignantly.

Marc shifted gears and went over other aspects of her life. He took his time and asked her about her education, her employment which amounted to twenty-three months total for the grocery chain. He made her admit that her father was paying her way through life.

"Isn't it true that William complained constantly about your freeloading ways, your drug addiction and an unwillingness to provide for yourself?"

"No," Hailey angrily blurted out.

"Really? This self-made man who, from nothing, worked day and night for years to build a successful business and he never once complained that you could not be bothered to so much as get a job, never once complained about it?"

Hailey sat silently while Marc simply stared at her for several seconds.

"Isn't it true your entire employment history amounts to being hired eight different times for a total of twenty-three months? Would you say that's accurate?"

"No, it must be more than that."

"Ms. Sutherland, I have a copy of your employment history with *Sutherland's* grocery stores in my hand," Marc said holding up a two-page document. "Would you like to change your answer?"

"Yes, that's probably accurate," she conceded.

"Eight different times your father gave you a job, you would work for a few months then quit. Is that an accurate description? Or were you fired?"

"I was never fired."

"Isn't it true your father not only disapproved of this but was furious about it and the two of you argued constantly about this?"

"I wouldn't say we argued constantly about it."

"But it was a source of serious friction between you, wasn't it?"

"I suppose so, yes."

"Your father died March 24th of last year. The Christmas before that, while at your father's home for Christmas dinner on Christmas Eve, the two of you had a huge argument about your lifestyle and he threatened to cut off the money if you didn't go back to rehab, clean yourself up and get a job and work."

"I wouldn't say we had a huge…"

"I have witnesses I can call, Ms. Sutherland," Marc interjected.

Hailey stopped, looked nervously around then admitted it happened.

"Isn't it true you did not go to rehab, did not clean yourself up or get a job?"

"He threatened to do this several times. I didn't think he would do it."

Hailey's answer was technically nonresponsive, and Marc could have requested Judge Carr order her to answer yes or no. Except, the answer she gave was far better than that.

"Isn't it true that this perfect Daddy's girl relationship you tried to get the jury to believe is total nonsense?"

"Objection, argumentative," Danica Kyle stood up and said knowing the damage was done.

"Sustained," Carr ruled.

"Isn't it true that after your father died you received a total, from his estate and the stock you owned in the business, of one-hundred thirty-thousand dollars?"

"Yes," she said. Then, unable to contain herself, blurted out, "Because of that bitch!" and pointed at Mackenzie.

"Your Honor," Marc started to object.

"The jury will disregard that last part of the witness's answer," Carr said to the jury. He looked at Hailey and sternly said. "No more of that."

"Isn't it true you blame your stepmother, Mackenzie, for this?"

"She is to blame."

"Isn't it also true that you're about to be evicted from your twenty-seven-hundred dollar a month apartment because the money is gone?"

"Objection, irrelevant," Danica said.
"Overruled," Carr said. "Answer the question."
"Yes," she admitted.
"I have no further questions."

Paige Sutherland was up next. Danica Kyle also conducted her direct-exam, and through no fault of Danica's, it was a disaster. Despite the time and preparation both Danica and Heather spent with Paige preparing her, Paige could not help herself. She came across as angry, bitter and spiteful. So much so that Danica had a difficult time keeping her on track. At least four times she insisted on making the point that she missed her father-in-law and her poor, dead husband and left no doubt whom she blamed.

By the time she finished an almost exhausted Danica Kyle happily turned her over to Marc. Marc was almost salivating because, apparently, Paige, like Hailey, had not been completely candid with the prosecution.

"Isn't it true you were having an affair with your husband's lawyer..."

"Objection, relevance," Danica almost yelled as both she and Heather jumped to their feet.

"May we approach?" Marc asked. He knew they would react like this and he was ready for it.

Carr waved them forward and hit the white noise button so they would not be overheard.

"Your Honor, they opened the door," Marc said. "All of this 'I'm so lonely and I miss my father-in-law and my husband is so much blather.'" Marc looked at Heather and said, "Be thankful I won't ask if she was screwing the old man, too."

"He's right. You opened the door," Carr said to the two women. He looked at Marc and said, "You better have proof of this."

"We do, your Honor. It's all been presented to the Office of Professional Responsibility and the lawyer, Simon Kane, is in quite a jam with them over it. Hey," Marc continued speaking to Heather, "it's not my fault she didn't tell you or you didn't find out."

Carr waved them back to their tables, overruled the objection and told Marc to continue.

"Isn't it true Mrs. Sutherland, you were involved in an illicit sexual affair with your husband's lawyer, Simon Kane, that began two years before your husband died?"

Paige sat silently staring daggers into Marc. If she had a gun Marc believed she would have used it.

"You son-of-a-bitch," she spat out at him.

"Is that a yes or no?" Marc calmly asked.

"Yes or no, Mrs. Sutherland," Carr said masking his amusement at the exchange.

"Yes," she curtly answered.

"Isn't it true this affair continued after your husband, whom you testified you miss terribly, died?"

"Yes," she snarled.

"Is it still going on?"

"No."

"Maybe you weren't quite as lonely as you claimed."

"Objection, argumentative," Danica said.

"Sustained. Move along, Mr. Kadella."

Marc paused for a moment to let the jury continue to see the venomous look in Paige's eyes. He decided he had done enough damage to her and ended his cross-examination.

"Redirect, Ms. Kyle," Carr asked.

Danica and Heather whispered back and forth trying to come up with a way to rehabilitate Paige's testimony. They quickly realized anything they did would likely make it worse.

"No, your Honor," Danica finally said.

Paige was excused and Carr called for a break. As Paige walked toward the gate, Maddy shifted around in her chair in case Paige attacked Marc. Maddy wanted to be in a position to counterattack, if necessary.

During the break, Heather and Danica hurried back to their office to confer with Shayla Parker. This being an election year, the Black Widow trial was closely monitored by Shayla. The media was still making veiled references to justice for the rich and Shayla desperately wanted a guilty verdict for the upcoming election.

Parker called Judge Carr on his private phone to let him know she needed thirty minutes with her subordinates. Her special friend, Judge Carr, quickly agreed with the request.

For the next half-hour the three prosecutors went over the case and came to the conclusion they were still in good shape. The damage done by putting Hailey and Paige on the witness stand did not harm the question of Mackenzie's guilt. The circumstantial evidence still pointed to her and only her. The consensus was that the case was closer than they thought at the beginning, but they still had it won, especially if Heather put on a typically terrific closing argument.

"We've got Adam Sutherland sitting in the hall outside the courtroom," Danica reminded them.

"You want to put another one of these out-of-control idiot Sutherland's on the stand?" Heather asked. "God only knows what dirt Kadella has on him that he didn't tell us about."

Shayla dialed her phone and Judge Carr answered right away. She told him they were done and would be along in a little while.

"Judge," she said using his formal title in front of her employees, "we need a favor. We've decided not to put on another witness today. At least, not the one we had planned. Could we get you to adjourn early?"

Shayla listened for a moment then said, "Thank you and um," she wheeled around in her chair and whispered, "I'll be sure to remember it at an appropriate time."

A very curious Marc Kadella looked up at the clock when Heather and Danica finally arrived. The mid-afternoon break had lasted forty-five minutes while everyone waited for them. A minute later, Carr entered the courtroom and motioned for the lawyers to come up to the bench.

"How long will your next witness take?" Carr asked Heather.

"I won't be able to finish him today unless we stay late."

"How about we give the jury a break and knock off early? I hear the weather could get bad later with three or four inches of snow to drive home in. Marc?"

"I have no objection," Marc said wondering where this came from.

The lawyers returned to their respective tables and Carr adjourned until Monday morning.

While they were waiting for the courtroom to empty a thought occurred to Marc.

"I was expecting Adam Sutherland to finish the day," Marc said to Mackenzie and Madeline. "I'm thinking, after the problems they had with Hailey and Paige they decided not to put Adam on. Maddy, he's on my witness list but we need to drop a subpoena on him."

Marc retrieved a subpoena from his trial case, filled in the blanks and gave it to her.

"Get him this weekend. I'm guessing they will finish up Monday with Cooper Thomas. I want Adam in the hallway first thing Tuesday morning. We'll start with him."

"Why is Adam so important?" Mackenzie asked.

"Another spoiled disgruntled offspring of William Sutherland," Marc said. "Plus, you'll see."

FORTY-SIX

Saturday afternoon Mackenzie was out on a walk for the first time in almost two weeks. Probation services had agreed to remove the ankle bracelet with her word to Judge Carr that she would stay within a one-mile radius of her home. Anything farther than that she was to call in and leave word as to when and where, even if it was a trip to her lawyer's office in Minneapolis.

After spending all week cooped up in court or at home, it felt wonderful just to be outdoors for a while. The early March weather was miserable. Temperature in the low-thirties and a wet, sloppy snowstorm was in progress that would drop five inches before nightfall. Mackenzie didn't care a whit. In fact, the cold and even the wet snow felt refreshing and reminded her of her childhood. Of course, she was dressed for it; winter boots, a fur-lined, hooded parka and jeans.

Mackenzie slopped along in the street in a wide circle staying just inside the one-mile radius. Even though no one was watching or monitoring her, probably, she would strictly adhere to the rules.

While she walked along she could not prevent her thoughts from wandering back to the trial. It was beginning to look like the biggest problem they had, the lynchpin that they needed to remove, was the computer access.

Ever since the prosecution was allowed to bring in the testimony about the searches on both Wendell's computer and Bill's for heart attack inducing drugs, the computer access had hung over the trial. Only Mackenzie had access to both computers at the times of the searches. And Marc was sure Heather Anderson was going to drive a stake through Mackenzie with that during her closing argument.

Half-way through her walk, Mackenzie decided to put it out of her mind. Shortly after reaching the turn to head back, she passed a small pond. The ice was mostly gone, and she stood in the street for ten minutes watching the ducks and geese calmly swim around. A rotten day that the waterfowl seemed to enjoy. She made a snowball out of the wet snow and threw it toward the pond. It landed in the water and several of the ducks squawked, jumped out of the water and flew a few feet away. She felt good just to be alive and outdoors.

Mackenzie returned home, punched the numbers into the front door keypad and let herself in. While removing her boots and coat in the foyer, a thought occurred to her. She hurried up the stairs and into what was Adam's bedroom.

Searching through several boxes of the junk Adam left behind, she finally found something that might help. A yearbook from Macalester College in St. Paul.

Sitting on the floor in Adam's closet, she paged through it and found what she hoped she would. "Maybe," she quietly said out loud to herself.

"Marc," Mackenzie said into her phone after calling her lawyer. "Hi, it's me."

"Hey, Mac. How are you?" he pleasantly answered her.

"Could you come over for dinner? I'd like some company and I have something to show you. I'll cook up a couple of steaks and…"

"We're not going to get involved while this trial is going on," he reminded her.

"I know. Believe me, you'll want to see what I have. Six o'clock?"

"Sure, see you then."

Marc was seated at the breakfast island in Mackenzie's kitchen sipping at a glass of some kind of red wine. Marc didn't know or care enough about wine to bother to ask. Mackenzie handed it to him and he took it.

"Okay, what do you have to show me?"

"In a minute," Mackenzie said as she handed him his plate. She sat down on a stool on the opposite side of the island from him. "You remember we are having a problem with the access to both the computers?"

"Thanks for reminding me, yes," Marc said.

"We've been trying to come up with a plausible other person who might also have access. Well, while I was out walking today, it occurred to me that it could be two people. One who had access to Wendell's and one who had access to Bill's."

"We could find a list of those," Marc said while chewing his ribeye.

"Let me finish. I remembered a couple of days ago, when we were talking about Adam, that when I was with Wendell, I heard Phillip mention a friend of his named Adam that Phillip said lived in Minnesota. He was talking to Wendell and I didn't think much of it at the time."

"Are you serious? Do you have proof?"

Mackenzie opened a drawer on her side of the island, removed the yearbook she found and slid it across the granite countertop to Marc.

Marc held it up and said, "Macalester College. Good school, if a bit pricey. This is Adam's?"

"Yes," Mackenzie answered him.

"Phillip's in here?"

"Yes."

"So they went to the same school. I'm not sure that's enough to…"

"Open the front cover, upper left-hand corner. Read the salutation."

"To my best bud: 'Partners forever'. And it's signed Phillip and what looks like Cartwright. Holy shit, they knew each other. God bless you, Mackenzie!"

"There's more. I started thinking about the times I overheard Phillip talking to Wendell about his friend, Adam. Each time, it was at least three and maybe four times, as soon as I walked in and they noticed me, they stopped. You know, like they were talking about me and I caught them. And once, I definitely heard Phillip use the word crystal before they knew I was there."

"Crystal meth?"

"I think so. I know Wendell was using. I didn't care as long as he didn't use around me. And Phillip was a total junkie."

"Died from a heroin OD," Marc said.

"I wish you could spend the night," Mackenzie softly said. "I'm so damn lonely and…"

"I know," Marc said. "Sorry, no. I can't stay."

"Madeline thinks I'm guilty, doesn't she?"

"I don't know what she thinks," Marc said.

"Liar," Mackenzie said with a weak smile. "Do you?"

Marc reached across the table and took her right hand in his left. "No, I don't," Marc sincerely told her.

Marc finished his meal, pushed his plate aside, picked up his phone and said, "Speaking of Madeline," and speed dialed her number.

"Did you get Adam Sutherland served?" he asked her.

"No, but I have a line on where he'll be tonight. I'll get him. You know, it's Saturday night and I should be on a date, not chasing your witnesses."

"Tell him I want him at 9:00 A.M. Tuesday morning," he said ignoring her complaint. "I think they'll wrap up their case Monday with Cooper Thomas. I'll start off with Adam."

"I know, you told me this before. Are you listening to me? You're destroying my social life."

"Call Gabriella, see if she's not doing anything," Marc suggested.

"I did, she's coming with me," Maddy admitted. "I'm going to serve him at First Avenue later."

"You two in that place. I should call ahead and warn them. Call me and let me know you got him. Behave yourselves."

"Yes, Dad, we will."

FORTY-SEVEN

"State your name and occupation for the record, please," Judge Carr's clerk politely told the witness as he took his seat on the witness stand.

"Cooper Stuart Thomas. I'm a licensed attorney at law here in St. Paul."

It was Monday morning, shortly after 9:00. Cooper was the state's last witness and Heather Anderson was counting on him to put the final nail in Mackenzie's figurative coffin. Heather hoped, more than believed, that when the jury heard Mackenzie knew about William Sutherland changing his Will, they would draw the correct conclusion and come back with a guilty verdict. In fact, Mackenzie not only knew about the new Will she coerced William into doing it.

Cooper Thomas was not a litigator and it showed. It took him the better part of an hour to settle down. Knowing this ahead of time and having dealt with hundreds of nervous witnesses over the years, Heather brought him along with soft easy questions to get him comfortable and talking smoothly. Mostly background things about him leading up to when he met Mackenzie Sutherland. Before Cooper began his testimony about how he came to know her, Judge Carr called the morning break.

While the people in the gallery were crowding through the exterior door, Maddy Rivers somehow managed to squeeze through coming into the courtroom and make her way to the defense table. As she passed through the gate, Maddy smiled and said good morning to Heather and Danica Kyle. The two prosecutors politely, even sincerely, returned the greeting.

"I think I hate her," Heather whispered to Danica. "That's not fair, what she has."

"No shit," Danica very quietly replied. "And on top of it she's so damn nice all the time. If she was a bitch that would actually help to hate her."

"And smart," Heather added.

"Hey," Maddy said to Marc. "Hi, guys," she said to the bodyguards, Butch and Andy. "Morning," she smiled giving Mackenzie a reassuring pat on the back.

"Got him," she said to Marc. "I caught him at his apartment about an hour ago and told him if he wasn't here at 9:00 tomorrow I'd send the sheriff to lock him up until we need him."

"Did he believe you?" Marc asked.

"Yeah, he did," Maddy said. "How are you?" she asked Mackenzie.

"Good," she answered. "Be sure to bill me for the time it took you to catch up with my worthless ex-son-in-law."

"Please tell the jury how you first became acquainted with Mackenzie Sutherland," Heather told Cooper when everyone was back from the break.

"As I recall, she was a reference from a mutual acquaintance," Cooper said.

"Before this had you ever done any representation for any of the Sutherlands or *Sutherland's* grocery stores?"

"No, I had not nor did anyone in my firm. As I said, she came to me for a prenuptial agreement. She was engaged to William Sutherland and they both had substantial non-marital assets to protect in the event of a divorce."

"How much was Mackenzie worth at that time?" Heather asked.

"Objection," Marc stood and said. "Relevance and attorney-client privilege, your Honor."

"This is already public knowledge, your Honor. We could present numerous newspaper articles that accurately reported her net worth."

"Overruled," Carr said.

Marc figured beforehand that Carr would overrule him. In fact, he wanted him to. Since Mackenzie had more money than William, a significant part of the defense was she had no financial motive to kill him. Marc objected to make sure all of the jurors were paying attention. He wanted them to hear this.

"I found out shortly after the prenup was signed that she was worth roughly forty million dollars," Cooper said.

Strangely, this revelation did not faze anyone in the courtroom.

"Why didn't you find this out before the prenup was signed? Isn't that supposed to be included in the prenup? Full disclosure of assets?"

"Normally, yes. There should be an addendum in which both parties list everything. Instead, as part of the prenup, they signed a separate section agreeing they were satisfied that full disclosure was made."

"So, Mrs. Sutherland could have withheld something and…"

"Objection," Marc jumped up again. "Speculation, assumes facts not in evidence, lack of foundation, take your pick, your Honor."

"All of them. Sustained," Carr ruled.

For the next half-hour, Cooper testified generally about what other things he had done for Mackenzie. Marc was able to keep most of the specifics out by using the attorney-client privilege objection. Most of it was for financial matters she needed her own lawyer to handle. Nothing of consequence concerning her relationship with William or any of the Sutherlands.

"About fourteen months ago, early December, Mackenzie came to me to discuss a divorce. William was cheating on her. She told me it wasn't the first time and she had had enough of it. She wanted to know if the prenuptial agreement could be broken."

"Why?"

"The prenup allowed for five million dollars in the event of a divorce if one of them was unfaithful. Mackenzie believed she could get more in a divorce without the prenup in place."

"What did you tell her?"

"I told her we could try but I didn't see any reason for a court to throw out the prenup. I didn't think we had sufficient grounds."

"Then what happened?"

"She told me to hold off on the divorce. About a week later she called and told me they were going to work on saving the marriage. It was a week before Christmas, the Christmas that was William Sutherland's last one.

"The next time I saw her was at our firm's Christmas party, the one we have for favored clients. She came alone and told me she was bringing William in right after New Year's Day to have William do a new Will. She also told me they wanted a postnuptial agreement to invalidate the prenup.

"On Monday, January fourth, both William and Mackenzie came to my office. Mackenzie waited in the reception area while I met with William to go over what he wanted in the new Will."

"And what was that?"

"Basically, he wanted to leave everything to Mackenzie except for a specific bequest of one-hundred-thousand dollars to each of his children, Robert, Adam and Hailey."

"Did he make any arrangement for his grandchildren, Robert's children?"

"No, not a dime."

"Nothing for college or…"

"Asked and answered," Marc objected.

"Sustained, move along."

"Mr. Cooper, did you draft the new Will and the postnuptial agreement?"

"I did," he answered. "William told me he wanted it done right away. He admitted he was anxious to save his marriage, and this was his way of showing his wife how much he wanted to do that."

"Did he indicate whose idea it was?"

"Yes, he did," Cooper quietly admitted.

"And whose idea was it?"

"Objection, hearsay," Marc said.

"Overruled, the witness may answer," Carr ruled.

Cooper hesitated for a moment, looked at Mackenzie as if to say, "sorry" then said, "William claimed it was Mackenzie's idea. But he said…"

"Nonresponsive, your Honor."

"He's your witness," Carr reminded her.

"When did they come in to sign the new Will and postnuptial agreement?" Heather said deciding to move forward.

"The very next day, January fifth."

Heather asked for and obtained permission to approach the witness. She took several documents with her and one-by-one she had Cooper identify State's Exhibits One through Six. They were the Last Will and Testament of William Sutherland, the postnuptial agreement and pages of Cooper's appointment's calendar to confirm the dates.

When all of those were entered into evidence and given to the jury to pass around, Heather had one more to deal with.

"Mr. Cooper, I'm showing a document marked for identification as State's Exhibit Eight, do you recognize it?"

"Yes," Cooper answered.

"Tell the jury, please, what it is."

"It is a signed, sworn affidavit I signed claiming Mackenzie Sutherland knew nothing about the new Will her husband executed in my office on January fifth last year."

"The new Will is State's Exhibit One you are referring to?" Heather asked.

"Yes, it is."

"Were you lying when you signed this affidavit, State's Exhibit Eight or were you lying today when you testified that she knew all about it, including what was in the new Will, State's Exhibit One?" Heather asked, being very clear to identify the documents for the trial transcript and record.

Cooper hesitated for a moment as if thinking about his answer. He looked at Mackenzie who stared back, her eyebrows slightly raised. Finally, Cooper admitted he lied when he signed the affidavit.

"Why?" Heather asked.

"To help her," Cooper said weakly shrugging his shoulders. "I believed she had nothing to do with William's death and I didn't want to see her get in trouble."

Heather, like a kid looking at a "Do Not Touch" sign, had all she could do not to ask the next obvious question: "Why would you think that?" No matter how she phrased it, she could not imagine an answer that would help her case.

"I have no further questions," she said instead, her better judgment winning out. She took the affidavit from Cooper, walked it over to the jury box, gave it to the foreman and returned to her seat.

"We'll break for lunch now," Carr said. "You may examine the witness at one o'clock."

FORTY-EIGHT

"Mr. Cooper, where were you when the police picked you up for questioning?" Marc asked beginning his cross-exam.

"Objection, relevance and beyond the scope of the direct-exam," Heather said.

"Bear with me, your Honor. It goes to credibility," Marc said in response. "And is the state claiming he was never questioned by the police?"

Heather stood silently not responding to Marc's question.

"Overruled," Carr said.

"I'm not sure what you mean?" Cooper nervously said.

"Were you at home, the office, on the street?"

"In the parking ramp attached to my building."

"What time was it?"

"Just before eight o'clock."

"In the morning?"

"Yes."

"You were arriving at your office for work?"

"That's correct."

"Were they waiting for you or did they follow you in?"

"Your Honor," Heather said.

"Come up," Carr said and gestured to the lawyers.

When the three of them reached the bench Heather sarcastically asked, "Are you gonna ask him if he stopped to pick up his dry cleaning on the way?"

"That's enough," Carr admonished her. "Where are you going with this?" Carr asked Marc.

"I want the jury to see the complete picture of what they did to coerce him into changing his story," Marc told him.

"We did no…"

"Stop," Carr told her. "Okay, I'll allow it."

Back at their tables, Marc continued by repeating the question.

"They were waiting for me," Cooper admitted. "Detectives Coolidge and Finney."

"Did they put handcuffs on you and arrest you?" Marc asked.

"No."

"But they made it clear you were not free to leave. That you had to come with them, didn't they?"

"Yes, they did."

"Were you intimidated by them?"

Cooper's eyes nervously shifted about and he lowered his head a little before admitting he was.

"Were you allowed to make a phone call?"

"I called my office to tell my secretary I'd be late."

"Did the detectives ask you any questions on the ride to the police department?"

"No, they barely spoke to me."

"Did they read you your Miranda rights?"

"Yes, when we got to the police department."

"Did you ask for a lawyer?"

"I mentioned it. I sort of asked if they thought I needed one."

"What did they say?" Marc asked.

"If I wanted one I could call one. It was up to me. I decided not to."

"When you got to the police department was Heather Anderson there?" Marc was doing a little fishing. He did not know the answer, but he had a pretty good idea, based on past experience. He figured she was there, and he wanted the jury to see how all of this went down to know it was a set-up.

"Yes, she was."

"At eight o'clock in the morning she was waiting for you at the police department and not her office. Is that what happened?"

"Yes."

"When you got there, the three of them, Heather Anderson, Detective Coolidge and Detective Finney took you into a small, windowless room with a cheap table and a few chairs around it, didn't they?"

"Um, no, there was a window."

"With bars on it?"

"Yes."

"There was also a mirror on one wall and a cage to lock people into, wasn't there?"

"Yes."

"And they sat you down at the table opposite that cage then left you in there looking at it, didn't they?"

By now, everyone in the courtroom, especially Cooper Thomas, was wondering how Marc could possibly know this.

"No, not right away," Cooper said. "They started talking to me first, for a while."

"They talked to you about your life, didn't they?"

"Well, yes."

"Your marriage?"

"Yes."

"Your children?"

"Yes."

"Your nice home on Sunfish Lake?"

"Yes."

"Your income from your law firm?"

"Yes," he answered becoming quieter with each question.

"And they told you there was a very good chance that you would lose all of this if you didn't cooperate with them, didn't they?"

"Objection," Heather jumped up and said.

"Overruled," Carr said before she even had a chance to say what her objection was. Clearly Carr wanted to know what happened in the interrogation room.

"Yes," Cooper said with more enthusiasm.

"And they also told you that you could be disbarred and even go to prison, didn't they?"

"Yes."

"Was that when they left the room? All three of them?"

"Um, yeah, I think it was," Cooper said.

"How long were they gone?"

"Twenty to thirty minutes. I'm not sure. It seemed a lot longer. It seemed like a couple of hours."

"So, let me be sure I understand you. After telling you they were going to destroy your life, possibly get you disbarred and put you in jail, they left you alone in a room looking at a cage to think it over. Is that correct?"

"Objection," Heather said trying not to yell.

"Overruled," Carr said.

"Asked and answered," Heather insisted.

"Overruled," Carr said again more firmly.

"Yes, I guess they did."

"You were pretty scared sitting in that room, staring at that cage, thinking about the life you had worked so hard for being taken away, weren't you?"

"Yes, I certainly was."

"What time was it when they came back into the interrogation room?"

"Around 9:15, I think, 9:20."

"Had you agreed to help them before they came back into the room?"

"No."

"It wasn't until they had told you, several more times, all of the bad things that would happen to you if you didn't cooperate with them and then you agreed to change your story, isn't that true?"

"Yes," Cooper agreed.

“Did they tell you that you had to wear a wire and try to get Mrs. Sutherland to confess to murdering her husband?” Marc asked, again doing a little fishing.

“Yes, they made me wear a wire, not to get her to confess to murder, they didn’t believe she would. They just wanted me to get her to admit she knew about William changing his Will before he did it.”

“When did you do this?”

“Later that same day. I called Mackenzie, Mrs. Sutherland, and went to her house.”

“Were the police listening and recording the conversation?”

“Yes, they were.”

“Did you listen to the recording afterward?”

“Yes, I did.”

“Was it accurate?”

“Yes, it was.”

“Did you try to get Mrs. Sutherland to make the admissions the police wanted?”

“Yes, I did.”

“Did she admit that she knew about the Will before William had you write it?”

“No, she didn’t.”

“In fact, she absolutely denied any such knowledge, didn’t she?” Marc asked.

“Yes, she did.”

“And the police recorded her denials?”

“Yes.”

“Did you signal to her in any way that you were wearing a wire for the police?” Marc asked even though it was a very risky question. If Cooper answered yes, this entire line of questions would have just blown up in Marc’s face. He basically had to risk it to remove any doubts anyone might have about Cooper doing that.

“No, I did not.”

“As far as you know, she had no idea and today is the first she has heard of this, isn’t that true?”

“As far as I know, yes.”

“One last question, Mr. Cooper. Isn’t it true that if Mackenzie Sutherland is found guilty in this trial, Adam, Hailey and Page Sutherland will inherit millions of dollars?”

“Objection, beyond the scope of direct,” Heather said.

“I’ll allow it, if you know, Mr. Cooper,” Carr said.

“Yes, I believe they will.”

“I have no further questions at this time. I reserve the right to recall, your Honor,” Marc said.

"Do you wish to redirect, Ms. Anderson?"
"Yes, your Honor."
"We'll take a short break first." Carr said.

During the break Heather and Danica put their heads together and decided what to do on redirect. Marc had scored some very significant points especially about coercing Cooper's cooperation. The two women decided to ask just a couple of questions to soften the damage.

"Mr. Thomas, was your cooperation with the police in any way dishonest?"

"No, not at all."

"You did so because you committed perjury when you signed the affidavit, did you not?"

"Objection. Leading and that is not a determination for the witness to make," Marc said.

"Sustained as to leading. He's a lawyer and an officer of the court. Overruled as to whether or not he believed he committed perjury."

"Yes, that was the reason."

"I have nothing further," Heather said.

"Mr. Kadella?"

"I have nothing for recross, your Honor. However, I move the court to dismiss this witness's entire testimony as obviously coerced and unreliable."

"Denied," Carr quickly ruled. "The jury can decide for itself how much weight to give to the witness's testimony. You may call your next witness, Ms. Anderson."

"The prosecution rests, your Honor."

"Mr. Kadella?"

"Move to dismiss the indictment on the grounds that the state has failed to meet its burden, your Honor."

"Denied. The defense will begin its case at 9:00 A.M. tomorrow."

While they waited for the courtroom to clear, Butch Koll came through the gate and pulled up a chair next to Marc.

"How did you know? How did you know what went on in that interrogation room?" he whispered.

"Because I've been in that very same room. I have a pretty good idea what they did to him. It's what I would have done too; find a way to scare the hell out of someone."

Andy, Butch's partner, had joined them by now and said, "It was pretty interesting to watch."

Marc shrugged his shoulders looked at the empty jury box, turned back and said, "We'll see if it does any good."

"Can I talk to you for a minute in here?" Mackenzie asked Marc nodding her head toward the conference room door.

"Sure," he answered.

The two of them went into the small room, each took a seat at the table and Marc looked at Mackenzie waiting for her to start.

"When are we going to talk about me testifying?" she asked.

"We already have, several times."

"No decision was made," she pointed out.

"With what we have done and coming up, I think I can make a good case for reasonable doubt. I don't think you can add anything by getting on that witness stand and…"

"I want the jury to hear me deny that I did this. And I think they want to hear me say it."

"If that was all there was to it, I'd agree. But it's not. You get on that witness stand and Heather Anderson will come at you like a heat-seeking missile. She'll make you look like a scheming, conniving serial killer who seduced rich, older men and poisoned them for their money. She'll do it and I can't stop her."

"She's going to try that in her closing argument anyway."

"Yes, she will," Marc agreed. "But I can punch enough holes in it to create reasonable doubt. If she is able to use your words, the things she'll get you to admit on cross-exam will be much more powerful. Right now, all she has is the testimony of others. There's a big difference."

"I hate what people are saying about me. I stopped reading the newspaper or watching TV news. I want to publicly deny it."

"I'm trying to keep you out of prison. I can't worry about what people think. Besides, you'll be surprised how quickly that dies down. One of the Kardashians will get married or divorced or have a baby and everyone will move on."

This last statement made Mackenzie laugh, a rare occurrence lately.

"Okay," she agreed.

"We'll see, but I'll only let you testify if I think it is absolutely necessary. And right now, the risk is not worth it."

FORTY-NINE

For the fifth or sixth time, Marc looked over his shoulder at the back of the courtroom. He had talked to Maddy last night and she had made arrangements with Adam Sutherland to bring him to court this morning. It was 8:55 and so far, no sign of either of them. Marc had his computer tech standing by in the hallway to testify in case Maddy didn't get Adam to the court on time. He was on the verge of sending Butch into the hallway to try to call her again when, much to his relief, Maddy came through the door.

"Hi, everyone," she said when she got to Marc's table. "He's in the hall. Pissed off, but here. Sorry I didn't call. I forgot to charge my phone. Sorry."

"Go babysit him until he's called. It should only be a few more minutes," Marc told her.

"Is the defense ready to proceed?" Carr asked looking at Marc.

"We are, your Honor," Marc stood and said.

"You may call your first witness."

"The defense calls Adam Sutherland."

A moment later, one of the court deputies held open the door to the hall and Adam, followed by Maddy, entered the courtroom. He sullenly walked up the center aisle, through the gate and to the witness stand.

Despite being almost forty-years-old, an age by which most people have become grown-ups, Adam retained the air of a petulant, sulky, teenager. And he dressed the part as well.

This supposed adult showed up for court wearing sneakers, tattered jeans an untucked, unbuttoned plaid shirt and blue T-shirt. His disheveled hair added perfectly to the image of someone who just got out of bed, put on whatever happened to be lying on the floor and came to court. Marc could not have been happier. Let the jury's first impression be an accurate one.

Adam was sworn in, took the stand and stated his name for the record.

"Mr. Sutherland, where are you currently employed?" Marc began.

"I'm, ah, between jobs."

"What and when was your last job?"

"Objection, compound question," Heather said.

"Overruled, you will answer," Carr said.

"I do, ah, computer consulting. I'm an independent computer tech," Adam said.

"How much money did you make as a computer consultant tech last year?"

“I haven’t done my taxes yet, I’m not sure.”

“Best guess. Give me a ballpark approximation,” Marc said.

“Oh, I can’t really say.”

“Fifty thousand?”

“Ah, no, not that much,” he reluctantly admitted.

“More than one hundred dollars?”

“Yeah, sure, probably,” Adam said nervously shifting in his chair.

Marc looked at Carr and asked, “Permission to treat as hostile, your Honor?”

“Granted,” Carr answered.

“Let’s be honest with the jury, Mr. Sutherland,” Marc said turning more serious. “Isn’t it true you do not have one legitimate source of income as a computer tech consultant?”

“Well, I ah…”

“Yes or no,” Marc said.

“Yes,” Adam quietly agreed.

“Isn’t it true that your last legitimate employment was six years ago with *Sutherland’s* grocery stores?”

Adam squirmed in his chair before reluctantly agreeing.

“At that time, your father gave you your eighth chance at gainful employment, you lasted a total of two months then your father personally fired you, didn’t he?”

“Yes.”

“For selling drugs at work.”

“Objection, your Honor…” Heather started to say.

“Overruled,” Carr said. “Answer the question.”

“No, I mean, I don’t remember why. I think it was for being late too many times.”

Nice try, Marc thought.

“So, for the last six years, you have had no visible means of employment, no way to support yourself legitimately, isn’t that true?”

“I got by,” Adam muttered.

“Your father helped you with that didn’t he?”

“Yeah, sometimes,” Adam admitted.

“The Christmas before your father died, the last Christmas you’ve spent as a family, your father and your sister Hailey had an argument, didn’t they?”

“Yes.”

“And in front of everyone, including you, he threatened to cut her off from his money. To stop supporting her didn’t he?”

“Yes, he did.”

“Mr. Sutherland, you purchased a new Chevrolet Corvette approximately three months before this, isn’t that true?”

"I guess, about then, yeah. So what? Don't I get to drive a nice car?"

Ignoring him Marc asked, "A car that cost almost sixty thousand dollars?"

"About, I guess. I don't remember."

"Isn't it true, the first time your father saw this car was at the same Christmas gathering?"

"I don't remember," Adam answered, the light in his brain finally coming on as he realized where Marc was going.

"And isn't it true he was very angry when he saw it? You're under oath, Mr. Sutherland."

"Yes, he was."

"And isn't it also true that after he told your sister to straighten up or he would cut off his support, he looked at you and said the same thing?"

Adam fidgeted around for several seconds, rubbed his hands and nervously looked around before quietly answering, "Yes."

"I'm, sorry," Marc said, "I didn't hear your answer?"

"Yes," he said more loudly.

"Your Honor, I object to this entire line of questioning as irrelevant," Heather stood and said to break up the questioning. She immediately regretted it.

"We're allowed to explore other people who had the same motive the prosecution is trying to attribute to my client, your Honor," Marc responded.

"Yes, you are. Overruled," Carr said clearly sending the message to the jury that Marc might be onto something.

Marc asked for permission to approach the witness stand and did so when Carr agreed to allow it.

"Mr. Sutherland, I'm showing you a document marked for identification as Defense Exhibit D. Tell the jury what it is, please."

"It looks like a resumé, but the name is missing."

Marc handed Adam another document and said, "Mr. Sutherland, I'm now showing you a document marked Defense Exhibit E. Do you recognize it? Take your time."

In less than thirty seconds, Adam looked at Marc and said, "It's my resumé. One I did many years ago."

Maddy knew this was coming. When Adam admitted it was his, she pushed a couple of keys on Marc's laptop and both resumés appeared on the TV side-by-side.

"Compare both documents, please."

Adam held up both, looked them over and quickly realized the one with the name redacted was the same.

"They're the same. They're both mine. I don't understand."

"Read the highlighted part on Defense Exhibit E, please."

Adam read it to the jury. It was the part that let the reader know he had received a degree in computer science.

"Mr. Sutherland, were you in the courtroom when the prosecution's computer expert, Bernadette Olson, was shown Defense Exhibit D and testified that the person with this degree in computer science would be able to hide internet searches on a computer?"

Marc was using a somewhat sneaky tactic to get Adam to remind the jury that Adam could have done the searches. Heather was trying to think of a way to object, but since Marc already told the jury what he wanted, an objection would be pointless.

"No, I wasn't," a somewhat puzzled Adam said.

Marc submitted the documents into evidence and walked back to his table. Before he sat down, he looked at Adam and asked, "Where did you go to college?"

"Macalester," Adam said.

"Here in St. Paul?"

"That's right."

Marc picked up the yearbook went back to the witness stand and handed it to Adam.

Marc and Adam quickly went through the formality of identifying the yearbook as Defense Exhibit G.

"Is this your yearbook, one you left at your father's house in Crocus Hill?"

"Yes, it is," Adam agreed.

"Open the cover and read the handwritten note in the upper left-hand corner please," Marc said.

"To my best bud, partners forever," Adam read.

"Read the signature."

"Phillip Cartwright."

A loud enough buzz went through the room to cause Carr to gavel for quiet.

"This is the same Phillip Cartwright, the son of Mackenzie Sutherland's ex-husband in Chicago, Wendell Cartwright, isn't that true?"

Adam sat quietly for several seconds. He licked his lips and shifted his eyes until Marc reminded him he was under oath.

"Yeah, so what?"

"Mr. Sutherland, bearing in mind we can subpoena your phone records and check your email, did you maintain this friendship over the years?"

"Yes," he admitted.

"Isn't it true you've been in rehab at least twice for drug use, paid by your father?" Marc asked changing directions for a moment.

"Objection, your Honor. Mr. Sutherland is not on trial."

Thank you, Heather, Marc thought. "I'm trying to show the jury that perhaps he should be," Marc interrupted Heather.

"Recess. I'll see the lawyers in chambers."

When they came back into court and started testimony again, Marc had successfully convinced Carr to allow him to pursue his theory that others had the same means, motive and opportunity as Mackenzie.

The court reporter read the last question back to Adam and he admitted he had been in rehab twice.

"Isn't it true that Phillip Cartwright died recently from a drug overdose?"

"Your Honor!" Heather jumped up and said.

"Sustained."

"How many times have you been arrested and charged with possession with intent to sell narcotics?"

"Objection…"

"Overruled."

"I don't recall," Adam answered.

"How about six? Does six sound about right?"

"Yeah, okay. But I was never…"

"Nonresponsive, your Honor."

"Answer only the question."

"You were arrested six times over the years for suspicion of selling methamphetamines and each time your father hired a defense lawyer who was able to get a plea down to a misdemeanor or a simple possession charge, isn't that true?"

"Yes," Adam conceded.

"Isn't it true you were the supplier of methamphetamines to your good friend, Phillip Cartwright? You're under oath."

"Your honor…" Heather started to say but Carr held up a hand to stop her.

"Let me advise you, Mr. Sutherland, you can invoke your Fifth Amendment right against self-incrimination and refuse to answer," Judge Carr told Adam.

"I refuse to answer on the fifth, what the judge said," Adam answered.

"Would you say Phillip Cartwright had the same level of computer expertise that you do?"

"No, he didn't," a puzzled Adam said.

"Did you help him do the searches for heart attack inducing drugs on his father's computer?"

"Your Honor," a frustrated Heather Anderson stood again to object. "Assumes facts not in evidence."

"There's just as much evidence that Phillip had access to Wendell's computer as my client, your Honor. Just as much evidence that he did those searches as Mrs. Sutherland. Calista Sutherland, a prosecution witness testified Phillip, as well as several others, had access to the Cartwright home and that computer."

"May we approach?" Heather asked.

When the lawyers assembled at the bench, Heather said, "It's a 'Do you still beat your wife' question, your Honor. It doesn't matter how he answers it."

"You're right and cleverly done but I see no legal reason that he can't answer it. But if he says no, you will not use it in your closing to say he did. Is that clear?"

"Yes, your Honor," Marc said.

"No, I did not," Adam indignantly answered after the bench conference was finished.

Marc sat silently for a moment looking over his trial notes. He decided he had received about all he could get from Adam toward reasonable doubt. He was about to pass the witness when a final thought occurred to him.

"I almost forgot," he said. "How's the Corvette doing?"

Heather considered objecting but decided to let it go.

"Um, ah, fine," Adam muttered.

"Really? I heard you took a loan out against it and because you couldn't keep up on the payments, it was repossessed. Isn't that true?"

"Temporarily," Adam reluctantly agreed.

"Oh, I see," Marc said. "So, your money problems are temporary. The drug business about to pick up or are you planning on inheriting?"

"Your honor!" Heather jumped up again.

"Withdrawn. I have nothing further."

The afternoon session, up to the break was taken up by Heather trying to rehabilitate Adam's testimony. It was a losing battle. Having barely an hour to work with him, there was no way she was going to turn Adam into a Boy Scout. The best she could do was to paint the picture that Adam's motive for William's death was thin. Even though his father had threatened to cut him off, this had happened before, and Adam did not take it seriously.

FIFTY

Marc looked up from the document he was working on and saw Maddy and Mackenzie returning from the women's restroom. During the break, Marc had checked with his next witness then decided another subpoena needed to be served.

The two women took their normal seats at the table, Mackenzie in-between Marc and Maddy. Marc folded the document into thirds and handed it to Maddy.

"This is for Detective Coolidge. It's probably not necessary but I want to be sure," Marc said.

"Tomorrow morning at nine o'clock?" Maddy quietly asked while reading the subpoena.

"Yeah, first thing Wednesday," Marc said.

"Why?" Maddy asked.

"It's Wednesday. I only have two more witnesses; Coolidge and Dr. Olson. Coolidge first, then Olson. Carr will want to wrap up so he can get at his favorite county attorney. He might push Heather on Olson's cross-exam to get out of here."

"Should I call him first?"

"You can. I'm sure he'll cooperate. He'll probably agree to meet you, so you can serve him."

"All rise," the judge's clerk, Tyrone, announced.

Carr took his seat while Maddy gathered her things to slip out and serve Coolidge. Carr told Marc to call his next witness.

"The defense calls Derek Miller, your Honor."

The deputy by the door opened it and a tall, almost six-foot-ten-inch, African-American came into the courtroom. As he passed through the gate he nodded slightly at Marc and went up to the stand. He was sworn in, took his seat and said his name, age and occupation for the record.

Derek had been recommended to Marc by his criminalist friend, Jason Briggs. He was a one-time basketball player at Purdue, played briefly in the NBA and now at age thirty-eight, was a computer science professor at Northwestern University in Chicago. There was not very much Marc wanted to get out of him. The first thing they did was to spend fifteen to twenty minutes giving the jury a detailed accounting of the professor's qualifications.

Derek was not a typical computer geek. Marc gave him one open ended question and in ten minutes he easily explained how someone with sophisticated computer skills could fake the searches on the computers. Marc showed him Adam's resumé and Derek admitted it would be possible for Adam to have done it.

On cross-exam, Heather did a good job of casting doubt on his testimony. First he had to admit that Adam's degree from college was almost twenty-years-old, an enormous amount of time in the tech world.

"If someone with Adam Sutherland's twenty-year-old degree had not kept up on the latest technology that would make your testimony quite different, would it not?" Heather asked.

"Objection," Marc said as he stood. "Assumes facts not in evidence. Specifically, that Adam Sutherland has not kept up on the technology for twenty years. He testified that he worked as a computer tech consultant..."

"And made absolutely no money doing it," Heather reminded the jury.

"Overruled," Carr said. "The witness will answer."

"Yes," Miller honestly answered.

"Adam Sutherland might not be able to doctor the searches and fake them the way you testified, isn't that true, Professor?"

"Yes, it is," he admitted.

She tried to keep going along this line of questioning, but Marc was able to stop it as repetitious. Heather then moved on to Derek's compensation. His fee for the work he had done examining the computers, the searches and testifying was over fifty thousand dollars, including travel, lodging and expenses. By the time Heather finished making the man look like a paid performer, Marc wondered if he had made a mistake having him testify. It was not Miller's fault. He did a very good job handling himself on the stand. Heather was simply very experienced at shredding the testimony of defense experts.

Marc tried to rehabilitate him on redirect exam, but it was a little weak. His problem was that he had not pursued Adam's current computer skills. A mistake for which he had only himself to blame. Despite TV and movies every lawyer in every trial will mess up something they later wish they had done a better job pursuing.

When Heather finished making Miller figuratively bleed and Marc completed his weak redirect, Carr called a halt for the day.

"I'm sorry, Marc," Miller said when he left the stand and met with Marc. "We should've been better prepared for that."

"And it's entirely my fault," Marc said. "Don't worry about it. We got enough to argue reasonable doubt. That's all we needed. Send me your final bill and I'll take care of it."

Wednesday morning, Judge Carr took his seat and told Marc to call his next witness. Maddy was in the hall keeping Max Coolidge company when the deputy opened the door and signaled for them to come in.

Maddy took her seat at Marc's table while Coolidge went up to the witness stand.

"Good morning, Detective Coolidge," Marc began. "Some things have come up that I need to ask you about.

"During the course of your investigation, you did not spend any time investigating Robert Sutherland as a possible suspect, did you?"

"We didn't believe…"

"Yes or no, detective," Marc cut him off.

"No, I did not."

"Did you investigate Paige Sutherland?"

"No."

"How about Adam Sutherland?"

"No," Max answered again.

"Hailey Sutherland?"

"No."

"Isn't it true that each of these people had the same means, motive and opportunity as you allege Mackenzie Sutherland had?"

"We didn't think so," Coolidge said.

"Because you didn't bother to look at them at all and if you had you would have found they all did, isn't that true, detective?"

"No, I wouldn't say so," Max answered.

"Really?" Marc asked.

For the next twenty minutes, Marc went over the testimony made during the trial about each of the Sutherlands, their money issues, their lifestyle, and dependence on their father. He drew special attention to the threats made to cut off the money, especially to Hailey and Adam.

One-by-one Marc also brought out the reality that each had access to the Crocus Hill house and William's personal computer.

"Objection," Heather said to try to end it. "The detective had no knowledge of these things and counsel is conducting his closing argument."

"He opened the door, your Honor, by denying these people had the same means, motive and opportunity as my client. I'm just showing the jury he would have found this if he had done a more thorough investigation."

"I'll overrule the objection, but you've made your point, Mr. Kadella. Time to move on."

"Detective Coolidge, isn't it true that this drug that allegedly caused William's heart attack, Interleukin 2, no one ever found out where it came from? How it was obtained?"

"That's true."

"Isn't it true that every one of the *Sutherland's* grocery stores has a pharmacy in it?"

"Yes, I believe so."

"Isn't it true that Hailey, Adam and Robert all worked for *Sutherland's* grocery stores at one time or another?"

"Yes, I believe so."

"Did Mackenzie Sutherland?"

"Not that I'm aware of."

"Did you investigate or do a search of any of these pharmacies to see if that was where the drug came from?"

Squirming in his seat, Max reluctantly admitted they did not.

"Were you involved in putting a listening device on Cooper Thomas in an attempt to get him to induce Mackenzie Sutherland to make an incriminating statement?"

"Yes, I was involved," Max admitted.

"Were you in the van listening to the conversation between Cooper and Mackenzie?"

"Yes, I was."

"And a recording of this conversation was made, was it not?"

"Yes."

"Did Mackenzie Sutherland incriminate herself regarding William's final Will and her knowledge of it?"

"No," Max quietly answered.

"Cooper Thomas tried to get her to do so, didn't he?"

"Yes."

"In fact, she denied any prior knowledge of the fact William Sutherland changed his Will and did not know what Cooper was talking about, didn't she?"

"That's what it sounded like."

"Was a transcript made of the recorded conversation," Marc asked while looking at Heather Anderson who was staring straight ahead.

"I don't believe so, no."

"Isn't it standard procedure to make a transcript of these recordings?"

"Not necessarily, no," Max said.

"Whose idea was it to not transcribe this recording, yours or the prosecution?'

"It wasn't my idea. I'm not sure whose idea it was."

"Are you aware that if a transcription had been made, that would have to be turned over to the defense?"

"Objection. He's a police officer not a lawyer." Heather said.

"Sustained," Carr ruled.

Marc thought it over for a moment. Even though Carr had sustained the objection, the jury got the message.

"I have nothing further, your Honor."

Heather conducted the state's exam of Coolidge. She did about as good a job of propping up the investigation as anyone could. There was no reason to suspect anyone else even though the cops knew there were other people with access to William's computer. And they knew some of these people might have motive.

"Why were you focused on the defendant?" Heather asked.

"You have to remember," Max began looking and speaking directly at the jury, "the Sutherland kids were all in favor of a second autopsy. Only Mackenzie opposed it. Then there was the information I found in Chicago. It was obviously too much of a coincidence that she inherited a lot of money from two husbands who died the same way. Plus, they both changed their Wills shortly before they died.

"Then, finally, there were the two computers. Wendell Cartwright's and William Sutherland's. Each with searches for the same type of drugs and only Mackenzie had access to both."

Heather passed Max back to Marc who asked, "In your analysis, only Mackenzie had access to both computers because you did not go looking for anyone else, isn't that true detective?"

"We didn't believe..."

"Yes or no," Marc slammed the door on him.

"Yes, I suppose so."

It was almost 11:00 and the clock was rapidly ticking toward Judge Carr's noon rendezvous.

Marc called his final witness, Dr. Oscar Johnson, his medical examiner expert. Johnson was almost the exact opposite of Alfredo Nunez. Where Nunez looked to be the epitome of the medical professional, Johnson came across as everyone's favorite uncle.

Since the decision of guilty or not guilty could very easily come down to which medical expert was more credible, Marc took a lot of time having Johnson tell the jury his credentials. He had spent twenty-four years with the Dane County coroner's office, the last ten as the chief pathologist and he still taught pathology at the University of Wisconsin-Madison medical school. Johnson had published four highly regarded books on the subject and to really impress this Minnesota jury, he routinely lectured and assisted at the Mayo Clinic in Rochester.

Marc walked him through the second autopsy of William and the toxicology reports from it. He had also studied William's medical records and the most recent EKG done a year before his death.

"Doctor, I want your medical opinion, what kind of medical condition was William Sutherland in?"

"Poor at best. Apparently Mr. Sutherland had led a fairly hedonistic lifestyle. Eating well, drinking, smoking and obviously disdaining any meaningful exercise. I'm surprised he lived as long as he did."

"Would you say, to a medical certainty, that the drug found in small, trace amounts in him, Interleukin 2, caused his heart attack?"

"To a medical certainty, absolutely not. Look, he was in such bad shape and the EKG of his heart showed it to be weak enough that if someone jumped out of the bushes and yelled 'boo' at him, he could have had a heart attack."

Stop right now, Marc thought. "Thank you, doctor," Marc said.

Heather went after him, but Dr. Johnson had testified at too many trials to let her get to him. Try as she might to use Dr. Nunez testimony to discredit him, Johnson would merely shrug, agree that was the opinion of Nunez then stick to his own opinion.

"Dr. Johnson, why would someone interject Interleukin 2, a cancer drug, into someone who does not have cancer, except to induce a heart attack?"

"I don't know," Johnson answered. "In fact, I don't know that someone did, do you?"

Heather tried to sidestep his answer but by now she had done all she could to bolster her expert's opinion and reduce his.

She finished right at noon and Carr looked like he wanted to bolt. Instead, Marc stood and rested his case.

The judge looked thoughtfully at the lawyers for a moment then called them to the bench.

"What do you say we give the jury a break and have closing arguments Monday morning? Any objection?" When the lawyers said no to the idea of a weekend off for the jury if not themselves, Carr continued. "I'll want requested jury instructions by ten o'clock Friday morning. We'll meet again then."

Carr adjourned with the usual admonishment to the jury to avoid the news until Monday at 9:00 A.M.

FIFTY-ONE

The flames were mostly beneath her silently beckoning, waiting for Mackenzie to make a misstep and plunge downward to be consumed for eternity. Occasionally a flame would shoot upward to take the vague shape of a hand and grab at her feet, attempting to grasp her bare ankles and pull her in.

Mackenzie was on a tightrope. It appeared to be a one-inch steel cable stretched taut from somewhere behind her to somewhere ahead. She was wearing a red silk nightgown although, to her knowledge, she had never owned one. Her arms, the elbows bent, were outstretched on each side for balance.

Mackenzie looked around at what appeared to be a cave or a large room with a high rounded ceiling that she could barely see. There was light smoke or fog, she wasn't sure which, drifting around the room making it difficult to discern the true dimensions of it. Mackenzie could not see where the cable ended and looking back, it went into the fog and disappeared. She tried moving forward but her bare feet felt like lead. An inch or two at a time was all the progress she could make.

Looking down trying to lift her feet and move them along, she finally noticed that the flames gave off no heat. Even when the occasional flame up would lap at the cable, she felt nothing from it. The misty cloud of fog or smoke continued to rise up from the flames and swirl about the room but there was no heat at all.

Mackenzie continued to inch along the cable making no progress. Feeling a slight, out-of-place vibration in the cable, she looked up to see a dark, gray apparition of some sort. It seemed to be barely five or six feet ahead, but she could not make out what it was. The creature, whatever it was, appeared to be large, at least ten feet tall. It seemed to have an almost humanlike form, but it was shifting and changing shape making it too difficult to tell what it was.

Mackenzie continued to watch though it made no threatening gesture. Perhaps that was why Mackenzie felt no fear. Oddly, she realized, she had no fear of any of this. Not the flames or the endless cavern in which she appeared to be nor the phantom ahead.

Finally, two glowing, red cinders appeared where its eyes should be then it began to shrink and take on a recognizable appearance. After a few seconds, the creature turned into an old man. He was bald, quite wrinkled, gray and totally devoid of color as if he was a character in a black and white movie.

He was dressed in rags and holding a long chain in his arms. The old man was looking down when he first appeared, floating two or three inches above the cable. After a few seconds, while Mackenzie continued to watch him, her feet on the tightrope, her arms still at her side for balance, the old man slowly raised his head to look at her.

Mackenzie, immediately recognizing the old man, audibly gasped and said, "You're Marley! You're Jacob Marley and that is your chain..."

"Yes," the tattered, shabby old man agreed. "I wear the chain I forged in life. I made it link by link and yard by yard."

When he continued Mackenzie spoke with him, "I girded it out of my own free will, and of my own free will I wore it."

"Why are you here?" Mackenzie defiantly asked.

"You know why I'm here," old Marley replied. "Your chain is waiting for you."

"I have done nothing that I should not have done," Mackenzie said with the same defiance.

While she stared at the old man he began to take on a different form. The dark almost formless apparition returned then began to change yet again. In its place was another man. A dark but extremely handsome man was now before her. He was wearing a black hooded cloak, the hood covering his head.

Mackenzie could see his face and the top of his head. He had thick, black hair, a well-trimmed mustache and goatee with no trace of gray and perfectly trimmed black eyebrows. *He was almost beautiful,* Mackenzie thought as she stared, mesmerized by his eyes, deep-set and coal black.

"What do you want?" Mackenzie asked.

"You know," the man answered with a melodious, baritone voice.

"No, I don't," Mackenzie weakly lied.

"Yes, you do," the man said as he reached his right hand toward her.

Mackenzie involuntarily began to reach toward the extended hand with her left one then stopped and looked at it. She quickly jerked her hand back and held it to her breast for the man's hand was a skeleton; there was no flesh covering it at all.

"What do you want?" she asked again.

"It is your time. You must come with me, now."

"But I'm not ready," Mackenzie pleaded.

"No one ever is," the man replied. "Your time is up. Old Marley is right. You forged the chain you made in life and it is time to cloak yourself with it and carry it for all of eternity."

"I'm not ready," she quietly repeated.

"No one ever is," he repeated as he again extended the fleshless hand to her.

"Ahhh!" Mackenzie burst out as she suddenly awakened, sat up and gasping for breath, looked around her bedroom.

After a minute her breathing normalized and she tossed the covers aside, got out of bed and headed downstairs. When she got to the kitchen she put some ice in a glass and filled it with water from the refrigerator door. Still a bit shaken by the dream, Mackenzie drank half the glass of water in one gulp then filled it again.

Leaning against the counter by the sink, she took two more swallows then said quietly out loud, "That was interesting and pretty obvious what it meant."

She sat on one of the stools at the breakfast island, sipped her water and thought about what happened. For the first time in a long time she wondered if her conscience was bothering her. *Interesting concept*, she thought.

"Maybe it's time to put an end to this," she softly said, holding her forehead in her left hand as she looked down at the granite countertop. *I wonder what kind of deal Marc can make for me?* she thought. *I'd still have money they don't know about and life after prison.*

Mackenzie sat silently for another two or three minutes contemplating her situation. She came to a decision, finished the glass of water and got up and put the glass in the sink.

"No," she said looking out the window above the sink. "No, it was just a dream. Besides you started this now see it through."

The morning after the Marley dream was the Monday when closing arguments were to be given. Butch Koll and Andy Whitmore picked up Mackenzie and delivered her to the courthouse a little early. They expected a larger than normal media presence this morning and were not disappointed. Butch and Andy literally muscled through the crowd with the help of two deputies to get her in the door to the back hallway. The doors were still locked but the guards let them in.

Butch helped Mackenzie remove her coat and hung it up on the coat rack along the wall. They had all stopped wearing the Kevlar vests by now. As he was doing this, Marc, along with Heather Anderson and Danica Kyle, came into the courtroom from the back area.

"Good morning," Marc said as he fist-bumped with Andy and Butch.

"Can we talk for a minute?" Mackenzie asked him.

The two of them went into the small conference room. Mackenzie sat down on one of the cheap plastic chairs while Marc closed the door.

"You okay?" he asked.

Mackenzie took a deep breath then said, "I'm a little scared, to tell you the truth. I've been okay until this morning."

Marc sat down next to her, took her hand and said, "That's pretty understandable."

She looked at him and said, "Tell me everything's going be okay."

"Everything's going to be okay," He smiled.

"Odd, I actually feel better," she said. "Were you in with the judge?"

"Yes, going over jury instructions again. We'll argue some more about them after closing arguments."

"Good morning ladies and gentlemen," Heather began her closing argument. "First of all, I want to thank you for your service and your patience."

Heather then took a few minutes to explain what the closing argument is. During a normal trial, unlike TV or the movies, there are rarely any great, dramatic moments where someone tearfully breaks down on the witness stand and confesses. There are no moments when an unknown piece of evidence magically appears to prove guilt or innocence. For the prosecution it is a slow, methodical process where the lawyers build their case one piece at a time from a number of witnesses. Then during the closing argument, those pieces are brought together and presented to the jury. It is also the prosecution's opportunity to argue to the jury why they must find the defendant guilty.

"This is a difficult case to prove," Heather admitted while slowly walking in front of the jury, making eye contact with and addressing each of the jurors. "There was no confession, no smoking gun, no eyewitness to the deed. This is what we call a circumstantial case. Basically, that means the evidence, the circumstances of the crime point to one person."

Heather went on to go over the facts that were not in dispute. William Sutherland was essentially poisoned by a cancer drug that, if administered improperly, can lead to a heart attack. There were searches for this drug on his computer. He changed his Will shortly before his death leaving almost his entire estate to his wife, Mackenzie and very little to his sons, daughter and nothing to take care of his grandchildren.

Heather then shifted to Wendell Cartwright. She was careful to be very upfront and clear that Mackenzie was not on trial for Wendell's death. Of course, this reminder was done with a figurative wink and nod to make sure the jury could not simply overlook this.

"Wendell's death and the circumstances of it was allowed in trial to show a pattern. A much younger woman seduces and marries an older, wealthy man. After a while he changes his Will and the beneficiary of his Family Trust naming this wife and cutting off his family. The wife, who was using a different name and altering her appearance, inherits everything shortly after the Will is changed when Wendell has a sudden, massive heart attack. On his computer are internet searches for heart attack inducing drugs." While this was being explained, the pictures of Mackenzie as Frances Cartwright and Mackenzie Sutherland appeared, side-by-side, on the TV.

Heather spent a half-hour going over what she believed the defense would try to use to create, reasonable doubt. When she finished Marc realized she had been quite effective at deflecting his some-other-dude-did-it defense. On the other hand, he also knew he could rebuild it.

"The defense tried their best to claim William Sutherland's heart attack was not caused by the drug found in his body. Their claim was he was a heart attack waiting to happen. Use your common sense, ladies and gentlemen. It was not a mere coincidence that someone introduced small amounts of Interleukin 2 into William Sutherland and then he dies of a heart attack. No matter what their expert said, this is simply too fantastic.

"The computer searches for the heart attack drug," Heather said then stopped then looked at each of the jurors. "Despite their attempt to show otherwise, only one person had access to both computers: Mackenzie Sutherland.

"Remember what I said in my opening statement, ladies and gentlemen. This case was about one thing and one thing only: Greed. Mackenzie Sutherland had more money of her own inherited from Wendell Cartwright, than William Sutherland. No matter. She wanted William's money too. And according to her lawyer, she convinced William to change his Will then shortly afterward poisoned and murdered him. The medical examiner drew a timeline for you that laid this out perfectly. There is no other rational explanation for what happened here. Beyond a reasonable doubt does not mean beyond all doubt ladies and gentlemen. Again, the only rational explanation is that Mackenzie Sutherland poisoned and murdered her husband for his money. Find her guilty and send her to prison where she belongs."

Marc began his closing the same way Heather did, by thanking the jury for their time and service. He then took a few minutes to remind them of their oath, to consider the defendant innocent until proven guilty and to hold the prosecution to their burden of proving guilt beyond a reasonable doubt. While he did this, he stood still in front of them while using light hand gestures looked directly at each of them until each nodded their head in agreement.

"Beyond a reasonable doubt, ladies and gentlemen. The prosecution must prove all of it beyond a reasonable doubt. When we're finished, probably this afternoon, Judge Carr will give you his legal instructions. He'll explain to you the elements of each crime charged. It is on the prosecution to prove, beyond a reasonable doubt, each and every element of the charges. If the prosecution fails to prove even one of those elements, beyond a reasonable doubt, then you must, and I do mean must, come back with a not guilty verdict for that crime charged."

Marc then discussed the weaknesses of the prosecution starting with the investigation. The police focused solely on Mackenzie and did not bother with anyone else.

"Their motive for accusing Mackenzie, greed, was not substantiated by a single witness or shred of evidence or testimony that Mackenzie was a greedy person. It's a fantasy made up by the prosecution.

"Further," Marc continued, "The means to carry out the crime. Again, no evidence, no testimony to show how she supposedly poisoned William. And there were other people who had access to William's computer to do the searches and pharmacies through which the drug could have been obtained, Pharmacies to which Makenzie did not have access. In fact, we showed there were others who had better opportunity and means than Mackenzie Sutherland.

"The health of both William Sutherland and Wendell Cartwright. The prosecution wants you to believe that it is too much of a coincidence that these two men, husbands of my client, could have both died of a heart attack," Marc said.

Marc walked over to the prosecution table and with his left hand, palm up, pointed it at Heather and Danica. "That's what they want you to believe. How could this happen, they want you to ask? How can you possibly believe she didn't murder them both? It can't be a coincidence that both husbands died from the same thing, a heart attack."

Marc moved back in front of the jury box and continued. "First of all, ladies and gentlemen, the medical testimony for both men was that they were in terrible physical and medical condition and were walking heart attack victims. As for coincidence, fifteen hundred people die from heart attacks or heart disease in this country," Marc paused for several seconds, sternly looking them over then said, "...every day! That's as many as died on 9/11, every two days. In fact, the odds of both of these elderly men in bad physical condition dying of a heart attack are a lot better than the prosecution wants you to know.

"The Wills of William Sutherland and Wendell Cartwright. The lawyer who wrote the new Will for Cartwright testified that, as far as he knew, Mackenzie knew nothing about Wendell changing the Will or the beneficiary of the Cartwright Family Trust.

"The lawyer who testified Mackenzie knew about the changes William made was clearly if not coerced then intimidated into saying..."

"Objection to the use of the word coerced or intimidated," Heather said.

"Overruled. The jury heard the testimony of Cooper Thomas and they can decide if he was coerced or intimidated for themselves."

"Coerced or intimidated into saying she knew about the changes to William Sutherland's Will. No matter how you slice it, he is a liar. He either lied when he signed the affidavit, when he had no reason to lie or, he lied in court after the police interrogation during which they made it clear they were going to destroy his life and possibly put him in prison. And she," Marc continued referring to Heather, "doesn't want you to believe Cooper Thomas was coerced in any way.

"Finally, ladies and gentlemen, as a reminder, the defense has no obligation to prove anything. It's not up to me to prove someone else obtained the cancer drug and fed it to William Sutherland. But we have given you several other people who had motive, means and opportunity, at least as much as Mackenzie Sutherland. Certainly enough to create reasonable doubt that someone else did it.

"Mackenzie Sutherland was wealthy in her own right. She didn't need William's money. There were people for whom that was not true. William Sutherland had threatened to cut off the money to at least two of his children. They couldn't survive without it and they knew nothing about a new Will. For all they knew, if their father died, they stood to inherit millions which would have solved their money problems.

"The lynchpin of their case," Marc continued turning to look at Heather and Danica, "is the belief that only Mackenzie had access to both computers. Even though, again, we had no obligation to do so, the defense has shown reasonable doubt about that. Adam Sutherland and his good friend Phillip Cartwright, acting together had access to both computers. And they each had the same motive: inheriting money.

"There is reasonable doubt throughout this case, ladies and gentlemen. The prosecution has failed miserably proving Mackenzie Sutherland did this. Do your duty, abide by your oath, obey the law and return a verdict of not guilty."

FIFTY-TWO

Marc trudged up the back stairs from the parking lot to the second floor. As he did, he stomped the snow off his shoes from the five inches that had fallen during the night. It was almost 11:00 A.M. and he was just now arriving at his office on this Monday morning.

"Any messages?" he asked the secretaries when he entered the suite of offices. Marc was hoping to have received word from Judge Carr that Mackenzie's jury was in.

"No, sorry, nothing yet," Carolyn answered him knowing what he was looking for, "Maddy called wondering the same thing."

"How did your settlement conference go?" Sandy asked referring to the divorce Marc was handling.

"We settled it," Marc said while hanging up his overcoat.

"Gary happy with the settlement?" Carolyn asked.

"It's Hennepin County. He's the husband. Of course he's not happy. But the good news is his cheating ex-wife was delighted," Marc said.

"No news on the Sutherland jury?" Barry Cline asked as he came through his private office door into the common area.

"No, nothing since last Thursday when they asked for a clarification on the elements of each charge and reasonable doubt," Marc said.

"Hung jury," Barry said.

"Looks like, but which way?"

"Hard to say," Barry answered him.

About a half-hour later, Marc received the phone call he was waiting for. Or, so he thought. It was Judge Carr's clerk telling him the jury had sent out a message wanting to see Carr.

"Have they reached a verdict?" Marc anxiously asked.

"Didn't say. The note just said they wanted to see him," Tyrone said.

"Hung jury," Marc quietly said.

"Probably," Tyrone replied, "but you didn't hear me say that."

"What time?" Marc asked.

"1:30. He wants everybody there including Mrs. Sutherland," Tyrone told him.

"We'll be there Tyrone and thanks."

While Marc was on the phone with Carr's clerk, Mackenzie Sutherland was sitting on a stool at the breakfast island in her kitchen. A package had been delivered to her and while wearing thick, rubber cleaning gloves, she was reading through the contents. The private investigator she hired had done an excellent job. The man came highly recommended from the P.I. Mackenzie used in Chicago. When she finished looking over the photos and reading his report, quite pleased with what he came up with, she placed everything back in the large manila envelope it came in. The rubber gloves were new, never used and a precaution against DNA and fingerprints.

When she finished she hid the envelope on a top shelf in one of the kitchen cabinets. She would keep the contents hidden there until she could figure out how to get to a FedEx office to send the documents to the reporter she had in mind. As she was climbing down from the three-step ladder, her phone rang.

"Hi, any news?" she asked Marc when she answered it.

Marc told her what was happening and the 1:30 court call.

"What do you think?" she asked.

"I think the jury might be hung. They deliberated all day Saturday and I don't know why they would want to see the judge if they had a verdict. I think they're hung up."

"Is that good?"

"Maybe, we'll see. Let's not get ahead of ourselves. How are you?" Marc asked.

Mackenzie took a deep breath which Marc could clearly hear then said, "Stressed. How do you do this for a living?"

"Well, don't take this wrong, Mac, but it's not my ass on the line. Maddy will be here in a few minutes then we'll come by and get you. I'll call Butch and Andy and have them meet us at your place. We'll get some lunch then go to court. See you soon."

"All rise," Tyrone proclaimed as Carr came out onto the bench.

Marc, Heather and Danica Kyle had spent fifteen minutes in chambers with the judge discussing the jury's note. Everyone, including Carr, expected to be told the jury was hung up. Marc argued forcibly for Carr to order a mistrial. If that happened, the prosecution would have to decide if they wanted to try the case again. Unfortunately, Marc was a minority of one wanting a mistrial.

Judge Carr was inclined to force the issue and make the jury continue their deliberations even through the upcoming weekend. Heather and Danica were all for that.

Marc, somewhat successfully, argued that if the jury had to go through the weekend they were going to get angry. In that case, there was only one person they could blame and take it out on and that was Mackenzie Sutherland.

Carr said he would hold off on that until he heard from the jury.

"Be seated," Carr intoned. After everyone took their seats, Carr looked at the jury and asked, "Mr. Foreman, where are we?"

The first juror selected, the retiree named William Stokes, stood to address the judge.

"We're deadlocked," Stokes told him with a touch of frustration in his voice.

"I see. Well," Carr continued, "I'm sorry but that's not good enough. I understand the difficulty and your burden but I'm going to order you to keep at it. Start over if you have to, but let's get a verdict.

"Is there anything else?" Carr asked Stokes, the disappointment on his face plain to see.

"No, your Honor," Stokes said as respectfully as possible.

Looking over all of the jurors, Carr said, "I'm sorry but you've only been at it for eight full days. I have to ask you to keep going."

While the jury was filing out, Carr told the lawyers he wanted to see them in chambers again.

Carr hung up his robe on a coat stand behind his desk while the lawyers took their usual seats. Maddy, Mackenzie and the two bodyguards waited in the courtroom.

Carr took his seat behind the big desk and asked, "How long do you think we should give them?"

Surprised that the judge would even ask for their opinion on this, Marc quickly blurted out, "One more day."

"Two more weeks," Heather said.

"I'm thinking it's Monday today, we'll give them until Friday. If they don't come back with a verdict, we'll see where they are. Have you two talked about a plea?" Carr said looking at Heather.

"My client maintains her innocence, your Honor."

"I could probably go with first degree manslaughter with no sentencing recommendation," Heather said. The statement regarding no sentencing recommendation was a clear signal to the judge to go easy to get a deal made. Heather was the one starting to worry about a hung jury.

"What's her score?" Carr asked Marc referring to her criminal history score.

"Zero, your Honor," Marc replied.

"I'd go thirty-six months," Carr said. "She'd be out in twenty-four."

"Shayla Parker okay with this?" Marc asked.

"I could sell it," Heather said.

"I could talk to her also," Carr interjected.

I'm sure you could, Marc thought.

"Does your client want to go through another trial?" Carr asked.

Marc held his tongue, afraid of what wiseass comment he might make. "I'll talk to her," Marc said. "Don't hold your breath," he said to Heather.

"Is she still in the courtroom?" Carr asked.

"Yes, I'll talk to her right now if you want to give me a few minutes," Marc replied.

As he headed for the courtroom he got the distinct feeling he had just been tag-teamed by Judge Carr and Heather Anderson. It annoyed him, but he wasn't surprised. Knowing how cozy Carr was with Shayla Parker this likely came about from a little pillow talk.

Marc brought everyone, including Butch and Andy, the two bodyguards, into the conference room. Maddy, Marc and Mackenzie sat down at the table while Butch and Andy stood along a wall.

Marc told Mackenzie what the offer was then waited for the question they always ask.

"What do you think?" Mackenzie asked Marc.

Marc hesitated for a moment before answering then said, "If they had offered this before trial I would have considered it a huge win. A hung jury is certainly in our favor. But they could decide to try you again. A different jury could…"

It was Andy Whitmore who said it, "Don't take it. You're winning by a lot. Sorry, I didn't mean to…"

"No, it's okay," Marc said to him. "You think we're winning?"

"Yeah, I do," Andy said.

"Me, too," Butch added.

"Right now, the jury is hung up in your favor. The worst that can happen is the not guilty jurors won't be able to persuade the two or three that are holding out for a guilty verdict. You'll see. I'd bet my house, if I had one, on it."

"Butch?" Marc asked.

"Yeah, I agree."

"Maddy?"

"The more I think about it, the more I think he's right."

"They're not coming back with a guilty verdict. It's either gonna be not guilty or hung and I'd bet hung," Andy said sounding quite sure of himself.

Marc was looking at Andy then he turned to his client and said, "Mac?"

She thought it over for ten to fifteen seconds then said, "I am not guilty and I'm not going to say I am at this point." She looked at Andy, smiled and said, "Andrew, I hope you're right. What are the odds that they want to try me again if it is a hung jury?" she asked Marc.

"I don't know," Marc shrugged. "It may depend on the vote count. If it leans in one direction, that may decide it for them."

"I'm telling you," Andy said. "It's nine to three or ten to two for an acquittal. Maybe even eleven to one. I spent a lot of time watching them and I think I have them read pretty well."

Andy stopped and looked over the people in the small room, all of whom were staring at him.

"And boy do I have my neck stuck out," Andy said breaking the tension and bringing a laugh from everyone.

"Mac," Marc said again. "I need to go tell them."

"No," she said almost defiantly. "We'll win again if we have to."

"Okay," Marc told her while feeling a touch of disappointment at the prospect of trying the case again.

Barely two days later, Wednesday afternoon at 2:00 P.M., everyone was back in court, including the media and court watchers. Marc had received another call from Tyrone, Judge Carr's clerk telling him the jury, once again wanted to see the judge. Nothing about a verdict.

Maddy and Mackenzie, despite periods of stress between them during the trial, were chatting amiably while they waited.

"I don't know why, for some reason I'm not the least bit nervous. I should be but I'm not," Mackenzie told her.

"That's good," Maddy replied. "No matter what happens, stay calm."

"I'll be okay," Mackenzie said.

The jury was led in and Marc closely watched each of them for some sign or expression. A couple of them stole a quick glance at the defense table but offered nothing to indicate what they were thinking. Less than a minute after the jury was seated, Carr was in his big chair telling everyone to be seated. Carr looked over the crowded room and sternly reminded everyone he would not tolerate any disturbances or demonstrations of any kind.

"Mr. Foreman," Carr said to Stokes who stood to address the court. "Have you reached a verdict?"

"No, we have not, your Honor. I'm sorry but we all agree we are hopelessly deadlocked."

Carr looked over the jury and asked, "Is that true?"

Twelve heads nodded up and down in concurrence.

He turned back to Stokes and asked, "No further deliberations will help?"

"Your Honor, we have been deadlocked since the very first vote. No one has moved an inch," Stokes told him.

"What's the vote?"

"Ten to two in favor of acquittal. Two holdouts for a guilty verdict and they won't move," Stokes said being careful not to look at the other jurors for fear he would give them away.

"And this has been true since you began?" Carr asked.

"Yes, your Honor," Stokes said.

"Take your seat, sir," Carr politely said. "I'm disappointed but I'm sure you did your best. I thank you for your efforts," Carr said looking over the jury.

He swiveled his chair around to face the courtroom and said, looking at the lawyers, "I have no choice but to declare a mistrial. We'll adjourn until 9:00 A.M. Monday morning. The lawyers will meet with me in chambers to set a date for a new trial." With that Carr rapped his gavel and fled.

Heather and Danica left through the back-hallway door. While Marc held off the media mob crowding the rail while Maddy, Mackenzie, Butch and Andy went into the conference room.

Marc faced the reporters and responded to their questions with simple, "no comments." After a few minutes, the deputies began to herd them out through the exit.

"Does that mean they're going to try me again?" Mackenzie asked when Marc joined them in the little room.

"I don't know," Marc said. "I'm going on Gabriella's show tomorrow to talk about the expense and waste of time and taxpayer's money. I can also make it look like this is a personal vendetta by Shayla Parker because it's an election year. We'll find out Monday if they are really going take another shot at this."

"That ten to two vote might dissuade them, don't you think?" Maddy asked.

"Yeah, and if they do try it again, Andy is going to help with jury selection. Nice call," Marc said.

Mackenzie's bail was continued but her travel restrictions were removed following the ruling of a mistrial. The next day, Thursday morning, Mackenzie was up early and on the road shortly after 7:00.

It was a chilly, early March morning and Mackenzie disguised herself with a hooded coat with the hood covering her head and most of her face. She was also wearing large, black sunglasses. Fortunately, the cool weather made wearing leather gloves less noticeable.

Her first stop was at a FedEx store in a strip mall in Stillwater off I-94. Mackenzie had the young girl behind the counter make a copy of the documents she had, picked up a FedEx envelope then left.

Mackenzie got back on 94 eastbound, crossed the St. Croix River into Wisconsin then took the first exit into Hudson. She parked in the Hudson FedEx lot and placed the copies she had made and copies of a dozen photos in the envelope. She addressed it and took it into the store and had it shipped for same day delivery. While accomplishing this, not once did she touch any of it without wearing gloves. Nothing could be traced back to her.

FIFTY-THREE

"Good afternoon, ladies and gentlemen, I'm Gabriella Shriqui and this is the *Court Reporter*," Gabriella smiled into the camera and began the taping of the Thursday afternoon show. It was originally scheduled to be taped at noon but was delayed while they watched a short press conference given by Shayla Parker.

"My guest today, and I'm delighted to have him back, is local attorney Marc Kadella." She swiveled in her chair to face Marc. They were using the more informal, intimate set of two stylish armchairs with a coffee table between them.

"Welcome back, Marc. Thanks for taking the time to come on the show."

"Always a pleasure, Gabriella. Besides, this way I get to check out your tits and ass to see if they…"

"Stop!" Gabriella said while holding back her laughter. Most of the crew was having a pretty good time with Marc's irreverent comment. "Is this the way this is going to go?"

"Maybe," Marc replied. "I should have warned you, I'm in a pretty good mood today. Stress release from the trial being over, for now."

"Okay," Gabriella began, "we're going try this again and you be a good boy."

"No promises," he said.

Gabriella looked at her producer, Cordelia Davis, who said, "We'll cut out the smartass stuff. Begin with reminding the audience who he is."

"For those of you who don't know, Marc is the defense lawyer who represented Mackenzie Sutherland in the Ramsey County trial for the death of her husband, William Sutherland, founder of *Sutherland's* grocery stores. The trial ended yesterday with a hung jury and mistrial."

Gabriella then had Marc briefly explain what a hung jury and mistrial meant.

"Did you know Shayla Parker, the Ramsey County Attorney, held a press conference at noon to announce that they will pursue another trial against your client?"

"Yes, I saw it on TV. I'm not really surprised. All along I had the impression that she was using this case for her personal, political agenda," Marc replied.

"That's a serious accusation. Why do you think this?" Gabriella asked.

"Because their case was thin to begin with and she was taking a lot of heat from the media about it because my client has money. Now she's going to make it worse by trying it again and wasting more of the taxpayer's money. She's lucky there wasn't an acquittal. The vote was ten to two in favor of a not guilty verdict. Two holdouts out of twelve people."

The two of them spent another six or seven minutes discussing the evidence, mostly to allow Marc to talk about the strength of his case and the weakness of the prosecution's. He used this as an opportunity to taint the jury pool even more than the local newspapers, TV and radio already had in the event of a second trial. The same media who had pressured the county attorney to try it in the first place were now piously wondering why Parker did and if it made sense to do a second trial.

"Hold it," Cordelia said, interrupting them. "That's pretty good and we have enough for the show."

"Anything else you want to cover, Marc?" Gabriella asked then said, "And don't make any smartass comments about my body parts."

"Only if the cameras are on," Marc smiled. "No, that's good. You can call me Monday after we meet with Judge Carr and I'll let you know the new trial date, if there is one."

"Why wouldn't there be?"

Marc shrugged and said, "They could come to their senses and change their minds."

On Sunday morning, Mackenzie once again awoke earlier than normal. She hurried downstairs and as she stepped off of the bottom stair she heard the newspaper thumping onto her front door stoop. Mackenzie was eagerly looking for a story as she had both Friday and Saturday mornings. She plodded across the cold, marble floor in her bare feet, tightening the belt of the bathrobe as she did so. After retrieving the St. Paul Dispatch Sunday paper, she went into the kitchen and took it from its plastic bag, opened it to the front page of the A section and delightfully smiled at the screaming headlines.

Almost laughing, she poured herself a cup of coffee and took a seat at the breakfast island. Mackenzie sipped her coffee while reading the headline's again, checked the time on the wall clock and wondered how long it would be before Marc called.

Mackenzie read through every word of the story twice, a story Mackenzie ignited when she drove over to Hudson to FedEx the documents and photos. What she sent to a well-known reporter at the St Paul paper was proof-positive documentation of the affair between Judge Otis Carr and County Attorney Shayla Parker. Dates, times, places, photos, credit card receipts from hotels and restaurants. Everything her P.I. had come up with to slam the both of them and to at least document the appearance of impropriety of Judge Carr presiding over her trial.

At precisely 7:15 Mackenzie's phone rang. She looked at the ID, pressed the talk function and said, "Good morning, Marc. You're up early."

"I've had at least a half-dozen phone calls from reporters already. I've just spent the last fifteen minutes watching the local news. Have you seen it?"

"Yes, I have the St. Paul paper right here. I assume you're talking about Judge Carr and Shayla Parker," Mackenzie answered him.

"I've been trying to decide if you had anything to do with this," he calmly said.

"What difference does it make? Besides, no one forced them to have an affair. So they got caught? So what?"

"And that's the same conclusion I came to," Marc replied. "Well, as long as we're both up, how about I take you to breakfast."

"I need time to shower and get ready," Mackenzie said.

"How long? Eight, eight fifteen?" Marc asked.

"8:30," Mackenzie said.

"Okay, 8:30."

"What does this mean as far as them trying this again?" Mackenzie asked.

"Well, they still could, but I don't see it happening. This would be huge grounds for an appeal, maybe."

"Why maybe?" Mackenzie asked.

"We might still have to show bias in the judge's rulings. Look, we're getting ahead of ourselves. We'll know more tomorrow. I'll see you in about an hour."

Around three o'clock that same Sunday afternoon, Marc received the phone call he had been expecting. Tyrone Carver, Carr's clerk, was calling with news about the Monday morning meeting with Carr. Not surprisingly it had been called off. Instead, they were to meet with Chief Judge Douglas Feller in his chambers at 8:00 A.M.

What's going on?" Marc asked Tyrone.

"I don't know any more than that, Mr. Kadella. You've seen the news, I guess."

"Oh yeah, I've had reporters calling me all day. How are you doing?"

"Okay."

"Listen, Tyrone, no matter how all this shakes out, I hope you don't lose your job."

"No, I'll be okay. I'll get another spot with another judge, I'm not worried."

"Good. I guess I'll see Judge Feller in the morning. Thanks, Tyrone."

At 7:55 Monday morning, Marc found Heather Anderson and Danica Kyle waiting for him in Judge Feller's courtroom. They greeted each other, shook hands and Marc asked, "So, what is it going to be?"

"Nothing's been decided," Heather said. "We just got the bombshell dropped on us yesterday, like everybody else."

Marc smiled and said, "Look, I'm not accusing you of anything, but you knew what was going on."

Heather tried her best to look innocent then rolled her eyes to the ceiling and said, "I have no idea what you're talking about."

"No press here this morning," Marc casually remarked looking about the empty courtroom.

"Yet," Danica said.

Feller's clerk came into the courtroom and led them back to his chambers. "Good morning," Feller said as they filed in. "Please take a seat."

They introduced themselves and when they were seated Feller said to Heather, "Are you going to try this case again?"

"I don't know, your Honor. It's not my call. The last word I had from Shayla, who is still the county attorney…"

"Not for long," Feller interrupted her. "She's supposedly tendering her resignation today. She'll be sending it to Governor Dahlstrom, Attorney General Peterson, the mayor and myself. At least that's what I've been told. I can tell you this, there will be a press release this morning. Otis Carr is taking an indefinite leave of absence."

"Then I assume it will be Paul Schmidt's decision," Heather said. "Paul's the chief deputy county attorney," Heather said to Marc.

"You know your office is going to be up to your ass in appeals over this," Feller told Heather.

"I know," Heather agreed. "Every lawyer that had a case before Carr is going to file. Fortunately, I don't handle appeals."

"Let's take a break," Feller said. "You call Paul Schmidt and find out what he wants to do with this case. Tell him from me, I'll assign another judge, but I think you're wasting the court's time. Go give him a call, then tell Carmen when you're ready."

When Feller said he thought they were wasting the court's time, Marc's heart took a big jump. This was not a casual statement. Although Feller could not order the prosecution to drop the case, letting Heather know the judge thought it was a waste of the court's time was the next best thing. Wasting the court's time was probably the number one "do not do" on every lawyer's list. Judges hated it and if you do it you'll likely pay for it.

As the three of them were passing through the courtroom's back door Marc said, "So, Shayla's out. That won't help her political career."

Heather set her briefcase on a table and said, "You know as much as I do. Let me see if I can get a hold of Paul," she continued as she removed her phone from a skirt pocket.

"I'll wait in the hall," Marc said to let Heather have a private conversation. "Let me know when you're done."

Barely five minutes later, Heather opened the hallway door and motioned for Marc to come back into the courtroom. She held the door for him and when they got to the tables inside the bar he sat down and looked at her.

"Okay, please keep this to yourself for now," Heather said to both Marc and Danica.

"It's true, Shayla's resigning today. She'll probably stay on for a few days until things settle down. That's according to Paul. Until then Paul will be making all of the major decisions.

"We both agreed, with everything that has happened it would be too costly and difficult to continue this case. So, we're going to go into chambers and ask for Judge Feller to put it on the record and dismiss."

"Don't forget to have my client's bail money returned and the Sutherland inheritance, the twenty-seven million, have the hold on it removed."

"Will do," Heather agreed.

FIFTY-FOUR

The weekend after the prosecution dismissed the indictment against Mackenzie Sutherland, Sunday afternoon to be exact, Madeline Rivers was mentally working through a dilemma. A couple of days after it was dismissed, Maddy had wrapped up a small investigation she was doing. Her bank account, thanks to Mackenzie Sutherland, was in the best shape it had been in since she could not remember when. Because of this, she decided to take a few days off and simply relax.

Maddy was not someone who could simply relax. Less than two days later, something that had nagged at her in the back of her mind returned. Maddy's curiosity got the better of her and she started doing some online research. Thanks to the internet, tracking down a great deal of information on someone was a lot easier on the feet than back in the old Sam Spade, gumshoe days.

The dilemma she was now thinking over on this dreary Sunday afternoon was because of what she had found. Maddy started off hoping she would not find what she did. Now that she had found it, she could not ignore it either. She sat cross-legged on her couch sipping a light chardonnay and blankly staring at the rain through her living room's bay window.

"Should've left well enough alone," she quietly said to herself. "When are you going to learn to mind your own business?"

Maddy picked up her phone off of the coffee table and punched the first number in her directory. It was answered before the first ring finished.

"Hey, sailor," she said, "want to buy a girl a drink?"

"Is she easy and open-minded?" the man said.

"Don't make me hurt you, Carvelli."

"What's up, sweetheart?" Maddy's good friend, fellow P.I. and sometime mentor Tony Carvelli asked.

"I need some advice," she said. "Can we meet today?"

"Sure," he said. "Come over and I'll make you dinner."

"The last time you offered to make me dinner I had to go grocery shopping for you. It would've been cheaper to take you to a restaurant."

"I got enough lasagna for two," Carvelli said. "And wine. Although, if you don't mind...."

"Here it comes," Maddy said smiling.

"You could pick up some salad. You know, one of those bags of salad," he said.

"Is that it?"

"Oh, uh, how about some French bread and Italian salad dressing. Stop at a *Sutherland's,*" Carvelli said.

"Anything else?" Maddy asked with a touch of sarcasm.
"No that should do it. See you in an hour?" he asked.
"About that," Maddy said finally laughing.

While Madeline cleaned up the dinner dishes in the kitchen, Tony sat at the dining room table looking over what Maddy brought with her. He had been at it for about twenty minutes when she finished in the kitchen, came back to the table, poured each of them a little more wine and sat down.

Tony made two separate piles of the reports and photos, picked up his glass for a small swallow then set the glass down. Maddy quietly waited in the first chair to his right.

"These two," Tony began patting the pictures and documents in the pile to his right, "I don't think so. The photos are close, but the dates would be a little thin. Too close to the one in Chicago. And they're both in California."

"I agree," Maddy said.

"But these two," Tony continued indicating the ones to his left, "I'm about ninety percent convinced, especially the one in Milwaukee. And if he's one then the one in St. Pete is a likely one too."

"Timing is right, and the name is the same for both," Maddy agreed. "The question is: what do I do now?"

Tony thought about the question for a moment, sipped his wine before saying, "What would you like to do?"

"I'd like to burn it all and forget I ever saw it," Maddy replied.

"Then do that," Tony said. "Except, you can't just forget it."

"I think Marc's involved with her," Maddy told him.

"Personally?"

"Yeah."

"He should've never broken up with Margaret," Tony said.

"From what Marc told me, that was pretty much a mutual decision."

"If it's even possible he might be involved with her, you have to show him this," Tony said referring to what Maddy had discovered. "Tomorrow."

"I know," Maddy sighed. "That's what I needed to talk to you about."

"Do you want me to be there?"

Maddy thought about it for a moment then said, "No, I can do it. In fact, I won't tell him we even talked unless I think it's necessary."

"Maddy's here," Carolyn told Marc. She was standing in Marc's doorway with Maddy behind her looking over Carolyn's shoulder.

Maddy had called in the morning while Marc was in court and had Carolyn block out Marc's entire afternoon schedule for her.

"Hi," Marc said as Carolyn stood aside to let Maddy into Marc's office. "Are you in trouble of some kind?" he asked wondering why she needed the entire afternoon with him.

She set her small satchel briefcase on Marc's desk, sat down and began by saying, "No, but I have something important to see you about. You remember that during the trial I had my doubts about Mackenzie's innocence?"

"What have you done, Madeline?" Marc seriously asked.

"Probably something I shouldn't have," she admitted. "Don't be mad at me, please. I've found some things I'm not sure what to do with. I'm not even sure I can or should do anything with this. I at least need to show it to you."

Maddy explained that despite the hung jury, she retained some doubts about Mackenzie. Instead of letting the doubts go, she spent the last few days researching the internet. She was looking for wealthy men with younger wives who died suddenly leaving the merry widow very merry indeed.

"I went back twenty years and you wouldn't believe how many there have been. I found over three hundred possible. I was able to eliminate most of them for a couple of reasons. The cause of death was usually from an illness of some kind, a lot of cancer, or the age of the widow at the time was wrong for Mackenzie.

"Then I took out the ones who died from other than a heart attack. That cut the list down to nine possibilities."

By now, Marc's initial annoyance was gone, and his lawyer's antennae were up and working. Plus, he was simply curious at where she was going.

"I did some more digging for pictures and information about the dead husbands, their wealth, who got what and pictures and descriptions of the widows."

Maddy reached into her satchel and removed everything she had shown Tony the night before. While she was separating the pictures and documents, she said, "I was able to eliminate five of the nine that way."

Maddy stood up and aligned the four sets of papers in front of Marc on his desk. With her right hand, she patted the two reports to her right, Marc's left, then said, "Go over these two first then the other two."

"You think these might be Mackenzie?"

"Please, Marc, look them over first. You want some coffee?" she said as she stood up.

Marc had picked up the first report then said, "No, grab me a Diet Pepsi from the fridge will you, please?"

Maddy left Marc alone for ten minutes while she chatted with the staff. Barry Cline came in from outside and greeted Maddy, who had done some investigative work for him as well.

"What's going on?" Barry asked.

"Sorry, I can't really get into it. I'm seeing Marc about something and he's reading over some documents for me," she vaguely replied.

Ten minutes later she re-entered Marc's office with the sodas. He was looking over the information on the second one.

He finished it a few minutes later then said, "These two are maybe, at best."

"Before you make any judgment check the other two, please."

It took him over thirty minutes because he went through both twice. When he finished he looked up at the wall past Madeline and softly said, "Holy shit." Then he said it again much louder.

Marc leaned forward, placed his left elbow on the desk, his chin in the palm of his hand, looked at Maddy and asked, "What do you think?"

"I want to know what you think," she replied.

He let his hand drop, folded them together on the desktop and said, "The first two," he paused a couple seconds before continuing, "I don't think so. The pictures aren't quite right, and they happened a little too close together, timewise."

"I agree, but they were possible," Maddy said.

"These other two," Marc said patting the papers on his right, "They're her. I suppose we could find a techie with photo comparison software to run an analysis, but I'm ninety percent they're her."

"The timing is perfect, and both men knew each other. Her marriage to Hayes wasn't long after Bauer's death. I'll bet that's how they met. And she married Cartwright, the guy in Chicago, not too long after Hayes' death. All heart attacks and either a quick burial or cremation."

"Could there be others?" Marc asked.

"I don't think so," Maddy replied. "If you draw the timeline for all four of them there isn't a big enough gap between them to allow for a fifth one. Possible, but not likely."

"Great, so she's only murdered four men and taken all of their money," Marc commented sarcastically. "How much do you think she got, total?"

"Close to a hundred million give or take a couple," Maddy said. "Marc, this woman is fucking evil!" Maddy rarely swore and when she did there was a good reason for it.

Marc sat silently looking at her for several seconds then said, "The question is: what do we do about it?"

"What can we do about?"

"Nothing," Marc said shrugging his shoulders and shaking his head. "We're still bound by privilege and there's nothing we can do."

"Even for things we found out after the trial that had nothing to do with it?" Maddy asked.

"Yes, absolutely," Marc answered her.

"Um, Marc, I may have made a big mistake."

"What did you do, Madeline?"

"I showed this to Tony last night. I wanted his opinion and…"

"Oh, that's not a problem," Marc said with relief. He picked up his personal phone, found Carvelli's number and speed-dialed it. Tony answered right away and in less than a minute it was understood that he would keep this confident also since Mackenzie was a client of his as well as Marc and Madeline.

When Marc finished with Carvelli, he said to Maddy, "About all we can do is see her and try to convince her to come clean."

"Do we have an obligation to do that?"

"A legal or ethical obligation, no," Marc continued. "A moral obligation, yes. I can't just let this slide."

"She's a psycho, evil, she-devil," Maddy said. "She might go after you, too."

Marc thought that over before saying, "First of all, you're coming with me. And," he again paused, "I don't think so. That's not the Mackenzie I knew when we were kids."

"Oh, and this is? And you think you need to drag me into it too? Thanks."

"Hey, you started it. Besides, better we find out," Marc said as he dialed Mackenzie's number

"I'm bringing a gun," Maddy said.

"Good idea," Marc said while he listened to Mackenzie's phone ring.

FIFTY-FIVE

"Why am I so nervous about this?" Maddy asked Marc just as Marc reached for the front doorbell of the Crocus Hill house.

He pushed it and said, "Because we're about to find out some things we might not want to know."

A smiling Mackenzie opened the door, took one look at Maddy and Marc and said, "Wow, this looks serious. Everything okay? They haven't changed their mind about retrying me, have they?"

"No, no," Marc smiled slightly. "Too late, we do need to talk."

"Okay," Mackenzie said and stood back to let them enter. She said hello to Maddy. Marc suggested the dining room table and they went in and took chairs. Mackenzie sat at the head of the table with Marc to her right facing the wall and Maddy to his left.

"Okay, what?" Mackenzie asked while a feeling of dread washed over her from head to foot. By the look on their faces, although she did not want to admit it, Mackenzie knew why they were here.

Maddy had laid her leather satchel with the research papers in them on the table. Marc reached in and removed all four sets of documents. He placed the one from Milwaukee regarding Kenneth Hayes and those from St. Petersburg and Joseph Bauer in front of Mackenzie. She looked at the cover page of each set of documents, read the name of each man, became visibly unnerved and sat back in her chair.

"I have to ask, Mac," Marc said, "What can you tell me about these two men?"

Mackenzie's initial reaction was to act indignant and tell them both to leave. Instead, she took a minute to think over the past twenty years then made a decision.

"Are either or both of you wired?" she asked.

Maddy looked at Marc who calmly answered for both of them. "Of course not. We're here as your lawyer and hopefully, still your friends."

"Are you still covered by attorney-client privilege?" she asked.

"Absolutely," Marc replied then reached over and squeezed her hand. This gesture of affection caused Maddy, the cynical ex-cop, to raise her eyebrows a bit.

Mackenzie, still holding Marc's hand, visibly sighed, looked each of them in the eyes and said, "I guess it's time to tell someone. Wait here a minute. I'll be right back."

Mackenzie left the room, turned right at the stairs and went upstairs to the second floor. When she did this, Maddy removed her .357 Ladysmith from the holster on her hip. She leaned forward, placed her left arm casually on the table while holding the gun on her leg, unseen, under the table.

“You won’t need that,” Marc said.

“I hope not,” Maddy replied.

True to her word, Mackenzie returned holding a manila envelope in her hands. She sat down next to Marc and said, “You can put the gun away, Maddy. I’ll show you everything.”

Mackenzie removed the papers from the envelope while a slightly embarrassed Madeline holstered the revolver. Mackenzie handed the documents to Marc.

Marc, with Maddy looking over his shoulder, scanned the first page, looked at Mackenzie and said, “A police report for criminal sexual conduct? Mac, why don’t you tell us what this is?”

“October eleventh,” she began. “Two days after my twenty-third birthday, I met a girlfriend for dinner at the Wild Onion on Grand in St. Paul. We met about seven-thirty, had a nice time, nice evening. Her name’s Becky. We had become good friends at the U and hadn’t seen each other for a couple of months. My birthday was a good excuse to get together and catch up.

“It was a Tuesday evening and we both had jobs; our first jobs after college graduation. I remember every detail. We split up about ten. She was parked a block away on Grand down the street toward the Cathedral. I was parked on a side street, Avon, what would that be, south, toward St. Clair?”

“Yes, south,” Marc agreed.

“Anyway, we split up in front of the restaurant. She went to her car and I went to mine.”

Mackenzie stopped and averted her eyes from Marc and Maddy. Looking down at the table top she continued. “I shouldn’t have parked there. The streetlight by my car was out and I noticed it when I got there. I was in a hurry, so I parked there anyway…”

“That doesn’t make what happened your fault,” Maddy said, understanding where this story was headed.

“I know,” Mackenzie agreed looking at Maddy with a wan smile.

“Go on,” Marc quietly said.

“Anyway,” Mackenzie continued. “I got to my car and the next thing I knew three young men were all over me. A tan colored Ford van had suddenly appeared, they jumped out, grabbed me, threw me in back, climbed in after me and took off.

“For the next two hours, I went through hell. It’s the only way to describe it. While one of them drove, the others tore my clothes off, took turns slapping, punching and kicking me until I couldn’t resist anymore. I tried, I really did but it was useless.

"One of them slapped a piece of tape over my mouth to shut me up and they taped my hands behind me. I laid on a small blanket, naked and scared to death while they drove me to their destination, Lake Phelan. It must have been about a half-hour because they drove right to it. I was so scared I could barely breathe. I thought for sure they were going to rape then murder me. They weren't wearing masks. They didn't make any effort to hide their faces. The only thing they did about their identities, I found out later, was to use fake names.

"On the way, even though I was horribly afraid, I tried to stay calm and think. I noticed a couple of things about the van, the inside. If I ever found it, I could identify it."

"That took some balls," Maddy said.

Mackenzie gave her the same simple smile then continued. "I decided I would cooperate and hopefully they would let me live. I thought maybe all they wanted was sex and if I went along with it I'd be okay.

"They took me to Lake Phelan, on the East Side of St. Paul, to a parking lot down the street from the pavilion. It was on the main street between the lake and the golf course. Phelan Parkway."

"You saw this from the van?" Marc asked.

"No, I found out later," Mackenzie said.

"Let her finish," Maddy quietly told Marc.

"When we got there, one of them told me I'd better not scream, or they would kill me. He then ripped the tape off my mouth. That's not like TV. It really hurts. I told them they didn't need to hurt me, that I'd cooperate. That just made them laugh."

Mackenzie paused again and wiped a small tear from her face as she recalled what happened. For the next hour, the four of them took turns raping, sodomizing and forcing themselves in her mouth. All the while for amusement, they laughed, joked around, hit, kicked and slapped her.

After sufficiently amusing themselves, barely conscious though she was, she recalled being dragged out of the van and onto a walkway bridge over a creek that ran into the lake. Two of them hoisted her up onto the bridge railing and pushed her battered, beaten and naked body into the creek.

"At first," Mackenzie continued, "I thought I was going to drown, and I felt relieved. At least they weren't beating me anymore. They weren't raping and hurting me anymore. I literally thought death would at least put an end to it."

She looked at both Marc and Maddy and said, "If you haven't been through something like that, you cannot understand how bad it was. I've thought about it many times. Hundreds. Trying to adequately describe what it was like and I can't do it. I really thought death would be preferable. At least the pain would stop.

"In a few seconds, I realized the water wasn't very deep. It was muddy and had a lot of weeds and sticks, but where I was it was only a couple feet deep. I managed to pull myself up so my head was onshore, on the grass. It was a picnic area. Of course, at that time of night and that late in the season there wasn't anybody around.

"I remember lying there for a while, I don't know how long. It had been a warm September, so the water was still warm, warmer than the air. My main memory was how much I hurt. Everything hurt, from the top of my head to my toes. It was very difficult and extremely painful to breathe too. I later found out I had a partially punctured lung. I laid there for a while, I don't know how long, maybe twenty to thirty minutes, I'm not sure. I remember how warm and nice the water felt and it made my injuries feel a little better.

"After a while I saw some headlights pull into the parking lot. I crawled out of the water and tried to stand. I couldn't at first. My knees buckled a couple of times. I finally managed to stay upright and stumble up to the car. It was only a couple hundred feet, but I hurt so bad it seemed to be a mile.

"I got up by the car and they saw me. A couple of teenage kids looking for a place to make out. I must have looked like I'd crawled out of a swamp.

"The next thing I knew I was in the backseat with the girl holding me. She had a coat around me. Her boyfriend was driving, and they got me to Regions Hospital where I woke up later that night. I don't even remember the ride there.

"It's all in there," Mackenzie said. Referring to the documents she had brought down from upstairs and given to Marc. "Including the medical report and the statements from the kids who found me. I want you to know I'm not lying. I didn't make this up."

"No one thinks you did," Marc quietly said.

"Two St. Paul cops came, two detectives. An older white man, probably in his fifties and a younger white man, in his mid-forties. They took my statement. My purse was gone with my money and ID; my clothes were gone, and I later found out, my car had been towed."

"Why wasn't there a female detective?" Maddy asked.

"Don't know. I asked about that later when it was obvious the two men couldn't find their way out of a bathroom and weren't particularly interested in what happened. I admitted to them that I had told those guys I would cooperate, and they said that could be construed as giving my consent.

"I pointed out to these two Neanderthals that even if I did consent to the sex I sure as hell didn't consent to the beating. The older one, the senior detective just shrugged and said, 'Their lawyers will just say they got a little carried away.' You can guess how much effort they put into the case."

"What time of day was that?" Maddy asked. "Was it the night it happened?"

"Yes, probably five, six o'clock in the morning," Mackenzie said.

"Night shift guys. Lazy assholes waiting for retirement," Maddy replied.

"Two, three weeks went by and nothing much was happening."

"Was it in the papers?" Marc asked.

"Oh, yeah," Mackenzie said. "For three or four days it was all over the news."

"Funny, I don't remember it," Marc said.

"They didn't use my name. They don't identify rape victims," Mackenzie reminded him.

"That's right," Marc agreed.

"Anyway, after three weeks or so with no news from the cops I decided to see what I could find. I was feeling a lot better, physically. Most of the bruises had healed, my six broken ribs were better and the three teeth they knocked out were replaced.

"I went online looking for the parking sticker I saw in the back window of the van. I figured they were college students, so I started checking the local schools. Even though the sticker in the window was facing out, I had a clear image of it in my memory. It took about ten minutes online for me to find it. Macalester College in St. Paul.

"I didn't bother to tell the two cops. I figured I'd find these guys faster myself. It took less than two days driving around the campus and the streets around Macalester. I found the van parked in a driveway of a house about a mile south, in Highland Park. It had the same cracked mirror on the passenger side and parking sticker. I also took a chance late that night to peek inside. It was unlocked, and I found the ceiling light was missing the plastic cover, just like the one I was kidnapped in. My torn-up clothes and the blanket with my DNA on it were gone. It also smelled like someone had thoroughly cleaned the inside with bleach. Because of that, there was no proof, other than my word that I was ever in the van."

"I can see where this is going," Marc quietly said.

"I went to the two detectives, Laurel and Hardy I called them, and told them what I found. They were both pretty pissed off I was interfering in their investigation. We had a big argument and I went to their supervisor who made them get off their lazy asses and go pick these guys up. They found all four of them living in that house they were renting."

"Where was your dad during all of this?" Marc asked.

Mackenzie hesitated to answer then simply said, "We never really got along. Mostly because of his drinking. I told him what happened, and he said I probably asked for it. That was the last time I have talked to him."

Mackenzie continued to explain what happened. Her assailants were picked up and she positively identified all four of them. They were arrested on multiple counts each of criminal sexual conduct, assault and attempted murder. Bail was set at half a million dollars each. It was a huge story for several days but quickly died down after bail was paid. Their families had retained multiple, high-priced lawyers for each of them.

"To make a long story a little shorter, they all got together, the lawyers and my attackers and shut things down. They denied everything and alibied each other. Because there was no evidence, no DNA or witnesses and the cops couldn't get one of them to flip, the prosecutor wouldn't pursue the case. She told me quote, 'I'm not going to take a case to trial I'm not absolutely certain I can win.' Later a woman cop told me this prosecutor was a politically ambitious bitch who liked to brag about her won-lost record. Would only go to trial if the case was an absolutely certain conviction and she wouldn't take a chance and fight if she couldn't be positive she would win. Plus, the quality of the defense lawyers scared her off."

"So, they declined to prosecute," Marc said.

"That's right," Mackenzie said. "I felt like an absolute idiot. Like trash that had just been tossed aside. They dismissed the case and these four spoiled assholes were laughing and having a grand old time when they left court."

"And these four were, David Bauer, Kenneth Hayes Jr., Phillip Cartwright and Adam Sutherland," Maddy quietly said, knowing all of the names from her research.

"That's right," Mackenzie agreed.

FIFTY-SIX

"I was devastated, absolutely crushed. These four spoiled, psycho, coddled rich kids had treated me like garbage. They took away everything from me; my life, my humanity, my dignity, the very essence that made me who I am. They just ripped it out of me, threw it away and sent me the message that I was nobody, that I was nothing. That my life was not mine and they could do whatever they want to me then walk away laughing. That's what rape does to you, Marc," Mackenzie said looking at her lawyer. "It leaves you empty. Your life is not yours. You are totally at the mercy of someone who can take you and do unspeakable things to you and there's nothing you can do about it.

"I spent the next year in therapy," Mackenzie continued. "Rape counseling, that kind of thing. It wasn't helping me in the least, but I went a couple times a month for ten or eleven months. It finally occurred to me why it wasn't helping. It was victim therapy. How to cope with being a victim. I know it helps a lot of women deal with it, but I didn't feel like a victim. I felt white hot anger at these little bastards doing this to me and getting away with it. I didn't want to be a victim, I didn't want to cope with being a victim and I refused to accept it. I wanted my life back. I wanted to be whole again. I wanted to be me again. I wanted justice and I knew if I wanted it I'd have to get it myself.

"I was twenty-three years old. I had ambitions, desires. I wanted marriage and children, a family. And these little bastards took that away from me for their amusement."

"So you decided to go after them," Marc said.

"I quit victimhood therapy and started researching them. I found out everything I could about each of them including their families. One of the things I found during all of this is that wealthy, successful people are not necessarily something you want to become.

"You would think that having money would at least free you from the worry of not having money. It doesn't. If anything, it makes it worse. They're obsessed with it, terrified at the thought of losing it, of not having it. They live in their privileged world but they're certainly not happy. And they're all a bunch of useless, pretentious assholes.

"So, I went after them. I decided to get them where I knew it would really hurt: their money."

Mackenzie explained her strategy and how she went about it. First was Joseph Bauer. She found out everything about him which wasn't much. Bauer was a married workaholic with virtually no social life. No real friends and a wife that was practically an arranged marriage who spent more time at the local synagogue than she did with her family.

Joseph Bauer was going to be seduced, probably for the first time in his life.

An affair that his wife, the Jewish Princess, quickly found out about, a divorce and the rest was easy. Joseph also accommodated Mackenzie by having a bad heart from years of overeating, no exercise, and too much work. The only thing she could not prevent was a healthy cash payoff to the original Mrs. Bauer. A cash payoff to the Princess that worthless David, one of her rapists, would fritter away. Mommy simply could not say no to him until the money was gone. Now both the Jewish Princess and David were currently facing poverty and a long drug-related prison sentence for him.

Joseph Bauer made his death easy. He already had a bad heart and needed to use nitroglycerin pills to control it. One day he misplaced the nitro pills, or so Mackenzie told the police. Mackenzie started a fight with him at work and before she knew it he was slumped over at his desk. She told the cops she did everything she could to find his pills, but he must have left them at home as he did sometimes. Of course, she didn't mention anything about the fight she deliberately started to bring on the stress to his heart.

During her marriage to Bauer, she became acquainted with husband number two, Kenneth Hayes, Sr. Already conveniently widowed, Mackenzie knew Hayes and Bauer were friends from college before she targeted Bauer.

Hayes met her at the Bauer home a few months before Bauer's death and Mackenzie had little trouble reeling him in. She moved to Milwaukee, a quick courtship and wedding and Mackenzie easily turned the smitten Mr. Hayes against his three children to change his Will and leave it all to her.

"Now there's a worthless life," she said. "An investment banker for a small successful firm with his name on it. You work your ass off twenty-hours a day. You socialize with the same set of dull, boring dipshits who know nothing except money and never relax and simply enjoy life. It helps to have one screwed up personality to get involved in it.

"After Milwaukee and Ken Hayes' untimely heart attack while driving home one day, a quick cash out and I was onto Chicago. You pretty much know that story.

"I'll say this for Wendell Cartwright. He was a useless waste of breathable air, but he did know how to party. I came home early once and found him in the hot tub with four naked women, all in their twenties. I just shook my head and went to bed. It wasn't long after that when Wendell was cremated."

Madeline was sitting back in her chair uncertain if she should be proud of Mackenzie or appalled. Probably a little of both.

"Then you moved back to St. Paul to get William Sutherland. Four men murdered…"

"I didn't admit to murdering anyone," Mackenzie corrected him. "Everyone of them died of natural causes. A heart attack."

"I suppose that's true," Marc quietly said.

"I wasn't attacked, beaten, horribly raped and almost killed by just the sons. Their parents, especially the men who created these little monsters did it to me, too. They are just as responsible for it by instilling in their kids the sense of entitlement that they have."

"And then bailing them out of trouble their entire lives and never making them accept responsibility for anything," Maddy interjected.

"Yes," Mackenzie agreed nodding at Maddy. "That's truer than you know. The things I found out, the family dynamics these people have are unbelievable. They bailed these little brats out their entire lives. Schools, jail and not just the four boys. Hailey Sutherland is a perfect example. All of their kids are useless. They have no sense of right and wrong. No sense of responsibility or accountability. They took my life and thought no more of it than stepping on a bug. So, I took the one thing they care about more than anything else. I took their money and their entitled lives. The same money they used to get away with taking my life, I used to take theirs."

The three of them sat silently for a full two minutes, uncertain what to say, Marc and Maddy each having the same problem of how to sort out their feelings about this. They both knew, or at least had been taught, that what Mackenzie did was wrong but having a great deal of difficulty believing it.

"What about Bob Sutherland?" Marc asked.

"What about him?" Mackenzie replied. "He threatened me, I shot him. Period.

"Marc," Mackenzie said after another moment of silence, "I found three other girls that they did this to. One more here in St. Paul. I tried to convince her to go to the police, but she wouldn't. Another one near Milwaukee and one by Chicago. There are likely others. I sent, anonymously, two million tax-free dollars to each of them. They should be compensated, at least somewhat."

"You could've gone to prison for the rest of your life," Marc said.

"I was never worried about prison. What they did to me put me in a worse prison than the state could put me in. No, prison never worried me. I was always ready to take any punishment the courts tried to give me."

"Why didn't you tell me about this before your trial?" Marc asked.

"Why? So you could plead me not guilty by reason of insanity? No thanks. Plus, it's not true. I knew exactly what I was doing. I would have told you and let you use it at sentencing if we lost."

"Why didn't they recognize you?"

"I never saw them after the attack. The closest I came to them was in the hallway at court after their case was dismissed. After the attack I was a bloody, beaten mess. Plus, I changed my appearance just enough. Just because they have money doesn't mean they're the smartest people."

Mackenzie turned to Marc then said, "My biggest regret is you," she smiled her sad smile. "I thought maybe I could have something with you, something resembling a normal life. I know now that's not possible, is it?" she asked him.

"No, it's not. I'm sorry but I don't see how," Marc replied.

Mackenzie took one of Marc's hands and said, "I'm glad I told you. I'm glad I got it out. I feel a lot of relief. I've been carrying this around for twenty years and..."

"What will you do now?" Marc asked. "You have plenty of money."

"Not as much as you think. I took over ninety-nine million from them. They're all dead broke now. I gave six million to those three other girls I found. I'm keeping four million and the rest I have already given away, mostly in large donations to rape counseling centers and battered women shelters around the country. I've put most of their money to some good use."

"You deserve more than four million for what they did," Maddy said.

Mackenzie looked down the length of the dining room table past Marc and Maddy. Her eyes teared up, her mouth curled down, and she looked immensely sad about the whole thing.

She wiped the tears from each eye and said to Marc, "I'll be leaving in a couple weeks. I just want to go live quietly somewhere.

"When I think back on it, it's all so tragic. So many lives destroyed, so many dead. And all because the police and prosecutors wouldn't do their job. I did what I was supposed to do, what so many women who are raped are afraid to do. Go to the authorities and let them find justice for you. But they refused because the prosecutor didn't want to risk her precious won-lost record." Mackenzie looked at Maddy, smiled and said, "Well, I got her ass, too. Guess who the prosecutor was?"

"Heather Anderson?" Maddy asked.

"No," Marc said realizing who it was. "Heather was in high school when this happened. So, it was you who leaked the news to the St. Paul paper."

Mackenzie merely nodded her head and smiled.

"Who?" Maddy asked.

Marc said to Mackenzie, "Go ahead, tell her."

Maddy suddenly realized who it was and said, "Shayla Parker."

"Yep," Mackenzie said. "And I found out her boss at the time who backed up her decision was the Chief Deputy County Attorney, now Judge Otis Carr."

Marc was sitting in his office, his shoes kicked off, his feet in a drawer pulled out from the desk. The window behind him above Charles Avenue was open letting the fresh, warm, mid-May air come in. Marc was taking a break, the papers from the case he was working on were scattered across his desktop. He sipped a Diet Pepsi while he read, for the fourth or fifth time, the handwritten letter he received the day before from Mackenzie, now back to her original name, Mackenzie Lange.

It was two months since she left and until yesterday, not a word from her. She was doing fine living somewhere she wouldn't say. Once again she apologized for the way things turned out between them but not for the things she had done. All she would say is she was doing much better, in no small part because of Marc's help. Mackenzie had started seeing a psychiatrist and even began attending a non-denominational Christian Church. She ended the letter with the thought that perhaps someday they would meet again. Marc knew that was unlikely even though in his heart of hearts, he could not condemn her for what she had done. The 'system' had chewed her up and spit her out. How would any of us have acted given the same circumstances?

Marc folded the letter and put it back in his center desk drawer. He thought back at the fallout of the Mackenzie Lange tornado.

After Shayla Parker resigned, she was investigated by the Office of Professional Responsibility. Her license was still suspended indefinitely while the investigation continued. Her political career and marriage were finished. In connection with that, over thirty appeals of trial convictions over which Otis Carr presided had been filed. There were not likely to be many more since most criminal cases, close to ninety percent, are resolved by plea agreements. Those would not be appealable.

Judge Otis Carr, seeing the clear and convincing proverbial handwriting on the wall, voluntarily resigned and retired his license. His Honor was going to be quite busy for a while trying to stave off bankruptcy and preserve enough of his pension to live on. Marc was intimately aware of his problems. The documents scattered on his desktop concerned a divorce he was handling. His client was Claudia Carr and she wanted to drain the blood from Otis, one drop at a time. Hell hath no fury…

As for Mackenzie's rapists, they had received more, long overdue punishment. Kenneth Hayes, Jr., the son from Milwaukee, drove his car off the road during a snowstorm a month or so ago. He wrapped it around a tree and was pronounced D.O.A. at the scene.

David Bauer's drug case in Florida was resolved with a plea agreement in federal court. David had been the weakest of the four of them, the ones who had committed the rapes and assaults. He was more of a "go along to be accepted" type. Surprisingly, he had enough sense not to flip on his Cuban cocaine conspirators. He took his deal and was now in a mean, maximum security prison in Atlanta doing twelve years for possession with intent to sell.

Hailey Sutherland had disappeared. Maddy had checked on her out of curiosity and could find no trace of her. She would eventually end up, about a year later, a Jane Doe in the Los Angeles' County Morgue. Just another street-hooker-heroin overdose tossed into a pauper's grave.

Paige Sutherland, Robert's widow, was doing fine. With her family's money she was still quite comfortable, and Simon Kane's Mercedes was back in her driveway three or four nights a week. Simon managed to get back into good graces with his firm after a thirty-day suspension of his attorney license. His wife was divorcing him while Simon was trying to find a polite way to get away from the clutches of Paige Sutherland. Wanting and having are often two very different things.

Shortly after the trial of Mackenzie Sutherland ended, Adam Sutherland was arrested with a pound of crystal meth in his car. He spent two weeks in jail before he convinced Paige to put up bail for him. Back on the street he found he had no friends and very few people who even acknowledged knowing him.

Adam's money, along with the nice apartment and the flashy Corvette were all long gone. He was living in a one room weekly rental flea-trap in East St. Paul. One day a neighbor detected a strong smell coming from his room. The cops were called and found him hanging from a ceiling rafter. He had apparently ripped the ceiling apart and looped a length of rope through the stud, stood on a chair and kicked it over. Without Daddy there to bail him out, apparently he couldn't face his fate.

Marc leaned back in his chair, laced his fingers behind his head and stared at the ceiling. After twenty or thirty seconds, he said out loud, "I ought to write a book, but who'd believe it?"

His personal phone rang and when he looked at the ID he said, "Well this is interesting."

Marc answered the call and after ten minutes of catching up, made a lunch date for later that same day with Margaret Tennant.

Thank you for your patronage. I hope you enjoyed Personal Justice
Dennis Carstens

Feel free to email me at: dcarstens514@gmail.com

Also Available on Amazon

A Marc Kadella Legal Mystery No. 5

Delayed Justice

ONE

"Would either of you care for champagne?"

The question was asked of the two casually dressed businessmen seated together in first class. The flight attendant, an attractive woman in her mid-forties smiled down at the one in the aisle seat waiting for a reply. His companion, the younger of the two, ignored her while glumly staring out of the window.

"Sure," the older man answered her. He lightly poked his partner with an elbow who turned and looked at the woman.

"Champagne?" she politely asked again.

"Um, yeah, why not? Wait, make it half orange juice, please. It's a little early."

They were barely twenty minutes out of George Bush Intercontinental Airport in Houston on a four-hour flight to Panama City, Panama. Both men had reclined their chairs taking advantage of the ample legroom available in first-class. The younger man was again staring out the window while the attendant went for their drinks.

"I hate this shit," the younger one whispered loud enough for his companion to hear.

"I know you've told me at least a dozen times. Relax, life's too short to worry about every little thing."

The younger man turned his head to his right to speak to his companion and said, "Life's too short is exactly it. I've been up and on the go since three A.M. to fly to a meeting with a sociopath who would think nothing of slitting my throat just to watch the blood drain out."

His traveling companion, Victor Espinosa, heartily laughed at the nervous man, Walter Pascal. At that moment the attendant brought their drinks and departed.

"Relax, Wally. Trust me, if Javier had anything like that in mind, he'd send some guys to Minnesota. He wouldn't bother having us fly to Panama. Besides, he has nothing to be upset about."

"I know," Walter said relaxing a bit. "He just makes me nervous. He's the scariest guy on the damn planet."

"He is that," Victor agreed. "But he's been damn good for business. At least we're not shoehorned into a sardine seat in back," Victor continued referring to the seats in coach.

A short while later the flight attendant reappeared and asked about refills. Walter handed her his glass and told her to wake him when they served the meal. Victor accepted a refill.

"Don't drink too much," Walter said as he turned his head, closed the window blind and relaxed to get some sleep.

A little more than three-and-a-half-hours later they felt the bump and heard the whine of the landing gear being extended. The aircraft was on its final approach into Tocumen International Airport and was right on schedule.

"Why is it these flights are always on time when you're in no hurry to get there?" Walter asked.

Victor laughed then said, "Relax. We'll be home by midnight. This is no big deal."

"Oh, I know. I'm just being…"

"A total pussy," Victor said.

As promised, a limousine was waiting for them as they exited the airport. Even though it was late May in Minnesota and a warm spring and they were dressed in light, casual clothes, the Panamanian heat and humidity hit them like a blast furnace when they stepped through the sliding glass doors.

"I wasn't ready for that," Victor said as they walked toward their ride.

There was a driver at the wheel and a serious looking Latino standing by the doors. A third man, one the Minnesotans both knew, exited the car as they approached. He looked at the two men, flashed a bright, warm smile and held out his right hand to greet them.

"Carlos, my friend," Victor said. "Thanks for picking us up."

As the two of them shook hands, Victor reminded the vicious cartel member who Walter was.

Carlos Rodriguez was one of the top lieutenants in the Del Sur — The Southern Cartel. It was one of the smallest of the major Mexican drug gangs but also one of the most successful. Most of their business came from acting as a go-between, almost a wholesaler, for the larger cartels in the northern area of Mexico.

The leader was a man named Javier Ruiz-Torres. Fifty-two years old, he was known as El Callado — The Quiet One. In meetings, he rarely spoke and when he did, it was normally to his top aide, Pablo 'Paul' Quinones.

Quinones was what the Italians called his consigliore or, in Spanish, consejero. Born into an upper-class family, Quinones was educated at Stanford and the Sorbonne in Paris. He spoke several languages fluently and was drawn to the wild side of business rising rapidly alongside El Callado.

It was these two men that the Minnesotans were being chauffeured to meet.

"Good to see you too, Victor. Come," Carlos said as he held the door for them. "He's anxious to see you. No luggage?" he asked.

"No, we have to return tonight," Victor answered as he and Walter slid across the tan leather seats.

The ride from the airport to the hotel normally took ninety minutes. With the two motorcycle cops guiding them through traffic, they were entering the Marriott Villa in less than an hour.

The limo pulled up to the walkway in front of the villa, stopped and the thug in the passenger seat jumped out to open the door. Again, the heat hit the two Americans in the face and Carlos led them to the villa's front door. As he did, both guests walked a bit slowly looking over the grounds. There was a beautiful pool with a view of the Pacific Ocean and to their left was the fifteenth fairway of a championship caliber golf course.

"Nice digs," Walter said.

"Sure is," Victor agreed as he finished counting the guards that he could see. An even dozen not counting Carlos.

In the foyer, another serious-looking Latino man wearing a holster with a small, fully-automatic machine pistol in it, awaited them. He quickly, but politely and thoroughly frisked them both for weapons. Satisfied, the guard led them into the living room while Carlos stayed at the door.

They entered the living room where the two men they were meeting were waiting for them. Seated by himself on a plush, off white, suede couch was the old man himself, Javier Ruiz Torres — El Callado.

To look at him you would never guess he was the ruthless head of a drug cartel. An attractive man with a well-tanned look, he could easily pass for a banker or any legitimate businessman, except for the way he was dressed. He wore expensive, soft-leather, brown loafers, tan slacks and a silk shirt. The only jewelry he wore was a simple gold wedding ring and a modest gold chain with a crucifix around his neck.

"Welcome to Panama," the second man said as he shook hands with each of them. This was Paul Quinones, the man to whom they would actually converse. "Please, have a seat," he pleasantly gestured toward two of several matching chairs in the room.

Quinones took one of the same chairs next to his boss — no one sat on the couch with El Callado — and asked, "Something to drink? It's a warm day today even for Panama."

"That Evian looks good," Victor said referring to the bottle on the glass-topped table between them.

Quinones made a gesture toward a doorway, said something in Spanish and a minute later a young Latina girl set a tray with four bottles, glasses and ice on the table. Quinones dismissed her, then filled the glasses with ice and water for all of them.

"You're undoubtedly wondering why you're here," Quinones began the discussion by saying. "First of all, let me assure you we are quite satisfied with your services."

This statement caused Walter Pascal to almost faint with relief. He had been doing his best not to stare at the sociopath on the couch. He was also struggling with his breathing in an attempt to appear calm.

"In fact, we're interested in increasing our deposits each month," Quinones said.

The three of them, with El Callado listening to his counselor's translations, discussed rates of return, investment strategies and finally fees.

"Since we are doubling our investment with your firm, a twenty-five percent reduction in your fees is acceptable to us," Quinones told them. Noting that Quinones did not put that statement in the form of a suggestion, let alone a request, Victor Espinosa quickly agreed.

The three of them toasted the new arrangement, smiles all around even from Quinones' boss. Then Ruiz Torres gestured to Quinones who leaned over so his boss could whisper in his ear.

"Get rid of them. I hate talking to bankers. They bore me," he said.

"Si, jefe," Quinones replied. He looked at his two guests and said. "Senior Torres asked me to express his gratitude to you for coming today. Unless you have anything else...?" he said with an inquisitive look.

"No, I don't think so," Espinosa answered.

"Good," Quinones said as he stood. "Carlos will have you back in plenty of time to make your flight."

The limo taking their guests back to the airport had barely pulled away from the curb when El Callado and his counselor were conferring.

"He is here?" Torres asked as Quinones held the lighter for his boss to light his eighty-dollar Cohina.

"Yes, Javier," Quinones answered him using his first name as he was allowed to do in private.

"I want that taken care of today."

"Yes, Javier. It will be," Quinones said retaking the chair he had used. "What did you think of the gringos?"

Torres blew a cloud of sweet cigar smoke than said, "They are bankers. What do I care?" he shrugged. "You are satisfied they do a good job with our money?"

"Sí, Javier. It comes out clean with a fourteen percent return."

"Good. When Carlos returns…"

"He is here. He didn't go to the airport."

"Good. Have him take care of the problem."

The six-seat Beechcraft was an hour out of Panama City when the pilot dropped to a thousand feet. Besides the pilot, there were three men in the plane. Carlos, who was in charge of the mission, a young man name Juan and the object of their attention, Rafael Ortiz.

The small plane began to bank slightly to the right while Rafael stared out the back-seat passenger window.

He had been told they were searching for a place for a new landing strip.

"It is all jungle," Rafael said to Carlos who was in the copilot's seat. "There's no good place for a landing strip."

Carlos turned around, nodded at Juan who jammed a hypodermic needle into Carlo's neck and emptied the syringe.

Rafael yelped, grabbed his neck and tuned to Juan who stared impassively back. Within seconds Rafael was completely immobile although still very conscious. Juan unbuckled his seatbelt, opened the plane's door and began to push Rafael out.

Rafael tried to speak, tried to beg or scream but nothing came out. All he could do was stare at the younger man with his eyes wide open while trying to understand why this was happening.

Juan managed to get the man positioned in the doorway. Juan looked at those terrified eyes, muttered the word traitor, spit in Rafael's face then pushed him out.

Crashing through the trees broke Rafael's neck and mercifully killed him before he hit the jungle floor. Within a few days the indigenous wildlife would leave only strips of clothing and bones. In barely three or four weeks the jungle growth would be grown back and if you walked within a foot of him, you would not have found Rafael's remains.

The unfortunate part of the poor man's demise was that he was not the traitor. That man was still very much alive and well.

About the same time Rafael was making his free fall into the Panamanian jungle, a meeting was taking place in downtown Minneapolis. It was being held on the twentieth floor of the LaSalle Plaza, a thirty-story glass and chrome beauty on the south edge of downtown. Suite 2010 held the office of CAR Securities Management, LLC. The three hundred square foot corner office, with windows overlooking downtown and the western suburbs, was where the meeting was being held. There were two men present. The forty-two-year-old founder and CEO, Corbin Andrew Reed, whose initials, CAR formed the acronym for CAR investments and the firm's CIO, Chief Investment Officer, Jordan Kemp.

Corbin Reed and Jordan Kemp gave meaning to the phrase 'opposites attract.' The two of them had met in college at the University of Minnesota twenty plus years ago and hit it off right away.

Corbin was six feet two and sported a slender waist and full head of hair. Never married, his numerous relationships with women rarely lasted longer than a weekend. Jordan was barely five-feet-six-inches and was almost as round as he was tall. He was also still married to the only girl he ever dated, and she had initiated that. The two men complimented each other perfectly. Corbin could sell ice to Eskimos and Jordan was a statistical genius. Despite being a small firm with barely twenty employees, including themselves, they had made each other into millionaires many times over.

For a man running a company making the millions this one did, you would never know it by the decorations of his office. Other than the office's size and plush carpeting, it was hardly the lavish office of a rich CEO.

"Did you hear from our guys?" Kemp asked Reed after taking a seat in front of his desk.

"Yeah, I did," Reed replied.

"And they made it out of there without getting their throats cut?"

"Yeah and with an assurance that all is well and we're going to see more money coming in."

"How much?" Kemp asked.

"Another ten mil each month," Reed said. "We'll put that to good use."

"Where are you with the Corwin guy? What's his name?"

"David. He's on the verge of practically begging me," Reed said.

Kemp looked out the window facing north of the fifty-story Corwin building and said, “How cool would it be to get our hands on that money?”

“Patience. Besides, it’s his aunt we need to snare. David is small potatoes compared to what she controls.”

While they waited in the passenger loading area, Walter said, “So that’s it. We get out of bed at three A.M., fly to Panama, damn near melt from the heat for a fifteen-minute meeting?”

“They’re increasing their deposits by ten million a month. For that kind of money, yeah, we go to a fifteen-minute meeting in Panama. By the way, I forgot to mention, the old man speaks English as good as you.”

“I don’t understand something. Ten million per month is nothing to these guys. What do they want?” Walter asked.

“They’re checking us out. We are getting him the best return for his money,” Victor said. “They have a lot of others to do this kind of business with, not just us. We’re being tested.”

TWO

In a continuing effort, albeit a losing one, to get some exercise, Marc Kadella took the stairs two at a time up to the second floor. The stairway had a steep angle and ran straight up. When he reached the top, he stopped for a moment to check his breathing, mildly pleased to find it had not increased.

"Making progress," he quietly sad. He then poked himself in the midsection and said, "Could do better."

Marc was a lawyer in private practice and as a sole-practitioner rented space in a suite of offices shared by other lawyers. His landlord, Connie Mickelson, a crusty, older woman working on her sixth marriage, did mostly family law and personal injury work. Also, there was Barry Cline, a man about Marc's age, who was becoming modestly successful at criminal and business litigation. The fourth and final lawyer was Chris Grafton, a small business, corporate lawyer with a thriving practice who was a few years older than Marc and Barry.

Marc was sandy-haired, blue-eyed of Scandinavian and Welsh ancestry. He was a little over six-feet tall, in his mid-forties and the recently divorced father of two mostly grown children; his son Eric, age nineteen and a daughter, Jessica, age eighteen.

He was returning from court where he made a deal for his client, a low-level drug dealer, to receive probation. The client was the son of a business client of Chris Grafton. Marc tried to steer clear of drug cases. He did not want to become known as a drug lawyer. With the pervasiveness of drug involvement in practically all criminal behavior, his attempts to stay away from it were becoming more and more difficult.

Marc's client, a sometime, sort of, college student, was busted for the fourth time holding enough cocaine and pot to prosecute for possession with intent to sell. And for the fourth time he was given probation, rehab and a stern lecture. Marc always marveled at how quickly drug dealers got turned loose with a promise to be good and not do it again. Despite what liberal politicians believe, it was becoming harder and harder to get these people sent to prison.

Marc entered the suite of offices and heard Sandy Compton, one of the secretaries, say into the phone, "Let me check. I'll see if he's available," and she put the caller on hold.

"You available?" Sandy asked looking at Marc.

"Who is it?"

"Mary Cunningham. Before you say anything," Sandy quickly continued cutting off the protest she knew was coming, "She's called three times. She says it's important."

"It's always important with her," Marc said heading toward his office.

While Marc was on the phone listening to the woman, one of his divorce clients, Chris Grafton appeared in his doorway. Chris listened while Marc repeatedly said, "uh huh, I see, you're right, I don't blame you."

Finally, Marc ended the call by saying, "Don't worry, Mary. We'll get it all straightened out in the end."

Marc hung up and Chris said, "What was that all about?"

"I don't have any idea. I didn't listen to a word she said. A woman scorned. She cheats on him, multiple times, he finally gets fed up and wants a divorce and she's mad at him. She should be thankful he doesn't own a gun. I don't know how he put up with her as long as he did."

"Why do you do divorce work?"

"It pays the bills. Plus, it reminds me how glamorous the practice of law is. What's up?"

"How did this morning go?"

"Great actually. I thought he'd at least get six months on the county. No jail time. Probation and another promise of going through drug rehab. Probation services gave him a good report," Marc told him.

"He knows how to play their game and con them," Chris said referring to probation services.

"Sooner or later, he'll end up with a tag on his toe, lying on a slab covered with a sheet. Does his dad know he's moving into heroin?" Marc asked.

"Are you serious? How do you know?"

"I'm not positive, but I think so. You may want to pass it along to Bert," Marc said referring to the father.

"Did the kid tell you that?"

"No."

"So it's not privileged?"

"Nope."

Connie Mickelson appeared in the doorway next to Chris. Connie was their landlord who shared office space with these two men and one other lawyer.

"Hey," Marc said to her. "Where have you been?"

"Ramsey County," she replied. "Listen, I heard a lawyer joke I haven't heard before."

"Okay," Marc said eagerly listening.

"Terrorists break into a conference room where the American Bar Association is holding its annual convention. They take a hundred lawyers hostage.

"The FBI arrives, and the terrorist leader tells them if their demands aren't met, they threatened to release one lawyer every hour."

"Not bad," Chris said, "but I heard a better one the other day.

"An anxious fifteen-year-old-girl comes home from school and asks her mother if you can get pregnant from anal sex. The mother says, of course. Where do you think lawyers come from?"

The three of them laughed, and then a voice behind them said, "I like that one."

"You looking to get fired?" Connie said to Carolyn.

"Right," Carolyn said. "I know where all the bodies are buried, remember?"

"She's got a point," Marc said.

Shortly before noon Carolyn buzzed Marc to tell him Tony Carvelli was on the phone. Carvelli was a private investigator Marc occasionally used and was also a good friend.

Carvelli was in his early fifties and due to his years on the streets of Minneapolis looked it but could still make most women check him out. He had a touch of the bad boy image they couldn't resist plus a flat stomach and a full head of thick black hair touched with gray highlights; a genetic bequest from his Italian father.

Carvelli was an ex-Minneapolis detective and had the reputation of being a bit of a street predator, which was well deserved. He looked and acted the part as well. Dressed as he normally was today, he could easily pass for a Mafia wise guy. Growing up in Chicago, he knew a few of them and could have become one himself and very likely a successful one. Instead, after his family moved to Minnesota he became a cop.

He was retired from the Minneapolis P.D. with a full pension then became a private investigator. Over the years he was able to build a nice, successful business doing mostly corporate security and investigations.

"What's up?" Marc asked when he answered.

"I thought I'd call and offer to let you buy me lunch," Carvelli said.

"That's awfully considerate of you. What's the occasion?"

"I just got a call from a guy I know who works for 3M, a high up the food chain executive type. He's got a kid in a jam and needs a defense lawyer. I told him I knew you and he recognized your name."

"What did he do?"

"I don't know the details. Drug bust. I didn't ask what or how or anything," Carvelli told him.

"I hate doing drug cases," Marc said.

"I know. Look, this guy, the dad, gets me a lot of business. Not just 3M but other corporate guys he knows. I would appreciate the favor," Tony pleaded.

Marc hesitated for a brief moment then said, "Okay. I may owe you one anyway. The dad has money?"

"Oh yeah. He can pay. Try not to gouge him too much."

"I won't," Marc replied. "I'm meeting the girls for lunch. Want to join us?"

"Maddy and Gabriella?"

"Yeah," Marc said.

"I need to talk to Maddy anyway. Where and when?"

"Axel's and I'm already late," Marc replied.

"See you there."

By the time Marc arrived at the restaurant, his three lunch companions were already there. He joined them at a booth and sat next to Gabriella Shriqui, across from Tony and Maddy Rivers.

Gabriella was a minor local celebrity. She started her career in TV news as a reporter for local Channel 8 covering local courts and criminal activity. This is how she first came in contact with Marc and Maddy.

She was excellent at her job and looked great in front of the camera. Gabriella was stop traffic gorgeous. The product of Moroccan Christian parents who immigrated to America when her mother was pregnant with her older brother. Gabriella had silky black hair six inches below her shoulders, light caramel colored skin that looked like a perpetual tan and dark, almost black, slightly almond shaped eyes.

A job hosting a half-hour show entitled *The Court Reporter* had opened up when the previous host was murdered. Gabriella had done a bit of work for the show and was given the job. The show was, as the title implied, about what was going on in the courts both locally and nationally.

Madeline Rivers was an ex-cop with the Chicago Police Department in her early-thirties. In her three-inch heeled, suede half-boots she liked to wear, she was over six-feet tall. She had a full-head of thick dark hair with natural auburn highlights that fell down over her shoulders, a model gorgeous face and a body worthy of Playboy. In fact, foolishly posing for that magazine was what led her to quit the Chicago P.D.

Maddy, as she was called by her friends, had moved to Minneapolis after quitting the Chicago cops following her Playboy pose. At the same time, she went through an ugly breakup when she found out the doctor she had fallen for was married. After arriving in Minnesota, she got a private investigator's license. Maddy was befriended by Tony Carvelli and she was now doing quite well for herself. It was through Tony that she had met Marc. They had done several criminal cases together and had become great friends.

Marc's appearance interrupted a conversation taking place between Tony and Maddy. Maddy was not as successful as Tony, although she was making a good living. A lot of her work came from advertising for investigating prospective boyfriends and on occasion, girlfriends.

With the advent of online dating services came a growing market for quietly investigating people who were beginning to date. Maddy had saved quite a few women from involvement with men of questionable character. Even so, it surprised her how many women did not heed Maddy's warnings and refused to dump a guy whom Maddy found out was a total sleaze.

Madeline also did some criminal work for a few defense lawyers, mostly Marc and his officemate Barry Cline. This was her favorite work. To help supplement her income, she handled the occasional wayward wife or husband in a divorce, which she hated.

"So, when I get some overflow stuff from my corporate security clients, you want in?" Tony asked Maddy.

"God, yes! Please tell me I can stop doing divorce work," Maddy said.

"Yeah, I can probably get you enough, so you can drop that," Tony assured her. "But don't be stealing my clients. Some of the guys I work for will like you, maybe a little too much."

"Hey, maybe I'll meet a rich executive type."

"Find one for me too," Gabriella laughed

While they ate lunch, the four of them chatted amiably. Marc told his lawyer jokes and Tony added two that he had recently heard. After the table was cleared, Tony told Marc about the drug case he had called him about. Tony gave Marc the father's name, information and of course, the son's name and information also.

It had been long established that anything said at these informal get-togethers was not to be used by Gabriella as a newsperson unless agreed upon.

"He's out on bail?" Marc asked.

"Yeah, Ramsey County," Tony replied.

"We need a good, juicy murder case," Maddy interjected.

"Yeah," Gabriella quickly agreed. "My show could use something spicy." She looked at Marc and continued, "How about a sex scandal murder involving some rich people or politicians?"

Marc looked at her and said, "You want me to see what I can do to create one?"

"Would you?" Maddy asked smiling.

He frowned at her across the table and said, "I'll do my best."

Changing the subject, Gabriella asked Maddy, "How's the new boyfriend?"

"Good, we get to listen to the girl-talk part of the conversation," Carvelli sarcastically said.

Maddy turned to look at Tony with a steely-eyed, stern expression.

Uh-oh, Marc thought, and then quickly said, "I always enjoy hearing about these things."

Maddy turned her head to Marc and gave him the same look. After a few seconds she looked at Gabriella and said, "He's great."

"Really? Wow! He is a bit of a hunk," she added. "Great, huh?"

"Well, he's you know, good. I mean he's okay… we're doing all right."

Tony looked at Marc and said while ticking off each item on his fingers, "She went from, he's great to, he's good to, he's okay to, we're doing all right all in one breath."

"He's history," Marc said.

"Probably tonight," Tony agreed.

Maddy scratched her nose with the middle finger of her left hand while looking back and forth at the two men. Gabriella had a hand over her mouth trying not to laugh.

"What's his name and what does he do?" Tony asked.

"His name is Rob Judd and he works for a small, local investment firm in their bond department. He makes a good living; he's good looking and not an asshole."

"Everything your dad told you to look for. Maybe you could murder him. That could make a great local story," Marc said.

"Why are you being so mean?" Maddy seriously asked.

"I'm sorry," Marc and Tony both said.

"We're just teasing you a bit," Marc added.

"Well, stop it," Gabriella said. "You guys have no idea how hard it is to find a nice guy."

"With a job," Maddy interjected.

"It's no easier for us," Marc said.

"How's Margaret?" Maddy asked.

"I don't know," Marc said and sighed. "I think she wants marriage and I'm in no hurry. In fact, the longer I live alone the more comfortable I get with it.

"I need to get back to the office," Marc said wrapping up the discussion.

Made in the USA
Middletown, DE
05 August 2021